THE GIRL IN THE GLASS BOX

THE GIRL IN THE GLASS BOX

A JACK SWYTECK NOVEL

JAMES GRIPPANDO

HARPER

An Imprint of HarperCollins*Publishers*

THE GIRL IN THE GLASS BOX. Copyright © 2019 by James Grippando, Inc. All rights reserved. Printed in the United States of America. No part of this book may be used or reproduced in any manner whatsoever without written permission except in the case of brief quotations embodied in critical articles and reviews. For information, address HarperCollins Publishers, 195 Broadway, New York, NY 10007.

HarperCollins books may be purchased for educational, business, or sales promotional use. For information, please email the Special Markets Department at SPsales@harpercollins.com.

FIRST EDITION

Library of Congress Cataloging-in-Publication Data
Grippando, James.
The girl in the glass box / James Grippando.
p. cm.
ISBN 978-0-06-265783-1
1. Swyteck, Jack (Fictitious character)—Fiction. 2. Legal stories. 3. Miami (Fla.)—
   Fiction.
PS3557.R534 G57   2019
813'.6—dc23   2018022312

19 20 21 22 23 LSC 10 9 8 7 6 5 4 3 2 1

For Tiffany

THE GIRL IN THE GLASS BOX

CHAPTER 1

Dominican women are the most beautiful women in the world. Julia Rodriguez had heard it said a thousand times since coming to Miami. Usually she just smiled and took it as a compliment.

"But you don't *sound* Dominican," people would also tell her. Sometimes it came from native speakers with an ear for *Dominicanismos*—like "chilaxing," which means exactly what it sounds like in English, and which was part of the Dominican lexicon long before American millennials embraced it. Other times, however, seemingly innocent questions about her accent felt more calculated, a passive-aggressive way of fishing for her exact ancestry. Or her immigration status.

"Another Haitian hot chocolate, Julia!" the waitress shouted from the end of the long coffee bar. Julia was behind the counter, working the espresso machine. She'd been on her feet for nearly eight hours, since five a.m.

"Coming up," she said.

Miami's January cold snap, with temperatures way down into the fifties, made Haitian hot chocolate a seasonal sensation at Café de Caribe, and Julia made it like no other barista in South Florida. She started by hand-shaving a ball of pure chocolate. Then she'd simmer cinnamon sticks, star anise, nutmeg, and *fèy bwadin* leaves, when she could find them at the markets in Little Haiti, but mace was a passable substitute when she couldn't. An enchanting aroma filled the coffee bar as she combined the ground chocolate, sugar, some vanilla essence, and a pinch of salt. The final step was to thicken with plenty of evaporated milk, which she crowned with shavings from the rind of a green bergamot orange, a shriveled, pungent limelike fruit.

Julia claimed it was her Haitian grandmother's recipe, no one the wiser that she had no idea who her grandmother was, let alone if she was Haitian. Sometimes she'd embellish even further, telling customers of a beautiful ebony woman with a French accent who'd migrated from Port-au-Prince and survived by selling delicious Haitian hot chocolate on the streets of Santa Domingo. Most Dominicans were of mixed European and African ancestry, and those who openly admitted to Haitian blood ran a unique risk; the country deported thousands of Haitian descendants every year, even if they were born in the DR. But the politics of island immigration mattered not to Julia's story, for in reality she'd never set foot in Hispaniola, be it the Dominican or Haitian side.

"Julia, can I see you in my office, please?"

It was the café manager. Duncan McBride was one of those people who liked to tell Julia that Dominicans were the most beautiful women in the world, though hearing it over and over again from the middle-aged gringo who approved her paycheck was just creepy.

"Be right there, Mr. McBride."

Julia watched out of the corner of her eye as the manager retreated to the office at the end of the hallway and closed the door. Her hands shook as she poured the hot chocolate into a porcelain cup and, for the first time all day, knocked it off the saucer and spilled it all over the counter.

"*Puchica,*" she said, instinctively reverting to her native tongue.

A coworker grabbed a clean hand towel and came to her aid. "I got it, honey. And by the way, in the DR it's *coño*, not *puchica*."

Every country has its own way of saying "damn." "*Gracias,* Elena."

Elena was Dominican and the first coworker to realize that Julia was not who she claimed to be. But they'd become friends, and, rather than ask questions, Elena had made herself an unofficial tutor in all things Dominican.

"Why would he call me to the office?" Julia asked with concern. "You think he's going to fire me?"

"No way. You're the best barista here."

"I told him I was Dominican when he hired me. You think he's on to me?"

"Don't worry about that. It's called the Café de Caribe, but hardly anyone here is from the islands. Eduardo's Mexican. Jorge's from Ecuador. Maria's from Peru. We're all the same to McBride."

Julia moved closer, speaking softly. "Is everyone else here legal?"

"Of course."

"Really?"

"Mmm-hmm. And we're also all doctoral candidates at the University of Miami who decided to sling coffee while working on our dissertations."

They shared a laugh.

"Just go see McBride and stick to your story. You'll be fine."

Julia thanked her with a smile, then made the long walk down the hallway to the back office and knocked lightly on the door.

"Come in," said McBride.

Julia opened the door and stepped into his windowless office, which was only slightly larger than a walk-in closet. Shelves lined the walls, and bags of coffee beans from eleven different countries were stacked from floor to ceiling. McBride was seated behind his metal desk.

"You wanted to see me?"

He asked her to close the door, which she did, and directed her to the only chair. Julia sat facing her boss, his desk between them. *No reason to panic*, she told herself.

"So, it seems we have a little issue, Julia." He laid a one-page document on the desktop and slid it all the way to the edge, facing her. It was the IRS form W-9 she'd completed and signed when she was hired.

"Payroll tells me that the Social Security number you gave us doesn't exist."

Julia was speechless. She'd cleaned houses for five months, sixteen hours a day, to save up enough to buy that number. "How can that be?"

"You tell me."

Julia was silent.

"Look, you're an awesome worker," said McBride. "Personally, I don't think this should even matter. You do the work, we withhold the taxes, and Social Security happily pays the money to some aging baby boomer. At the end of the day, the only thing this phony number means is you can't claim benefits from a system you paid into. Where's the foul?"

"Are you saying I can keep working here?"

"It's not that simple."

"But I really need this job."

"I understand. You're desperate. You're probably even a little pissed off. I'm sure you talk to other employees, and right now you're thinking, 'Why me?' Between you, me, and the coffee beans, here's the situation. It's probably less than one in a hundred new hires that we actually verify the Social Security number. Our lawyer tells us to do random spot checks just in case we ever get audited by ICE, so we can say we have a compliance program and avoid the big fines. Your bad luck: you're the one in a hundred."

"So . . . I can't work here?"

"No. Unless—"

"Unless what?"

"Unless we come to an understanding."

"What kind of understanding?"

McBride reached across the desk for the W-9, but rather than retract it, he knocked it over the edge. His pedestal-style desk had an open front, and the paper fluttered to the floor, landing at the tunnel-like gap between the pair of side cabinets that supported the desktop.

"Pick that up, Julia."

Julia was sure he'd knocked it to the floor on purpose, but she was on the verge of losing her job and chose not to make an issue of it. She leaned forward from her chair and reached down for the paper. She nearly had it when McBride's foot shot from the opening and landed on the paper. He pulled it back toward him, drawing the paper farther under the desk. Julia glanced through the opening and got an eyeful. McBride's pants were halfway down his thighs.

Julia froze.

"Do we have an understanding, Julia?" McBride took his swollen member in hand. It was obvious that he'd been thinking about this conquest for some time. "We can help each other here, Julia."

It suddenly occurred to her that there was no lawyer and no ICE compliance program—that she was not the randomly chosen, one-in-a-hundred new hire whose Social Security number had come back invalid. McBride had singled her out for his own pleasure.

"Julia?"

He wanted an answer, so Julia decided to give him one. The center drawer was suspended by metal slides beneath the desktop. Julia reached up through the opening, grabbed the back of the drawer, and pushed it open with all her strength. McBride squealed like the pig he was, as the metal face of the drawer slid forward and slammed directly into his state of self-arousal.

"You little bitch!"

Julia jumped to her feet, flung open the office door, and bolted from the room. She was half running, half walking as she hurried past the coffee bar.

"What happened?" asked Elena.

Julia was too upset to tell her. She grabbed her purse from under the counter and continued to the door.

McBride emerged from his office with his shirt untucked, but his trousers were pulled up. "You'd better run!" he shouted down the hallway. "I'm calling ICE right now!"

Julia kept going. The door had barely closed behind her when it burst open again. Four of her coworkers flew out of the Café de Caribe at the speed of Olympic sprinters, apparently having taken McBride's ICE threat more generally than he'd intended.

Julia dug her car keys from her purse, got in her car, and fired the ignition. The engine whined as it always did, and then it made a strange clicking sound that she'd never heard before. Julia made the sign of the cross, begged the Lord to forgive her for what she'd done to McBride, and turned the key once more. The engine started.

"Gracias, Señor Jesús," she said, and her eyes welled with tears as she steered out of the parking lot.

CHAPTER 2

Julia drove straight to Miami's Little Havana neighborhood.

Julia was what sociologists called the new face of Little Havana—the influx of Central Americans who moved in as the Cubans moved up and out of the immigrant neighborhood they'd established. The Nicaraguans had arrived first, driven by political and economic unrest in the 1980s. Then came the Hondurans, fleeing poverty; Guatemalans, escaping their civil war; and Salvadorans, running from gang warfare and the highest murder rate in the Western Hemisphere. The Cuban immigrant success story transformed Coral Gables, Key Biscayne, and other upscale areas into Hispanic upper-middle-class enclaves. Central Americans took over the *barrios* left behind, especially the East Little Havana community, close to the Miami Marlins baseball stadium and north of Southwest Eighth Street—the famous "Calle Ocho." Where there were once Cuban sandwich shops selling *media noches*, there were now Nicaraguan cafeterias selling *queso frito* and *nacatamales*. Julia could have starved to death searching for a tortilla in the original Little Havana. Now they were sold on every street corner.

"Let's go, let's go," she muttered under her breath. She was behind the wheel, stuck in traffic just two blocks from her duplex. The sleek white architecture of the domed baseball stadium glimmered in the South Florida sun, casting shadows on the boarded-up businesses across the street. The school day had just ended, and a group of children walked along the sidewalk, headed for houses and apartments that had been painted orange, red, or other bright colors to look more like home. Julia looked for her daughter, but these girls were clearly middle schoolers. She could hardly believe that Beatriz was in the ninth grade.

Julia's old Chevy inched forward. The traffic light had cycled from red to green and back to red again. She'd barely moved. Angry motorists all around her blasted their horns. The old man in the intersection selling bags of lychee nuts from his bicycle just shrugged, as if to say, *Don't blame me.*

"I am so sorry," Julia said to no one, but she was suddenly thinking of her four coworkers who'd fled the Café de Caribe after McBride threatened to call ICE. They could no more afford to lose their jobs than she could. Julia had taken everyone down in a desperate act of justifiable penis-cide.

Julia shook off the guilt and focused on the problem at hand. She had a teenage daughter at home alone, with ICE possibly on the way. She dug her cell phone from her purse one more time, hoping for a miracle, but she'd missed last month's payment, and she knew it was futile: no service.

Gotta get home.

A delivery van suddenly pulled away from the curb. Julia was still two long blocks from home, but she could get there faster on foot than fighting traffic. Parking on the street was normally impossible, so Julia seized the opportunity. She zoomed into the open spot and hoofed it down the sidewalk. Her duplex was at the end of the block-long coil of razor wire that ran like a man-eating slinky atop a chain-link fence, right next door to Little Havana's "cheapest" used-tire garage, SEÑOR GOMAS—GOMAS USADAS MÁS BARATA!

Julia was winded from the two-block sprint from her car as she hurried inside. She locked the door with the chain, caught her breath, and shouted, "Beatriz!"

A response didn't come quickly enough. Julia ran to the kitchen. Beatriz was at the table staring into an open algebra textbook.

"Why didn't you answer me?"

Beatriz looked up from her homework. "Did you say something?"

"Ay. Never mind. You need to pack a suitcase."

"Where are we going?"

"Your aunt's house."

"Why?"

"Because ICE is coming."

Beatriz rolled her eyes. "You always say ICE is coming."

"This time is different. My boss turned us in, and he knows our address."

"Why would he do that to you?"

"Because he's a—" she started to say, then stopped herself. "It doesn't matter why. Just go to your room and pack a bag."

"It's hardly *my room*," Beatriz said, grumbling. Mother and daughter shared the one bedroom, which wasn't actually a bedroom. It was once the dining room of an old single-family house that had been chopped into three apartments for five different families.

Julia chased her all the way to the dresser, threw a suitcase on the bed, and unzipped it. "Pack enough for at least two weeks."

"Two weeks!"

"Yes. We have to stay away from this house till I'm sure ICE isn't coming."

"You know, Mom, if ICE comes, you don't have to answer the door."

"What if they break down the door?"

"ICE can't enter anyone's house unless they have a search warrant from a judge. If they knock on the door, you just don't answer."

"Who told you that?"

"Every immigrant knows that."

"Yeah, all the ones back in El Salvador."

"No, Mom. Mr. Perez told me. My social studies teacher."

"Is Mr. Perez going to be our lawyer and keep us from getting deported if ICE does beat down the door?"

"You're impossible."

Julia yanked open a dresser drawer and threw a handful of Beatriz's clean socks into the suitcase. "No, I'm your mother. Get packing."

Beatriz started by picking up her favorite jeans from the floor. Over the next five minutes, mother and daughter systematically worked their way through the rest of their possessions, some things landing in the suitcase, other things being left behind. When the bag was full, Julia zipped it up, and Beatriz grabbed her school backpack.

"Let's go," said Julia, and she wheeled the bag out of the room. Beatriz followed her to the door, and the last thing Julia grabbed on her way out was the small crucifix that hung on the wall. She put it in her purse, locked up the house, and hurried down the steps toward the street.

"Does Tía know we're coming?" asked Beatriz.

"No, I didn't have a chance to call her."

"How do you know we can stay there?"

"Because she's my sister."

"Can I drive?"

"Two more years. Get in the car."

Julia climbed into the driver's seat. The passenger's-side door didn't open from the outside—Julia had bought the car that way—so she reached across the front seat, lifted the handle, and pushed it open for Beatriz.

"I forgot my algebra book!"

"Ay, Beatriz. Where is it?"

"On the kitchen table."

"Do you need it?"

"Yes! Do you want me to flunk algebra?"

Julia sighed and handed her the key ring. "Hurry!"

Beatriz raced into the house. Julia waited, squeezing the steering wheel tightly, as if it were a stress-relief ball, and nervously checking out every passing vehicle.

Hurry it up, girl.

There was no way to know if or when ICE was on its way. But she had to take McBride at his word. It was common knowledge that immigration raids and deportations were on the rise. In the Little Havana neighborhood alone, more undocumented immigrants had been arrested in the last three weeks than in her first six months in America. Julia knew two women personally who'd been picked up and given the choice between voluntary deportation or a months-long wait in jail for an immigration hearing. They took the one-way flight to San Salvador.

She blasted the horn, but still no Beatriz. "What the heck are you doing in there, girl?"

Julia's heart was pounding, and then it sank. She didn't like the look of the approaching vehicles. A Miami-Dade police car led the way. Behind it was a white van with a wide blue horizontal stripe on the side—the markings of Homeland Security. They were a half block away and closing fast. Instinct told her to duck down behind the dashboard, but Julia froze for a moment—just long enough for law enforcement to spot her.

The orange swirl of the police beacon hit her in the eyes. A blaring siren pierced the neighborhood. Julia had no car keys; she couldn't make a run for it even if she'd wanted to. But Beatriz's words suddenly replayed in her mind: *ICE can't enter anyone's house unless they have a search warrant from a judge.*

Julia slid across the bench seat and jumped out of the car on the passenger's side. The police car and ICE van screeched to a halt in the street. Julia launched herself across the sidewalk and ran as fast as she could toward the house. The front door opened. Beatriz screamed from the doorway. Julia was ten feet from her daughter when a man twice her weight took her down like a linebacker making an open-field tackle. Julia hit the ground hard.

"Don't move!" the ICE officer shouted.

"Mami!" Beatriz screamed.

Unless they have a warrant.

"Shut the door, Beatriz!"

"No, Mami!"

"Beatriz, just shut the door! Now!"

The ICE officer grabbed Julia by the elbow, yanked one arm behind her back, and cuffed her wrist.

"Quieto!" he shouted in bad Spanish—*Key, Ate, Toe*—as he cuffed the other wrist.

Julia was on her belly and bleeding from where her chin had hit the concrete. But she had a clear line of sight to the front door and could see the tears in Beatriz's eyes.

"Go!" she shouted, purely on adrenaline.

Beatriz disappeared behind the closed door. Another ICE officer charged toward the house and banged on the front door. Julia was close enough to hear Beatriz fasten the chain lock on the inside.

Good girl.

The ICE officer commanded her to her feet and told her to get in the van.

Only then did Julia begin to feel the pain.

CHAPTER 3

On Wednesday morning, Jack Swyteck went food shopping with Abuela. This wasn't just the dutiful grandson taking his grandmother to the grocery store. This was Jack's biweekly lesson in Cuban culture.

"What you like for eating, *mi vida?*"

Mi vida. Literally it meant "my life," and Jack loved being her *vida.* "*Camarones?*" he said.

"*Ah*, shreemp. *Muy bien.*"

It had been their routine since Abuela's arrival from Cuba, Jack speaking far less than perfect Spanish and Abuela answering in broken English. Over the years, he'd improved from about a C minus to a B plus in Abuela's gradebook, doing the best he could for a grown man who was half Cuban by blood but had been raised 100 percent gringo by his Anglo father and stepmother—which was precisely the point of his trips with Abuela to *la tienda.*

Mario's on Douglas Road was the neighborhood market in an area that began to establish itself as Cuban American with the first wave of immigrants in the 1960s. Decades later, after hundreds of small Hispanic businesses had been squeezed out by *El Walmart, La Target,* and the like, Mario's Market was virtually unchanged, owned and operated by the Sires family since the Nixon presidency. A cup of *café con leche* was still just thirty-five cents at the breakfast counter in front. Nine aisles of food were stuffed with the basic essentials of life, including twenty-pound sacks of long-grain rice, *bistec de palomilla* sliced to order, delicious caramel flan topping, an assortment of cooking wines to satisfy the most discerning chefs, and glass-encased candles painted with the holy images of Santa Barbara and San Lazaro. Established customers could buy on credit, and the best Cuban bread in town, baked on the premises, could be purchased straight from the hot ovens in back. All you had to do was follow your nose or, for the olfactory deprived, follow the signs and arrows marked PAN CALIENTE. Jack had driven past the store a thousand times on his way to the courthouse, and he would have kept right on driving for the rest of his life had his grandmother not come to America and opened a whole new set of doors for him. Abuela always seemed to be preparing a meal or planning the next one, as if on a mission to make up for living nearly half her life under Fidel Castro with virtually nothing to cook and nothing to eat.

Jack's life had changed drastically since that very special day when he'd first laid eyes on his maternal grandmother. Jack had since married. He and his wife, Andie, had given Abuela her only great-grandchild. His law practice was actually making money, though Jack was still a bit too ideological for his own financial good—still a sucker for fighting the good fight for clients who could never pay him, everyone from homeless children to death row inmates. Abuela liked to call him *Doctor*, a title of respect that old Cubans showed *abogados*.

Abuela was now well into her eighties, forgetful at times but still Jack's window to the past—to his mother's roots. Of course, there would always be the gaping hole of a life that was never lived, the tragedy of a mother who died of preeclampsia soon after bringing her son into the world. Jack's father had told him stories about Ana Maria, the beautiful young Cuban girl that Harry Swyteck had fallen head over heels in love with. Jack knew how they'd met; he knew about the fresh yellow flower she used to wear in her long brown hair; he knew how jaws would drop when she walked into a party; and he knew that when someone told a joke, she was the first to laugh and the last to stop. All of those things mattered to Jack, but even on those rare occasions when his father did open up and talk about the wife he'd lost, he could offer Jack only a snippet of her life, just the handful of those final years in Miami. Abuela was the rest of the story. When she talked of her sweet, young daughter from Bejucal, her aging eyes would light up with so much magic that Jack could be certain that Ana Maria had truly lived. And Abuela could be certain that she *still* lived, the way only a grandmother could be certain of such things, the kind of certainty that came when you took a grandchild by the hand, or looked into his eyes, or cupped his cheek in your hand, and the generations seemed to blur.

Jack carried the bagged groceries to his car, helped Abuela into the passenger's-side seat, and got behind the wheel.

"There's a girl for you to meet," she said as the engine started.

Jack smiled sadly. Abuela had once been so determined for Jack to meet "a nice Cuban girl" that she'd phoned into Cuban talk radio and shared his phone number live on the air. They'd been having a very good morning so far, but this remark had rekindled Jack's fears that her mind was slipping in old age.

"Abuela, you know I'm married now, right?"

She rattled off something in Spanish that was far too advanced for Jack's ear, but he got the gist of it, something to the effect of, *You might think I'm a crazy old woman, but I have a photographic memory,* which could well have been true, except that Abuela still shot in film, so to speak, and not everything got developed.

"This girl's name is Beatriz," said Abuela. "She's fourteen years old. And she needs your help, *Doctor.*"

Jack met with Beatriz in Abuela's dining room.

Abuela was a frequent customer at Café de Caribe and had heard about Julia and Beatriz Rodriguez from a barista named Elena. "My grandson will help," Abuela had promised, which of course was before she'd even bothered to check with Jack. Not that Jack had a say in the matter: he'd found Beatriz and her aunt waiting in a car outside Abuela's apartment upon their return from

Mario's Market. Abuela was right in one respect: most immigrants depended on volunteer lawyers who were willing to represent them for free. Unlike people held on criminal charges, immigrant detainees are not afforded the Sixth Amendment right to legal counsel. Since deportation is not formally considered a punishment, but an administrative consequence for violating a civil law—crossing the border—they have no right to an attorney paid for by the government.

Beatriz's aunt Cecilia helped Abuela put away the groceries in the kitchen while Jack spoke in private to his prospective client. Beatriz was a bright young girl and fluent in English. The conversation was going just fine but for the fact that every ninety seconds Abuela would poke her head into the room and say the same thing in Spanish: "You can help this poor girl, right, Jack?"

Nobody could say *pobrecita* like an *abuela*.

"Do you know where ICE took your mother?" asked Jack. He and Beatriz had moved past the preliminaries, and it was time to get to the important questions, though Jack was mindful that he was speaking to a child.

"No. Nobody knows. That's why I'm so scared. Do you think they could have deported her already?"

"How long has she been gone?"

"They picked her up two days ago."

Less than forty-eight hours. "The only way she'd be gone that quickly is if she's been deported in the past."

"As far as I know, this is the first time she's been to this country."

"That's important," said Jack. "What nationality is your father?"

"Salvadoran. Like my mom and me."

"Is he still in El Salvador?"

"I don't know."

"Is he alive?"

"No idea."

"When is the last time you saw him?"

"I . . . I don't remember."

Jack made a few notes on his pad, then continued. "How long have you been in Miami?"

"Since July."

Jack counted in his head. "About seven months. How is it that your English is so good?"

"My mother was a housekeeper for a UK businessman and his family for over ten years. They had a daughter my age. They were hoping I would teach her Spanish, so they let us play together. The girl was nice, but honestly she was a little lazy. My English ended up much better than her Spanish."

"I can relate." Jack was thinking of his trips to Mario's Market and Abuela's lessons in Cuban culture. He shifted subjects. "Tell me how you got here—to Miami, I mean."

Beatriz sighed, as if overwhelmed by the question—or, more likely, the journey.

"My mom saved up for two years. One day she came to me and said, 'We leave tonight.' We got on a bus to Guatemala, and when I woke up the next morning we were at a town called Tecun Uman. From there you have to cross the river to Tapachula, Mexico. It's a bizarre place. Dozens of rafts made out of tractor-tire inner tubes. If you speak Spanish, it costs a dollar to cross. Two dollars if you want a raft with no guns or drugs on it. If you're from Haiti or Africa—I even met some people from Nepal—it's ten dollars. My mom nearly flipped when I loaned five dollars to a girl from Nigeria: 'Beatriz, we still have four thousand kilometers to go!'"

Jack pulled up a map on his iPhone. Forty-three hundred, to be exact.

Jack listened as Beatriz recounted the journey. The first thinning of the ranks was on the Mexican side of the river, where migrants in the hands of unscrupulous smugglers parted company with their cash and landed in the Tapachula detention center, Latin America's largest, where they awaited deportation to their home country. The luckier ones continued north in groups of five or larger, by bus or on foot, up the "Mexican corridor" and all the way to the

U.S. border. Along the way there were the handlers, the cons, the gross men with an eye for pretty thirteen-year-old girls who looked "fresh." Fear became their friend; they were afraid to stop moving, and even after they crossed the border, speed was critical. Any undocumented immigrant detained within one hundred miles of the U.S. border was subject to expedited deportation. Beatriz and her mother spent their last dollars on a bus trip from Texas to Miami. After all that, her mother had landed in a detention center—the crock at the end of the rainbow.

"What have you done so far to find your mother?"

"My aunt has been asking around, trying to figure out where to start."

"There's actually a website," he said, as he accessed the Internet on his smartphone. "I use the bureau of prisons online inmate locator all the time."

"My mom is in prison?"

Effectively she was, but Jack tried to be sensitive. "I'm talking about the ICE detainee locator. It's different from the bureau of prisons." *Sort of.*

Beatriz provided her mother's full name and date of birth, which Jack entered.

"Hmmm."

"What does 'hmmm' mean?" asked Beatriz.

"Looks like your mother is not in the system yet. That's nothing to be alarmed about. ICE has over forty thousand beds in the detention program. It can take a few days for an update."

"Why doesn't she call my aunt and let us know where she is? Isn't she allowed to make a phone call?"

"I'm sure she'll call as soon as she can. Making a call from a detention center is not as easy as it sounds."

"What's it like in one of those places?"

Jack didn't see any point in trying to sugarcoat it. "It's a jail, basically."

"Will she be safe?"

Jack hesitated. Did detainees inflict violence on other detainees? Every day. Were there reported cases of male guards assaulting female detainees? Hundreds of them. Would Julia get all the medical attention she needed? Maybe. Maybe not. The inside of an ICE detention center was like the dark side of the moon, completely off the map except for the rare instances of abuse so appalling that they blip onto society's ethical radar.

"Your mother sounds like a woman who can take care of herself," said Jack, opting in the final analysis for a little coating of sugar.

"Will there be men in there with her?"

"That's an excellent question, Beatriz. Some facilities are for men only, like Krome Detention down in Homestead. That could be why it's taking a while to get your mom into the online database. They need to find a bed in a facility that takes women."

"And children?" she asked with trepidation.

"That's where immigration law is hard to separate from immigration politics. One thing I can say is that children stopped at the border have bigger problems than you do. Especially where you have an aunt who's legally in this country and willing to take you in."

"So, what will happen to me?"

"How long can you stay with your aunt?"

"She's finishing a master's degree at Florida International University this year. I'm guessing her student visa expires when she graduates."

"We'll sort that out. But let's take one step at a time. First, we have to help your mother."

Abuela rushed in from the kitchen, hugged Jack, and planted a kiss on his cheek. "*Gracias, mi vida!* I knew you would help!"

Obviously Abuela had been eavesdropping on a privileged lawyer-client conversation, but Jack let it go. It wasn't lost on Jack that his own mother was not much older than Beatriz when Abuela had put her on an airplane for a better life in Miami—and they had never seen each other again.

"Yes, I will help."

Cecilia entered the room. "And to your question, Beatriz: of course you can stay with me."

Abuela wasn't the only eavesdropper.

"*Gracias,* Tía," said Beatriz.

Cecilia hugged her niece, and it suddenly seemed as though they were holding each other up. Jack wondered how many minutes, not hours, of sleep they'd had since Julia disappeared.

"How long will this whole process take?" asked Cecilia. "Until we know if Julia is being deported or not, I mean."

"It varies. But I would expect it to be months before Julia has a final hearing."

"As far as Beatriz having a place to stay, my student visa is good through next December."

Eleven months. "You should look into renewing it. This could take more than a year. Especially now that Julia has a lawyer on her side."

"Will Julia stay in detention all that time?"

"Not necessarily," said Jack. "ICE could release her if she posts a bond. It's like getting out on bail before a criminal trial, except this isn't a criminal case."

Beatriz shook off her fatigue, alarmed again. "What if ICE decides not to release her?"

"We don't know that yet."

"But let's say they don't let her out? Can I visit her?"

"I wouldn't recommend that anyone who's not legal visit an ICE detention center. Cecilia is fine."

Beatriz shrank. "Well I'm not *fine.* You mean I can't see my mom?"

"Not while she's in detention," said Jack.

"So it could be months before I see her again."

"I didn't say ICE won't release her on bond."

"You didn't say they will."

"We won't know until I talk to the deportation officer assigned to the case."

"You're a lawyer. If ICE won't let her out, there has to be something you can do! Can't you make them do it? Can't you sue them and make them let her go?"

"I—"

"Of course!" said Abuela. "My grandson will get your mother out. Don't you worry about that."

Jack was about to inject the usual legal disclaimer—"We'll see" or "I'll do my best"—but before he could open his mouth, Beatriz sprang from her chair and threw her arms around his neck.

"Thank you, Mr. Swyteck. Thank you from the bottom of my heart."

"Pobrecita," said Abuela.

Jack glanced at his grandmother and drew a breath. "You're welcome" was all he could bring himself to say.

CHAPTER 4

How you like Club Fed so far, *chica*?"

Julia glanced at the detainee in the next bunk. There were forty-two women in Julia's pod—seven rows of bunk beds, three up and three down. All detainees wore orange jumpsuits; most were Hispanic. Julia had landed in the bunk beside a Bahamian woman who seemed nice but never shut up, and who liked to call her *chica*. The woman's name was Nellie.

"Nice," said Julia.

Nellie laughed so hard it echoed off the windowless walls of solid concrete.

"What's so funny?" asked Julia.

"You are, *chica*."

Julia felt anything but funny. Exhausted. Angry. Depressed. But not funny.

Transport and processing had taken all night and into the morning. After the open-field tackle on her front sidewalk, ICE officers locked her in the back of the van, and then they just sat there—literally, just sat there for nearly five hours. The van didn't move. All Julia could figure was that ICE was playing a game of "wait and see," betting that eventually Beatriz would come out. Or maybe they thought someone truly dangerous was inside. They finally tired of waiting and took her someplace in Miami—whether it was a local police station or an ICE facility, Julia couldn't say—for fingerprinting, paperwork, and collection of personal items. She spent the next four hours in a holding cell with eleven other women. Sometime in the middle of the night the guards came, emptied the pen, and loaded the women onto an old school bus. The windows were painted black, so there was nothing to see. Julia fell asleep for some period of time during the trip, though she wasn't sure how long. When she woke, the bus unloaded and Julia found herself in the yard, standing in the shadow of a guard tower outside the gates to what Nellie called "Club Fed."

"Did you meet your deportation officer yet?" asked Nellie.

"No."

"You will. Soon. Just remember: they are not your friend. Everything you say to them, they will figure out a way to use it against you."

Julia didn't feel much like talking, but she suddenly realized that Nellie might be a source of something that so far had been in very short supply: information.

"How long you been here?" asked Julia.

"Seven months."

Puchica. "Why so long?"

"That ain't long. The lovely Miss Brazil over there?" she said, indicating two rows over. "Ten months. Next to her, Miss Trinidad and Tobago? Over a year. Things don't move fast here. The first thing ICE does is decide if your case meets the requirements for expedited deportation, which is, like, *boom*, you're gone. If you're not one of those quickies, you land here, and these folks ain't in no hurry to see you go. Every night you sleep in that bunk, ICE pays them eighty-five bucks."

Julia blinked, confused. "ICE pays *who*?"

"This place."

"What is 'this place'?"

Nellie laughed again. "You kill me, *chica*."

"I'm serious. I saw the sign. I know it's Baker County. But what is that?"

"It's a county-owned jail. You think this little shithole town in the middle of nowhere needs a jail with five hundred beds? They fill the place up with you, me, and all these other warm bodies."

"How far are we from Miami?"

"Miami? Shit, *chica*. You a long way from Miami."

Julia must have slept longer on that bus than she'd realized.

"I need to call my daughter. When do they let us use a phone?"

Nellie laughed again. It was annoying on some level, but Julia gave her the benefit of the doubt. After seven months in this factory of broken spirits, anyone would be desperate to find something to laugh about.

"Is there no phone?"

"Oh, yeah. There's a phone. You gotta pay the girls from Honduras ten dollars to use it."

"They own the phone?"

"Sort of. They see you use the phone, they come collect the phone tax. You don't pay, you spit out your teeth."

Julia was no stranger to gangs and their highly effective methods of collection.

"I really need to talk to my daughter."

"Join the club."

"You have a daughter?"

Nellie's expression changed. Even forced laughter seemed a remote possibility. "She's three." Nellie settled back onto her bunk, clasped her hands behind her head, and looked up at the ceiling. "I miss her so much."

Julia felt compelled to say something encouraging. "You'll be together soon, I'm sure."

Nellie shook her head, still staring at the ceiling. "No. I'm gonna lose her."

"Don't say that."

"It's true. The legal aid lawyer told me."

"You have a lawyer?"

"Yeah. We all do. A really nice young lady from Jacksonville who volunteers her time."

Julia looked around her pod. On her way to her assigned bunk, the guard had taken her past the central tower, an octagon-shaped surveillance station overlooking eight pods that stretched out like the spokes of a wheel, each as big as Julia's, each filled to capacity.

"There's one lawyer for everybody?" asked Julia.

"Yeah. Unless you can afford your own. Which I recommend. These volunteers mean well, but you can end up like me. Screwed."

"Why do you say that?"

"Because it's true. I got picked up for shoplifting at the mall. Public defender told me to take a plea to get no jail time. What he didn't tell me is that taking the plea would get me deported. Karen—she's the nice legal aid woman from Jacksonville—tried to keep me here on what they call humanitarian grounds, because I have a daughter. We lost my appeal last week. She says there's nothing more she can do for me. Just a matter of time 'til they need my bed for somebody new."

"Where will you go?"

"Haiti."

"You don't sound Haitian."

"I was born in the Bahamas, but my parents were Haitian, so the Bahamas says I'm not a citizen."

"Do you know anybody in Haiti?"

"Nope. Don't speak the language, either. Get yourself a good lawyer, *chica*. That's my advice."

"How am I supposed to pay for a lawyer?"

"I dunno. Make like the girls from Honduras and find yourself a racket. Ten bucks here, ten bucks there. It adds up."

The irony struck her. Thousands of people fled the hell of El Salvador's gangs every day. Now she was stuck in legal purgatory, forced to pay a "phone tax" to the girls from Honduras.

A guard approached, and he seemed laser focused on Julia. He stopped at her bedside. "A-one-eleven-six-zero-zero-eighteen."

Julia didn't immediately comprehend.

"That's you, *chica*. You're a number now," said Nellie.

Her all-important alien number. "Right," said Julia. "That's me."

"Let's go. Time to meet your deportation officer."

Julia rose from her bunk.

"Hey, *chica*," said Nellie. "Remember what I told you: not your friend."

Julia nodded in appreciation, and then followed the guard down the concrete corridor.

CHAPTER 5

F ound her," said Jack.

Jack had checked the ICE detainee locator before going to bed on Wednesday night, and he checked again first thing the next morning. He was surprised and relieved to get a hit, and he immediately called Julia's sister to share the news with her and Beatriz. His next move was to call Theo Knight.

"Dude, it's Jack."

Theo was Jack's best friend, bartender, therapist, confidant, and sometime investigator. Jack especially liked to use Theo on pro bono cases. Theo worked cheap, sometimes refusing any pay at all, trying to pay back a debt that Jack recognized as no debt at all.

Theo was a former client, a onetime gangbanger who easily could have ended up dead on the streets of Overtown or Liberty City. Instead, he landed on death row for a murder he didn't commit. Jack had literally saved his life. With his civil settlement from the state, Theo went on to open his own tavern—Sparky's, he'd called it, a play on words and a double-barreled flip of the bird to "Old Sparky," the nickname for the electric chair he'd avoided. Sparky's had done well enough to get him a second bar. Of course Theo needed a second bar. After four years of living eight feet away from death, Theo had developed a simple credo: Anything worth doing is worth overdoing. Though Jack often cringed at the things Theo said and did, he'd come around to accepting the fact that he needed a little bit of Theo in his life.

"You up for a road trip?" asked Jack.

"Where to?"

"Macclenny."

The line went silent. Theo had hung up on him. Jack suddenly recalled that Macclenny was about ten miles away from the town of Raiford and Florida State Prison, where Theo had lived on death row. Jack redialed, and Theo immediately picked up, his tone laden with incredulity.

"Seriously? A road trip to Macclenny?"

"It's a seven-hour drive. I need a driver."

"Oh, hey, no problem. And can we stop at the museum of Confederate memorials on the way up?"

"Theo, I'm doing this case for free, and I have work to do for my paying clients on the way up. Help me out."

The pro bono button was the right one to push, and Jack knew he had his driver as soon as Theo asked, "What's the case about?" At six-feet-six, Theo could be intimidating as hell, but he was pretty much a pushover for a story like Beatriz's. They were on the road by nine thirty. Jack phoned the visitation office, confirmed that attorneys could visit without an appointment, and left a message for Julia to call him. He wasn't technically Julia's lawyer until she said yes, but Jack put the odds of her saying no right up there with the likelihood of Theo making it all the way to Macclenny without mentioning their last case for an immigrant.

"Hey, whatever happened with Ricardo?"

They hadn't even left Miami-Dade County.

"You really want to know?"

"Yeah. Kid was cool."

Ricardo Fuentes was a nineteen-year-old Mexican college student who dreamed of making it on Miami Beach as a stand-up comic. He had a pretty good run with his deportation shtick—the twenty-first-century version of gallows humor—until ICE caught his act, figured out that he'd overstayed his visa, and deported him.

"You can visit him next time you're in Chalupa."

Jack's cell rang. It was from the Baker County Facility. He thought it might be Julia, but it wasn't.

"Mr. Swyteck," a woman said in a southern drawl, "this here is ICE officer Cindy Johnson"—*Aaahs offisuh*—"badge number fifty-seven, four-two-oh-six. I am the deportation officer for Julia Rodriguez."

Jack thanked her for calling and jumped straight to the sixty-four-thousand-dollar question. "Has ICE determined the amount of Ms. Rodriguez's bond for release yet?"

"Well," she began. *Wha-ell.*

What followed was an entirely unnecessary but seemingly unstoppable recitation of the various levels of priority that ICE assigned to detention of detainees under the Immigration and Nationality Act, from those convicted of capital murder to the catchall category of those who "otherwise obstruct immigration controls." Jack interrupted her a few times to get specifics about Julia, but she persisted undaunted, as if reading from a script. Theo continued to drive somewhere north of eighty m.p.h. as Jack took notes. They were passing Yeehaw Junction when, finally, Officer Johnson delivered the bottom line.

"Say that again," Jack said into his phone.

She did. Jack asked a couple of follow-up questions, but the ICE officer had "no further information at this time." The call was over. Jack put his phone away.

Theo glanced over from the driver's side. "What's the verdict?"

Jack was still trying to process it. "Julia Rodriguez is a Level One detainee."

"What's that?"

"Aliens who pose a danger to national security or a risk to public safety."

"What does that mean?"

Jack glanced out the window at the passing cow pastures. "It means she's ineligible for release on bond."

CHAPTER 6

Jack and Theo rolled into Macclenny around dinnertime.

The town was basically one street—a strip mall and a few mechanic shops—just under an hour's drive from Jacksonville and ten minutes through fields and forest to the Georgia line. For ICE, Macclenny was perfectly located: not too close to a metropolitan center with a high density of volunteer lawyers who make the work of deporting people more difficult, and easily reached by interstate from anywhere in the Southeast, where immigration is forever on the rise.

Theo was hungry, so they stopped for dinner at a Mexican restaurant on Sixth Street. A cheery waitress greeted them.

"What kind of tequila you got?" asked Theo.

"I'm sorry," she said with a big smile. "We don't have tequila."

It was downhill from there. Jack ordered the chicken enchiladas. Theo went for the beef tacos.

"What kind of Mexican restaurant has no tequila?" Theo said, grumbling.

"What kind of Mexican restaurant has no Mexicans?" said Jack.

Theo looked around, checking out both customers and servers. "Damn straight. This whole town's like a Latin-free zone."

Classic Theo: a bit overdone, but pretty much spot on. Baker County was over 80 percent "white only" (non-Hispanic, no mixed race), and nearly all the rest of its twenty-seven thousand residents were African American. The vast majority of its Hispanic immigrant population was locked up at Florida State Prison or the county jail.

It was dark when they reached the detention center, and lights from the low-slung, four-building facility glimmered on the prairie like an ocean freighter in the night. Regular visitation ended at six p.m., so the parking lot was empty as Jack and Theo pulled up. Attorneys could visit until ten p.m., but the vast majority of detainees were unrepresented, so there was only one lawyer ahead of Jack at the intake window. When his turn came, Jack identified Theo as his legal assistant, which drew a double take from the intake officer. Her thoughts quickly went in the wrong direction.

"There's no physical contact allowed."

"Excuse me?"

"Your 'legal assistant,'" she said, making air quotes. "He's not a boyfriend, is he?"

Theo sidled up to Jack and put his arm around him. "You got a problem with that, sweetie?"

Jack pushed him away. She'd clearly meant no contact between detainees and visitors, but Theo had flustered her, and she buzzed them through the security door.

A neckless ICE officer named Winston met them on the other side. "How we all doin' tonight?" he said with a Cajun accent.

"Fine," said Jack.

"Would be better if that Mexican restaurant served tequila."

"Let it go, Theo," Jack muttered.

Winston laughed. He knew the restaurant and raved way too much about the enchiladas, which really weren't that good, but Jack agreed, just to be agreeable. It was like buying insurance, in case Theo hauled off and said something to piss the guy off.

Winston checked the name on Jack's badge. "Swyteck, huh? You related to Harry Swyteck?"

"I'm his son."

"You don't say? Good man, Harry was. I worked down at FSP

when your daddy was governor. Busy time. Gotta respect a man who has the courage to flip the switch on Ol' Sparky—that's what we called the electric chair, back in the day when an execution was an execution."

"Ah, the good ol' days," said Theo.

Jack was fresh out of law school when Governor Swyteck signed the death warrant for Theo Knight, not to mention several other of Jack's death row clients who weren't nearly as lucky—or as innocent, for that matter.

Winston took them down a long hallway, at the end of which they passed a barred window that looked out to a gravel yard. Puddles of standing water glistened in the security lights.

"Had rain today," said Winston. "Girls missed their hour of rec time. Makes 'em restless being cooped up all day, so you boys behave yourselves. Know what I mean?" he said with the wink of a dirty old man.

Jack caught Theo's eye, shooting him a look that said something along the lines of *You can kick his ass now.*

Winston led them up a flight of stairs to an elevated octagonal guard booth at the hub of the surrounding pods. The walls were lined with panes of one-directional glass, each providing a clear view of the pods below. It was like looking down on a rat maze, women and guards maneuvering their way around one another and past the bunks and fixed tables that were laid out with linear precision. Jack wondered how these detainees coped with the lack of privacy. Even when men were not watching through windows, a guard in the watchtower booth sat with eyes glued to the screens, scrutinizing the captured images of women with no place to go.

A second guard joined them as they continued down the corridor to the attorney visitation room. They happened by a woman in her cell who was getting dressed. Jack averted his eyes to respect what little privacy she had, but her bare back attracted a leering glance from Winston as they passed.

I'm serious, thought Jack, wishing Theo could read his mind. *Kick this guy's ass—now.*

They stopped at the metal door at the end of the hallway. Winston unlocked the door.

"Attorneys only at this point," he said to Theo.

"What makes you think I'm not a lawyer?"

Jack intervened. "I need Clarence Darrow here for two minutes."

"All right," said Winston. "I'll give you two minutes. And tell your daddy Winston from death row says 'hey' when you see him."

"I definitely will," said Jack.

Jack entered first, and Theo followed. The guard closed the door and locked it from the outside. Julia was seated at a small table. She rose to greet Jack as he approached.

"Thank you for coming."

"I'm glad I can help."

Beatriz was a pretty girl, so Jack was in no way surprised to see that Julia was an attractive woman, even in prison garb. She'd put her hair in braids, probably to keep life simple in jail, but it made her face even more striking. Jack probably should have given Theo a heads-up: he seemed tongue-tied through the introductions, without words for the first time since they'd left Miami.

Julia returned to her chair; Jack and Theo sat opposite her at the table. They were surrounded by windowless walls of yellow-painted cinder block. Bright fluorescent lighting lent their meeting room all the warmth of a workshop.

"How are you holding up?" asked Jack.

She shrugged. "Just going through the motions, I guess. I don't feel in control of anything."

"We aim to change that," said Jack. "But first, I met Beatriz. What an amazing young woman."

"Thank you," she said. "Is she taking good care of Cecilia?"

They shared a smile, which Jack took as a very positive sign. Maintaining a sense of humor was critical. "Your sister is in very capable hands."

Her smile faded. "I miss my girl so much."

Jack sensed an emotional slide was coming, which he'd anticipated. Cue Theo. "So, my friend Theo here is not going to stay long. I just wanted you to meet him and know that he's part of the team. If for any reason, any time of day, Beatriz ever feels afraid, feels threatened, or just needs a ride, she calls this guy, okay?"

Julia smiled with her eyes, but more at Theo than Jack. "Thank you."

"You're problem," said Theo, a clumsy combination of "You're welcome" and "No problem."

Jack winced. *"What?"*

Julia smiled and tried not to laugh. "I know what he meant."

Jack rose. Theo followed his lead, said good-bye to Julia, and walked with Jack to the exit. At Jack's knock, the guard opened the door from the outside. Theo said nothing on the way out. He simply mouthed the word *wow*.

The door closed and Jack went back to the table.

"So, can we talk about the elephant in the room?" said Jack.

"I'm sorry—what?"

Her English was good, but the idiom was obviously lost on her. "Never mind. What I mean is that I spoke to your detention officer. I'm told that you're a Level One detainee."

Julia nodded, her eyes cast downward.

"You want to tell me about that?"

"Don't know what there is to tell."

"Then let me start," said Jack. "I find myself in a really uncomfortable position here. My *abuela* promised Beatriz that I would get you out of here. I never guarantee anything but, honestly, I pegged you as a pretty strong candidate for release on bond. You have a daughter. She's enrolled in public school. Your sister is legal and lives in Miami. You have a job."

"*Had* a job," she said.

"Cecilia mentioned that to me. We'll talk more about Mr. McBride, but let's sort this out first. Why did ICE label you a Level One alien with no bond?"

"Honestly? I have no idea."

"Do you expect me to believe that?"

"I'm not a terrorist, if that's what you're worried about."

"Level One goes way beyond terrorism. For example, if you were deported in the past—for any reason, even a traffic ticket—you'd be Level One this time."

"I've never been in this country before."

"That's what Beatriz told me. So we can rule that out. What about a criminal record?"

"What about it?"

"If you've ever been convicted of a felony? That could put you in the Level One category."

"What do you mean by a felony?"

"Any crime punishable by more than a year in prison."

"Okay."

"Okay what?"

"Okay, I'm thinking."

"What is there to think about? Have you ever been convicted of a crime?"

"Not . . ."

"Not what?"

"Not in this country."

"In El Salvador?"

"*Sí.*"

"Did you go to jail?"

"No. No jail time."

"What was the crime?"

Her expression tightened. "I don't want to talk about it."

"We have to talk about it. How long ago did this happen?"

"Six years. I was twenty-six."

"We're clearly not talking about some juvenile offense. I need to know the crime you committed."

More silence.

"Let me explain something," said Jack. "I do a lot of criminal defense work. Sometimes my clients tell me everything; sometimes they don't. I defend them either way. Your situation is different. This is not a criminal case. If we are going to keep you from being deported, we can't simply assert your right to remain silent under the Fifth Amendment to the Constitution and say the government failed to prove its case beyond a reasonable doubt. The rules are different in deportation. You're an undocumented immigrant in violation of federal law. Period. Unless we come forward with evidence and prove some basis for you to stay, you're gone. Do you understand?"

She nodded.

"So let me ask the question again. What was the crime?"

She remained silent.

"Julia, if you don't talk to me, I can't help you."

A tear rolled down her cheek.

"Maybe you need a different lawyer," said Jack, rising.

"Stop," she said.

He was bluffing, but it seemed to have worked. Jack lowered himself back into his chair. He waited. Julia continued to struggle, but Jack sensed that she was almost there.

"Julia," he said in a soft voice, "what was the crime?"

She looked away, then back, wringing her hands on the tabletop. And then she told him.

CHAPTER 7

Manos arriba!" the Mexican police officer shouted. Hands up! The seven migrants on the side of the road complied. Three men were from Honduras. Two others were from El Salvador. The silver-haired woman and her teenage granddaughter were from Ecuador. They were about an hour north of Mexico's southern border with Guatemala.

"My name is Hugo Ramirez," the younger Salvadoran whispered to his much older friend.

"Ramirez?" he whispered back. "Since when?"

"Don't give them your real name. No matter what they do to you."

The trip from San Salvador, destination *los Estados Unidos*, had started out fine. Hugo Martinez—aka Ramirez—made it through Guatemala, rafted across the Mexican border at the San Pedro River, and piled into the back of a cattle truck with seventeen other migrants, all headed for "La 72," a migrant shelter in the city of Tenosique. The driver stopped halfway there, somewhere in the farmlands of the Tobasco region, and demanded more money. Most of the migrants coughed up the extra cash. The five men objected. The old woman and her granddaughter simply didn't have any more money. The driver called the local police, who arrived in an SUV two minutes later—way too quickly for this not to have been coordinated.

"On your knees!" the police officer said.

The prisoners did as they were told, their hands still in the air. A second police officer went down the line, one by one, patting the migrants down and emptying their pockets. He collected every-thing of value—money, wallets, passports—in a paper bag. Then he handed the bag to the truck driver through the open window.

"*Gracias*," the driver said. The engine started, and the prisoners watched the cattle truck pull away with a dozen migrants in the back, seven short of capacity.

A third cop climbed out of the police SUV and walked toward the prisoners. "What's the situation," he asked his deputy.

"No documents, Sergeant."

"Our passports are on the truck!" one of the Hondurans said.

"Quiet!" said the sergeant.

The old woman came forward, pleading on behalf of her grand-daughter. "Please, sir. Please don't take us to Tapachula." She was referring to Siglo XXI in Tapachula, Mexico's largest detention center. It was no place for a woman of any age.

"Don't worry, you are not going to Tapachula." The sergeant's tone was anything but reassuring.

On his order, the deputies put the old woman and her grand-daughter in the back seat of the SUV and crammed the five men into the cargo compartment. It was tighter than the back of the cattle truck. The pile of sweaty bodies reached all the way up to the ceiling, and the mere act of breathing was a struggle. They bounced around in the back for thirty minutes as the SUV traveled down a nearly impassable road. Finally, they stopped at a run-down warehouse. Hugo overheard one of the officers say they were in Cárdenas.

The rear door creaked opened, and the police officer ordered the migrants out of the SUV. Hugo's leg was asleep from the way his friend had been lying on it, and he nearly stumbled as his foot hit the dirt. They lined up at the side of the road, the Ecuadoran woman and her granddaughter at one end, Hugo and his friend at the other end. The SUV had kicked up a cloud of dust, and as it settled around them, a band of Mexican men approached from the warehouse. Three men were armed with machetes. The fourth, apparently the leader, carried an automatic rifle. The sergeant smiled and shook hands with him, as if they were old friends. Money changed hands, blurring the lines between lawbreakers and law enforcement.

"Welcome to the ransom hotel," the sergeant told the migrants. "You are now the property of Los Zetas."

Zetas. Mexico's most notorious crime gang, arguably the most brutal in all of Latin America, and law enforcement's chief suspect in the disappearance of tens of thousands of men, women, and children who never made it to the U.S. border. It was enough to send chills down the spine of any migrant.

The man with the gun approached the teenage girl. He grabbed her by the chin, forcing her to look him in the eye. "Are you a virgin, *chica*?"

She didn't answer.

He chuckled. "We'll get a lot of money for you, my flower."

The old Salvadoran man looked at Hugo with despair. "We're dead men," he whispered.

Hugo's gaze traveled from one Zeta to the next, as he sized up the opposition. "Yes," he said quietly, narrowing his eyes with resolve. "But I'm taking that motherfucker with me."

CHAPTER 8

I t was Friday afternoon, and Jack was in the Orlando Immigration Court.

A lawyer from the Department of Homeland Security, Office of the Chief Counsel, was seated on the opposite side of the courtroom. A black-robed immigration judge was at the dais, his gaze fixed on the flat-screen monitor on the wall. Julia's image was on the screen; all Baker County Facility detainees appeared for immigration hearings via teleconference to Orlando.

"Jack Swyteck, on behalf of the respondent, Julia Rodriguez," Jack said for the record.

"Simone Jerrell," said the DHS lawyer. "For the United States of America."

It was a standard announcement, but Jack wondered how such words must have felt to a refugee locked up in a county jail, appearing via video conference from a little town in north Florida, up against the entire "United States of America."

"Good morning, all," the judge said, "I'm Judge Alvin Greely. Now before the court is Ms. Rodriguez's request for release on bond pending a final hearing on the government's demand for deportation."

Jack's conversation with Julia at the Baker County jail the night before had left no doubt in his mind that she should petition for release immediately. It normally took at least a week or two to get on the calendar, but Judge Greely had an opening, and Jack grabbed it.

The judge continued, "I understand from Mr. Swyteck's filing that ICE opposes release on any terms."

Jerrell rose to address the court. DHS lawyers don't wear uniforms, but if ever they might, Jerrell had nailed it: navy blue suit, white blouse, red scarf. "That's correct, Judge. The respondent has a prior felony conviction."

"What is the nature of the felony?"

"She violated Article 133 of the penal code of El Salvador."

The judge scratched his salt-and-pepper beard. "Unfortunately, I don't have the Salvadoran penal code committed to memory, Counselor, so you're going to have to elaborate."

Jack rose, eager to seize control. "My client terminated a pregnancy in the first trimester."

"Which is a first-degree felony under Salvadoran law," said Jerrell.

The judge paused to consider it. "When did your client have this procedure?"

"Six years ago," said Jack.

"Is this the entirety of her criminal record?"

"Yes," said Jack. "And I would also like to point out that she is the primary caregiver to her fourteen-year-old daughter, who is enrolled in the Miami-Dade County public school system."

Judge Greely leaned forward, peering out over the top of his reading glasses. "Ms. Jerrell, am I to understand that this is the kind of felony that should keep a mother separated from her daughter?"

Jack took heart in the judge's question, but it seemed only to invigorate his opposing counsel.

"This is not a trivial matter," said Jerrell. "Under Salvadoran law, an abortion is a crime punishable by up to fifty years in prison."

"Fifteen years?" the judge asked, obviously surprised.

"Not fifteen," said Jerrell. "*Fifty*. It's considered aggravated murder. Not to be flip, but illegal immigrants are denied bond and deported every day in this country for offenses far less serious."

The judge took a deep breath, then nodded, seeming to acknowledge the letter of the law. "Mr. Swyteck, does Ms. Rodriguez concede that she was convicted of this crime?"

"My client concedes that she pleaded guilty under an agreement with the prosecution that allowed her to serve no jail time."

"It doesn't matter if she served no jail time," said Jerrell. "The crime is punishable by more than one year in prison. It meets the definition of a felony under the U.S. Immigration Act."

"I understand the government's position," the judge said.

Jack said, "I would also like to make the court aware of certain extenuating circumstances."

"Tell me," the judge said.

"My client terminated the pregnancy under circumstances that most people would agree should never be a crime." Jack glanced at Julia on the video screen and proceeded lightly, sensitive to the fact that it was still a source of shame in the backward ways of her old *barrio*. "She was sexually assaulted."

Jack's announcement seemed to have caught the government attorney off guard, but Jerrell collected herself, reloaded, and fired away. "I have two responses to that, Judge. One, there is nothing in the criminal record to confirm that Ms. Rodriguez was sexually assaulted. Two, even if she was, there are no exceptions under Salvadoran law. Rape, incest, saving the life of the mother—it doesn't matter. Ms. Rodriguez violated the statute, she is a convicted felon under the laws and constitution of her home country, and under the laws of this country she should be denied release from detention pending her deportation."

Another deep breath from the judge. Prior to the hearing, Jack had checked his bio online. They were exactly the same age, but Greely looked fifteen years older. The carved-in-wax worry lines on his face were testimony to the burnout rate among immigration judges, who, on average, managed two thousand cases a year.

"I hear what you're saying, Ms. Jerrell, but my inclination is to order release and set bond at the statutory minimum of fifteen hundred dollars."

Jerrell took a step forward, pressing her point. "With all due respect, release of this detainee would be completely at odds with current immigration policy, which disfavors the release of detainees who are prioritized for deportation."

Jack had officially heard everything: a legal argument based on White House policy. It would never fly in a regular courtroom, but immigration judges weren't part of the independent judicial branch. They were employees of the U.S. Department of Justice and its Executive Office for Immigration Review, which meant that the attorney general could direct immigration judges on how to interpret the law and, if the attorney general didn't like that interpretation, he could fire them.

Jack tried another angle. "Judge, I would also point out that no credible argument can be made that Ms. Rodriguez is a flight risk. She just wants to take care of her daughter. If bond is posted, she isn't going to disappear. She will return for her scheduled hearing."

"Flight risk is not the issue here," said Jerrell. "Federal law states that she should not be released from detention if she is a flight risk *or* if she's a danger to the community. Mr. Swyteck conceded that she's a convicted felon."

"Terminating a pregnancy after a sexual assault doesn't make her a danger to the community," said Jack.

"I tend to agree with Mr. Swyteck," said the judge.

Jerrell was backpedaling, but she showed no sign of panic.

"Fine," said Jerrell, as she retrieved a file from her trial bag and then approached the bench. "We would also bring to the court's attention this criminal complaint, which was filed against Ms. Rodriguez this morning."

She offered a copy to the judge, crossed the courtroom, and handed a copy to Jack.

"I've never seen this before," said Jack.

"You're seeing it now," said Jerrell, her voice taking on an edge. "The manager of Café de Caribe, where Ms. Rodriguez was employed prior to her arrest, filed this criminal complaint with the Miami-Dade Police Department this morning. Mr. McBride's affidavit states that he fired Ms. Rodriguez and called ICE after she was caught red-handed stealing his wallet from his office."

"What!" Julia shrieked over the video conference.

Her words startled the judge and the lawyers. Jack suddenly had to backtrack on his talk about no right to remain silent in immigration proceedings. An alleged crime changed the whole ball game.

"Julia, don't say anything until we've talked in private."

The judge took a minute to read McBride's affidavit, then addressed the DHS lawyer. "What is your position, Ms. Jerrell?"

"Given the totality of the circumstances, which include a criminal complaint and a prior felony conviction, Ms. Rodriguez's request for release on bond should be denied."

"So ordered," said the judge. "The respondent shall remain at the Baker County Facility without bond."

"We will appeal the decision," Jack said for Julia's benefit.

"That's your right," the judge said. "Anything else?"

"No," said Jerrell.

Jack had one request. "Judge, is there any possibility that my client could be transferred to South Florida?"

"Mr. Swyteck, there are over four hundred thousand detainees in the system and not nearly enough beds. Florida is especially overcrowded. Just yesterday I had to enter an order transferring seventy-five detainees to Texas because Krome Detention had them sleeping on the floor. You can file a motion for transfer, but I wouldn't hold my breath, if I were you."

"But—"

"Next case," he said, ending it with a bang of his gavel.

Counsel for another detainee hurried forward to take Jack's spot at the respondent's table. The flat screen went black, and Julia's image was gone.

"Thank you, Judge," said Jack.

For nothing.

CHAPTER 9

Jack was back in Miami early Friday evening and met Theo at the Café de Caribe. He ordered a Haitian hot chocolate, which sounded much more interesting than anything else on the menu board, but the barista told him it was no longer available. He took a decaf and joined Theo in a booth by the window. A framed old map of Latin America and its coffee-producing regions hung on the wall behind him.

"How was the trip back?" asked Theo.

Jack groaned.

With McBride's criminal complaint, Julia's detention in Macclenny was no longer just inconvenient; it was nearly unworkable. Theo had dropped Jack off at the Orlando Immigration Court for Julia's hearing and continued on to Miami. Jack's plan had been to fly home from Orlando, but McBride's criminal complaint against Julia changed everything. Jack couldn't just call his client. There was no such thing as a "private" phone conversation with an ICE detainee. He ended up renting a car, driving to Macclenny, meeting with Julia, driving to Jacksonville, and then flying to Miami.

"Honest to God," said Jack, glancing at the old map on the wall, "it would be easier if she was in El Salvador."

"She may be there soon enough."

"Not funny."

"Sorry."

Jack signaled a server to their table and asked to see the manager.

"I'm not sure he's here," she said.

"He is," said Jack. "I called an hour ago. Whoever answered the phone said he's here till eight."

"Is something wrong?" she asked.

"You could say that," said Theo. Jack had filled him in by phone from the airport.

"We just need to speak to him," said Jack.

"Sure." She turned and headed to the back. Jack stirred a packet of sugar into his coffee.

"So, what is Julia's status?" asked Theo.

"Undocumented."

"I didn't mean immigration status."

Jack was messing with him. He'd been waiting for this follow-up since Theo had tripped over "You're problem."

"You mean is she married?"

"Yeah."

"She was. Her husband left her two years ago."

"So she's divorced?"

"No, when I say 'left her,' I mean he just disappeared. There's been no divorce, so she's technically still married. Why do you want to know?"

"No reason."

Jack smiled to himself. Since getting married, he'd observed that there were two questions unmarried men raised for "no reason." Marital status of a mutual acquaintance was one. "Is your wife coming?" was the other.

"Can I help you gentlemen?" said McBride. "I'm the manager."

Jack did the introductions with full disclosure, meaning that he identified himself as Julia's lawyer.

"I'm not sure I should be talking to you," said McBride.

Theo rose and put on the face that had ensured his survival as a "Grove Lord" when he was growing up in the ghettos of Miami's Coconut Grove. "Have a seat," said Theo, towering over McBride.

"Well, okay, I have a couple minutes," said McBride. He slid into the booth. Theo sat right next to him. McBride shifted closer to the window, putting a sliver of comfortable space between him and Jack's oversized friend.

Jack had a copy of the typewritten affidavit that the DHS lawyer had presented in court that afternoon. He laid it on the table. "That's your signature?" asked Jack.

"Yeah, uh-huh."

"Not every criminal complaint lodged with a police department has a sworn affidavit attached to it. Who asked you to sign this?"

"Ms. Jerrell did. The ICE lawyer."

"When did she ask you?"

"Yesterday."

"Was it also her idea for you to file a formal complaint with the police against Julia?"

"I'm—I'm not sure I should be answering these questions."

Theo spread out a little, placing his massive forearms on the table, his bulging triceps pressing against McBride's shoulder. "Go 'head and answer, Mr. Coffee."

"I wouldn't say it was Ms. Jerrell's idea. I'd been meaning to call the police ever since I caught Julia in my office stealing my wallet."

"I see," said Jack. "Now, did Julia actually steal your wallet? Or did it drop out of your pocket when you were pulling your pants down?"

McBride bristled. "I don't know what you're talking about."

"I'm talking about the real reason you called to sic ICE on Julia."

"I need to get back to work, fellas."

"So soon?" said Theo. "We were having so much fun."

"Let me out of this booth."

Jack locked eyes with him. This wasn't a TV drama, and the purpose of this meeting hadn't been to break him on the spot and elicit a tearful confession. The point was simply to send McBride a clear message that he wasn't going to get away with this.

"Let him go," said Jack.

Theo rose, and McBride eagerly slid out of the booth. But he didn't scamper away with his tail between his legs. "Julia might think she's in the driver's seat with you and your big black friend here. But it's my word against hers, and she's a proven liar."

"You haven't proved anything," said Jack.

"Julia told everybody here she was Dominican. Even wrote it on her job application. Lying about your nationality is not a good thing when you're looking at deportation. Now get out of my café, both of you. And if you ever come back, I'm calling the police."

McBride turned and left.

"Nice guy," said Theo.

"A real peach."

"Why would Julia lie about her nationality?"

"I don't know," said Jack.

"You want me to drive you back to Macclenny so we can ask her?"

Jack kept his laughter to himself as he rose from the booth. "You don't have a thing for Julia, do you?"

"No! Why would you ask that?"

"No reason," said Jack. "No reason at all."

CHAPTER 10

"'d like to make a phone call, please," Julia told the guard.

It was Saturday morning. Julia's pod had the early breakfast shift—six a.m.—but she was skipping it. She'd called Cecilia after Friday's videoconference hearing to tell her the bad news. She didn't get to talk to Beatriz, who was in school, so they agreed that Julia would call first thing Saturday morning before Beatriz left for her weekend volleyball match.

Two women approached as a guard escorted Julia from the dining hall.

"Don't forget about us," the bigger one said.

Fortunately, Julia had enough money in her commissary account to cover both the cost of the long-distance phone call and the ten-dollar Honduran phone tax.

"No problem," said Julia.

It was a two-minute walk past the guard tower to the phone bank. Only about a half dozen inmates were ahead of her, but some of them may also have been holding a spot for a friend. All Julia could do was wait. A little more time to choose her words was probably a good thing. She needed and wanted to speak to Beatriz, but she still wasn't sure how to explain. Julia tried to script something out in her head, but it was hard to think clearly. From the moment ICE had cuffed her in front of her own daughter, she'd felt untethered from reality.

"When you're done," said the guard, "just wait right here. One of us will walk you back."

Julia assured him that she had no place to go.

Forty minutes passed. She knew that the volleyball match was in Palm Beach County, which meant that Beatriz needed to leave the house no later than seven, and Julia was getting nervous. The line was moving, however, and she was getting close enough to over-hear some of the women speaking into the phones. She lost count of the number of times she heard "Don't cry, baby," or words to that effect. She was far from the only mother slated for deportation.

"Hey, you gonna use the phone or not?" the detainee behind her asked.

A phone at the end of the row had opened up. Finally, it was Julia's turn. She went to it, and her hand shook as she dialed Cecilia's phone number.

Please, someone answer.

On the second ring, she heard Cecilia say hello. She was about to bring Beatriz to the phone, but Julia stopped her.

"Did you explain everything to Beatriz? She understands I'm not coming home?"

"Yes. She understands."

"How did she take it?"

"Fine. Teenage girls are really tough."

Julia smiled sadly. "You're such a bad liar, Cecilia."

"Yeah, I know. Let me get her. She's dying to talk to you."

Julia's grip around the phone tightened. The wait seemed much longer than it was. She hoped she was strong enough to get through this.

"Hi, Mommy."

That voice—it almost killed her. "Hi, girlfriend."

"When can I see you?"

A second near-mortal wound. "I don't know."

"I want to come see you."

Jack had explained the danger of visiting an ICE detention center. "Honey, Mr. Swyteck said that's not a good idea."

"I don't care what he said. Tía said she's going to visit. I want to see you, too."

Cecilia was legal, but Julia didn't want to mention her daughter's immigration status over the telephone. Jack had warned her that ICE was listening, and the sign on the wall—ALL CALLS ARE MONITORED BY LAW ENFORCEMENT—reinforced his words.

"You and Mr. Swyteck can talk about this another time."

Julia changed the subject, trying to make it about Beatriz. School. Boy problems. Today's volleyball match. Anything but ICE. The diversion worked for a few minutes, but reality came back around.

"I can't believe this is happening to us," said Beatriz, her voice shaking.

A lump came to Julia's throat. "Don't worry about things you can't control, honey. That's Mr. Swyteck's job."

The woman in line behind her grunted something to the effect that Julia's time was up. Julia wasn't aware of any time restriction, but it was seven o'clock anyway, and she didn't want to make Beatriz late for her match.

"Beatriz, I have to go now," she said into the phone. "We'll get through this. It's in God's hands."

"I know."

"I love you."

"I love you, too."

Julia hung up, and the next detainee in line practically knocked her to the floor in her rush to the phone. Julia stepped aside, and a guard approached to walk her back.

"I don't feel like eating," she told him. "Can I just go back to the pod?"

"Actually, you got a visitor," he said.

"Me? Who?"

"Dunno, sweetie."

I'm not your "sweetie." She thought it but didn't say it.

Julia followed the guard down the long corridor. She focused straight ahead, her gaze like a laser, making no eye contact with anyone inside the cells she passed on the left or right. She wasn't technically "in jail," but she felt imprisoned in every sense of the word. Hearing her lawyer announce in immigration court that she was the victim of sexual assault had only exacerbated the pain, stirring up a past that she'd managed to compartmentalize and suppress for years.

At the end of the cell block, the door buzzed open to the visitation area, which was like a long hallway. A line of detainees sat on one side of the glass and their visitors sat on the other. The guard directed her to bay number three. Julia didn't recognize the woman on the other side of the visitation glass.

"Are you sure she's here to see me?" Julia asked the guard.

"Yep," he said. "You got thirty minutes."

Julia took a seat on the stool and picked up the phone.

"Julia Rodriguez?" the woman asked over the intercom.

"Yes. Who are you?"

"Sandra Watson," she said, as she held her photo ID up to the glass. "I'm a counselor with the north Florida chapter of the Coalition to Stop Sexual Violence against Migrants."

"I didn't ask to see a counselor."

"Most women in your position don't. I wanted to make you aware that our organization is here to help all women in detention who are victims of sexual assault."

"How did you know about me?"

"Immigration hearings are public record. We have volunteers who monitor them."

It was nice on one level, but Julia was starting to feel like nothing about her life was private anymore.

"Okay. Well, I guess I can call you if I need you."

"I was hoping we could talk a little now. Get to know each other. Tell you what our coalition has to offer."

Julia said, "Fine," then she listened as Sandra explained the organization. She told Julia about herself, too. Sandra and her five-year-old daughter fled Guatemala and were placed in family detention at the T. Don Hutto Residential Center, a former state prison in Texas. They were part of the ACLU's first wave

of class actions against an Obama administration policy of locking up children with adults in facilities that were built to house
criminals—which had seemed unthinkable, until even worse
things came along. Sandra was also the victim of sexual assault.

"Maybe you'd like to tell me about your situation," said Sandra.

"Maybe."

"I understand yours was six years ago."

"Right."

"Was your attacker ever punished?"

"No."

"Do you know who he was?"

Julia didn't answer.

"I can understand if you are afraid to say his name. I was afraid,
too. But just a simple yes-or-no answer would be a good start. Do
you know who did this to you?"

She hesitated, then answered. "Yes."

"Okay. That was good. Do you know his name?"

Julia felt something rising up within her, a combined rush of
anger, hate, and fear that touched her core. "Yes," she said into the
phone.

"Can you tell me his name?"

The feeling inside her only intensified, and suddenly it was as if
his hand were around her throat all over again. Julia shook her head.

"I totally get it," said Sandra. "But the more information you
give me, the more chances we have to help you."

Julia stared back through the glass, but her flight instincts took
over, and she couldn't fight the urge to run away. "I have to go now."

"Just take your time."

"I'm sorry," said Julia. "I have to go."

She broke eye contact with the woman on the other side of the
glass, placed the phone in the cradle, and called for a guard.

CHAPTER 11

J ack could have spent the entire weekend in the office. For a
sole practitioner, working for one client meant that other work
didn't get done. Julia's case had seriously cut into his prep for
the upcoming trial of a real estate developer accused of defrauding
his investors out of a half billion dollars. Jack was representing the
kingpin's right-hand man, a twenty-year-old high-school dropout
who was so good at cooking the books, he could have had his own
show on the Food Channel. He was also the most polite crook Jack
had ever defended, as evidenced by the way in which he'd followed
Jack's advice to assert his constitutional right not to bear witness
against himself before the grand jury:

*"Mr. Cookson, did you disclose to investors that over a million dol-
lars of their funds would be used to purchase Rolex watches and other
jewelry?"*

"I'll take the Fifth, please."

And on it went for another forty-five minutes—*"I'll take the Fifth,
please. I'll take the Fifth, please"*—as if he were asking for another
slice of Grandma's cherry pie. Lawyers had put up with worse for an
up-front cash retainer, but it wasn't worth another weekend behind
his desk. It was debatable whether the influence was conscious or
subconscious, but Julia's separation from Beatriz had left Jack determined to spend Saturday morning with his daughter.

"Let's go fly a kite," said Jack.

"Yay!" shouted Righley. "Can we bring Mommy?"

"Yes, Mommy's allowed."

"And Max, too?"

Max was their golden retriever. "Let's ask him if he wants to come."

Righley whispered into Max's ear and reported back immediately. "Max says yes. He thinks kites are fun."

And delicious, no doubt. "Okay, Max can come."

They piled into the SUV, Righley strapped into her car seat behind Jack, and Max with his big head sticking out the window behind Andie's headrest.

Righley was Jack and Andie's only child, and she'd been angling to fly a kite at Matheson Hammock Park since her fourth birthday. Her party had been at the park's picnic area, and it also happened to be a perfect day for the kite boarders to launch from the narrow strip of beach on Biscayne Bay. Righley and her friends had watched from shore and loved everything about it: the music that played from the vans while surfers set up their rigs; the cool wet suits; the colorful kites that soared into a cloudless blue sky, sending the surfers skimming across flat seas and flying into the air like feathers caught in the breeze.

"Kites!" said Righley, as Jack steered into the parking lot.

A woman in a neon-pink wet suit was doing about thirty knots, twenty-five feet above the bay, before splashing into the shallow blue-green waters.

"You don't think Righley's under the impression that she came here to do *that*, do you?"

"If she is, it's your fault," said Jack.

Andie was unlike any woman Jack had ever known, and not just because she worked undercover for the FBI. Jack loved that she'd been a Junior Olympics mogul skier before blowing out a knee, that she wasn't afraid to cave dive in Florida's aquifer, and that in her training at the FBI Academy she'd nailed a perfect score on one of the toughest shooting ranges in the world.

"I resent that," she said with a smile.

Righley was her mother's daughter and was of course hugely disappointed to find out that she would be flying a kite with her feet firmly on the ground, not soaring into the air with Max on board. They went for ice cream at the concession stand to make things better. Jack and Andie watched from the picnic table as Righley introduced Max to a new friend.

"Are you going back to Macclenny this week?" asked Andie.

"Hope not."

"How long is that case going to last?"

Jack knew what she was really asking. The understanding that made it possible for a criminal defense lawyer to marry an FBI agent was that she didn't tell him which clients to defend and he didn't tell her which crooks to investigate. But Jack's pro bono work was in a different category: his working for free hit them both in the wallet.

"Hard to say," said Jack. "My client is getting a raw deal, but I have an idea on how to turn things around fast."

"Anything you can tell me about?"

Jack's ice cream was melting fast. He changed hands and let Max the vacuum cleaner lick the soft serve from his vanilla-cream-covered fingers. "I might take this to the media."

"Why do you think that's a good idea?"

"Because I don't think a woman should be considered a convicted felon under U.S. immigration law for having an abortion after getting raped. And I think that makes a pretty compelling news story. Don't you?"

"Yes, if it's true."

"I believe her."

"Wow. A lawyer who believes his client. That should be more than enough to make you the lead story on every fake-news website out there."

Jack didn't bother telling her about McBride. What happened or didn't happen in his office at Café de Caribe was a classic he said, she said scenario.

"I hear you," said Jack, which Max apparently understood to

mean "Here, boy." With one swoop of Max's tongue, the rest of Jack's ice cream cone disappeared.

The need for corroboration weighed on Jack's mind, and after five years of marriage, Andie was pretty good at reading him. After getting their fill of kite flying, Andie drove Righley and Max home. Jack took an Uber to visit Julia's sister.

Cecilia was in Miami legally, but her two roommates were not. They lived in a vintage-sixties neighborhood where every house on the block looked virtually the same, a ranch-style shoebox painted either beige or yellow. Some still had the original jalousie-style windows—a burglar's best friend—which accounted for the prisonlike security bars on each window. There was not a blade of grass anywhere. Front yards were paved or bricked over, like used-car lots, to accommodate more cars and more people than a two-bedroom, one-bath house was ever designed to handle. Backyards were nonexistent. Narrow side yards between houses were several inches deep in loose pea gravel, on which the crunch of footfalls in the night warned the undocumented of an ICE raid.

Jack and Cecilia sat on folding lawn chairs on the stoop outside her front door. Jack had called earlier with a heads-up that he wanted to talk about Julia's sexual assault, and the only place out of Beatriz's earshot was on the stoop.

"Julia is seven years older than me," Cecilia said. "She was married and Beatriz was eight years old when all this happened, but I was still living at home."

"When did you find out about it?"

"After she got arrested."

"I didn't mean the abortion. I meant, when did you find out that she had been sexually assaulted."

"I know what you meant. The first I heard anything about a sexual assault was when Julia got arrested for having an abortion."

"I take it she didn't report the assault to the police."

"No."

"Which doesn't mean much," said Jack. "Even in this country most sexual assaults go unreported. I imagine the number of unreported assaults is even higher in El Salvador."

Cecilia didn't reply.

"Where did your sister have her procedure?" asked Jack.

"I don't know. Someplace not safe. She was bleeding when she checked herself into the hospital. That's how she got caught. A nurse in the emergency room turned her in. The police came out and took her to jail as soon as the doctors said she could leave."

Jack tried to imagine such a dilemma—the choice between staying home and risking death or going to the hospital and risking arrest. "Did she tell anyone at the hospital that she was sexually assaulted?"

"As far as I know, she didn't tell anyone until she was in jail."

Jack detected a hint of skepticism. "Somebody must have believed her if the prosecutor agreed to no jail time."

"That prosecutor took a lot of heat."

"Do you mean from the Church?"

"The Church, the courts, the lawmakers—you name it. Most people thought Julia said she was raped just to stay out of jail."

"What do *you* think, Cecilia?"

"You're asking about my sister."

"That's why I want to know what you think. Julia's credibility is going to be an issue in her case, starting with the abortion and continuing all the way through her former employer's accusations of theft. Do you believe Julia was telling the truth when she said she was sexually assaulted?"

She shifted uncomfortably in her lawn chair. "What do you want me to say, Mr. Swyteck?"

"I just want your honest answer."

She glanced over her shoulder, as if checking to see if her niece was listening, then looked Jack straight in the eye. "I don't know," she said. "That's the most honest answer I can give you."

CHAPTER 12

Hugo's knees buckled, and he dropped to the cold Mexican-tile floor. The pain was unlike any he had felt before, the kind of pain that came from two nights without sleep—and hours of electric-shock interrogation from one sadistic monster.

"God, have mercy," he prayed, as he inspected the burn marks on his bare chest.

Hugo spent his days locked in a windowless room about the size of a closet. In fact, he was pretty sure that it was once a janitor's closet, as it still smelled like cleaning fluids. He ate there, slept there, and marked the passage of time by counting the meals he was served. Nine so far, so three days, he figured. The only time he got out was when a guard took him down the hall to the bathroom. They rarely even bothered to blindfold him. The Zetas were in so tightly with the local police that they didn't seem to care if their hostages could identify them.

Hugo heard the jingle of keys outside the door. "In the corner," the guard said.

Hugo went to the far corner and sat, which was the routine. The guard opened the door and placed a bottle of water on the floor. Another temporal indicator: day four, he presumed.

The guard ordered him to face the wall, which he did. Then he tied Hugo's hands behind his back and led him down the hall. Another hostage was being escorted from the bathroom when they arrived. Hugo had counted nine other hostages this way, including a pregnant woman. He had yet to see the silver-haired

Ecuadoran woman and her teenage granddaughter from the cattle truck, and it sickened him to think of where they might be.

The guard untied his hands and opened the bathroom door. The
stench had nauseated Hugo the first time, but he was getting used
to it.

"Two minutes," the guard said.

Hugo entered. The guard left the door open and stood right outside in the hallway.

Los Zetas made the journey through Mexico a Latin American
migrant's worst fear. They grabbed headlines with brazen atroci-
ties, like the massacre of 265 migrants who were buried in mass
graves in the northern state of Tamaulipas, or the disappearance of
43 college students in the southern state of Guerrero. Sensational
media coverage fueled the gang's kidnap-for-ransom industry,
striking so much terror in the migrant community that even the
poorest families of Honduras or El Salvador somehow managed to
come up with thousands of dollars in ransom to spare their loved
ones from rape, torture, and violent death.

Hugo took all of his two minutes, if only because the small
window in the bathroom was his only view of daylight. The guard
fastened his hands behind his back but didn't take him to his
closet. The guard blindfolded him, and Hugo knew what that
meant. Prisoners were blindfolded only for a trip to the "party
room."

The guard led him down the hallway, and with each step the
music—coming from somewhere—got louder. When they stopped,
it sounded as if they were standing right outside a dance club.

A shrill scream rose above the music, and it was clear that no
one was dancing.

The guard opened the door, yanked off Hugo's blindfold, and
pushed him to the floor. Hugo slid to the corner, where two other
men were seated on the floor with their backs to the wall. A group
of men at the counter raised their beer bottles and cheered Hugo's
arrival.

"Got the Salvadoran again," the guard said. "The one you asked for, El Lobo."

El Lobo. The wolf. Hugo recognized him as the man with the assault rifle who'd paid off the Mexican police. He'd swapped out his rifle for a semiautomatic pistol.

"We'll get to him," said El Lobo. His piercing gaze shifted to the man seated on the floor next to Hugo. "What's your name?"

"Paco."

"Your turn."

Paco climbed to his knees, pleading. "No, please!"

"Crank up the music!" El Lobo told his men.

Music was part of the ritual. It was Hugo's impression that these savages enjoyed the macabre incongruence of party music and the shrill screams of torture victims.

"My family will pay!" Paco said, groveling. "I'll give you the phone number."

He shouted out a string of digits, and one of El Lobo's thugs wrote it down.

"Call them," said Paco. "You'll see. They will pay fast!"

"Of course they will pay," said El Lobo. "And when they hear you scream, they will pay more. Put him on the grill," he told his men.

"No!"

The grill was a metal table in the center of the room. The men grabbed him, stripped him naked, and threw him on the table. One man took his ankles and another took his wrists. They stretched him the length of the table and strapped him down tight, as if placing him in a medieval rack. A fat guy stood at the foot of the table with a length of hardwood handy, ready to swing it at Paco's arches like a baseball bat if he resisted in any way. Another guy with a wild look in his eyes—definitely on drugs—tended to the electric transmitter on the small table near the victim's head. He smiled perversely as he connected the wires, one by one, to the victim—to his chest, his abdomen, and finally his genitals.

They called him El Electricista. The Electrician.

"Just dial that phone number," Paco pleaded. "There's no need for this!"

"*Bueno*," said El Lobo. "You better hope they answer."

El Lobo punched the numbers on his phone. Paco was so nervous that Hugo could hear him breathing across the room. El Lobo broke the silence, speaking into his cell phone in a bright and cheery voice.

"Hello, I'm calling with some excellent news about our friend Paco." He held the phone for Paco. "Keep it short."

"It's me, Paco! I've been kidnapped. Just do what these men say! Please, just—"

El Lobo pulled his cell away. "Stay on the line," he said into the phone.

"Don't hurt me!" said Paco.

El Electricista laughed as he forced metal beads down the prisoner's throat—electrodes that would make the voltage cut like lightning through his insides.

"Swallow!"

Paco obeyed.

At the turn of the dial the current flowed. Paco's entire body tensed and then quivered. There was suddenly a bizarre symphony of howling from El Lobo's men and the bloodcurdling screams of a man who probably wished he was dead.

"Find us some money," El Lobo told Paco's family, and he ended the call.

El Lobo walked across the room to Hugo, placed his boot on Hugo's leg, and then bore down directly on one of the burn marks from the electrode. He'd undergone the treatment on his first day at the ransom hotel—or was it the second? It didn't matter. Hugo tried not to show how much it hurt.

"Rest up, my Salvadoran friend. You're back on the grill in ten minutes."

El Lobo walked away.

The hostage beside Hugo had reached his emotional limit. "*Ay*," he said, his voice quaking. "We should have just done like the others and paid that stupid truck driver the extra money."

"No."

"What did it get us? Now we have to pay ransom."

"I will never pay," said Hugo. "I will never give them a phone number."

"We will, or they will kill us. We will end up like those college students," he said, referencing the forty-three who "disappeared" in Guerrero.

"No," said Hugo, his resolve only strengthening. "I will kill them. One by one, I will kill every one of them. And I will escape."

The man chuckled without heart. "And after this miraculous escape, where will you go, Hugo?"

"Miami."

"Miami?" the man said with bemusement. "What's in Miami for a man from El Salvador with no clothes and no money?"

"The most beautiful Salvadoran woman in the world."

"Really?" the man said with another mirthless chuckle, clearly not believing any of it. "What's the name of this beautiful woman?"

Hugo looked past the grill, gazing into the fog of the middle distance. "Julia," he said. "Her name is Julia Rodriguez."

CHAPTER 13

How a Monday-morning flight to Jacksonville could cost more than business class to Paris was beyond Jack. Rather than fret over airline economics, though, he burned a few more frequent-flier miles and, for good measure, scrimped on the Jacksonville-Macclenny leg, snagging a great deal on a rental car that was only slightly smaller than the Barbie convertible Righley got for Christmas. He was with Julia in the Baker County Facility attorney visitation room by midmorning.

"Didn't expect you back so soon," said Julia.

"Me neither," said Jack.

Cecilia's "I don't know" response to the sexual assault question didn't sit well with Jack. He wanted to do all he could for Julia, but any crimp in her credibility could put her beyond the help of any lawyer. That was the simple reality of a deportation hearing. He laid it out that bluntly for her, because he had to.

"Are you saying I have to prove I was raped?" she asked.

"Right now, you have two strikes against you. One, a felony conviction under the law of El Salvador and, two, McBride's accusation that you stole his wallet. If we can convince the immigration judge that you had an abortion because you were raped, I believe he will disregard the felony conviction, even though the statute has no exceptions. But if he doesn't believe you on that, he won't take your word over McBride's police report. ICE wins. You'll get out of here only when you're deported."

"I get it. But how am I supposed to prove something that happened six years ago in another country?"

Jack hesitated. He'd interviewed and cross-examined scores of crime victims in his career. There was no template. A question that might mean nothing to one victim could send another to dark and unimaginable places.

"Walk me through the case in El Salvador. How did you convince the prosecutor that you were sexually assaulted?"

"I don't want to go through that again."

"I understand."

"I don't think you do."

"You're right. I'm sorry. I hate when people say they understand when they can't possibly. Let's see if I can do a better job of explaining where I'm going with this, all right?"

"Sure."

"I want to explore a claim of asylum for you. Do you know what asylum is?"

"I know that everybody here wants it."

"And obviously not everybody here qualifies. You might, as the victim of sexual violence."

"Do you have any idea how many women in this jail are victims of sexual violence?"

"I don't doubt it for a minute. And I don't want to mislead you: to get you asylum, we have to prove a lot more than the fact that you're a victim of sexual violence. We have to prove that the violence is connected to government action, and that you have a credible fear of it happening again if you're deported."

"How do we do that?"

"Let's put that aside for the moment. Nothing else matters if we can't prove step one: you were sexually assaulted."

"So we're back to where this conversation started. I have to convince the judge I was raped."

"Yes. And again I'll be honest. Going into immigration court is like going back to the bad old days. The social bias against believing a woman's claim of sexual assault is real in any courtroom. But at least in the criminal courts there have been some improvements.

Like the old laws that required corroborating evidence to prove rape. Those have been repealed."

"What's corroborating evidence?"

"Something other than your own testimony. Like a rape kit, for example. Or a witness to the crime."

"So we don't need a witness in my case. Is that what you're saying?"

"That's in a criminal court. I know this sounds crazy, but it's easier to prove rape in a criminal prosecution than in an immigration case. I'm not talking about 'the law,'" he said, making air quotes. "I'm talking reality. We're going to need more than your testimony."

"So we do need a witness?"

"That's one form of corroborating evidence. But the fact is that most sexual assaults don't have witnesses."

She lowered her eyes. "What if mine did?"

It wasn't the response Jack had expected. He proceeded cautiously. "Was there a witness in your case?"

She nodded.

Jack hesitated again. A "witness" could mean a lot of things. Gang rape was one of them. "Is that why the prosecutor in El Salvador believed you?"

Again she nodded.

"How many witnesses were there?"

She took a moment, then raised her index finger.

"One?" asked Jack.

She nodded.

Jack gave her more time, then asked the question that had to be asked. "Who was it?"

She didn't answer.

"Julia? Can you tell me the name of the witness?"

Her gaze was fixed downward, somewhere on the floor. "I talked with a counselor on Friday. Sandra is her name. She helps victims like me."

"Did you tell her about the witness?"

"No. She said I could call her if I wanted to."

"Would you rather talk to her about this? Should we ask her to come back?"

Julia took a deep breath, but she didn't answer.

"Julia, should I get the counselor? Or can you tell me?"

"I can tell you," she said softly.

"Okay. Good. Take your time. What's the witness's name?"

Jack waited. Finally, Julia looked up, her eyes welling with tears.

"Beatriz."

CHAPTER 14

A midafternoon flight from Jacksonville landed Jack in Miami before rush hour. Beatriz and her aunt met him at his office. It was near the criminal courthouse in an old neighborhood that was transitioning from single-family homes to a mix of residential and commercial, where historic residences were being converted into art studios and professional office space.

"Cool house," said Beatriz.

Jack's office dated back to the 1920s, ancient by Miami standards, built in the old Florida style with a coral-rock facade and a big covered porch that made you want to pull up a rocking chair.

"The very first owner was a famous Miami pioneer, Julia Tuttle," said Jack.

Beatriz smiled. "Julia," she said, giving the dearly departed Ms. Tuttle the Spanish "Hoolia" pronunciation. "Like my mom."

Jack hadn't made that connection, but he liked it. "Yeah, like your mom."

Jack led them inside. The previous owner was the Freedom Institute, where Jack had worked as a young attorney fresh out of law school. Four years of defending death row inmates proved to be enough for Jack, so he struck out on his own as a sole practitioner. A decade later, when his mentor passed away and the institute was on the brink of financial collapse, Jack came up with a plan to save it, which eventually meant buying the building. The Freedom Institute operated rent-free upstairs in the renovated bedrooms. Jack and his longtime assistant ran his practice downstairs.

"Wow," said Beatriz.

Jack's career had its share of ups and downs, but lately it had been up, and his renovation of the old "Hoolia" house reflected better times. The original floors of Dade County pine had been sanded and refinished. The high ceilings and crown moldings had been restored. The bad fluorescent lighting, circa 1970, had been replaced in a total electrical update. The living room was an impressive reception area decorated with oriental rugs, authentic antiques, and silk draperies.

Beatriz stopped at the edge of a gorgeous Sarouk rug. "Should we take our shoes off?"

"People have done much worse than walk on that rug." Jack was thinking of the night that he'd hit big on one of his contingency-fee cases, and Theo had stopped by to help him celebrate with "shots of tequila, no training wheels"—no salt, no lime. It hadn't been pretty.

Jack led them to what was once Julia Tuttle's dining room, now his private office. Rather than take the power position behind his desk, they each took an armchair near the fireplace that had once been the house's only source of heat. Jack didn't want to jump right into business, so he asked Beatriz about the *Star Wars* T-shirt she was wearing. He was failing miserably in his attempt to convince her that there was blue bantha milk in his refrigerator when Cecilia reminded them that the meeting had a purpose.

"Beatriz and I talked about what happened to her mother," Cecilia said.

The transition was too abrupt. Beatriz fell silent and drew her hands into her lap, tightening them into twin balls of tension.

"Let's ease into this a bit," said Jack. "You know what we came here to talk about, right, Beatriz?"

She nodded.

"We all know something bad happened to your mom in El Salvador. Let's just call it 'the situation,' okay?"

"Okay."

"How old were you when the situation happened?"

"Eight."

"Where were you when it happened?"

"Home."

"Where in your house?"

She wrung her hands. "I can't remember."

"Do you remember where your mother was?"

She paused, as if trying to recall. "I don't."

"Was anyone else in the house?"

Another long pause to search her memory. "Not that I remember."

Cecilia jumped in. "She doesn't remember much."

"That's okay," said Jack, keeping his focus on Beatriz. "I just want to know everything you can remember about the situation."

Beatriz breathed in and out. "I remember I was home with my mom. And I remember hiding in a closet."

"Why were you hiding in the closet?"

Her struggle continued, and Jack saw more pain than strain in her expression. "I don't know."

"Do you want a minute to think about it?"

"I said I *don't know*," she said sharply.

"That's fine," said Jack, keeping his voice gentle. "Is there anything else you can remember?"

Her eyelashes fluttered, as if powering her recall. "I remember talking to a man about it."

"About the situation?"

"Right."

"Was your mom there for this conversation?"

"No."

"Who else was there?"

"A police officer."

"Was this in your house?"

"No. I think it was the police station. It was a long time after— after the situation. They asked me a lot of questions."

"Was this after your mother was charged with a crime?"

"I have no idea."

"Do you remember what you told them?"

"No."

"Do you remember anything at all?"

Beatriz shook her head.

Jack could have probed further, but Beatriz appeared to have had enough. And Jack wanted a word in private with Cecilia. He told Beatriz to wait where she was while he and Cecilia stepped out. Jack closed the door on the way out and led Cecilia to the reception area in the old living room.

"Did Julia change her mind about this?" he asked.

"I don't understand your question."

"At our meeting this morning, Julia told me that Beatriz was a witness to the crime. From what I heard in there, I get the impression that Julia had second thoughts about putting her daughter in this position, so she called Beatriz while I was flying back from Jacksonville and told her not to get involved."

"That's not what's going on."

"How do you know?"

"I just know."

"*How* do you know?"

"Because that's what a good mother would do."

Jack hadn't expected that. "Are you saying Julia's not a good mother?"

"No, I'm sorry," she said with a shake of her head, chiding herself. "I didn't mean that. This is all just so stressful."

"Cecilia, is there something you should tell me about your sister?"

"No. That was just a stupid remark I made. It makes me sad to see what Beatriz is going through day after day, and sometimes I get mad at Julia for it, but this is not her fault. Just forget what I said."

Jack didn't answer right away. He let the silence linger, taking note of how Cecilia handled it.

"Seriously," said Cecilia. "Nobody told Beatriz to get amnesia."

"Okay," said Jack. "But if Beatriz isn't under her mother's order to forget everything, we have a child witness with some seriously suppressed memories."

"I don't know what to do about that."

"I have a couple of ideas," said Jack.

"I hope at least one of them is good."

Jack gazed toward his office, thinking of Righley, thinking that Beatriz had been just four years older than his own daughter when she'd witnessed something no child should ever witness.

"So do I," he said.

CHAPTER 15

The light in Hugo's closet switched on, and he felt the barrel of a gun pressing up under his chin.

"Don't shoot," he said, barely moving his mouth.

"Soon, you will beg for this bullet." It was El Lobo, and he smelled like tequila. "Now get up. We're going to the party room."

The party room. *Not again.*

Hugo felt the barrel of the gun against the back of his head, as El Lobo tied his wrists behind his back. He did a poor job of it. Much more slack than usual. *Definitely drunk.*

With his hands behind his back and a drunken Zeta breathing down his neck, Hugo walked down the hallway as directed and entered the party room. El Lobo's men were seated on barstools around the grill, but there was no hostage. The men were using it as a card table. Two empty bottles of tequila were on the floor. A full bottle was being passed around. In the middle of the table was a pile of cash.

"Keep walking," El Lobo said.

The barrel of the gun felt glued to the base of his skull as Hugo stepped forward. The drunk Zetas welcomed him with merriment as El Lobo shoved him toward the grill.

Hugo's throat was going dry. "I will never give you a phone number," he said with defiance.

"Shut up!"

Hugo showed no reaction, but the response cut through him like a knife. El Lobo had a frightening edge to his voice. Tequila could make men mean, and a meaner El Lobo was not a good thing.

"Kneel," said El Lobo.

Hugo lowered himself to his knees, his gaze cast toward the floor. El Lobo grabbed him by the throat.

"I'm going to give you one more chance: Give us a phone number."

El Lobo released his grip, and Hugo coughed in his struggle for air. "Kiss my ass," he said, coughing again.

El Lobo gathered the nylon rope that El Electricista used to tie the prisoners to the grill. Then he went to the small table in the corner of the room, picked it up, and smashed it to pieces on the floor. He grabbed one of the broken table legs with one hand and held the loop of rope in the other.

"My friends," he shouted to his fellow Zetas, "I give you the garrote!"

The men responded with a rhythmic chant, as if they were at a soccer game: *"El garrote, el garrote, el garrote!"*

"Quiet!" shouted El Lobo, and then he stepped closer to Hugo. "You ever heard of the garrote, Señor Hugo?"

Of course he had. The gangs of El Salvador were always looking for more inventive ways to murder their rivals. But Hugo said nothing.

"Let me show you." El Lobo dropped the loop over Hugo's head like a noose. Then he fed the table leg through the rope and turned it quickly, tightening the slack. It squeezed around Hugo's neck, but not too much.

"The rules are simple, my friends. I deal each of you one card. Low cards take a shot of tequila and add fifty pesos to the kitty. High card turns the garrote. Just *one* turn. And here's the payoff: if it is your turn of the garrote that makes the Salvadoran give us a phone number, you take the pot!"

The men rolled with laughter, loving it, except for one skeptic, a fat guy who was naked from the waist up and covered with tattoos. "What if he won't give a phone number and just dies? Who gets the pot?"

El Lobo smiled at the man's stupidity, then reached down and tapped Hugo not so gently on the face. "He'll give us the phone number," El Lobo said, still smiling.

The men laughed. The fat one poured a round of shots, which the Zetas belted back in a toast to El Lobo and his imaginative games.

"Let the tournament begin!" shouted El Lobo, as he dealt the first round of cards.

The losers groaned, took their hundred-proof medicine, and anted up their fifty pesos each. The Zeta who'd been dealt a king of hearts gave the table leg another turn. Hugo's head tilted back, and the noose gripped his neck. He had no intention of giving up a phone number, but even if he'd wanted to, he could never have forced the words from his mouth.

El Lobo dealt another hand. The losers drank a shot of tequila. Another winner turned the garrote. Hugo groaned, but it was more like wheezing. His vision blurred.

Still another hand was dealt. Ace of spades topped queen of diamonds.

Drink, drink, drink!

Another turn of the garrote.

Hugo could no longer bear it. His body twisted, his feet slid out from under him, and he rolled to the floor. One of the men—another winner?—grabbed him, maintaining pressure on the garrote as he buried his knee into Hugo's sternum. Hugo was pinned on his back, completely at the man's mercy. His head pounded with congestion, like the worst sinus headache imaginable. His eyes bulged. His face flushed red. It was as if he could hear nothing but his own desperate grunts, but then he heard something more.

El Lobo was shouting at him, demanding a phone number.

Hugo struggled to make out the words, wanted to answer if it would end this suffering. But it was all running together.

The garrote tightened further. Hugo tasted blood in his mouth as small bleeding sites erupted in the moist, soft mucosa of the lips and mouth. The shouting continued, except that to Hugo's ears it no longer seemed like shouting. It sounded like . . . singing. As he struggled to remain conscious, El Lobo and his gang were singing to him like a choir of angels.

The explosion that followed left Hugo aghast. A crimson shower of blood and gray matter left him wondering if his head had actually exploded, but El Lobo was suddenly on top of him, lifeless, with a gaping hole in the top of his shattered skull.

"*Coño!*" Hugo shouted, shocked to discover that he had a voice. There was no pressure on the garrote, but his excitement was short-lived, as mini-explosions erupted across the party room. The windows shattered, woodwork splintered into pieces, and Zetas dropped to the floor in pools of their own blood.

"*La policía!*" a wounded Zeta shouted. He shot out the lights with a pistol, raised an Uzi to the window, and returned the spray of gunfire.

Hugo played dead in the darkness, gaining strength and continuing to recover from the garrote as bullets flew overhead. Another Zeta dropped to the floor, shot dead. A bullet skipped across the tile inches from Hugo's face. Maybe it was a police raid. Maybe a rival gang had declared war. Whoever was showering the Zeta stronghold with bullets seemed to draw no distinction between kidnapper and hostage.

Gotta get out of here!

Hugo wriggled his hands free from behind his back—El Lobo's tying had been sloppy indeed—and took the automatic pistol from El Lobo's dead hand. In the darkness, he slithered across the floor to the door, which was already pockmarked with bullet holes as another spray of gunfire from somewhere outside the building sent more splinters flying.

Hugo counted at least three dead Zetas on the floor. Two others, maybe a third, were at the windows returning gunfire. Hugo could stay in the party room and die with the criminals or he could make a run for it.

Hugo checked the pistol. Nine millimeter. Semiautomatic. Fifteen rounds in the magazine and one in the pipe. He took a deep breath, said a quick prayer, and flung open the door. The *pop-pop-pop* of gunfire was all the warning he needed to keep his head low as he launched himself into the hallway.

CHAPTER 16

Nope," said Andie. "No way are you going to El Salvador."

Jack was in bed, Righley had been down for hours, and Andie was sitting on the edge of the mattress brushing her hair. She had green eyes from her Anglo father, but that raven-black hair was from her mother, who was a descendant of the Yakama tribe in central Washington's Yakima Valley. Jack didn't have to look far to get the "we're all immigrants" message.

"If I'm going to make a case for asylum, I have to prove that my client was sexually assaulted in her home country. Her daughter witnessed it but has no memory of it. The last thing I want to do is resurrect those memories for Beatriz."

"How does going to El Salvador solve anything?"

"I get off the plane, I go straight to the courthouse, and I meet with the prosecutor who decided that Julia should get no jail time for violating El Salvador's law against abortion. Obviously he believed she had been sexually assaulted, or he wouldn't have made that recommendation. I get an affidavit from him saying exactly that, and I come home."

"Can't you just call him?"

"I've been trying. He won't call me back. If I go see him, I know I can make it happen."

"One problem."

"What?"

"You're not going."

"Can we talk about this, please?"

"Jack, no. First off, plane tickets aren't free. Who's paying for all this?"

"I'm using miles where I can, so it's really not much so far. And I started pulling tax info for the accountant this week. Last year was my best ever practicing law. We can afford to give something back."

"And I love it that you think that way. I truly do. So forget that. Money's not my real issue. Jack, do you realize that, other than actual war zones, San Salvador has the highest murder rate of any city in the world?"

"Let's not exaggerate."

"I'm not exaggerating. I work for the FBI. I know these things. Eighteen homicides a day in a country that has fewer people than the state of Massachusetts. The rate is like twenty times higher than the worst city in the United States. This is an entirely unnecessary risk. You're a married man with a four-year-old daughter."

"And an eight-year-old golden who still thinks he's a puppy."

"Fine. Make fun, Jack."

Jack slid across the mattress and sat right beside her. "Hey, I'm sorry. I don't mean to be a jerk."

"I know," she said with a smile. "You just can't help it."

"Absolutely true. And this big jerk has a really big problem. I need something more than my client's testimony to convince an immigration judge that she was the victim of sexual assault. I'd like to be able to do that without psychologically scarring her daughter."

Jack held his wife, and she leaned against him. The warmth of her body through the silk nightie felt good.

"There are ways to minimize the trauma for Beatriz," said Andie.

"What are you thinking?"

She pulled away from him, unfastened the long gold chain around her neck, and dangled her pendant in front of him. Slowly, it swung back and forth before his eyes, and Jack followed it.

"You want to have sex tonight," she said, talking like a hypnotist. "You *really* want to have sex tonight."

Jack tried not to laugh. "Hypnosis?"

She stopped. "Yeah. Why not? We've used it on child witnesses. Some people say it works. Maybe it does."

The pendant started swinging again.

"What do you think, jerko?" she asked.

"I'm kind of a skeptic," said Jack. His gaze drifted away from the pendant, meeting Andie's. She looked amazing. "But for some reason, I suddenly want to have sex tonight."

Andie laughed, put the talisman on the nightstand, and pulled Jack into the sea of blankets.

Jack knew exactly which psychiatrist he wanted Beatriz to see, and on Thursday afternoon Elaine Moore, M.D., was available.

Dr. Moore was not the world's biggest proponent of hypnotically induced memory recall. She used hypnosis in her practice, but she used it cautiously. So cautiously that, in one of his capital cases at the Freedom Institute, Jack called her as an expert witness to *attack* the use of hypnosis in a police homicide investigation. It was Dr. Moore's testimony—"Uncorroborated, hypnotically elicited memories can lead to the wrongful imprisonment of innocent people"—that had won a last-minute stay of execution for Jack's client.

The session with Beatriz lasted about an hour. One of the very first things Jack had done for Julia was the paperwork naming Cecilia as Beatriz's health-care surrogate. It was intended for medical emergencies, but it also allowed Cecilia to sign the medical consent form for both the hypnosis and the videotaping of the session. Jack met with Dr. Moore in her office, without Beatriz or her aunt, to watch the video.

"Do you want to start from the very beginning, pre-hypnosis?"

"Better fast-forward," said Jack. "I might go under just watching you do it."

"It doesn't work that way, Jack." She smiled, seeming to understand that he was kidding. "Just so you know, Beatriz wanted her aunt with her, but she's off camera."

Dr. Moore cued up the video to about the middle of her session with Beatriz. Jack watched the screen. Beatriz was seated in a chair with eyes closed and shoulders slumping. All sign of worry and nervousness had vanished from her expression. *Peaceful* was the word that came to Jack's mind.

Dr. Moore adjusted the audio and, with a push of a button, the screen came to life.

"Beatriz?" the doctor in the recording said in a soothing voice. "What can you see?"

"It's dark."

Of course it's dark, your eyes are closed, was Jack's initial reaction. But he quickly picked up on the fact that she was recalling a dark place.

"Can you see anything?" the doctor asked her.

"Lines. White lines. Light."

"What else?"

"It smells like Mommy's clothes in here."

Dr. Moore hit PAUSE. "It took us a while to get to this point. She was hiding in a closet. Her mother's clothes were hanging above her. The white lines she's talking about are the slats on a typical closet door."

"Got it," said Jack.

The video resumed.

"Can you touch the lines, Beatriz? Can you feel them?"

"Uh-huh. On my face."

Jack said, "So her face is pressed up against the closet door?"

"Right."

The video continued.

"What do you see now?" the doctor asked her. "I want you to think hard and tell me what you see."

A minute passed, and Jack watched the transformation on the

child's face. The peacefulness evaporated before his eyes. Something seemed to rise up inside her, forcing the words from her mouth in Spanish.

"Stop!" Beatriz shouted.

Another minute passed. The expression on Beatriz's face was one of horror.

"Stop what?" the doctor asked, prodding, also having switched to Spanish.

"Stop! Stop hurting her!"

The child's anguish was getting harder for Jack to watch, but he didn't dare turn away.

"Stop! *Papi*, stop!"

Jack felt chills.

"That's enough!" Cecilia shouted, suddenly appearing on-screen. She hugged her niece and held her tightly in her arms. Dr. Moore stopped the video.

"Obviously Beatriz came out of it there," the doctor said.

"Is *'Papi'* who I think it is?" asked Jack.

"Yes. I spoke with Beatriz afterward. *Papi* is what she called her father right up until the last time she saw him."

"So what she saw—" Jack started to say, then stopped to catch his breath. "Beatriz saw her father sexually assault her mother?"

"That's one interpretation," said Dr. Moore.

"Do you have another one?"

"Yes, absolutely. That's why I'm skeptical of the use of hypnosis in police investigations. Another perfectly sound interpretation is that Beatriz was playing in the closet and happened to catch her parents having sex in their bedroom. That's a traumatic event for a child."

"Even more traumatic for an adult," said Jack, trying not to imagine it.

Another psychiatrist might have found it inappropriate, but she knew Jack well enough to appreciate the sometimes warped sense of humor that allowed death penalty lawyers to maintain their sanity.

"You see my point, right, Jack?"

"I do."

"It's my view that the underlying response to hypnosis always implicates some level of fantasy and imagination. So be careful with this."

"I will be."

"You shouldn't take anything you heard in that video at face value. You need corroboration. Do you get my drift?"

"I do," said Jack. "The way I see it, Beatriz's mother could use a little refresher on the free flow of information between a client and her lawyer."

CHAPTER 17

Beatriz climbed out of bed before dawn. It had been a sleepless Thursday night, and her alarm wouldn't sound for another forty minutes, but she couldn't take another minute of lying there on her back, wide awake, staring at the ceiling.

What do you see, Beatriz?

She had no memory of seeing Dr. Moore speak those words, but she couldn't stop hearing that voice in her head.

Tell me what you can see?

She stood motionless beside the bed, alone in the darkness of what Cecilia called the "spare bedroom." With no closet and barely enough room for a twin bed and a dresser, it wasn't much of a bedroom; and it was a "spare" only in the sense that neither Cecilia nor her three roommates used it, but it was rarely unused. An endless stream of friends and relatives passing through Miami had slept there on the journey to somewhere else, someplace better.

Beatriz took one step and stopped. The ceramic floor was cool beneath her feet, but she suddenly felt a rush of fear and anger inside her that burned like an electric current. The mini-blinds on the window were closed, but there was just enough of an opening for the light of a streetlamp to shine through the slats. White lines of light in the darkness, like the slatted closet door in her parents' bedroom.

What do you see, Beatriz?

She lunged at the dangling cord and yanked it so hard that the entire set of mini-blinds came crashing down from the window frame. It made a terrible metallic racket when it hit the tile floor, like exploding soda cans, and Beatriz let out a scream so loud that she frightened herself. As she fell to the floor, sobbing, a light blinked on in the hallway. Cecilia came running into the room, switched on the bedroom lamp, and saw the mess.

"Beatriz! Are you all right?"

Cecilia lifted her niece from the floor, sat her on the edge of the bed, and held her. "Beatriz. What happened?"

Beatriz could barely sit up. "I saw it again," she said, choking back tears.

Her aunt stroked her head gently. Beatriz waited for her to ask her *what* she saw again, but the question didn't come. Cecilia seemed to know.

"It's all right, baby," she said, rocking her sister's child. "Everything's going to be all right."

Alarmed by the commotion, Cecilia's roommates suddenly appeared in the doorway. Cecilia assured them that everything was okay. They said nothing to suggest that Beatriz was no longer welcome, but the room had been a bit of a teenage mess even before the mini-blinds were splayed across the floor, and Beatriz suddenly felt like an intruder, or at least like a burden.

"I need to get ready for school," she said.

"It's early," said Cecilia. "Why don't you try to get a little more sleep."

"I can't sleep."

Her aunt let her go, and Beatriz made her way down the hall to the bathroom. A single bathroom for three women and a teenage girl was not without problems, but Beatriz had no complaints. A hot shower was not something to be taken for granted. At some point in the life of this old house, probably when the neighborhood was considered upper middle class, a previous owner had ripped out the bathtub and installed a walk-in shower like Beatriz had never seen before. The door was glass. The two side walls were made of glass blocks, floor to ceiling. When the water was hot enough, and with the light shining through the blocks of blurred glass, tiny rainbows shimmered in the rising steam. Beatriz liked to turn on the shower, sit inside the glass box, feel the splash of hot water on her face and body, and let the rainbows rise from nowhere.

"Beatriz?"

She stirred, confused. Water was falling from above, but it was lukewarm, not nearly as hot as she liked it. She heard knocking but not on the shower door. Someone was in the hallway at the bathroom door.

"Beatriz, are you okay in there?" It was Cecilia.

The water in the shower stall was three inches deep. *Must've fallen asleep.*

Beatriz rose, turned off the shower, and wrapped herself in a towel. Her aunt was right outside the door when Beatriz opened it.

"You're going to miss your bus if you don't hurry, sweetie."

Panic struck. Beatriz was working on the "perfect attendance" award at school—zero absences, not a single tardy slip. She was determined not to blow it, even though her twenty-minute ride on a school bus from her house in Little Havana was now a forty-minute ride on a city bus from her aunt's house. Beatriz hurried to her bedroom, dressed in record time, and grabbed her backpack on the way out of the house. She ran all the way to the bus stop and caught the Number 11 bus just a split second before the driver closed the hydraulic doors. There were plenty of open seats. She took one about halfway back and slid all the way over to the window, catching her breath and pulling a comb through her wet hair, as the bus pulled away from the curb and merged into morning traffic.

Beatriz was peering out the window, alone with her thoughts, when a stranger sat down beside her. Beatriz had been the only passenger to board at her stop, so for some reason the man had moved from somewhere in the back of the bus to be next to her. She shifted closer to the window but didn't say anything.

"I know your mother," the man said.

She didn't look directly at him, but with a cut of her eyes she caught a glimpse. She was certain she'd never seen him before. "Who are you?"

"Your mother used to work for me at the coffee shop."

Beatriz had yet to hear a full explanation of why her mother had rushed home from work at Café de Caribe and told her to pack their bags, but the vibe she was getting from this man was not a comfortable one.

"What do you want?" she asked.

"I need to get a message to your mother. Unfortunately, she's kind of hard to reach these days. So I want you to deliver it to her."

Beatriz was reluctant to say yes or no.

"Will you do that for me?" he asked.

"I guess so."

"Her lawyer came to see me. He's giving her very bad advice. Tell your mother that no one is going to believe her. The judge will believe me."

Beatriz was silent. The bus slowed as they approached the next stop.

"And tell her that calling me a liar is a very foolish thing. Because I have ICE on speed dial. And I know where you live."

The bus stopped and the doors opened. McBride rose, walked to the front, and stepped off the bus.

It gave Beatriz a chill to see him standing on the sidewalk, watching her through the window as the bus pulled away.

CHAPTER 18

Jack decided that his next visit to Julia would piggyback on the wallet of a paying client. The following week, he had a sentencing hearing before a federal judge in the Northern District of Georgia for a white-collar client who would soon be wearing orange. Macclenny was in the final analysis "on the way" to nowhere, but Hartsfield-Jackson Atlanta International Airport via Jacksonville with a side trip to the Baker County Facility worked just fine.

They met in the usual room, at the usual table, in the usual chairs. Julia wore the same orange that Jack's convicted Georgia client would be wearing for the next ten years. Julia even looked bored, no spark in her eyes and no hope in her voice. The monotony of prison life was unbearable for the guilty or the innocent, the convicted or the uncharged, the inmate or the detainee. And detention was prison, no two ways about it.

"Beatriz delivered quite the surprise last week," said Jack.

"I heard."

"From whom?" Jack hadn't told her.

"Cecilia. I called Beatriz over the weekend, and my sister filled me in."

Jack gave her another quick lecture about no privacy on jail telephones, but that was not at all the point of his visit. "You didn't tell me that the man who sexually assaulted you was your husband," said Jack.

"You didn't ask."

"You told me you didn't know the man who raped you."

"I'm not sure I actually said that, but it wouldn't be a lie if I did. By the time Jorge did this to me, I felt like I didn't know him."

"Don't be cute with me, Julia. The identity of the man who sexually assaulted you is critical information. If Beatriz was a witness, how did you think I would not find out?"

"She was in a closet. It was dark. She heard me screaming and knew I was being attacked. She never told me or anyone else that she saw the man who was hurting me."

"Are you telling me that this session with Dr. Moore was the first time Beatriz identified your attacker?"

"As far as I know, yes. Now I regret that I even told you she was a witness. I would never have brought her into this if I'd thought this would come out. Do you think I *wanted* her to know that her father raped her mother?"

"She's always known it. The hynopsis just helped her recall."

"And now she'll never forget it," said Julia, her voice shaking. "I can't believe I did this to her. What kind of terrible mother am I?"

Jack recalled his conversation with Cecilia—when she'd withdrawn her words—and wondered if the similar accusations had been laid in the phone conversation between sisters.

"You can't beat yourself up about these things," said Jack.

"I should have told you it was Jorge."

"Why didn't you?" asked Jack. "Was it because you wanted to keep it a secret from Beatriz?"

She looked away. "Partly."

"What's the other reason?"

She looked him in the eye. "Truthfully? I'm scared."

"Of what?"

"Him."

"Still? You said he left two years ago."

"Yeah, but you have to understand that this was not a onetime thing that happened six years ago. This started before Beatriz was even born, and it kept on going until the day he left. He always told me he'd find me if I ever told anyone what went on inside our house."

"Do you have any reason to think he'd actually find you here?"

She paused, as if not sure how to answer. Or maybe she just wasn't sure Jack could ever understand. "Have you ever lived with someone who controlled everything you did, everything you said, everywhere you went? Have you ever felt worthless, like nothing you ever do is right? Have you ever been afraid to have your own thoughts? It doesn't matter where I go, Jack. Even inside this place—a detention center for *women*—I sometimes find myself looking over my shoulder. I have no reason to think he won't find me, no matter where I go."

"I'm sorry you have to live like that."

"Me, too. He's been gone for two years, but it's always on my mind. When I applied for the job at Café de Caribe, people thought I lied about being Dominican and part Haitian to work in an island coffee shop. But that's not it. Sometimes I wish I could just reinvent myself. Be someone else. Does that make any sense?"

"It does. And all of this could be part of your final hearing on deportation. But right now we have to focus on getting you out of detention."

"Does this change anything?"

"It might. The reason this came up in the first place is that you were convicted under El Salvador's ban on abortion. ICE took the position that you were a convicted felon ineligible for bond. The judge seemed willing to disregard that conviction if you terminated the pregnancy because you were sexually assaulted."

"I *was* sexually assaulted."

"Yes. But I know what ICE will argue. The El Salvador law has no exception for rape, and this is not a case under U.S. immigration law where the judge should recognize one."

"Why not?"

"Because you and Jorge were husband and wife, and if the child had been born, he or she would have been Beatriz's full sibling."

"Do you think the judge will agree with that argument?"

"He shouldn't, but he might. Immigration judges work for the

Department of Justice. They aren't bending over backward to find reasons to keep you here."

"Okay, let's say the judge agrees with ICE and says I violated the law of El Salvador, no exception. Then what?"

"Then you're a convicted felon under U.S. immigration law. There's no way you'll be released on bond, and it's almost a certainty that you'll be deported after the final hearing."

"That's just not right."

"We're working in an arena where anything that can be used against you will be used to the fullest. That's the way ICE operates."

She looked away, thinking. "What if I didn't want the abortion?"

"Then why did you get one?"

Her gaze shifted back to Jack. "I didn't have a choice. Jorge wanted it. He found the doctor who did it. I don't even know what kind of doctor he was. Jorge took me to the house and we did it in the bedroom. He stood there and watched to make sure it was done. He paid for it."

Jack considered it, thinking aloud: "Your abusive husband rapes you and forces you to get an abortion. You don't sound like a criminal to me."

"So you think we can win? I might get out of here on bond?"

"I'm liking our case," said Jack. "But there's a big 'if.'"

"If what?"

"If we can prove it. We have your testimony, and we have Beatriz's."

"Not Beatriz. Cecilia and I talked about it. This is too much for her. I won't let Beatriz testify."

The decision didn't shock Jack, and it sounded nonnegotiable. "All right, then. We have your testimony."

"Isn't that enough?"

"I guess it will have to be," said Jack.

CHAPTER 19

It's not enough," said Jack.

Theo grabbed Jack's half-empty beer glass from the bar top, refilled it from the tap, and placed it back in front of Jack. "How's that?"

"Thanks, but I meant Julia's testimony. By itself, it's not enough to convince an immigration judge to release her on bond. Have you been listening to anything I've been saying?"

Jack's flight from Jacksonville had landed him in Miami early that evening, and he had driven straight to Cy's Place, the jazz club that Theo owned and operated. It was named after his sax-playing uncle, Cyrus Knight, who'd played in Miami's Overtown Village, once known as Little Harlem. Happy hour had just gotten under way, and cocktails were starting to flow at the big U-shaped bar. The Friday-night musicians were setting up, and in an hour or so Cy's Place would ooze that certain vibe of a jazz-loving crowd, with crowded café tables fronting a small stage for live music. It was at one of those tables that Jack had proposed to Andie.

"Yeah, I'm listening," said Theo. "You got a dog-breath case. What else is new?"

"It's not a dog-breath case. I just need more evidence."

"Uh-huh. See that short guy over there?" he said, indicating with a jerk of his head.

Jack glanced down to the other end of the bar. "What about him?"

"He's not short. He just needs more height."

Jack drank his beer. "I take your point. But my case is not impossible. I can get more evidence."

"Yeah, how? Julia won't let her daughter testify. She's so scared of her husband that she thinks he might track her down inside a women's jail, so don't be surprised if she folds on you, too. That will leave you with zero witnesses." Theo rinsed a couple of cocktail glasses in the sink behind the bar. "Sounds like you got a dog-breath case to me."

Jack glanced up at ESPN on the flat-screen TV, thinking. Theo wasn't off the mark. It wasn't just a question of whether the judge would believe Julia. It was entirely possible that she'd fold on the day of the hearing, too afraid to testify about certain things or to testify at all.

"There is another way to go about this," said Jack.

"Yeah, but isn't it a crime to bribe an immigration judge?"

Jack ignored it. "Andie put the kibosh on a trip to El Salvador when I mentioned it before. But I think I need to go."

Theo extended his hand across the bar top. "It's been really nice knowing you."

Jack didn't take the offered handshake, so Theo withdrew it. "You honestly think I can't go to El Salvador without getting myself killed?"

"No. I think you can't ignore a direct order from Sergeant Henning without getting yourself killed."

"*Agent* Henning. They don't have ranks like that in the FBI. But never mind that. The only thing I can say to you is this: I'm going to El Salvador."

Theo leaned into the bar, resting his forearms on the polished granite top. "Let me ask you a question. Julia seems cool, not to mention gorgeous."

"You really do have a thing for Latin chicks, don't you?"

"Who doesn't? But forget that. I just wanna know: Why you puttin' so much of yourself into a case like this?"

"I could give you about a hundred reasons. I'll give you one. In all the years you've known Abuela, how many times has she asked me for a favor? Me as a lawyer, I mean."

"I'm gonna say none."

Jack slapped the bar top. "Close enough, dog breath!" he said like a game-show host. "And for being so smart, you have won this prize chosen especially for you: a round-trip ticket to the exotic and always exciting San Salvador!"

"Cool. Like old times."

Jack took another drink. "But safer."

Theo smiled. "Sure, Jack. Whatever you say."

They landed at Monseñor Oscar Arnulfo Romero International Airport on Monday, midmorning. Theo haggled over the airport's departure tax, which went nowhere, but Jack was able to lock the cabdriver into a flat fare for the thirty-mile trip north, away from the Pacific coastline, and into San Salvador.

"Where in the city?" the driver asked in Spanish.

Jack had a printed map and circled the building to avoid any confusion. "Office of the General Prosecutor."

The route took them through the dry terrain south of the city, then through the *barrios*, some lower-middle-class apartment buildings and some dirt-poor shacks, many of which appeared to be abandoned. According to the driver, entire families would just pick up and go, forced from one town to the next by gangs who recruited their children and stole whatever money their working relatives in the United States sent back to El Salvador. The backdrop for such problems was a city nestled in natural beauty. Several of this tiny country's twenty volcanic cones flanked the metropolis, the most stunning of which was the mile-high Boquerón Volcano, touching the sky at over six thousand feet.

In the distance, a green agricultural field stretched across a hillside. "Is that sugarcane?" Theo asked the driver.

"The cemetery," the driver answered in Spanish, and Jack understood most of his explanation, which he translated for Theo.

"He says all the cane fields in El Salvador are cemeteries. It's where gangs like MS-13 dump the bodies. Bus drivers who won't pay extortion. Kids who refuse to join the gang. The cane cutters find them during harvest season. When the fields are combed over, the bones—mountains of bones—turn up. Many of the bodies have been hacked to pieces. Bodies missing legs, missing hands, missing their head."

"Maybe Captain Henning had a point," said Theo.

It was lunchtime, and the driver recommended a quick stop at a *pupusería*, which was the Salvadoran version of a diner dedicated to the confection of *pupusas*, the country's iconic dish. It was like a tortilla, made with corn dough and filled with cheese, pork rind (*chicharrones*), refried beans, or tropical vine flower (*loroco*). Topped with tomato sauce and a kind of tropical sauerkraut known as *curtido*, it was foolish to eat a messy *pupusa* with your bare hands, but that didn't stop Theo from being "that guy." Twenty minutes and as many napkins later, they were on the road again. The driver dropped them at the curb in front of the building and warned them not to wander too far into *El Centro*, which wasn't safe. Before pulling away, he asked Jack to tell the president about the gangs when he got back to the United States, as if Jack had a direct line to the White House. Jack told him he'd try.

The prosecutor in Julia's abortion case had never returned Jack's phone calls from Miami, so Jack's only official appointment was with a criminologist who worked in the same building. Israel Tovar was a portly man who thought carefully before he spoke, with more than twenty years of experience in the Office of the General Prosecutor. He and his assistant were the only forensic investigators in the country who did exhumations. Jack thought Tovar would be a good starting point on the disappearance of Julia's husband.

"He's been missing for two years," said Jack. "His wife and daughter have no idea where he is."

Tovar nodded, as if he'd heard such words too many times before. He rose from behind his cluttered desk and invited Jack to walk with him to a huge map on the wall that was covered with colorful dots.

"Each dot is a burial site," he said.

Jack studied the map. Most of the dots—he estimated about fifty—were in and around San Salvador. Dozens more extended toward La Libertad, Santa Ana, and Sonsonate. Not a single one of El Salvador's fourteen departments was free of dots.

"The purple ones are wells," said Tovar, "and the green ones are clandestine cemeteries that my team has already excavated. The blue and red dots are wells and clandestine cemeteries that haven't been explored yet, where there should be more bodies. The yellow dots are mass graves from the civil war that have been excavated. Fifteen at last count, about fifty-five bodies found. The orange dots—ten or eleven there—mark places where I know there are more victims. Just haven't gotten there yet."

"How long you been doing this?" asked Theo.

"Fifteen years. We started with two or three clandestine graves. I'm sorry to say that now we're the country with the most clandestine graves in the world."

"How many bodies have you recovered?" asked Jack.

"About five hundred. We pull them from wells, septic tanks, caves, you name it."

"Cane fields?" asked Jack, checking the taxi driver's story.

"Yes, cane fields, too. You get to notice patterns after a while. Gangs have their own signatures, kind of like serial killers. Those who kill in San Vicente, in the middle of the country, dig circular graves. In the west, it's rectangular graves. In La Libertad, San Salvador, and San Miguel, we find oval-shaped graves. And the bodies tell a story, too. The victims might be naked or put in the ground facedown. Some are marked with a stake and bottles, with wire tourniquets twisted around their necks. Some have been buried alive—you can tell from their body language. Other gangs dismember their victims and cover them with lime. The most gruesome sites are for members of a competing gang. And of course the majority of them are young."

Jack could have told him that Julia's husband probably deserved what he got, but he let Tovar finish the point he was making.

"So you ask me about a woman's husband who disappeared two years ago never to be heard from again. Tell me where you'd like me to start, Mr. Swyteck."

Jack took another look at all the colorful dots. "I wish I could. But maybe there's something else you can help me with."

"Please," said Tovar.

"There's a prosecutor I was hoping to meet," said Jack.

CHAPTER 20

I t was Hugo's first crossing of the Rio Grande. But it was not his first trip to America.

Hugo was a child when he and his parents fled a twelve-year civil war that had displaced thousands and turned countless Salvadoran families into refugees. Because they reached the United States before 2001, his entire family qualified for El Salvador's Temporary Protected Status under U.S. immigration law. They settled in Los Angeles, at the intersection of 18th Street and Union Street, the cradle of Barrio 18. Gangs ruled, and on his fourteenth birthday, Hugo tattooed the gang symbol "18" onto his neck. His mother endured more heartache than any mother should bear, and finally his father kicked him out of the house. An arrest on illegal weapons charges sent him bouncing between detention centers and correctional facilities in South Central Los Angeles. There he found God, but not even He could save Hugo from deportation to El Salvador. Hugo wanted no more of gangs, but a promise of loyalty to any Salvadoran gang was a lifelong commitment. With "18" inked onto his neck, he feared that his only options in San Salvador would be a life of violence with "18" or death at the hands of rival gangs, like Mara Salvatrucha, who would happily run a blade across that tattoo and slit his throat. Before he boarded the ICE flight, however, one of the prison ministers in Los Angeles gave him a tip.

"Go to the Ebenezer Church in the Dina neighborhood of San Salvador," she'd told Hugo. "There's a bakery in the back of the church. Ask for a woman named Julia."

Hugo found the church. He found Julia working in the bakery. He found an angel from heaven—who was married to the husband from hell.

"Is it time yet?" his friend asked in the darkness. It was Paco, the last man on the grill at the ransom hotel. The police raid in Cárdenas had left most of the kidnappers dead. Hugo, Paco, and two other hostages had used the confusion to their advantage, disappearing into the night, and in the morning had caught up with another group of northbound migrants.

Hugo checked the watch he'd taken from the wrist of a dead Zeta. "Almost midnight," he said.

A group of about twenty migrants had been waiting on the Mexican side of the border since noon. Their "coyote," a term that could mean anything from a paid guide to a human smuggler, would lead them across the Rio Grande at the southernmost tip of Texas, west of Brownsville and about sixty miles upriver from where the fourth-largest river system in the United States emptied its snow-fed waters into the Gulf of Mexico.

"You scared?" asked Paco.

It was a cool and cloudless night. Hugo's gaze was fixed on the starlit horizon on the other side of the river, as he kept a sharp eye out for any "stars" that moved at the speed of an ICE patrol helicopter.

"After all we've been through, Paco, you want to know if I'm scared about crossing a river?"

Paco chuckled, but it broke off nervously as their coyote approached and said, "Time to go."

The group gathered at the base of a hill about a hundred yards from the riverbank. Their coyote, a young man named Esteban, did a head count. Five men, eleven women, five children. Two of the children, a boy and his older sister, were traveling on their own, no adult to look after them. Esteban gave final instructions. Anything that can't get wet goes in the plastic bag. Be aware of the undercurrent; when you step on the bank on the other side, you'll be about 200 yards down from where you entered on the Mexican side. If you encounter border patrol anywhere after crossing, keep your hands out of your pockets and never run *toward* them.

"Is the water polluted?" one of the women asked.

They were about a hundred miles downriver from Nuevo Laredo, where broken old pipes sent raw sewage flowing like a waterfall—up to five million gallons every day—into the Rio Grande. "I wouldn't drink it," said Esteban.

They were told not to move until Esteban gave the signal. There were coyotes with other migrants in the area, and a group to Hugo's right suddenly made its move in the darkness. Hugo was relieved to see that his group was not the first to cross; someone else would be the border patrol guinea pigs.

"I think we're next," Paco whispered.

"Yeah," said Hugo.

"Look me up if you ever come to Chicago."

"I will."

"I would like to meet your beautiful woman in Miami. Juanita?"

"Julia."

"Does she know you're coming?"

"No. I haven't talked to her since she left San Salvador."

"Did she tell you she was going to Miami?"

"No."

"How do you know she's there?"

"Because I know her husband is there."

Paco smiled, confused. "What are you going to do? Find her husband and say, 'I'm here for your wife'?"

The question set Hugo thinking about how the pendulum had swung in his life—from Barrio 18 to Ebenezer Church and then back again. Whatever religion he'd found in prison was lost in El Salvador.

"No," said Hugo. "I'm going to kill him."

CHAPTER 21

Who names a church after Scrooge?" asked Theo.

He and Jack were in the back seat of a taxi, and Theo was reading their destination from the map, silently mispronouncing the *Iglesia* Ebenezer. In fairness, if Jack hadn't googled it, he wouldn't have known that Ebenezer was a location mentioned by the books of Samuel as the scene of battles between the Israelites and Philistines.

"Better than the Church of Fagin, I guess," said Jack, but the Dickens allusion was lost on his friend.

It was day two of their trip to San Salvador, and they'd spent the night at one of the city's safest hotels in the quiet Zona Rosa district. The neighborhood around the church was another matter. It was controlled by the notorious 18th Street gang, and the cabdriver offered repeated warnings, even trying in broken English to make sure his foolish American passengers appreciated the *"daohn-jeer."* Jack understood. Julia had told him about the bakery behind the church, and he knew better than to wander around the *barrio*.

The cab stopped behind the church. Even in broad daylight, the only safe place for a cabdriver to sit and wait was outside a major hotel, so Jack tipped him generously and told him to circle back in exactly one hour. Theo led the way and Jack hurried behind him across the sidewalk and into the bakery.

The first thing Jack noticed was the wonderful smell, like any bakery. But the tattoos on the arms, necks, and faces of the bakers told the real story. Some were recognizable objects: flying cars, exotic flowers, or indigenous goddesses. Some were nonsensical—except as gang symbols. Julia had told him that, except for a few volunteers like her, everyone who worked at the church bakery was a former gang member.

"Are you Mr. Swyteck?" a man asked in English. He was considerably older than the other workers, and he was the only one without tattoos. Jack had called ahead to set up a meeting with Julia's old boss, and Jack recognized the voice from their phone conversation.

"Marco?" asked Jack.

He confirmed it with a smile and a handshake. "My beautiful Julia," he said, smiling sadly. "How is she?"

Jack had explained the sobering situation in their phone conversation, but Marco said that he'd prayed for a miracle before going to bed last night and was hoping that her release had come to be. Jack hated to disappoint him, but Marco got over it and invited Jack and Theo into his office to talk in private.

"What do you think of our little bakery?" asked Marco.

"Nice," said Jack.

"Makes me hungry," said Theo.

Marco brought them a sampling of fresh breads and cookies. Theo ate while Jack and Marco talked, starting with a point of curiosity on Jack's part.

"How do you get gang members to work in a bakery?" asked Jack.

Marco smiled. "They've turned to God."

"And the gangs are okay with that?" asked Jack.

"Normally anyone who tries to leave a gang is killed as a traitor. Religious experience is an exception for almost all the gangs—the Mara Salvatrucha, the 18 South, the 18 Revolutionaries, the Mirada Locos, the Mara Maquina, the Mao-Mao. But I would say the Revolutionaries 18 has lost the most soldiers to God."

"But the men who work here still have gang tattoos," said Jack.

"Yes. That is because desecration of any gang symbol, including removal of a tattoo, is punishable by death. But it doesn't matter what worldly symbol is on their skin. As long as they dedicate themselves to God, they are welcome here. And the gangs leave them alone."

"I don't mean to insult your efforts," said Jack, "but what if somebody fakes it just to get out of the gang?"

"They are still welcome here. But if they don't lead a pious life, they will answer to the gangs."

The colored dots on Israel's map of clandestine graves suddenly popped into Jack's mind.

"Let's talk about Julia," said Jack.

"Wonderful person," said Marco. "She was a tremendous help to me here for many years. Literally worked for food so she and her daughter could eat."

"What can you tell me about her husband?"

Marco's expression soured. "What do you want to know?"

"Have you ever met him?"

"Yes."

"When is the last time you saw him?"

"Seven or eight months ago. He came asking for Julia."

"Does she know this?"

Marco shook his head. "No. I told him never to come back here again and to leave Julia alone."

"Julia told me that she hasn't seen him in two years. He left her."

"That's true. He left her because I told him he must go."

"And he listened to you?"

"Mr. Swyteck, I live and work in a war zone. I've picked up bodies from the street right outside this church. I've kept dozens, maybe hundreds of men from becoming another body on the street. On occasion, I have been known to call in favors. When I tell Julia's husband he must go, he knows he *must go*."

"I like this guy," said Theo.

It was a welcome moment of levity, but the mood soon turned serious. "I think I know the answer to this question," said Jack, "but I have to ask. Why did you tell him to go?"

"I could tell you stories. But I won't."

"I would like to hear the truth," said Jack.

"You will. Wait right here."

Marco rose and stepped out of the room. A minute later he re-turned. Three young women were in his company. Jack and Theo rose as Marco introduced each woman by her first name only.

"These women volunteer here, like Julia did," said Marco. "This bakery would shut down without their help."

The women said nothing, and their solemn expressions told Jack that they were not in the room to be congratulated.

Marco spoke to them in Spanish, thanking them for their hon-esty in advance, and telling them how important this was to Julia. Then he continued, still in Spanish.

"Please raise your hand like this," he said, demonstrating, as if swearing an oath, "if you have ever been sexually assaulted."

The woman in the middle was the first to raise her hand. The other two joined.

Marco looked at Jack and asked, "Did you understand my question?"

Jack had been taken aback, but he'd gotten it. "Yes."

Marco addressed the women. "Keep your hand in the air if you were assaulted by Señor Jorge."

No one lowered her hand.

"Keep your hand up if you were sexually assaulted by Señor Jorge more than once."

Their hands didn't move.

Marco thanked them on behalf of himself and Julia, adding that there is no shame in being a survivor of sexual assault. Then he dismissed them, and it was just the men in the room.

"Is there anything else you need to know about Julia's husband, Mr. Swyteck?"

Jack wondered how many other victims there might be. "No," he said. "I think I got it."

CHAPTER 22

Beatriz?"

She heard a woman calling her name, but Beatriz couldn't respond. She couldn't even open her eyes.

"Beatriz, wake up."

Beatriz forced her eyes open but couldn't lift her head from the pillow. Such a hard pillow. The hardest, flattest pillow she'd ever felt. She turned her head, and as her face rolled to one side she sensed the cool veneer of something that didn't feel like her pillow at all.

Someone shoved her shoulder, which made her start.

"That's it. Wake up, girl."

The voice belonged to her math teacher, but Beatriz had no idea what Ms. Alvarez was doing in her bedroom.

"Open your eyes now."

Beatriz wiped away a little pool of spittle that had gathered on the desktop beside her mouth. She wasn't in her bedroom. Her lashes fluttered, and she was beginning to orient herself.

"You slept through the entire class," her teacher said.

Beatriz slowly raised her head from the desktop. Her gaze swept the room and finally came to rest on the algebraic equations written across the whiteboard. It was definitely her math class, but she and her teacher were the only people in the room.

"I missed class?" she asked with concern.

Ms. Alvarez took a seat in the student desk beside her. "I'm afraid so."

"Why did you let me sleep through class?"

"You were out cold."

"I can't miss class!"

"Honey, relax. We all know what you're going through at home. Are you not sleeping at night?"

"No," Beatriz said quietly.

"You're looking skinny to me, too," Ms. Alvarez said, cupping her hand around Beatriz's bony wrist. "Are you eating breakfast, lunch, and dinner?"

"Not really hungry."

"Is there anything you want to talk about?"

Beatriz shook her head.

"You sure?" Ms. Alvarez asked. "I'm a good listener."

Beatriz had told no one about the man on the bus. Ms. Alvarez was her favorite teacher. She wished she could tell her, but what would that accomplish? A phone call to ICE on that man's "speed dial"? Even if he'd dragged her off the bus and raped her, she couldn't have called the police.

"There's nothing to talk about."

"Okay. But at some point we will have to talk about your grades. Two weeks ago you had a ninety-eight. Zeroes on homework are killing you. You have to turn something in. Even if it's incomplete it's better than a zero."

Beatriz nodded.

"Come see me after school today. We can work through it together."

"Okay."

"Great. It's a date," Ms. Alvarez said, and then continued talking, but Beatriz was hearing none of it. She was looking past her teacher, staring out the window behind her, and her gaze was fixed on a man wearing a uniform.

Beatriz let out a shriek that startled her teacher, and she shot from her desk like a launched missile.

"Beatriz!"

Ms. Alvarez chased after her, but Beatriz kept running across the classroom, out the door, and down the hall. Her teacher called her name, but in heels Ms. Alvarez was no match for Beatriz's quick feet. Beatriz tried the first door she came to and flung it open, looking for someplace to hide. A class was in session, and a roomful of heads swiveled in her direction in a collective display of confusion. Beatriz continued to the next door, and then to the next until she found an empty classroom. She pushed a desk against the door to barricade it closed, switched off the fluorescent lights, and ran to the window.

The man in the uniform was still in the parking lot.

She went from window to window, lowering the blinds as quickly as possible. Behind her, the desk at the door began to move. The door pushed open. Ms. Alvarez entered the empty classroom.

"Don't tell him I'm here!" Beatriz shouted.

Ms. Alvarez watched as Beatriz struggled with the dangling cords to the blinds and shut herself off from what was outside the windows.

"Don't tell *who* you're here?"

Beatriz stopped. She was out of breath from the run, the excitement, the fear. "ICE!"

Ms. Alvarez crossed the room to the window and peered between slats in the closed blinds. Then she went to Beatriz and held her tightly, speaking in a soothing voice.

"Honey, it's the security guard."

"Huh?"

"It's okay. That's Mr. Thompson. It's not ICE."

Beatriz gasped, frightened by the memory of the ICE agents who'd taken her mother, even more frightened by her own paranoia. But she trusted Ms. Alvarez and knew she would never lie to her.

"I thought—"

"I know what you thought, honey."

Beatriz could no longer stand on her own two feet. She felt comfort in Ms. Alvarez's arms and didn't want to separate from their embrace. Together, they lowered themselves to a seat on the tile floor. Then the tears began to flow, and Beatriz pressed herself against her teacher like a child even younger than she was.

"I want my mom," she said, sobbing.

Ms. Alvarez stroked her head. "I know, honey. I know."

CHAPTER 23

The cabdriver picked up Jack and Theo outside the Ebenezer bakery precisely one hour after dropping them there, as promised. But they weren't going straight back to the hotel. Jack gave him the address.

"You're going to Soyapango?" the driver asked, not hiding his surprise.

The criminologist at the public prosecutor's office had been unable to arrange a meeting with the prosecutor in Julia's case, but he'd come through in another way. He found the defense lawyer who'd negotiated Julia's plea with the prosecutor. Gabriel Santos was in private practice in Soyapango, on the east side of San Salvador.

"Is it not safe?" asked Jack.

"It depends."

"On what?"

"Do you feel lucky?"

Jack glanced at Theo, who said, "I won't tell Lieutenant Henning if you don't tell Lieutenant Henning."

"*Vamos*," said Jack.

The driver pulled away from the curb, leaving the comforting smell of the bakery behind them. He cruised steadily above the speed limit, choosing not to stop at a couple of red lights that Jack, too, would have punched through. Then they stopped for no apparent reason. The driver pointed, and Jack spotted the police tape. An entire block was cordoned off, the street and sidewalks empty except for a smattering of police officers and a bus with the windshield shot out and the driver's side riddled with bullets. Jack could tell that it was an old American school bus, once yellow, now painted in bright reds, greens, and blues for its second life as a public bus in Central America. Its driver, however, would have no second life, no second chance. Death was dealt evenhandedly to any driver who let it be known that he was fed up with the "protection" payments that bankrolled the gangs and their drugs, jewelry, and motorcycles.

"*Otro muerto*," said the cabdriver.

"Another one dead," Jack said for Theo's benefit.

"I think I could have figured that one out," said Theo.

The cabdriver followed the detour, doing a nice job of maneuvering around stopped and slow-moving vehicles, shaking his head as they passed petrified drivers who had no business being anywhere near the east side, much less lost in Soyapango. Jack's meeting was scheduled for two p.m., and the driver dropped them in front of the lawyer's office with five minutes to spare.

"Be back in—"

One hour, was what Jack was going to say, but the driver pulled away, tires squealing, before he could finish.

"I don't think he's coming back," said Theo.

"You don't say?" said Jack.

Jack turned and faced the building. On the front door, behind iron bars, was a sign that read ABOGADO. They were in the right place. Jack phoned the office on his cell, and Santos unlocked the door and the bars to let him and Theo inside.

Santos was extremely personable and, typical of Salvadorans, a gracious host, offering coffee, pastries, and possibly even his right arm, had Jack asked for it. He led them to his private office in the back of the suite and immediately apologized for the revolver lying on his desktop, which he'd kept handy ever since the bodies of two men and a woman were left on the steps of the public prosecutor's office in Soyapango. They appeared to have been tortured.

"Can't be too careful," he said, as he tucked the gun into the top drawer.

Jack agreed, and after a few more pleasantries the conversation turned to Julia. Santos didn't keep files on cases dating back six years, so he spoke from memory.

"Rodriguez," he said, straining his recall. "Yeah, nice lady. No money for a lawyer, but nice."

"How did she get you to represent her?"

"It's a criminal charge," he said. "In El Salvador, the accused has the right to legal assistance, and if she can't afford it, the state has to provide her with court-appointed counsel."

It struck Jack as ironic that, even though Julia was effectively facing the same charge in a civil deportation proceeding, she had no right to court-appointed counsel under U.S. law.

"You got a good result for her," said Jack.

"Yes. No jail time."

"How did you manage that?" asked Jack.

"It wasn't easy in Julia's case. If the woman denies she had the procedure, the prosecutor has a tough case. But in cases like Julia's, where something goes wrong and the woman ends up in the hospital, they panic. They're scared of dying—bleeding to death. So they tell the doctor or the nurse what happened. Then they get reported. Prosecutors like to take those cases to trial."

"Why didn't they take Julia to trial?"

"Special circumstances."

"Because she was sexually assaulted, you mean?"

"Not exactly," said Santos. "She said she was sexually assaulted by her husband."

"I'm not sure I understand," said Jack. "Did the fact that she was raped by her husband make the prosecutor more or less inclined to take Julia's case to trial?"

"Less. Much less."

"I don't follow that logic."

"That's because you don't know this prosecutor. *Mucho machismo.*"

"So?"

"He wasn't cutting Julia a break and giving her no jail time because she was sexually assaulted."

"Because her husband forced her to have it?"

"No. That never really factored into it."

"Then why?"

"The prosecution just wanted the case to go away."

"But why?"

"Because no man should be prosecuted for raping his wife."

Jack was stunned, silent.

Santos shrugged. *"Machismo."*

CHAPTER 24

Jack exited the terminal at Miami International Airport and was immediately struck by how much warmer it was in subtropical Miami than in tropical San Salvador. Such was the difference between twelve feet and three thousand feet above sea level. Jack removed his jacket, said good-bye to Theo, and waited in the cab line outside "Arrivals."

Jack had initially thought his meeting with Julia's Salvadoran lawyer was a home run. It turned out, however, to be more like a ground-rule double. That a public prosecutor had gone out of his way to avoid prosecuting Julia's husband for sexual assault was definitely something Jack could have used in Julia's claim for asylum. Getting Santos to repeat what he'd said privately in a publicly filed affidavit was another matter.

"I practice in these courts every day," he'd told Jack. "I can't publicly humiliate one of the lead prosecutors."

Jack was finally next in line for a cab and climbed into the back seat. The driver happened to be a Salvadoran named Gustavo. Jack didn't mention it, but Gustavo must have been so much happier not having to pay half his wages to the 18th Street gang for "protection."

"A donde?"

It bugged some of Jack's friends when people in the service industry assumed that they spoke Spanish. Most of them, however, didn't actually want their English-only sons and daughters driving taxis on the streets of Miami.

Jack gave Gustavo the address to Cecilia's house. She'd been texting him. Said she was "very worried" about Beatriz. It was after dark, just about seven p.m., when Jack reached the house. Cecilia invited him in, but it was not the typical warm Salvadoran welcome.

"We have a serious problem," she said.

Beatriz was in her room, and Cecilia's roommates were in the kitchen. Cecilia didn't offer him a seat in the tiny living room, so they talked while standing just inside the front door.

"There's something wrong with Beatriz," she said.

"What do you mean by that?"

"She doesn't shower, brush her hair, or even change her clothes. I don't remember the last time I saw her eat anything. She's skinny like a rail. I'll bet she's lost ten pounds. I checked her backpack this morning. Beatriz never showed me, but there's a note from every single one of her teachers saying that she hasn't turned in any homework. On her last math quiz she didn't even answer any of the questions. Blank page. She's flunking everything. My niece is normally an A student."

"Poor kid. She's obviously depressed."

"*I'm* depressed. This goes way beyond that."

"She wasn't this bad the last time I saw her. Did something happen since last week?"

"She wasn't sleeping at night," said Cecilia. "She woke up before sunrise one morning, screaming. An hour later I found her asleep in the shower. I honestly think that's the last time she bathed."

"Are kids giving her a hard time at school?"

"I don't think that's it. I called her math teacher, Ms. Alvarez. Beatriz freaked out yesterday at school. She thought ICE was coming to get her."

"Oh, boy. Can I talk to her?"

"Probably not."

Jack detected a hint of anger in her voice. "What do you mean 'probably not'?"

"I'll show you."

Cecilia led Jack down the hall. Beatriz's door was closed, but Cecilia didn't even bother to knock or call out her niece's name before opening it. She entered, and there really wasn't room for the bed, the dresser, and two visitors, so Jack stood in the doorway.

Beatriz was asleep but not beneath the covers. She lay atop the comforter, still dressed in street clothes. Jack was immediately alarmed to see how thin and pale her face looked.

"Those are the same clothes she was wearing yesterday morning when I sent her off to the bus stop."

"How long has she been here like this?"

"Since she got home from school yesterday. Thirty-some hours now."

"Have you tried to wake her?"

"No. The poor girl probably didn't sleep for a week. I'm letting her rest. Look how exhausted she is. We're standing here talking right next to her and she doesn't even stir."

Jack moved as close as he could to the bed. Beatriz's breathing seemed normal. Her lips were very dry.

"You said she wasn't eating. Has she at least been drinking water or anything?"

"I don't know. Not much, I'd guess. She hasn't gotten up to go to the bathroom."

Jack took Beatriz's wrist, which felt unusually bony even for a teenage girl, and checked her pulse. Seventy seemed normal, but the fact that she didn't stir upon his touch, and that her hand dropped limply at her side when he released her wrist, gave him concern. He just didn't like the way she looked. Didn't like it at all.

"We should call a doctor," Jack said.

"No," Cecilia said, and her body language underscored the firmness in her voice "What we should do, Mr. Swyteck, is stop treating this child like a piece of evidence—like a *thing*—in my sister's case."

"That's not fair, Cecilia."

"Yes, it is. That morning Beatriz woke up screaming? That was the day after your friend the psychiatrist hypnotized her."

"We're not going to do that again."

"You got that right," said Cecilia, "because I am not going to allow it. Those papers that you had Julia sign in the jail—they named me Beatriz's health-care surrogate. It's time for me to step in and protect my niece."

"That's fine," said Jack. "You should take her to see a doctor."

"Don't tell me what to do."

"I'm just saying that it would be a smart thing for you to consider, as health-care surrogate."

"Maybe. But right now, as the head of the house where Beatriz lives, the smart thing for me is to tell you to leave her alone. Leave her out of this deportation nightmare, and tell my sister to stop being so damn selfish."

Cecilia's eyes were like burning embers. They were standing barely a foot apart in the tiny bedroom, and Jack felt he was finally meeting the tougher of the two Rodriguez sisters.

"I'm going to leave now, Cecilia. But Beatriz is still Julia's daughter. Take her to a doctor. Or you will hear from Julia's lawyer."

Jack stepped out of the room, walked to the front door, and let himself out of the house. Before getting into his car he stopped and looked back at the house. Maybe Cecilia was right and Beatriz was just exhausted. But she'd seemed more unconscious than asleep.

Jack pulled his phone from his pocket and dialed 911 for an ambulance.

CHAPTER 25

Duncan McBride was a party animal. At least for another hour. It was Safari Night at Club Cheek-ah, a Miami strip club that boasted the hottest Latina babes in South Florida. The artwork on the marquee made it clear that the "cheek/*chica*" double entendre had nothing to do with their pretty faces.

McBride downed another shot of tequila in the front seat of his car, alone. It was coming up on two a.m., and this was his third trip of the night to "the well" for refueling. Drinks inside the club were crazy expensive. Experience had taught him that the affordable way to sustain a buzz was to head to the parking lot every ninety minutes or so, get in his car, knock back three or four shots of inexpensive firewater, and then just suck up another twenty-dollar cover charge on reentry. He had it down to a system. A night at Club Cheek-ah would cost him nearly a week's salary. He did it once a month.

"Party time," he said to himself, liking that handsome dude looking back at him in the rearview mirror. He shoved the bottle of tequila into the glove box, knocking the maintenance manual, his car registration, and a few other papers to the floor in his haste. He gathered them up and shoved them back in the box, pausing to take another look at one document in particular. A process server had ambushed him in the parking lot at Café de Caribe that morning and served him with the subpoena to appear as a witness in Julia's immigration case. The caption said it related to an "Emergency Motion to Reconsider Release of Detainee on Bond" filed by attorney Jack Swyteck. It made McBride chuckle.

We'll see about that, Swyteck.

He closed the glove box and climbed out of the car a little too quickly. Tequila head rush. He let it pass. Then, with a spring in his step, he crossed the parking lot to the club entrance, coughed up the cover charge for a third time, and stepped into the swirling lights and blaring dance music. His pockets weren't exactly bulging with cash, but if he played it smart, he had at least one more lap dance in his budget. A brunette wearing nothing but a pair of purple five-inch heels gave him a smile and, with a graceful turn, offered an eye-popping look at her round, firm bottom.

"Like what you see, cutie?"

Dancers at Club Cheek-ah hailed from virtually every South American and Central American country on the map. McBride had his favorite.

"Dominican women are the most beautiful women in the world," he said with a smile.

"Thank you, sweetie. You're cute, too."

This one was smokin' hot. He'd had his eye on her for hours, but she'd paid him no mind. Some "suit" had monopolized her all night, but finally he'd gone home to his wife. Now she belonged to McBride.

"I'm Sherida," she said, and with a comely expression she led him past the line of pole dancers to a booth in the back. Sherida sat dangerously close to him, but he knew that the road to his desired destination was paved with twenty-dollar bills. The lap dance was a well-honed art form at Club Cheek-ah. Completely naked women worked on very drunk men, and the old saw about a fool and his money played out on a nightly basis.

This is going to be so good.

"How about a bottle of champagne?" she asked.

McBride hesitated. That would set him back about two hundred bucks. Not really within his budget, but this Dominican with the perfect ass was the gold standard.

"No problem," he said.

Sherida signaled to the bartender, an exaggerated gesture that made her breasts rise before McBride's eyes. He would have liked to pull her even closer, but club rules forbade any physical contact that wasn't dancer-initiated. It was strictly enforced—which McBride had learned the hard way.

"What's your name?" asked Sherida.

McBride told her, and Sherida told him what a "big strong" name it was, how cute his eyes were, how much she loved his smile—all the things men heard from naked women who worked for tips. McBride wanted to enjoy it, but his head was buzzing. Too many tequila shots on that last trip to the car. He never actually passed out, but too often he overdid it, which made him sweat, which made him stink, which turned off the dancers. He could feel the dampness in his armpits. The odor couldn't be far behind. The polite thing would have been to excuse himself and slather on the overpriced cologne sold by the attendant in the men's room, but he didn't budge. He didn't want her to latch onto someone else.

The server brought the overpriced bottle of champagne. McBride reached into his pocket for his wallet. It wasn't there. He checked the other pocket. No wallet. Panic set in. He rose, patted himself down, checking every pocket twice. It wasn't anywhere.

"Somebody stole my wallet."

Sherida rolled her eyes. "That's what they all say."

"No, I mean it. My wallet is gone."

Sherida said something in Spanish and signaled for the bouncer. In a flash, a man dressed all in black who was at least a foot taller than McBride arrived at the table.

"Give this loser the boot," said Sherida. "No money."

"No! I have lots of money. Somebody took my wallet."

"Yeah, yeah. Let's go, pal."

McBride wanted to plead his case, but the guy had more muscles than Brussels and showed no sign of a sense of humor.

"Maybe it's in my car," he said to Sherida.

"Yeah, whatever."

The bouncer grabbed him by the arm and showed him to the exit. The buzz from all that tequila and the anticipation of Sherida bouncing up and down on his lap had dissolved into drunken embarrassment. It was getting difficult to put one foot in front of the other. The lot was about half full, and as he staggered across the pavement, trying to remember where he'd parked, he hardly noticed the guy sitting on the trunk of his car, smoking a cigarette.

"Hey, buddy," the man said. "Did you lose your wallet?"

McBride stopped and struggled to focus. The man was holding up a wallet for him to see.

"Hey, yeah! Where'd you find it?"

"Bathroom floor."

McBride had no memory of going to the men's room. He walked toward the man, smiling with gratitude. "Thank you so much."

The man took a long drag from his cigarette, then opened the wallet. "Gotta make sure it's you," he said as he read from the driver's license. "Duncan McBride?"

"That's my name."

He exhaled, blowing a cloud of smoke into McBride's face. "You the Duncan McBride who works at that coffee shop, Café de Caribe?"

"That's right. I'm the manag—"

It was the combination of things—both the knife at his throat and the speed with which the man moved—that silenced McBride midsentence. The man's face was right in front of McBride's, his eyes black as coal.

"Don't hurt me," McBride pleaded.

"Don't resist. Keys. Nice and slow."

McBride's hand shook as he dug the car keys from his pants pocket. The man snatched them away, and the trunk popped open. "Get in."

McBride emitted a whimper, completely involuntary, and the twitch of the six-inch serrated blade at his throat told him that he didn't dare scream. The man shoved him into the trunk, his face toward the spare tire, and then he bound McBride's wrists behind his back with the ease and quickness of someone who had done this before.

The trunk slammed shut, and McBride lay in a tight ball in total darkness, his head resting on the wheel well as the engine started and his car pulled away.

CHAPTER 26

J ack was back in the Orlando Immigration Court, Judge Greely presiding. Simone Jerrell from the Department of Homeland Security was seated on the opposite side of the courtroom. Julia appeared by videoconference from the Baker County Facility, just like at the last hearing, except that she looked more worried this time. A teenage daughter in a hospital four hundred miles away could do that to a mother.

"Good morning, everyone," said Judge Greely. "I understand that the detainee has filed an emergency motion seeking reconsideration of this court's previous denial of her request for release on bond."

"Correct," said Jack.

The judge flipped through the stack of pleadings before him. "Before we get to that, has the respondent asserted any defenses on the merits to the department's application seeking Ms. Rodriguez's deportation?"

"Yes, Your Honor," said Jack. "We are asserting a defensive claim for asylum, based on the failure of her home country of El Salvador to protect her from sexual violence."

"Did ICE conduct a credible-fear interview?" the judge asked.

Typically, the first step in an asylum application was an interview by ICE to determine whether the applicant had a "credible fear" of further persecution if ordered to return to her home country—a prerequisite to asylum.

The DHS lawyer rose. "Ms. Rodriguez has not been interviewed."

"Why not?"

"This is an awfully belated claim of asylum," said Jerrell. "As far as I can tell, it's based on a sexual assault that allegedly happened some six years ago."

"There's more to it than that," said Jack.

"For your client's sake, there had better be," the judge said. "But we'll address that at the final hearing. For now, tell me why your client should be released on bond prior to that hearing, Mr. Swyteck."

"As you may recall, the court was inclined to release Ms. Rodriguez on bond until the department introduced into evidence a criminal complaint filed by a Mr. Duncan McBride, who is the manager of the coffee shop where Ms. Rodriguez was employed. Today, it was our intention to prove that Mr. McBride filed that complaint to retaliate against Ms. Rodriguez for rejecting his unwanted sexual advances."

The judge shuffled through the papers in the file before him. "I see you have submitted an affidavit from Ms. Rodriguez so stating."

"Yes. I also intended to cross-examine Mr. McBride here today," said Jack. "He was served with a subpoena commanding his appearance in court, but he has ignored the subpoena."

The judge didn't look happy. "Ms. Jerrell, that criminal complaint from Mr. McBride is the chief reason I ordered detention. Where's your witness?"

"We don't know," she said sheepishly.

"Excuse me?"

"No one has seen Mr. McBride for at least two days. He hasn't been to work. He seems to have gone missing."

Jack jumped on it. "Judge, if that's the case, this court should order my client's release effective immediately."

"That may be a little hasty," said the judge. "Ms. Jerrell, if I gave you another week to locate your witness, would that help?"

"That would be satisfactory."

Jack glanced at his client's image in the monitor. Her expression conveyed the same "two-against-one" dismay that Jack was feeling.

"Judge, our request for release can't wait a week. Ms. Rodriguez's daughter is in the hospital. A report from her physician is attached to our motion in the file. This proceeding against her mother has taken a terrible toll on her emotionally. It's manifesting itself in malnourishment, severe dehydration, and depression."

"Not to be flip," said Jerrell, "but we all want our mommies. That's not grounds for release on bond. I would also point out that this is not a case in which the detainee overstayed a validly issued visa. She entered this country illegally, which means that she could be charged with a crime."

"But you haven't charged her criminally," the judge pointed out.

"No."

"And they never will," said Jack. "Because then it would be a criminal proceeding, and the government would have to pay for her lawyer. Judge, this effort to mischaracterize my client as some kind of dangerous criminal is all bluster. There is no evidence in the record to support her detention, and I disagree with Ms. Jerrell's cynical dismissal of our humanitarian argument as an 'I want my mommy' defense. This is a very serious matter."

"All right, all right," said the judge. "Here's what I'm going to do. I will order the release of the detainee on humanitarian grounds. Bond is set at two thousand dollars."

Jack could live with that. Two thousand dollars really meant coming up with only two hundred, the customary 10 percent required by a bail bondsman.

"However," the judge continued, "if and when the child's condition improves, the government can file a motion to return Ms. Rodriguez to detention."

"Excuse me?" said Jack. "If her daughter gets better, my client goes back to jail?"

"I've made my ruling."

"Thank you, Judge," said Jerrell.

"Next case," said the judge.

The immigration-court shuffle was on, with the next detainee appearing on-screen from Baker County, and another attorney stepping up to replace Jack at counsel's table. Jack grabbed his bag and headed toward the public-seating area on the other side of the courtroom rail.

"Swyteck, you got a minute?" asked Jerrell.

After the "mommy" remark, he was in no mood to speak to her. "Sorry, I don't."

"Come on. Thirty seconds."

"Urgent call to make," said Jack, reaching for his cell. "Gotta phone your names in to the Harvard Foundation ASAP."

"What are you talking about?"

"You and Judge Greely," said Jack, deadpan. "I'm nominating you for Humanitarians of the Year."

Jack felt the weight of Jerrell's glare as he turned and headed for the courtroom exit.

CHAPTER 27

Jack picked up Julia at the Baker County Facility.

Nothing moved quickly in jail, but the drive from Orlando was over two hours, which was also how long it had taken Cecilia to go door-to-door in her neighborhood, collect the bondsman's fee, and wire it to Mickey's Bail Bonds in Macclenny. Julia had already been released and was waiting outside the complex with her bag packed when Jack pulled up in his rental car. He'd never had a more grateful client—not even on death row.

"Thank you, thank you, thank you!" she said over and over.

Jack put her bag in the back seat, and they headed to the airport in Jacksonville. He'd planned to use the time alone in the car to tell her more about his trip to El Salvador, but Julia had other ideas. All she wanted was to borrow Jack's cell.

"No need," he said. "Open the glove box."

She did and found a cell phone. "Should I use this one?"

"It's yours. It's prepaid."

"You are just the best. If you weren't married, I'd kiss you."

"It's actually from Theo—your 'getting out of jail' gift. He's kind of an expert on the subject."

"That's so sweet of him."

Sweet. Not a word Jack had often heard in the same sentence with "Theo."

Julia had the main number for the hospital written on the palm of her hand, and she asked the switchboard operator to connect her to Beatriz's room. Jack picked up enough of one side of the conversation to understand that Cecilia had answered, Beatriz

was asleep, and the sisters were in disagreement as to whether
Cecilia should wake her. Julia ended the call in frustration.

"I can't believe she won't put Beatriz on the phone."

Julia didn't have a full appreciation of Beatriz's condition, and
Jack decided to leave the medical update to the hospital physi-
cians. Julia filled the rest of the ride with calls to worried friends
who'd been sending prayers and asking about her. By the time they
boarded the plane, the string of sleepless nights in jail had finally
caught up with her. Jack let her rest on the flight to Miami and then
drove her to the hospital.

"You're coming up to the room, right?" asked Julia.

Jack didn't want to intrude on a mother-daughter reunion, but he
hadn't seen Beatriz since the ambulance had taken her away. "You
sure it's okay?"

Spanish idioms were often beyond Jack's fluency, and the expression that Julia rattled off reminded him of something Abuela
might have said. "Of course it's okay," she added, as if Jack was
already part of the family.

The University of Miami/Jackson Memorial Hospital was
Miami's premiere public hospital, which meant that in addition
to its stellar reputation for groundbreaking research in everything
from cancer to spinal injury, it was also a workhorse for the world
of Medicaid and the uninsured. Parking anywhere near the main
entrance was impossible, so Jack and Julia entered through the
ER. The waiting room was a virtual cross section of lower-income
Miami, one night's share of nearly a quarter million visits an-
nually. An old Haitian woman hung her head into a big plastic
bucket that reeked of vomit. A homeless man with no legs slept
in the wheelchair beside her. A single mother comforted a crying baby as her four other children played leapfrog on the floor,
shouting at one another in Spanish. Jack got it that there was a
cost to treating undocumented children, but he wasn't second-
guessing his decision to call an ambulance.

They were issued visitor badges at the registration desk, and after a painfully slow elevator ride, the doors finally parted at the third floor. Polished tile floors glistened beneath bright fluorescent lighting, an assault on the eyes that rivaled snow blindness. Cecilia met them at the pneumatic doors to the pediatric suite, and the sisters locked in a tight embrace, which triggered Latin tears of joy by the bucketful.

"She's awake," said Cecilia.

Julia shrieked with excitement and raced down the hallway. Jack and Cecilia followed, and by the time they reached the open door, Julia was leaning over the bed rail and had Beatriz in her arms. Jack waited in the hall with Cecilia, giving Julia a moment alone with her daughter.

"I think I owe you an apology," said Cecilia.

They hadn't spoken since Aunt Cecilia had turned into a mother bear on steroids. But Jack had endured much worse, from clients taking a swing at him to witnesses spitting in his face. "No problem," said Jack. "We're all under a ton of stress."

The pediatrician arrived and asked to speak to Beatriz's mother. Julia pulled herself away from her daughter, choosing to get the medical update in the hallway, out of Beatriz's earshot.

"I'll sit with her," said Cecilia.

"Actually, she wants to talk to Jack," said Julia.

That seemed to hurt Cecilia's feelings, and Jack wasn't sure what was up, either.

"Fine. I'll be in the lounge," said Cecilia.

Jack knocked lightly on the doorframe and entered the room. Beatriz was sitting up in the bed at a comfortable angle. Fluids flowed into her veins from an IV bag suspended from a pole on the other side of the bed. She turned her head and smiled.

"Hi, Mr. Swyteck," she said softly.

Jack pulled up a chair to her bedside and sat down facing her. Her color was much better, and some of the sparkle she'd lost had returned to her eyes. "How are you feeling?"

"Much better, now that my mom's home."

"I'm sure."

"Thank you for helping us."

"You don't have to thank me. I'm glad to help."

Her smile faded, and a crease of a worry line appeared between her eyes. "This thing that happened to me. It was really scary."

"That's why I called an ambulance."

Beatriz turned very serious. "Could you hear me?"

"I'm sorry. Could I hear you when?"

"When you and Cecilia were talking to each other in my bedroom. Did you hear me tell you to call the doctor?"

Jack looked at her with concern. "Honey, you didn't say anything when I was in your room."

"Yes, I did!" she said in a hushed but urgent voice, taking care not to let anyone outside the room hear them. "I was yelling to you at the top of my voice. 'Call the doctor! Mr. Swyteck, call the doctor!'"

"You must have dreamed that."

Her head rose from the pillow. "No! It wasn't a dream!"

"Okay," Jack said in a calm voice. "Don't get yourself worked up over this."

She settled back into her pillow.

"You were dehydrated," said Jack. "You weren't eating or sleeping. It was—"

"It was like I was in the box," she said, her gaze fixed on the ceiling.

"What?" asked Jack.

"I could see you standing there over my bed. I could see Tía, too."

"That's not possible. Your eyes were closed."

"I don't care what you say. I *saw* you both. And I could hear what you were saying. I was talking to you, but you weren't listening. Or maybe you couldn't hear me, because I was inside the box."

"What box?"

"A glass box," she said. "It was all around me."

Beatriz turned her head on the pillow, peering over the bed rail as Jack's gaze met hers. She looked terrified, and Jack had no idea how to respond.

"Did you tell your doctor about this?" he asked.

Beatriz nodded.

"What did she say?"

"Not much. She said they did an MRI and a bunch of other tests while I was asleep, but they didn't find anything for me to worry about."

Jack smiled just enough to reassure her. "It sounds like they took very good care of you."

Beatriz nodded, but it was not without trepidation—and fear. "I just don't want to go back in that box."

"Good news!" said Julia, as she entered the room. "You're being discharged, baby. The doctor says I can take you home tonight!"

Beatriz shot an uneasy glance at Jack, then smiled weakly at her mother. "That's great, Mom."

"This is one of the best days of my life," said Julia. She went to Jack and hugged him. "Thank you so much."

It was a heartfelt embrace, but Jack was looking over Julia's shoulder toward Beatriz, who still seemed to be recovering from the secret she'd shared with him.

"You're welcome," Jack said to his client.

CHAPTER 28

Night fell and streetlamps blinked on as Julia and her daughter stepped off the bus at their corner of Little Havana. They walked side by side, each with a bag over one shoulder, passing countless bench billboards for ABOGADOS DE ACCIDENTES, English lessons for Spanish speakers RÁPIDO, and other necessities of immigrant life. They were about a block from their house.

"What was it like in the detention center?" asked Beatriz.

The question was a bit out of left field, and there were so many ways to answer it. Julia went with the benign option. "Boring," she said. "Really boring."

Their little duplex next to the used-tire shop wasn't much, and the fence that protected Señor Gomas actually had more razor ribbon than the fence around the Baker County Facility. But to Julia, at least on that night, it was like checking into the Ritz. The doctors at Jackson had decided that it would serve Beatriz better to sleep in her own bed than to spend another night in the hospital for observation. Amen to that. As for Julia, anything was better than a bunk in a detention center.

"What was the worst thing about the place?" asked Beatriz.

"Missing you."

"Other than that."

"Worrying about you."

"Mom, stop, I'm being serious," Beatriz said.

Her tone struck Julia as a highly Americanized teenage whine—part of the "melting pot" experience, Julia figured. "I'm serious, too," said Julia. "The whole time I was there, I couldn't stop thinking about you."

"Forget about me for a minute. I want to know about the place. Tell me the worst thing about a detention center."

Julia stopped to think, and in the glow of the streetlamp, Beatriz stood there, waiting. A car passed, and then another. Beatriz wasn't a little girl anymore, and she deserved a thoughtful response.

"Not knowing," said Julia.

"Not knowing what?"

"How long you're going to be there, or where you're going to end up."

They started walking again. Then Beatriz asked, "Do we know where we're going to end up?"

Julia put her arm around Beatriz's shoulder. "Mr. Swyteck is a very good lawyer."

"But do we *know*?"

"Let's take it one day at a time, girlfriend."

They stopped at the front door, and as Julia dug the key from her bag, they exchanged an uneasy glance. The memory of Julia pinned beneath the weight of an ICE officer and Beatriz closing the door on them was still raw. Julia turned the key, opened the door, and took a step inside. The light switch clicked when she flipped it, but the light didn't go on.

"Great. The electric bill didn't get paid."

"Tía paid it," said Beatriz. "She came by and picked up the mail every day."

Julia toggled the switch up and down. Nothing. "Bulb must be burned out." She took another step inside, but Beatriz stopped her with an arm tug.

"What, honey?"

"It's so . . . dark."

Julia was suddenly reminded of that little girl with her head under the covers asking Mommy to leave the light on. It really hadn't been *that* long ago. She crossed the dark room and switched on a lamp, which brightened everything but the expression on Beatriz's face.

"Smile, baby," said Julia. "We're home."

Beatriz closed the door. "I guess so."

Julia opened her bag and dug out the last thing she'd packed before the ICE arrest, the crucifix that she'd grabbed on her way out of the house, and she rehung it on the wall hook next to the door. "We're safe here," she said.

"It feels weird to me. I don't know why."

Julia planted a kiss on Beatriz's forehead. "I have an idea. How about a cup of Haitian hot chocolate?"

Beatriz rolled her eyes. "Mom, in case you haven't noticed, we're not Haitian."

"We're not Italian, either, but you love spaghetti. One Haitian hot chocolate, coming up. Go unpack," she said, as she headed to the kitchen.

Julia laid her bag on the counter and then checked the cupboard, running the list of ingredients through her mind. She had almost everything she needed, though the powdered stuff would have to sub for the freshly shaved cocoa bean. She laid a cutting board and a kitchen knife on the counter, grabbed a saucepan, and took it to the sink to add a little water. The faucet hissed and Julia froze. Her gaze locked onto the back door like a laser. She turned off the water and walked slowly to the end of the kitchen counter for a closer look.

They had no backyard. Behind the house was just a narrow alley, and the only reason they used the back door was to take out the trash. The door wasn't completely closed. At least it didn't appear to be. It seemed a little off, protruding maybe an eighth of an inch beyond the frame. Julia tried to recall the last time she'd taken out the trash. She couldn't remember, but it didn't matter. She would never have been so careless as to leave the door ajar.

Assuming it was ajar.

Julia took the knife from the cutting board, held it tightly in her hand, and continued around the counter toward the back door. Five steps and she was there. She laid her hand on the panel and pushed.

The door moved.

Her pulse quickened. She turned the knob, but it just spun around loosely. The back door had been jimmied open.

"Beatriz!"

A shrill scream came from the other end of the house.

"Beatriz!" she shouted over and over again as she ran from the kitchen and down the hallway, the kitchen knife her weapon. She found her daughter standing in the doorway to the bathroom. The light was on, and Beatriz's hands covered her eyes. She was shaking but otherwise unable to move.

"Oh, my God," said Julia, gasping at the sight.

She held Beatriz tightly and pressed her daughter's face against her shoulder. Julia took one more look at the bloody and mutilated body in the bathtub, and then took her daughter to the bedroom. Beatriz was crying, and Julia was trying not to cry as she helped her daughter onto the bed.

"It's okay, it's okay," said Julia, trying to calm Beatriz, even though she knew things were far from okay. She stroked Beatriz's head with one hand and with the other dialed Jack on the disposable cell. Thank God he answered.

"Jack, we need you," she said, breathless.

"What's wrong?"

"Please, come quick," she said in a voice that shook. "Duncan McBride is dead."

CHAPTER 29

Jack broke the speed limit on every street between Key Biscayne and Little Havana, and he even rolled through a few stop signs. Even so, by the time he arrived, Julia's house was an active crime scene.

An ambulance and the medical examiner's van were parked on the street, a seeming contradiction between life and death. Police cars from Metro-Dade and the city of Miami cordoned off the immediate area, some with blue beacons swirling. Uniformed officers, crime scene investigators, and detectives were coming and going at the direction of the officer posted at the open front door. Jack parked next door in the driveway entrance to Señor Gomas' Used-Tire Shop. A media van from *Action News* pulled up right next to him, joining four other local TV stations that had already staked out a position for a live report on their late-evening broadcasts. Curious neighbors watched from behind the yellow police tape that ran the length of the sidewalk.

"Swyteck!" a woman shouted.

Jack turned and saw Heather Brown from the *Miami Tribune* rushing toward him. Heather had covered several of Jack's capital cases. He knew her well, and it was a safe bet that she'd been the first journalist on the scene.

"Can't talk now," he said, as he continued down the sidewalk. She walked with him.

"I need to talk to your client."

Jack stopped. Heather was one of those reporters who seemed to know everything, but he was still curious: "How did you know that?"

"I'm addicted to police radio. Got here before the cops did. She said you told her not to talk to anyone."

Jack had told her exactly that. He'd also told her to let the police inside and then hole up in a neighbor's house across the street, down the block, or around the corner—anywhere but in the other half of the duplex, where it would be impossible for Julia to open the door and let Jack in without having a microphone and a TV camera shoved in her face. "I'm not going to let her talk to the media, Heather."

"I got some good stuff," she said. Heather was the ultimate horse trader—a client interview in exchange for the nuggets she'd coaxed out of a loose-lipped cop or investigator on the scene. She had Jack's attention.

"Such as?"

"Victim's name?"

"Lame."

"Time of death, less than twelve hours."

"You're getting warm. I'll think about it."

"Hey! We had a deal."

Heather had obviously never gone to law school. Jack stopped on the civilian side of the yellow police tape, flagged down a Metro-Dade officer, and asked to see Assistant State Attorney Phillip Arnoff. The Miami-Dade State Attorney's Office always had a prosecutor on duty to cover a possible homicide investigation. After hanging up with Julia, Jack's first call had been to a friend in the Homicide Unit, who'd told him Arnoff was on duty.

Arnoff and a homicide detective named Barnes came out of the house to see Jack. Heather made it clear that she wasn't about to leave Jack's side, so Jack, Arnoff, and the detective walked across the street to the neighbor's house. The detective asked to question Julia, and Jack said he'd allow it as long as her lawyer was present. Jack, Julia, the prosecutor, and Detective Barnes gathered around the neighbor's kitchen table. The detective asked standard questions—how she'd known the victim, how long, when she'd last seen him. Then Julia told him about the door being jimmied, Beatriz's scream, and what she'd found in the bathroom.

"He was in the tub. There was so much blood."

"You mean everywhere in the room?"

"No. On him and in the tub."

Both the prosecutor and the detective were taking notes. "Do you have any idea who would want this man dead?" the detective asked.

"Have you already ruled out suicide?" asked Jack.

"A fair question," said Arnoff. "The answer is no—that's the medical examiner's job."

The detective smiled a little, clearly having something to add. "But I will tell you that I've been doing this for almost twenty years, and I've never seen a man slit his own throat from ear to ear so viciously that he nearly decapitated himself. So pardon me if my questions have a slight bias toward a homicide investigation."

"Thanks for being so forthcoming," said Jack. "You can answer, Julia."

"No. I don't know who would want Mr. McBride dead."

The detective turned the page on his notepad. "How long were you out of the house before you came home and found Mr. McBride's body?"

"Pretty long."

"A few hours?"

"No. Since the seventh of January."

That raised the detective's eyebrows. "Three and a half weeks? That's a long vacation."

"It was no vacation."

"Then what was it?"

She told him, and Jack explained her immigration status.

"I see," said the detective.

"Interesting," said the prosecutor. "Was Mr. McBride in any way involved in your deportation case, Ms. Rodriguez?"

"I'll answer that," said Jack. He figured he might as well be straight about it: Arnoff would find out soon enough, and Jack didn't want it to appear that he was trying to hide anything.

"Duncan McBride was a witness against my client. He claimed that Julia was fired for stealing his wallet. That was a lie. He fired her because she rejected his sexual advances."

"I see," said the detective.

"Interesting," said Arnoff.

It was becoming their new favorite routine.

"Mr. Swyteck," said Arnoff, "would you mind giving me the name of the Department of Homeland Security lawyer who is handling Ms. Rodriguez's case?"

"Jerrell," said Jack. "Simone Jerrell."

"Thank you. That's helpful. Is there anything else you'd like to tell us, Ms. Rodriguez?"

"I didn't kill him, if that's what you're asking me. How could I? I just got out of detention."

"Fair point," said Arnoff. "But I put a lot of stock in motive, and in my experience, you don't have to be free and out on the street to want a man dead and get something done about it. So pardon me in advance if I don't let this be the end of it." Arnoff tucked away his pen.

Julia was about to respond to the insinuation, but Jack stopped her.

"I need to get back to the crime scene," said the detective.

They rose and shook hands. Jack gave each man his business card. "Call me, not my client, if there's any follow-up."

"Oh, we'll follow up," Arnoff said, tucking Jack's card away. "Count on it."

The men said good night. Jack walked them out the front door and watched them cross the street to the crime scene. Julia joined him on the front step.

"I don't want them talking to Beatriz," she said.

"Neither do I."

"Will they?"

Jack was still watching the assistant state attorney on the other side of the street, but he was thinking of his talk with Beatriz in the hospital, just the two of them. Arnoff was on his cell phone as he ducked beneath the police tape, and Jack wondered if he was already talking to ICE.

"They will," said Jack, "over my dead body."

CHAPTER 30

Julia was back to cleaning houses. Condo cleaning, technically speaking. Miami had more condos than coconuts, and it was Julia's impression that in a metropolitan area of five million people, no more than seven or eight of them actually picked up after themselves.

Their duplex in Little Havana remained a crime scene for two days, and even after the police padlock was removed, she and Beatriz refused to go back. Theo and one of his busboys from Cy's Place volunteered to move their belongings to Cecilia's place, where Julia could have the spare bedroom and Beatriz would sleep on an air mattress in the living room until they could find a new place. The landlord wouldn't refund Julia's deposits, but she couldn't bring herself to put another one of her problems on Jack. Cleaning two condos a day was the only way to stay financially afloat.

"Hey, Cinderella. Back to work."

Stella had caught her gazing out the floor-to-ceiling window, admiring Miami's skyline from a glass box on the seventy-third floor of the tallest residential tower south of New York City.

"Oh, sorry."

"I was kidding," Stella said with a little laugh. It was her full-time job to keep the apartment immaculate for the Colombian owner who visited once a month, and for his mistress, who lived there year-round. Stella had heard about Julia's situation at their church, and she'd been able to convince Señorita-Sleeps-Till-Noon that she needed a second housekeeper five hours a week.

"San Salvador has three tall buildings," said Julia. "The tallest is about that high," she said, pointing to a thirty-story high-rise on the bay. I was counting how many are taller than that."

"How many are there?"

"I was at thirty-three when you busted me. I lost count." Her gaze drifted back to a city of glass on a blue-green bay that glistened in the sun on a cloudless afternoon. "It's so unbelievably beautiful."

Stella smiled with her eyes. "I hope you and your daughter get to stay."

"Thanks. Me, too."

Julia finished at five o'clock. Stella stayed every night till eight and cooked dinner, just in case *la señorita* deigned to eat, which she usually didn't. Julia took her forty dollars in cash, thanked Stella profusely, and rode the express elevator down to the lobby. Two security guards kept an eye on her as she left the building, either checking her out or perhaps making sure that she didn't walk out the door with a piece of museum-quality artwork.

Her bus stop was at the westerly bend on Brickell Avenue, where the relatively quiet residential stretch of the south Brickell area yielded to the mixed-used high-rises and office buildings of north Brickell and Miami's bustling Financial District. Nestled in the midst of towering giants of steel and glass on the waterfront was St. Jude Melkite Catholic Church, one of the area's few remaining historical buildings. Over the decades, St. Jude's had managed to withstand several powerful hurricanes and, even more impressive, a string of building booms that sent countless other architectural gems the way of the wrecking ball. Julia had a twenty-minute wait for her bus, so she stepped into the chapel, admiring the Romanesque arches surrounding a beautifully tinted ceiling as blue as the South Florida sky. Painted icons graced the altar and surrounding walls, and arched windows of stained glass commemorated various saints. Rows of old wooden pews stretched before her. She knelt before the cross and the Sacred Heart.

From all accounts, Duncan McBride had suffered a terribly violent death. He'd been missing for days. Ligature marks around his wrists and ankles indicated that he'd been taken alive and held captive. Multiple bruises and cigarette burns on his arms and chest confirmed torture. The amount of blood in the bathtub meant that his killer had taken him there alive and then slit his throat. And yet Julia couldn't bring herself to feel sorry for him. For that, she prayed for God's forgiveness.

Julia left the church and walked to the corner. The sun hung low in the sky somewhere beyond the trees and buildings, and long shadows stretched across Brickell's four divided lanes. Two Haitian women were waiting at the bus stop when Julia got there. Their traditional maid uniforms removed all mystery as to what they were doing on Brickell Avenue. Julia took a seat on the bench and watched the traffic pass.

It was then that she saw him.

Julia wasn't completely sure at first glance. Passing cars and the palm trees in the landscaped median gave her a less-than-perfect line of sight to the other side of Brickell Avenue, but a second look confirmed that it was him. He was standing on the sidewalk beneath the sprawling limbs of an old oak, staring straight at her. Julia didn't know what came over her, but she followed her first impulse. She went in the opposite direction.

Julia walked quickly, as fast as she could without breaking into a dead run, her stride lengthening as she approached the church. She hurried up the stone steps, pushed the heavy door open, and ducked inside. She knew he had seen her, seen where'd she'd gone, but she prayed that he would get the message and understand that Miami was her clean slate, that she'd left "what might have been" in San Salvador, and that she didn't want him to follow.

The door opened; her prayers were unanswered.

Julia fell against the wall, on the verge of hyperventilation, and it wasn't from the attempted getaway. The door closed behind him. He just stood there, looking at her the way only he looked at her.

"Hugo," she said, breathing out his name. "*What* are you doing here?"

Jack rode with Theo to Julia's house in Little Havana. The busboy who'd agreed to help Theo move out Julia's belongings was a no-show. Jack was curious to see how Miami-Dade homicide had left the crime scene, so he pinch-hit. A crime scene cleanup crew was inside the house when they arrived. A man dressed in coveralls was carrying out a bucket of something.

"Damn, that was a lot of blood," the man said.

That was saying something, coming from a crime scene cleaner in Miami.

Fortunately for Jack's back, Julia and Beatriz didn't have much. He and Theo cleaned out the kitchen first. The only furnishings in the living room that didn't belong to the landlord were a couple of lawn chairs and a small bookcase containing Beatriz's schoolbooks. They left the bedroom for last, which was just personal items, towels and linens, and their clothing.

"I can't touch these things," said Theo.

He was staring down into a drawer of undergarments.

"Don't look at me," said Jack.

Jack opened a suitcase. Theo removed the drawer from the night-stand and dumped everything inside—no hands. As he shoved the drawer back into place, he noticed the framed photograph on the nightstand, next to the lamp. He picked it up for a closer look.

"Who's this guy?" asked Theo.

Jack checked it out. There were only two people in the five-by-seven photograph, Julia and a man.

"It's not her husband," said Jack.

"How do you know?"

"Because I recognize the place. It's outside the bakery where Julia worked in San Salvador. The manager told me her husband was banned from going anywhere near there."

"A woman doesn't keep a photograph on her nightstand for no

reason. And they seem pretty chummy for two people who just work together."

Theo handed the photo to him, and Jack couldn't disagree. Julia's arms were around the man's neck, and her head was on his shoulder.

"And what's with that tattoo on his neck?" said Theo. "Eighteen? Looks like gang shit to me."

"All the men who work in the bakery are former gang members," said Jack.

Theo looked out the window. He seemed disappointed. More than disappointed. Jack put the framed photograph in the suitcase with Julia's other belongings.

"Theo, can I give you some advice?"

Theo didn't answer, but he was smart enough to know what Jack was going to say.

"I like Julia," said Jack. "Love her daughter. I want to help them. But you should forget about Julia. She's a little dangerous. Even for *you*, I think she's dangerous."

CHAPTER 31

Funny, isn't it?" asked Hugo.

They were in the church vestibule, their faces lit only by flickering sconce candles and the iron chandelier high overhead.

"Funny?" said Julia.

Hugo took a step toward her, but she recoiled, which made him stop. "Funny that I would catch up with you," he said, glancing at their surroundings, "in a church."

Julia knew what he meant. The last time they'd seen each other was in the Iglesia Ebenezer. It was the day before she and Beatriz had boarded a bus for Guatemala, their first step to Miami.

"You didn't even tell me you were leaving," said Hugo.

"I couldn't," she said, struggling. "I couldn't tell anyone."

"You can tell me anything, Julia."

She shook her head. "Jorge came back."

"I knew it. You didn't have to leave because of him. I told you I would take care of him."

"No!" she said. "That's not what I want. That's not who I want you to be."

"Want?"

Julia looked away. *"Wanted,"* she said, underscoring the past tense.

Silence hung between them, and she worried that if she didn't say something fast, he would come to her. "Are you here legally?"

"What do you think?"

"What did you come here for?"

"You know what for."

Julia took a breath. "You have to go back. You can't stay in Miami."

"Since when do you work for ICE?"

That made her chuckle, and they both smiled. Then Hugo turned serious. "I'm not going back to El Salvador," he said. "Unless you do."

"Please, don't stay in Miami."

"I can't promise you that I won't."

"It's too dangerous, Hugo. I think Jorge is here. It's no different now than it was in San Salvador. Jorge never lets go of his *things*. If he thinks you came here for me, he will kill you."

"Let him try."

"Don't talk tough," she said angrily. "That tattoo on your neck, that's not who you are. Jorge is different. He fooled me for a while, but that didn't last. Jorge is Eighteen to the core, now more than ever. And he's never going back."

"I knew all of that before I came here, Julia."

"Then you should never have come."

"I'm glad I came."

"Have you lost your mind?"

"No," he said, his expression tightening. "But Jorge has lost his home-field advantage. May the best man win."

Hugo gave her that look again, that smile that would come from the other side of the Ebenezer bakery and make her feel safe. Then he pushed open the door and left her alone in the back of the church. For a moment she stayed where she was, leaning against the wall, and then she hurried out the door and called to him from the top step.

"Hugo!" she shouted, her voice strangely flattened by early evening darkness.

He kept walking toward Brickell Avenue.

"Hugo, do not go looking for him!"

He didn't even glance back at her.

"Promise me, Hugo!"

Rush-hour traffic was at a bumper-to-bumper standstill. Hugo weaved between cars across four lanes. Finally, he turned as he reached the sidewalk, raised his phone, and snapped a photo. He checked it and smiled, tapping his heart with two fingers the way athletes do when sending love to someone in the stands.

Julia watched from the church, her heart sinking, as Hugo disappeared into the stream of pedestrians on the other side of the street.

H o!" Jack shouted.

Theo hit the brakes, and the back of the SUV stopped a foot away from Cecilia's front door.

"You're supposed to stop on the first 'ho,' not the third," said Jack. "I'm not Santa Claus."

Backing up to the front door would make it easier to unload Julia's belongings, but Theo was more interested in what was across the street than what was behind him. "I think Julia just got off that bus."

The bus pulled away, spewing diesel fumes as Julia stepped down from the curb.

"You almost parked in her new living room," said Jack.

"I got distracted."

Jack pushed open the passenger door. "I told you she was dangerous," he muttered as they climbed out of the SUV.

"I heard you the first time, Santa."

Julia crossed the street, approached their SUV, and thanked them profusely for their help. Jack could tell something was wrong, even before she asked him if they could speak in private. Theo said he could handle the unloading. Jack and Julia went for a walk around the block.

"The papers you filed in my deportation case," she said. "Who can see those?"

"It's a public record. Is there anything specific you're worried about?"

"The part of my affidavit where I say McBride harassed me at work. You mean anybody could see that?"

"Anyone with access to the Internet."

As they neared the intersection, Jack suddenly realized that he was in one of the old neighborhoods that he'd sped through on his bicycle on the way to the park as a kid. These overcrowded houses filled with multiple immigrant families once had been middle-class starter homes for young married couples. Time flew by. Neighborhoods changed. Immigrants kept coming.

"I think my husband knows what McBride did to me," she said, and then she stopped to look him in the eye. "And I think he killed him."

Jack didn't say anything.

"You don't seem surprised," she said.

"He was already high on my list of suspects. I heard some pretty terrible things about him from your old boss and three other women at the church bakery. You weren't the only woman he sexually assaulted. The man is a serial rapist."

"He's also the most possessive human being on the planet. If he knew that McBride even tried to lay a hand on me, he would kill him."

"That part I understand. But here's what I don't get: Why would he kill him in your bathtub instead of somewhere out in the Everglades, where the police would never find the body?"

"He doesn't care if the police find the body."

"This goes beyond not caring. Your husband went out of his way to make serious trouble for you."

"You don't get it at all, Jack. Jorge wasn't trying to help my case by killing ICE's witness against me. He wasn't trying to hurt my case, either. This isn't about my deportation case at all. This was a warning to me."

"A warning about what?"

"McBride would never have harassed me if I hadn't been asking for it. That's how my husband thinks. Now McBride is dead. Killing him in my house is Jorge telling me, 'See what you caused, Julia? This is your fault.'"

There was a perverse logic to what she was saying. It also put a finer point on Jack's advice to Theo: *Even for you, I think she's dangerous.*

"But to be McBride's killer, Jorge would have to be *here*, in Miami," said Jack.

"I believe he is."

"Have you seen him?"

"No."

"Have you heard from him?"

"No."

"What makes you believe it?"

She started walking again. Jack went with her, passing in the shadow of a ficus tree so old that its sprawling roots had displaced entire sections of the sidewalk. It was like walking an obstacle course.

"Julia, why do you think your husband is in Miami?"

"A friend came to see me today," she said. "From El Salvador."

"That's a pretty good friend to come all the way from San Salvador."

"Hugo is an old friend. We worked together in the church bakery."

"Is that Hugo in the picture that was on your nightstand?"

She stopped and looked carefully at Jack, as if to ask him how he knew about that.

"Theo and I saw it when we picked up your things," said Jack.

"Oh, right. Yes, that's Hugo. He told me Jorge is in Miami."

They rounded the corner. An old woman was curbing her Chihuahua on one of the only patches of grass on the block. Just ahead, Theo was standing in the driveway next to the SUV, texting someone.

"How does Hugo know where your husband is?"

"I have no idea."

"Is it because Hugo is in Barrio Eighteen?"

"Hugo is not in Eighteen."

"He was. I saw the tattoo on his neck in the picture."

"That was in the past."

"How else would Hugo know your husband is in Miami, other than gang connections?"

"I didn't ask him how he knows."

Jack stopped. "Let's put aside what Hugo said. Here's what we know. Hugo is a very good friend of yours. At some point in his life, Hugo was deep enough into the Eighteenth Street gang to wear it on his neck. Hugo is definitely in Miami, and McBride is dead. Your husband might be here; he might not be. So, if you can arrange it, I'd like to talk to Hugo."

"You think Hugo killed McBride, don't you?"

"I didn't say that."

Julia paused to consider the words Jack had chosen, as if to make sure she appreciated every nuance of her second language. "You're right, Jack. You didn't say it. But you didn't deny it, either."

She picked up her pace, leaving Jack behind.

"Julia," he said, and she stopped at his call. Jack wasn't sure if this was the right time or place to ask, but he needed to know: "Why did you never divorce Jorge?"

Julia was gazing back in his direction, but her face was a silhouette in the backlight of the corner streetlamp, and Jack couldn't tell if she was actually looking at him or not.

"Jorge said he'd kill Beatriz if I divorce him. Is that a good enough reason?"

He didn't doubt the honesty of her answer, but something in her tone told him that this trip around the block had changed things between them. "That's good enough for me," he said.

Julia continued down the sidewalk to her sister's house. "Theo!"

she said, as she started up the driveway. "I forgot to thank you for the cell phone you gave me. That was so sweet of you."

Sweet. There was that word again, and this time Jack liked it even less than the first time Julia had used it.

Jack started to follow but immediately stopped, realizing that he'd just stepped in a fresh pile of Chihuahua shit.

CHAPTER 32

Jack wasn't surprised. Less than a week after the murder of Duncan McBride, ICE filed a motion requesting the court's "immediate reconsideration of the detainee's release on bond for humanitarian reasons." As written, the motion was based solely on the door that Judge Greely had left open at the previous hearing: improvement in Beatriz's medical condition. But Jack's guard was up for an underhanded effort to link Julia to the murder of the chief witness against her. Judge Greely scheduled a hearing in Orlando on what, coincidentally, would be the one-month anniversary of Julia's arrest.

Jack and Julia met in his office for two hours on the afternoon before the hearing. Jack drove her home to her sister's house after the prep session. He wasn't just being nice. Julia said it was important for Jack to talk to Beatriz, and unfortunately Beatriz was in no shape to leave the house.

"She's been getting worse every day," said Julia, "ever since the judge reset the hearing."

Jack followed her through the living room to the kitchen. "Did you tell her the judge might put you back in detention?"

"No, but I left my copy of the order right there on the counter after I read it, and I guess Beatriz was curious to know why I was so upset. I didn't leave it there for Beatriz to read it, but in typical teenager logic, her response to that was 'You didn't tell me *not* to read it.'"

"Is she as bad as the last time?" asked Jack.

"Not yet. But I'm afraid we might be headed there. Can you talk to her?"

"Sure."

"She's in Cecilia's room. She lies there after school until it's time to go to bed."

Since Julia had moved in and taken over the spare bedroom, her daughter had been spending the nights on an air mattress in the living room, which probably wasn't helping the situation. Julia went down the hallway to her sister's bedroom to tell Beatriz that Jack wanted to talk to her. A minute later she came back for Jack and took him to see Beatriz.

"I'll be in the kitchen if you two need anything," said Julia, and she left them alone.

Beatriz was at the far edge of the mattress, lying on her left side and facing the wall, still wearing her school clothes. There was no chair in the room, and sitting on a bed alone in a room with a teenage girl didn't seem like a good idea, so Jack half leaned and half sat on the edge of the low-slung bureau.

"I guess you heard we've hit another bump in the road," said Jack, trying to downplay it.

"Is that what you call it?" Beatriz said, still facing the wall. "A bump in the road?"

"That's really all it is."

"Easy for you to say. You can see your mother anytime you want."

"That was my *abuela* you met. My mother died when I was just a few weeks old."

The wall was suddenly not so interesting to her. Beatriz rolled onto her other side and looked at Jack. "Sorry. What did she die from? If it's okay to ask."

"Yeah, it's okay. I'm not sure they had a name for it then, but now it's called preeclampsia. Women don't die from it now as much as they used to. But this was, geez, a hundred and fifty-seven years ago."

She smiled a little. Jack saw an opening. "Have you been taking care of yourself, Beatriz? Eating? Sleeping?"

Beatriz shrugged.

"I know this is an emotional roller coaster, but you can't run yourself into the ground thinking the worst is going to happen."

Beatriz looked off to the middle distance. Her mother's return had rekindled the sparkle in her eyes, but it was gone again. "When Mr. McBride was killed, I thought that would be good for me."

Jack thought he understood what she was saying—that it would be good for Julia's case—but he wanted to be sure. "How would it be good for *you*, Beatriz?"

She touched her hair the way nervous teenage girls do. "I never told you, but I talked to him."

"You talked to McBride? When?"

"The day after I was hypnotized. Friday morning. On my way to school, on the Metrobus."

Beatriz sat up in the bed. Jack listened as she shared every detail, from the way McBride seemed to appear from nowhere, to his parting threat, *"I have ICE on speed dial."*

"This was almost three weeks ago," said Jack. "Why didn't you tell me before?"

She was still sitting up, still looking at him, but the clouds in her eyes seemed heavier.

"Beatriz? Did you tell anyone about this?"

Jack waited for an answer, but Beatriz was no longer looking directly at him. Her gaze shot past him. Or through him.

"Beatriz, this is important. I'm going to ask you something, and I want you to tell me the absolute truth. Have you had any communication at all with a friend of your mom's named Hugo?"

No response.

"Did you tell your mom's friend Hugo that Mr. McBride threatened you on the bus to school?"

Beatriz continued to look past him and drew a breath. Finally, she lay back on the bed, rolled over, and once more faced the wall.

"Beatriz?"

There was a light knock on the doorframe. Julia entered, and she was openly disappointed to see Beatriz still trapped inside the cocoon she'd crawled into after school.

"Nothing from her?" asked Julia.

Jack watched as Beatriz seemed to drift away again, then he slowly looked away, his gaze coming to rest on Julia. "I wouldn't say 'nothing,'" said Jack.

CHAPTER 33

I t was Jack's third time in Judge Greely's courtroom in a month: one for the hometown ICE with Julia's detention, one for the away team with her release on bond, and now the rubber match. This time, Julia was not appearing by videoconference. She sat at Jack's side at counsel's table.

"Your Honor, the Department of Homeland Security renews its request for prehearing detention," Simone Jerrell said, "based on a drastic change of circumstances."

Unlike the previous hearings, a handful of reporters were seated in the gallery behind Jack and his client, on the public side of the rail. The brutal murder of the government's chief witness had triggered media interest, most of it legitimate, some sensational, referencing Julia's case as evidence that it wasn't just Mexico sending its murderers across the border.

"Is it the government's position that Ms. Rodriguez is connected to the murder of Mr. McBride?" the judge asked.

"No," said Jerrell, "at least not at this preliminary stage. But we may well take that position at the final deportation hearing."

"Then what are the 'changed circumstances' that justify Ms. Rodriguez's detention prior to the final hearing?"

"This court released Ms. Rodriguez on humanitarian grounds because her daughter was hospitalized. Her daughter is now out of the hospital and back at school. She is living in her aunt's house. I would note that her aunt is in this country legally, and it was her aunt who admitted her to the hospital and who serves as health-care surrogate. It's clear that the child's every need as a minor can be met by her aunt. There is no compelling humanitarian interest to justify the release of Ms. Rodriguez purely on humanitarian grounds."

The judge looked to the other side of the courtroom. "Mr. Swyteck, what do you say to that?"

Jack rose. He'd expected Jerrell to spice up her written motion with at least a verbal allusion to the fact that the chief witness against Julia had been found dead in her bathtub. But it appeared that DHS was serious about putting Julia back in detention based solely on the improved health of her daughter.

"Your Honor, the picture is not nearly that rosy. Since the government announced its plan to put my client back in detention, her daughter has been in a steady state of decline. If we lose this hearing and Ms. Rodriguez is ordered to return to the Baker County Facility, I fully expect that her daughter will be readmitted to the hospital within a matter of days."

"Let me see if I understand this," the judge said. "This court cannot order the detainment of Ms. Rodriguez as long as her daughter is in ill health, and her daughter will be in ill health only as long as Ms. Rodriguez is in detainment. Is that your argument, Mr. Swyteck?"

Jerrell interrupted. "That's exactly it. Mr. Swyteck is trying to box this court into the immigration version of catch-twenty-two."

"Good book," said the judge. "And a pretty good argument, too, wouldn't you say, Mr. Swyteck?"

"I agree only with the first half of your statement, Your Honor."

"What support do you have for your position?"

"I'd like to present the testimony of an expert witness, Dr. Eric V. Johansson. He's a psychiatrist."

"I wasn't planning to turn this into a full-blown evidentiary hearing," the judge said. "Can't you submit your expert testimony by affidavit?"

"I believe it's important for the court to hear Dr. Johansson, live, in order to overcome the expressed concern of an immigration catch-twenty-two. That doesn't seem like too much to ask if the court is giving serious consideration to sending Ms. Rodriguez back into detention."

The judge sighed as he scanned the courtroom, seemingly overwhelmed by the number of lawyers queued up for hearings on the afternoon docket. "How much time do you need, Mr. Swyteck?"

"Twenty minutes," said Jack.

Judge Greely checked with his judicial assistant, who said there was nothing available. "I'll make room on my lunch hour tomorrow," the judge said. "Can the respondent's expert witness be here then?"

"Dr. Johansson will appear by video conference from Stockholm."

"Sweden? Why Sweden?"

"Because he's the world's foremost authority on *de apatiska* and *uppgivenhetssyndrom*."

"I have no idea what you just said, Mr. Swyteck."

"The literal translation is 'apathetic child.' And in scientific literature, the medical condition that justifies the release of my client on humanitarian grounds is known as resignation syndrome."

"Never heard of it," the judge said. "And I should warn you that just because a doctor with fancy letters after his name labels something a 'syndrome' doesn't mean I'm going to buy it. But I'll listen."

"That's all we ask," said Jack.

"See you tomorrow at noon."

"Thank you," said Jack, pleased enough to give his client a little thumbs-up as they left the courtroom.

CHAPTER 34

A re you sure this is real?" asked Andie.

Jack had called home to get a Righley fix and to let Andie know that he'd be spending another night in Orlando. Judge Greely's warning about doctors and their flaky "syndromes" had been playing over in his mind since the hearing. Andie was his reality check whenever he thought he might be getting too far out there on the zealous advocacy spectrum, so he decided to run "res-ignation syndrome" past her.

"You sound skeptical," said Jack.

"I *am* skeptical. 'Oh, my kid is sick unless I get asylum.' How do you know these families haven't just found a doctor who's so eager to attach his name to a new syndrome that he's willing to look past the fact that it's all a game the family is playing to win asylum?"

Jack didn't know. That was the truthful answer. Judge Greely would preside over Julia's final hearing, so it was important not to lose all credibility right out of the gate at a preliminary hearing. It was Dr. Moore, the psychiatrist who'd hypnotized Beatriz, who'd put Jack in touch with Dr. Johansson. Jack said good-bye to Andie, recited *Olivia Saves the Circus* from memory to Righley—he'd read it to her a hundred times—and then called Dr. Moore. She had an idea.

"I want you to meet one of the *apetika*," she said. *The apathetic.*

"I'm not going to Sweden. Salvadoran gangs I can handle. Ten below zero? Forget it."

"No worries. There's a rehab center in Uppsala where some of these children have been sent to recover. Dr. Johansson and other doctors on his team participate in patient evaluations by video from Stockholm or wherever they're located. I've done it myself. I'll ask him if you can join tomorrow morning's rounds."

"He'll need the parents' consent."

"He'll get it. This would give his research added validity if you could get a U.S. Immigration Court to recognize the syndrome."

"Or we can all crash and burn together."

"It's your call. My advice is that you take a look at these children with your own eyes. Then decide if you want to go forward in court."

Jack saw little downside to the proposal. "Sounds like a plan."

"Good. Set your alarm, Counselor. Nine a.m. in Stockholm is three a.m. in Florida."

"No problem," said Jack, but that was before the Matchbox Twenty song about that certain hour started playing over and over again in his head, keeping him awake till three a.m. And he was feeling lonely.

G od morgon from *Sveeden*," said Dr. Johansson.

Jack was alone in his Orlando hotel in front of his laptop. He could hear the doctor's voice, but the real-time transmitted image on his screen was an examination room more than two hundred miles away from Dr. Johansson's office. A physician from Doctors of the World and a nurse stood beside an examination table, but there was no patient in the room.

"Jack, the child we have selected is a nine-year-old girl who, for purposes of this call and to protect her privacy, we will call Sophie. She is from the former USSR. Four years ago, Sophie and her parents were stopped in their home country by men in police uniforms. They turned out to be local mafia. Sophie was in the car, so she saw her mother attacked. Sophie and her mother escaped, but her father did not."

"She's been like this since then?" asked Jack.

"No. Her mother brought her to Sweden, seeking asylum. They lived here for three years. Sophie went to school here and was very active. Loved ballet. She became fluent in Swedish. Her mother doesn't speak the language, so Sophie translated for her when the letter came from the Migration Board denying their request for asylum. That is when her condition began to deteriorate.

"Can you bring her in, Dr. Lunsford?"

The camera followed Dr. Lunsford as he went to the door and opened it. Sophie's mother, a woman with dark eyes and a sad but serious expression, wheeled her into the room. Dr. Lunsford lifted the girl from the wheelchair and laid her on the table. Sophie appeared lifeless in many ways, her eyes closed and limbs just dangling from her body. But as the doctor positioned her on the table, she looked anything but dead. Her hair was thick and beautiful. Her skin was perfect and with good color. There was a sweetness in her expression that punctuated what a pretty little girl she was. She seemed to be sound asleep. A Sleeping Beauty.

"How long has she been like this?" asked Jack.

"Eleven months," said Johansson. "She's nourished through a feeding tube in her nose, but we remove it when we can. She doesn't open her mouth, so there's a risk of choking."

Jack watched as the doctor and nurse ran through the basic examination. Pulse: normal. Blood pressure: normal. Reflexes: normal. Everything was normal, except that nothing was normal.

"What does Sophie feel when she's in this state?" asked Jack.

"It's a complex answer," said Dr. Johansson, "but it's probably best to show you. Dr. Lunsford, could you do the honors, please?"

Dr. Lunsford disappeared from view on Jack's screen and returned a minute later holding a plastic bag filled with ice cubes. The nurse rolled up Sophie's sweatshirt to expose her belly. The doctor placed the bag of ice on her bare skin.

Sophie didn't move.

"Could you check her heart rate, please?" asked Dr. Johansson.

The nurse did. "Sixty-two again," she said. "No change."

Jack could hardly believe his eyes, recalling his own reaction the time he'd fallen asleep by the pool and Righley had decided to see how long it would take for a cherry Popsicle to melt on his chest. The world would never know.

"What is Sophie thinking during all of this? Or is she thinking?"

"We hope she will tell us one day," said Johansson. "The best anecdotal description I've heard is from a boy from Russia named Georgi. He spent eight months in bed until his family was granted asylum, and only then did he recover. He said it was like he was underwater, but he wasn't drowning. He was in some kind of capsule made of very thin glass, and if he moved or spoke, it could cause the glass to shatter. He was in constant fear that the water would pour in and drown him."

"The glass box," Jack said softly, like a reflex.

"I'm sorry?" said Dr. Johansson. "Did you say something?"

Jack was staring at the screen, saddened to think of Beatriz in such a state for months. "I was just going to say that I'm looking forward to your testimony later today, Dr. Johansson."

"It will be my pleasure. I hope it helps."

"So do I," said Jack.

CHAPTER 35

The respondent calls Dr. Eric V. Johansson," said Jack.

The hearing started promptly at noon. Dr. Johansson appeared on the monitor while seated behind a desk in his Stockholm apartment. He was a broad-shouldered man of full face made even fuller by a heavy salt-and-pepper beard. His leather-top desk was clear of clutter, save for an elaborately carved wood pipe that lay beside a tin of tobacco. The window behind him was as black as the cold Nordic winter night.

The witness was sworn, and Jack questioned him from counsel's table, seated beside Julia, starting with Dr. Johansson's professional qualifications.

"I am a fellow in the Department of Women's and Children's Health, Division of Neonatology, at Stockholm University," he said in precise English, albeit with a Scandinavian accent. "For the past five years, I have also overseen clinical studies in conjunction with the Centre for Research Ethics and Bioethics at Uppsala University in Sweden."

"What type of clinical studies have you conducted?"

"They relate to resignation syndrome."

"Can you please explain to the court what resignation syndrome is?"

"Sure. It is a relatively recent diagnosis that has been recognized by the Swedish National Board of Health and Welfare since 2014. It affects certain children. There is global and severe loss of function, which progresses in stages, beginning with anxiousness and depressive symptoms, in particular lethargy. Stage two is stupor, and, finally, the child exhibits a complete lack of any responsive behavior, even when presented with painful stimulus. At this late stage, patients are seemingly unconscious with eyes closed, incontinent, mute, and sustained by a tube feeding."

"Are these children in a coma?"

"No, that would not be an entirely accurate statement. There are similarities, but the brain is not injured."

"How many cases of resignation syndrome have you seen in your research?"

"There are hundreds that I'm aware of. More than one hundred fifty last year alone."

"You said it affects 'certain children.' What children?"

"Resignation syndrome affects children and adolescents seeking asylum or undergoing the migration process."

"What is it about the migration process that triggers the syndrome?"

"The most severe cases arise from deportation orders directed at the child or a parent. In simple terms, the child responds to the emotional trauma by disconnecting from the conscious part of his or her brain. Most vulnerable of all are children who have witnessed extreme violence, often against their parents, or whose families have fled a deeply insecure environment."

Jerrell rose. "Judge, I object to this entire line of questioning."

"On what grounds?" the judge asked.

"First of all, no qualified physician or psychiatrist has diagnosed Beatriz Rodriguez with resignation syndrome, and there is no evidence in the record that the child—as opposed to her mother—has suffered any kind of physical or emotional trauma to trigger the syndrome."

Jack didn't want to get into Beatriz's suppressed memories elicited by hypnosis. "Judge, we are offering into evidence the complete hospital record for Beatriz. While there is no formal diagnosis, the court can easily see that she exhibits many of the symptoms that Dr. Johansson just described."

"That may or may not be the case," said Jerrell. "But more to the point, I did some research last night. This syndrome has *never* been diagnosed in *any* child outside of the country of Sweden."

The judge addressed the monitor. "Is that true, Doctor?"

"Technically speaking, yes. But I believe that this is because Sweden has such a long and well-known history of welcoming asylum seekers. The drastic change in government policy and increased deportation of refugees in recent years has created social incoherence in the minds of migrant children. They flee persecution or violence in their home country with the expectation of staying in Sweden; they assimilate to Swedish culture; and then they are faced with an order of deportation. We have found that when the child's family is granted permanent residence, this eases the trauma and kick-starts recovery."

"My question," Judge Greely said, "is whether this so-called syndrome has been recognized outside of Sweden."

"Every culture recognizes some range of physical symptoms available to the unconscious mind when a life veers off course and produces psychological conflict. Your country is no exception. In the 1980s, doctors in California documented dozens of cases involving Cambodian refugees who had lost their ability to see for no apparent reason other than the fact that they saw family members tortured during the Pol Pot regime. The refugee children diagnosed with resignation syndrome exhibit similar psychic wounds. They feel totally helpless, so they become totally helpless."

"I'll take your response as a no," the judge said. "Mr. Swyteck. I've heard enough. No more junk science in my courtroom, please."

"Excuse me?" the doctor said indignantly. He looked about ready to throw his pipe and tobacco tin halfway across the globe and squarely at the judge's head.

Jack interceded before things got worse. "There are certainly critics, Your Honor. But Dr. Johansson has been documenting this syndrome in peer-reviewed scientific journals for over fifteen years."

"It's *junk*," said Jerrell. "Thank you for calling it by the right name, Judge."

"Don't be so quick to thank me," he said. "Ms. Rodriguez, it's your lucky day. I happen to know from the nine other women who appeared before me yesterday afternoon, and from three more this morning, that Baker County Facility is at full capacity, with a waiting list for female detainees as long as my arm."

"But—" said Jerrell, at a loss for what to say next.

"Don't push it, Ms. Jerrell. Even if we had a place to put her, it is this court's opinion that the department has not shown that Ms. Rodriguez is a danger to the community. I understand that she's technically a convicted felon under Salvadoran law, but she terminated a pregnancy after she was sexually assaulted."

"According to Mr. Swyteck."

"Does the department have evidence to the contrary?" the judge asked.

"I can provide a sworn affidavit to that effect," said Jerrell. "I spoke to the Salvadoran prosecutor. Ms. Rodriguez told the hospital emergency room physician that her husband was the father."

The judge turned a suspicious glare toward Jack. "Mr. Swyteck, does your client deny making that statement?"

"No. But it doesn't change anything."

"I'll be the judge of that."

Jack had hoped to hold his evidence of domestic abuse until the final hearing, not only because it was good strategy, but also to avoid putting Julia through it twice in a public courtroom. But Jerrell had forced his hand.

"Ms. Rodriguez was sexually assaulted by her husband, who then forced her to have an abortion at an unlicensed, back-office clinic that nearly killed her," said Jack.

"That's not even grounds for asylum," said Jerrell. "I don't condone domestic violence, but asylum is for a victim of persecution *by her government*, not for a woman abused by her husband."

It was a serious issue, but Jack had researched it. "A victim of domestic violence can be granted asylum if two circumstances are met. One, she is unable to leave the relationship and, two, her government either condoned the private actions or demonstrated an inability to protect the victim. We can satisfy both conditions."

"Mr. Swyteck is grossly overstating the law," said Jerrell. "In the history of immigration jurisprudence in this country, the Board of Immigration Appeals has issued one opinion—*one*—in which a Salvadoran woman was granted asylum based on domestic violence, and it was vetoed by the attorney general because it didn't apply a strict enough standard."

Judge Greely held up his hands, parting the lawyers like a boxing referee. "Counsel, we have now moved way beyond the question of whether Ms. Rodriguez should be detained until her final hearing on asylum. The department's motion to return the respondent to detention is denied. Ms. Jerrell, if you don't like my ruling, tell ICE to find someplace to put all the undocumented immigrants you want detained. Especially women.

"But, Mr. Swyteck, I intend to fast-track your client's request for asylum. Frankly, I'm dubious. You had best be prepared to address the question that Ms. Jerrell just raised about persecution by the government of El Salvador. This is a U.S. court of immigration, not an international court of family law and marital disagreements."

An interesting word choice: "disagreements." *Talk about dubious.*

"Understood," said Jack.

"Next case," the judge said with a bang of his gavel.

Jack gathered his papers and led his client to the court exit as quickly as possible, before Jerrell could request an alternative form of "detention," such as house arrest. They exited through the rear double doors, and Julia stopped him at the first reasonably private place they came to, away from the crowd outside the courtroom, just beyond a long wooden bench in the hallway.

"Did the doctor from Sweden say 'feeding tube'?" she asked.

Jack had expected the usual self-centered litany of "me-me-me" worries that he heard from most clients, but it was suddenly obvious to him that a mother would have a different set of priorities.

"A feeding tube is in extreme cases," said Jack.

"What if we lose the asylum argument? What if the judge deports me? Wouldn't that be an extreme case?"

"A legal worst case doesn't have to mean a medical worst case."

The words didn't have the intended effect. Julia's concern only heightened, and Jack assumed it was for both herself and her daughter.

"The judge said he was 'dubious' about asylum," she said. "What does that mean, exactly?"

If his years of death penalty work had taught Jack anything, it was never to lie to a client, never to promise the moon when your whole case could crater.

"It means we have work to do," said Jack.

CHAPTER 36

Jack switched his phone out of "airplane mode" as the short flight from Orlando touched down in Miami. His e-mail in-box populated before his eyes, one message after another. It was the usual late-afternoon Friday onslaught, as lawyers launched the electronic court filings that they'd been holding on to all week, timing their release just right, assuming the principal objective was to ruin your adversary's weekend. One message caught Jack's eye. It was from the public prosecutor in El Salvador. After weeks of stone silence and no reply to Jack's repeated requests, the prosecutor was willing to meet with Jack and discuss Julia's case.

"Why do you think he changed his mind?" asked Julia. She was in the seat next to him as the plane taxied across the runway. Jack had a theory, but he didn't share it. Ruining someone else's weekend was not his style.

Andie wasn't thrilled about a second trip to El Salvador, but Jack promised to bring his "bodyguard." On Tuesday morning, he and Theo were on their way to San Salvador. Jack's assistant had snagged a couple of last-minute cheap tickets on a discount Internet site. Jack was stuck in the middle seat in the last row, mouth breathing for three hours to deal with the bathroom stench. Theo fared better.

"I still don't see how you got upgraded to first class," said Jack, as they exited customs.

"Cuteness counts," said Theo.

"Yeah. That's gotta be it."

They took a taxi into the city, ate lunch, and then went straight to the justice building for a two p.m. meeting. Theo waited in the reception area as Jack met with the prosecutor in his office.

"*Buenas tardes*, Señor Swyteck," the prosecutor said.

Jack answered in kind, and his Spanish was good enough to ensure that the remainder of the meeting would be conducted in English.

"Have a seat, please," he told Jack.

Raul Espinosa was about Jack's age, short in stature but long on self-confidence. He wore his hair combed straight back, more gray than Gordon Gecko's in the first *Wall Street*, but nowhere near as gray as Gordon Gecko in the sequel. He had dark eyes and handsome Latin features, though there was something oddly distracting about the skin above his upper lip. It lacked the healthy color of the rest of his face, and Jack could only surmise that he'd recently shaved off a mustache. Someone had probably told him being clean-shaven would make him look younger, a supposition Jack based on Andie's reaction to his after-forty foray into the "five o'clock shadow" that so many men in their twenties sported: "It makes them look sexy, Jack. It makes you look homeless."

"I'm glad you decided that a meeting would be productive," said Jack.

"I hope it will be," Espinosa said, as he walked around to the other side of his desk and took a seat in his leather chair. He was polite enough to ask about Jack's flight, recommend a restaurant for dinner, and exchange a few other pleasantries. Jack caught himself glancing around the room, checking out the framed newspaper clippings on the walls, the awards on the prosecutor's desk, the tropical fish in the saltwater aquarium on the credenza—anything to keep himself from staring at that white ghost of a mustache beneath Espinosa's nose.

"Let me be direct with you as to my objective," said Espinosa, turning to business.

"Please," said Jack.

"I want you to leave Jorge Rodriguez out of your client's claim for asylum in the immigration court."

Jack had suspected as much from the moment he'd read Espinosa's e-mail on Friday; it was the theory he'd decided not to share with Julia on the runway. "I'm sorry, but that's not possible," said Jack. "Domestic violence is the basis for Julia's claim for asylum."

"Half the basis," said Espinosa. "The other half is that the government of El Salvador—specifically, *this prosecutor*—does nothing to protect its women from abuse by their husband. Or, worse, condones it."

"It's not personal," said Jack.

The prosecutor chuckled. "We have fifty homicides a week in El Salvador. None of them is personal."

"Jorge Rodriguez sexually assaulted his wife and three other women."

"Not three."

"Yes, I met them on my last trip."

"You must have missed the fourth."

"Is that supposed to be funny? The man is a serial rapist who raped his wife and then forced her to have an abortion that almost killed her. He doesn't deserve your protection."

His expression turned very serious. "Yes, he does."

"How can you possibly say that?"

"It was our agreement."

Jack was without words for a moment. "Your agreement?"

Espinosa leaned forward, his hands folded atop his desk as he looked Jack in the eye. "Jorge Rodriguez is a gang informant. Information he provided to us has helped us solve more than a dozen homicides and led to the conviction of the killers. He is in our witness protection program."

There was a moment of disconnect, as the prosecutor's words were just so far from what Jack had expected to hear. "You agreed not to prosecute Mr. Rodriguez for the rape of his wife and three other women?"

"Four other women. In exchange for information."

"And that was your decision?"

Espinosa shrugged. "As you say in English: you do what you gotta do."

"That's fine. Then you understand I'm doing what I have to do for my client, which means that I intend to prove in court that her husband sexually assaulted her."

"I wouldn't care if that was all you intended to prove. But as I said, that's only half your case. If you go into a court of immigration in the United States and argue that the prosecutors of El Salvador will not protect their women from sexual assault, then I must defend the honor of my office. I will be forced to contact the attorney from your Department of Homeland Security."

"And tell her what?"

"El Salvador is not a third-world banana republic that is unable or unwilling to protect the victims of domestic violence. This office chose not to prosecute Mr. Rodriguez for one reason only: our country is being destroyed by gangs, and Mr. Rodriguez cooperated with law enforcement in our war on these lawless gangs. It's that simple."

Jack gazed at him from the other side of the desk, taking the time to measure his words. "That's a very clever argument, Mr. Espinosa."

"I don't know if 'clever' is the right word. It's simply the truth."

"Your version of the truth? Or Simone Jerrell's? Or was it a collaboration?"

"I'm not sure what you're implying."

"Honoring this supposed agreement with Jorge Rodriguez allows you to save face as a prosecutor, and it puts my client on the next deportation flight from Miami to San Salvador. Pretty convenient how that version of 'the truth' works for both you and U.S. immigration authorities."

The prosecutor smiled thinly. "Convenience is a good thing."

Jack rose. "Except when it's not."

Espinosa rose and showed Jack the door. "Have a very nice flight back to Miami, Mr. Swyteck."

"Thank you. And allow me to apologize in advance."

"For what?"

"For the severe inconvenience that I promise I will cause you."

CHAPTER 37

Assistant State Attorney Phillip Arnoff was in his office that Tuesday afternoon when he got the phone call he'd been hoping for. It was from Miami-Dade detective Danny Barnes, who was heading the Duncan McBride homicide investigation.

"We got our break," said Barnes.

The bouncer on duty for Safari Night at the Club Cheek-ah had told Barnes that McBride went to his car at least twice to "liquor up," and a comparison of tire tracks from the club parking lot to tracks outside McBride's apartment confirmed that his car had been there. Safari Night was the last time anyone had seen McBride alive, and no one had seen his silver Honda sedan since then. Anytime a vehicle went missing in a homicide case, Miami-Dade Police kept a sharp eye out along the Miami River. Stolen cars and the incriminating evidence they contained, along with tons of other stolen goods, could easily disappear forever on one of the Venezuela-bound freighters that set sail from Miami every day.

"You actually found McBride's car?" asked Arnoff.

"You bet we did," the detective said.

"Don't inventory it until I get a warrant," said Arnoff.

"We don't need a warrant to inventory a stolen vehicle."

"I know. But I got Simone Jerrell and ICE breathing down my neck in that deportation case that McBride was part of. Feds do everything belt and suspenders."

"Fine, I'll wait," Barnes said, grousing. "We're at Seabird Terminal B, just down the street from the Miami River Rapids Mini Park."

"I'll meet you there."

The shipping area near Miami River Rapids Mini Park was up-river, closer to the airport and well away from the upscale river-front development in downtown Miami. Many of the older sketchy cargo terminals had been shut down and rebuilt in Miami's effort to compete with Savannah and other East Coast ports for the ever-increasing imports from China. Still, the seedy underbelly of commerce continued to flow through South Florida, some of it as polluted as the river itself. Huge cranes worked around the clock, hoisting mountains of metal containers onto Caribbean-bound freighters. Some carried electronics and other dry goods. Others carried vehicles with the VIN scratched off. Trucks and four-wheel-drive vehicles were in particular demand, as any Miamian who *used to* own a Range Rover would attest.

The State Attorney's Office was next door to the criminal court-house, and in less than ninety minutes Arnoff had a warrant. He drove quickly to the Seabird Terminal B and parked along a chain-link fence that was topped with military-grade razor ribbon. The pair of Dobermans on the other side of the fence provided a second line of deterrence to would-be thieves. A uniformed MDPD officer led Arnoff to the crime scene tape that encircled the team of investigators and McBride's silver Honda. The doors on both the passenger's side and driver's side were wide open. Barnes was inside and already searching the vehicle, with his flashlight aglow.

"You didn't wait for the warrant," said Arnoff.

"You didn't move fast enough."

"I told you that ICE—"

"Fuck ICE," said Barnes. "We don't need a warrant."

Arnoff didn't argue the point. "Anything of interest?"

"Half-empty bottle of tequila in the glove box."

Arnoff nodded. "That confirms what the bouncer told us about McBride going to his car to do shots."

"That's not all McBride did in his car," said the detective. "I've seen enough dried semen to say with confidence that Mr. McBride jerked off in his front seat on at least one of his trips out of the Club Cheek-ah."

"Some things I just don't need to know," said Arnoff.

"Hmm," said Barnes, but he wasn't responding to Arnoff. His flashlight was aimed at the console. "That could be interesting."

"Tell me," said Arnoff.

"We went through McBride's office at the café and his apartment with a fine-tooth comb. Didn't turn up a single ashtray or tobacco product."

"So he wasn't a smoker," said Arnoff, following his point.

"Nope. Not a smoker. Yet we have two cigarette butts in the ashtray of his car. Both the same brand, so probably one smoker."

"Should be enough dried saliva there for a lab specimen, wouldn't you think?"

"I would think."

"Nice work, Detective."

Barnes gathered the cigarette butts with sterilized tweezers, dropped them into an evidence bag, and sealed it. "Hel-*low* DNA," he said.

CHAPTER 38

Jack didn't care if the Hacienda Real was the best steak restaurant in El Salvador. He wasn't going to eat anywhere on the recommendation of Raul Espinosa.

"But I love steak," said Theo.

"I found a place that has the best craft beer in the country."

"I can live without steak."

Cadejo Brewing Company was in San Salvador's Zona Rosa, a popular area filled with some of the city's best hotels and restaurants. Cadejo brewed its own beer in the enormous steel vats in a back room. The hostess spoke enough English to give Theo a tour, which was intended to help him choose a brew he liked, but as Jack could have predicted, he ordered one of each—and not the sampler size.

"Really nice IPA," said Theo.

They were seated on stools at the bar, Jack with a seasonal draft and Theo with six different glasses lined up in front of him. A waitress hurried past them on her way to a table, carrying a tray of burgers and chicken wings that smelled delicious.

"Are you really going to drink all of those beers?"

Theo sucked down the rest of the IPA in a couple of swallows. "You say that like it's a bad thing, Jack."

Jack tasted his beer.

"You're sipping," Theo said with disapproval. "A man doesn't *sip* beer. He drinks it."

"Sorry. I'm not much in a drinking mood. This is not what you'd call a good day."

Theo started on the pilsner. "Honestly, I don't get it. There's so much low-hanging fruit for ICE to go after. Seems like this Simone Jerrell is devoting way too much effort to deporting Julia and her daughter."

"I agree."

"Almost makes you think ICE is using her to get to somebody else."

It was the prison mind-set at work, the added value that Theo Knight brought to Jack's legal brainstorming sessions. "Like her husband," said Jack.

"Or that guy in the picture. The gangbanger with his IQ tattooed on his neck."

"Hugo," said Jack. "Eighteen is the name of the gang."

"I been in a gang. And I been in places where they kill you in a minute for being in the wrong gang. If Hugo tattooed the name of his gang on his neck where everyone can see it, 'eighteen' is his IQ."

"Señor Swyteck?"

Jack swiveled around on the barstool. The first thing he'd done after the meeting with the prosecutor was to call Julia's old lawyer for a follow-up meeting. It was Gabriel Santos who had suggested they meet at Cardejo after work. Jack thanked him for coming and bought him a beer.

"What did you think of our highly ambitious prosecutor, the esteemed Mr. Espinosa?"

"We think he's an asshole," said Theo.

"Well," Santos said, raising his glass, "then it's unanimous."

They drank to it, and then Jack provided more details about his meeting with the prosecutor. Santos listened and seemed to understand the predicament.

"If you have to prove that the Salvadoran government is unwilling or unable to protect married women from sexual assault, then it sounds like you have a tough case."

"Yes," said Jack, "unless I can rebut Mr. Espinosa's testimony that he chose not to prosecute Julia's husband because he became an informant. Which is where you come in."

"Me?"

"Last time we talked, you said that the prosecutor's machismo was the reason Jorge Rodriguez was never punished for assaulting Julia. You said it was Espinosa's personal belief that no man should ever be punished for raping his wife."

"That is true."

"How do you know that's what Espinosa believes?"

"Because he said it. We were standing in the hallway outside the courtroom trying to resolve the charges against Julia. He said it to my face."

"That is exactly the kind of evidence I need for Julia's asylum case. The fact that Espinosa would say such a thing to Julia's lawyer proves that the prosecutor's office is unwilling to protect a married woman from domestic violence."

"What would you like me to do?" asked Santos.

"I want you to sign a sworn affidavit stating exactly what Espinosa said to you."

Santos shook his head. "I told you before. Attacking a prosecutor is suicide for me professionally. I deal with these people every day. I'll be a marked man. Everyone in that office will bust my balls every chance they get."

"My experience is the opposite," said Jack. "Prosecutors walk all over you if they think you're afraid to do the right thing."

"I practice in the Soyapango District, Mr. Swyteck, not the fancy halls of Brickell Avenue."

Every professional and businessperson in Central America equated Miami with Brickell Avenue, where there were no courthouses. The halls where Jack actually practiced were anything but fancy.

Santos drank from his beer. "May I propose a solution?"

"Go right ahead," said Jack.

"A hundred thousand dollars should compensate me for the aggravation this will cause me."

Jack coughed on his beer.

"Whoa," said Theo, "somebody came here to see Mr. Green."

"It's a reasonable number," said Santos.

"Mr. Santos, the rules don't allow me to pay witnesses for the evidence I need to prove my client's case. I could be disbarred for that."

"Then pay me in cash. No one needs to know."

"Look, I'm not going to pay you."

"Then I can't help your client."

"You're the only person who *can* help her. Theo and I were talking earlier. She's getting a raw deal. We think ICE is taking it out on her to get to someone else. Possibly her husband."

Santos laughed.

"Why is that funny?"

"Because you said her husband was in the Salvadoran witness protection program."

"That tickles your funny bone, does it?"

"It's funny that you think he would still be alive. They lost four last week. Twenty a month are murdered. There's no *protection*, and there's money to be made inside the police departments for giving up the names of informants to the gangs. If what Mr. Espinosa told you is true, if Julia's husband went into witness protection, I give it a one-in-a-hundred shot that he's still alive. One in seventy-five that they'll find the whole body. One in fifty that they'll find a piece of it."

He finished his beer with a long tilt and then climbed down from his stool. "You don't have many cases in El Salvador, do you, Mr. Swyteck?"

"No."

"Good thing. Let me know if you change your mind about my proposed solution." He slapped Jack on the back and headed to the exit.

Theo started on the red ale, brew number three. "Ten to one they find his body in pieces someday."

"Five to one," said Jack.

"So if this dude Santos is right and witness protection got Jorge Rodriguez killed, who slit Duncan McBride's throat like a gang-banger?"

Jack thought about it, but not for very long. "Another gang-banger."

CHAPTER 39

Beatriz arrived fifteen minutes early to her math class. The door was open, and Ms. Alvarez was alone in the classroom grading papers at her desk, which was perfect. Beatriz had a surprise for her favorite teacher, and she didn't want to make a big deal out of it in front of her classmates.

"Happy Valentine's Day," she said, as she stepped into the classroom.

Ms. Alvarez put down her red pencil, and Beatriz laid a small tray of candies on the desk.

"That's so sweet of you, Beatriz. Thank you."

"In El Salvador, Valentine's Day is not just for your sweetheart. We call it El Día de Amor y Amistad—the Day of Love and Friendship. You have been a good friend. So I brought you Salvadoran treats."

"They all look so good."

"This is what street vendors will be selling all day today in San Salvador. Meringues, chocolate-covered strawberries, rainbow-colored marshmallows—all sorts of things that we buy for our friends. The marshmallows are my favorite. Try one."

Ms. Alvarez did, and it made Beatriz smile to see her teacher's eyes light up. "Good, huh?"

"Delicious."

The intercom on the wall crackled, and the voice of the school principal, Mr. Henderson, filled the classroom: "Ms. Alvarez, is Beatriz Rodriguez in your next class period?"

"Yes," said Ms. Alvarez. "Actually, she's here with me right now."

"Can you bring her to my office, please?"

"Before class or after?"

"Now, please. Thank you."

The intercom clicked off, and Beatriz's happy mood had switched to worry just that quickly. She'd known of only one other student called down to the principal's office in that fashion, and it was to tell the girl that her father had died.

"What do you think this is about?" asked Beatriz.

"I don't know."

"Will you go with me?"

Ms. Alvarez nodded. "Sure. I'll walk you there."

Beatriz's mind raced with possible reasons to be summoned to the principal, and none of them was good. Nerves had so gotten the best of her that she didn't even realize she was holding Ms. Alvarez's hand, let alone crushing all the bones in her fingers. Ms. Alvarez led her to the administrative suite, and the assistant showed them into the principal's office.

Beatriz had never stood this close to Mr. Henderson, and his imposing size would have surprised her had she not known by reputation that he was a former high school football star. He directed her to the chair and asked Ms. Alvarez to stay. It was the three of them behind the closed door.

"Beatriz, there is a Detective Barnes here to see you. He's with the Miami-Dade Police Department."

Beatriz felt as if she'd been punched in the stomach. "Is ICE with him?"

"No. This has nothing to do with ICE."

Good news, but it didn't relieve all anxiety. "What does the man want?" asked Beatriz.

"He said he wants to speak to you."

"What about?"

"He's with the Homicide Unit. I assume it has to do with—well, I'm not going to assume anything. He just wants to talk."

News of the body found inside Beatriz's house had traveled far and wide. Every kid in her high school knew about it, so it was no surprise to Beatriz that the principal was aware of it, too. "What if I don't want to talk to him?"

"Then you can tell him that."

"Can't you or Ms. Alvarez tell him for me?"

"I'm sorry, but no. I can't stop the police from doing their job. As principal, the only thing I can do is notify your mother that the police came to the school and asked to talk to you."

"Did you call my mom?"

"Yes, but I didn't get an answer."

Beatriz felt her hands shaking. Ms. Alvarez spoke up for her. "Can't you tell the police that we're waiting to hear back from her mother?"

"No," said the principal, his voice firm. "That's the school policy, which was written by very smart lawyers who read the court opinions and tell us what to do in these situations. We notify the parents. We don't interfere with an investigation. High school students are old enough to tell the police if they're willing to talk or not. That's the law. There's nothing more to discuss."

Ms. Alvarez tried to soften the situation. "It will be okay, Beatriz. Just tell them that you don't want to talk, or that you don't want to talk without your mother being there. You can do that."

Beatriz wasn't sure she could—no matter what the smart lawyers or the Supreme Court said about it. Ms. Alvarez gave her a half smile of encouragement, and it seemed to help a little. She drew a breath and let it out. "Okay. I'll tell him."

Mr. Henderson rose and led Beatriz out of his office to the other end of the administrative suite. It was a part of the building that Beatriz had never seen before, never even knew of its existence, and she felt like a stranger in the secret halls of school discipline. They entered a conference room at the end of the hall. Waiting inside were Detective Barnes and a woman who said her name was Officer Cabal. Neither was wearing a police uniform, but that didn't make it any less scary. Barnes asked the principal to leave. He and Cabal then sat on one side of the table, and Beatriz sat on the other.

"Good morning," said Barnes, and he kept right on talking, giving Beatriz no opening to say what she was feeling, and when the opportunity to speak finally arose, and Beatriz tried to tell him that she didn't want to be in the room without her mother, the words simply wouldn't form in her mouth.

"Would that be all right, Beatriz?" the detective asked.

"Huh, what?" Beatriz had heard him speaking to her, but everything he'd said was like gibberish.

"I was just wondering if you could answer a few questions for us," said Barnes.

Beatriz didn't trust him one bit, but there was something about the whole situation that made her want to comply. "I guess so."

"Good. These are going to be real simple. Can you read English?"

She still didn't trust him. She glanced at Officer Cabal, who seemed nice.

"It's okay," Cabal said in a soft voice. "It's not a trick question."

"Yeah," said Beatriz. "I read English fine."

"Very good," said Barnes. "But let me ask the question another way. If you had to read something and it was very important that you understood every word, would you rather read it in English or in Spanish?"

She glanced again at Cabal, then answered in a soft voice. "Spanish."

"Good to know," said Barnes.

There was a file on the table at Officer Cabal's elbow. She removed a one-page, typewritten document and placed it directly in front of Beatriz. It was in Spanish.

"What is this?" Beatriz asked in Spanish. Cabal was fluent, and the conversation continued in Beatriz's native tongue.

"It's a form," said Cabal. "Detective Barnes would like you to read it and sign it. You have to sign it to give us your consent."

"My consent to what?"

Cabal reached under the table for the box that was at her feet and placed the box on the table. Beatriz watched as she opened a kit of some kind and removed a plastic tube, a pair of latex gloves, and what looked like giant Q-tips.

"This is all very simple, Beatriz. And it won't hurt a bit. All I want is for you to open your mouth for a few seconds. Then I take this little stick," she said, holding it, "swab the inside of your cheek with the cotton tip, and we're done. Signing that form says it's okay for me to do that."

"Why do you want me to do it?"

"Because I want to help you."

"Help me what?"

"Help you get out of here. If you don't sign this form, Detective Barnes will have no choice but to keep you here and ask you all kinds of questions about your parents."

"Like what?"

"Oh, Beatriz. Don't get me started, because if I do, then Detective Barnes here will really get going. And once he starts down that road, this could take hours. It's going to be so unpleasant for you. Much worse than me putting this little piece of cotton in your mouth for two seconds. *Two seconds.* That's it. And then you can go, no questions asked."

Beatriz was thinking about it. She wasn't sure if the detective understood her conversation with Officer Cabal in Spanish, but the next question was from him and in English.

"So, Beatriz," said Barnes, "tell me this: When was the last time you saw your father?"

Cabal spoke in Spanish. "See what I mean? Two seconds, Beatriz. Just sign, open your mouth, and we're done."

Cabal reached across the table and offered Beatriz a pen. Beatriz stared at it, but her hand didn't move.

Barnes asked, "When's the last time your mother saw your father, Beatriz?"

Beatriz blinked hard.

"Sign," said Cabal. "If you do, I'll make him stop."

Beatriz took the pen.

"That's it," said Cabal. "Sign and we go home."

Beatriz put the pen to the paper, and then she signed her consent.

CHAPTER 40

Jack was home early with enough flowers, candy, and balloons for the three generations of Valentines. Andie was showering and getting ready for their night out, but Righley and Abuela were all hugs and kisses as he came through the front door.

"I love you, Dada."

Jack picked her up and nearly melted on the spot, but Abuela was not so impressed.

"*Español, por favor,*" she said like a schoolteacher.

"*Te quiero, papi.*"

"*Muy bien,*" she said, adding what Jack translated as, "At least there's hope for someone in the family."

"Do you think I don't understand these things you say right in front of me?" Jack asked.

Abuela gave him a kiss, and all was just fine. Righley took her by the hand and led her to the kitchen to cook her favorite dinner in the whole world: "'Fraidy-cat noodle soup," a four-year-old's play on "chicken," which Abuela said was hilarious, even though the pun had to be way beyond her grasp. Jack went to the wine chiller, looked for something in line with the chocolatey theme of the holiday, and selected the Mother Tongue Shiraz from Australia's Barossa Valley. He poured Andie a glass and was headed toward the bedroom when his cell rang. It was Julia's number. He felt guilty letting the call go to voice mail, but it was Valentine's Day, after all.

Andie was still in the shower, and Max was lying on the floor in front of the closed bathroom door. It was his one and only trick: standing guard when Andie was in the shower. And he was good at it. Jack could walk into the room with a pork chop around his neck, and Max wouldn't leave his post. That still didn't keep him from throwing Jack a look with those big brown eyes, as if to say, "So, where's *my* candy?"

Jack's phone pinged with a text from Julia—"Emergency, please answer"—and his phone rang a moment later. He took the call.

"Jack, thank you for picking up! I think they're after Beatriz!"

"What? Slow down. You think who's after Beatriz?"

"The police. They went to her school today and took a DNA swab from her."

Jack put Andie's wine on the dresser and walked across the hall to his home office, listening. Julia recounted everything second-hand, parts of which she'd gathered from Beatriz and other parts from the school principal.

"This is insane," said Julia. "How could that detective even think that my daughter would slit a man's throat?"

"No one thinks Beatriz is a killer," said Jack.

"How do you know that?"

It took a constitutional law scholar to understand the rights of teenagers in police interrogations on school property, but Jack knew enough to draw some inferences. "If Beatriz was a suspect in the murder of Duncan McBride, Detective Barnes wouldn't just show up at her school and trap her in a conference room. An ambush like that could jeopardize their whole case."

"Then what do they need her DNA for?"

Andie appeared in the doorway, a glass of wine in hand. "Who you talking to, honey?"

Jack asked Julia to hold. "A client."

"Okay. Reservation is at eight. This wine is delicious. Come have a glass with me before we go."

"I'll be right there."

Andie left, and Jack returned to his call. "Julia, is there a time tomorrow morning when we can talk more about this?"

"Do you think they're just harassing me?" she asked.

"Do I think who is harassing you?"

"The police. Is that why they did this to Beatriz?"

"I really don't think so."

"Then why would they collect DNA from someone who's not a suspect. What's the purpose?"

Jack was reluctant to get into the science of DNA, but it wasn't fair to leave her thinking that the police were just harassing her and Beatriz. "My guess is that they're looking for a partial DNA match."

"What does that mean?"

"Let's say the police find DNA at a crime scene that doesn't belong to the victim. A drop of blood. A hair follicle. Some kind of body fluid. The logical thing to do is to get a DNA sample from the suspect and see if there's a match, right?"

"But you said that's not what the police did here."

"Exactly. Sometimes the police can't get a DNA sample from their suspect. So they might take DNA from someone who's related to their suspect. Depending on how much DNA that relative shares with the suspect, the police could get a partial match."

"Wait a sec. You're saying the police think they know who killed Duncan McBride, and Beatriz is related to that person?"

"Right now, that's the best explanation I have for what happened to Beatriz today."

"Am *I* a suspect?"

"No. That wouldn't make sense. Beatriz obviously has a lot of your DNA, but the police know where you are. They could get a warrant to force you to give them a DNA sample."

There was silence on the line, and Jack could almost imagine the wheels turning in Julia's head.

"Oh, my God," she said, as the realization set in. "It's Jorge."

"No, they *think* it's Jorge."

"I told you it was him," she said, her voice racing. "Hugo told me he's here. Jorge is in Miami!"

"I wouldn't jump to that conclusion. Your old lawyer in San Salvador thinks it would be a miracle if Jorge is still alive."

"Mr. Santos doesn't know my husband. Why would Jorge be a murder suspect if he's not even here? Why would the police be checking Beatriz's DNA for a partial match if he's not in Miami?"

"The police could have any number of persons of interest. Sometimes they just want to rule things out."

"Jack, I have to get out of here."

"Out of where?"

"Out of Miami."

"You can't do that. You posted a bond to get out of detention, and one of the conditions is that you cannot leave Miami-Dade County. If you violate that condition, you forfeit your bond, and Judge Greely will send you back to detention."

"You don't understand," she said, her voice rising with panic. "You don't know half of what Jorge did to us. We have to get out of here!"

"Julia, you can't go anywhere."

"I'm sorry, Jack."

"Julia, listen to me."

"I have to go."

"Julia!"

There was silence on the line. Julia was gone.

CHAPTER 41

C y's Place was packed with its traditional Valentine's Day crowd: men and women with no date, Theo included.

Theo was behind the bar mixing his signature drink, the Flaming Wild Banshee. One-fifty vodka and a dash of jalapeño juice, so named for the standard warning Theo issued to the bravehearted. "Light it up, belt it back, and try not to end up running through the bar like a flaming wild banshee with your hair on fire." Theo was serving one up for a lonely and indecisive businessman from Philly who'd exercised the poor judgment of ordering, "Whatever you recommend, good sir."

Theo set the flaming shot glass on the bar top, which usually triggered a reaction, but this guy was too deep into self-pity to notice that the flickering blue flame was threatening his eyebrows.

"I hate this day," the man said, grumbling.

"Alexander Graham Bell Day?"

"Valentine's Day."

"Never heard of it. February 14, 1876. Alexander Graham Bell patented the telephone. Why the fuck people send roses to their girlfriend to commemorate it, I have no idea."

"I'll drink to that," the man said, and he belted back the banshee.

Theo's cell rang. It was Jack, and Theo answered in his mushy voice. "Aw, you remembered. I love you so much, Jackie."

"I got a problem," said Jack. "Julia's freaked out, thinks her husband is in Miami, and wants to get the hell out of town."

"I thought that guy was dead. Is he here?"

"Nobody's actually seen him, as far as I know, but the police seem to think he could be in Miami."

"The Miami police?"

Jack gave him thirty seconds on the DNA, a subject near and dear to Theo's heart, as it was DNA that had sprung him from death row.

"Whaddaya want me to do?" asked Theo.

"If Julia so much as crosses the county line, she'll end up back in detention. Judge Greely said Baker County Facility was full, but ICE will find room for anyone who violates the conditions of release on bond."

"So you want me to stop her?"

"Andie will kill me if I bail out on dinner. Can you just go by Julia's place and calm her down? And yeah, make sure she understands that she cannot go anywhere."

"Sure, I can get someone to cover the bar for an hour or so."

"Thanks, buddy."

"No problem," said Theo. "And by the way: Happy Alexander Graham Bell Day."

Julia cleared the plates from the table and took them to the kitchen sink.

Beatriz had said nothing during dinner. She'd eaten nothing, hadn't even taken so much as a sip of water. She just sat there, and when Julia was finished, Beatriz had gotten up and gone to take a shower before bed. At least she was bathing. Still, it was like night and day, the difference between the girl who'd left for school so excited about the Valentine's Day treats for Ms. Alvarez and the zombie at the dinner table.

"Are you going to be okay here?" asked Cecilia.

Julia's sister was going out for the night with her roommates, celebrating in Salvadoran fashion the "friends" component of El Día de Amor y Amistad.

"Yeah. Go have fun."

Cecilia told her to call if she needed anything. The front door closed, and it was just Julia and her daughter in the house. She hoped.

He can't be here. Please, God. Don't let him be here in Miami.

She'd panicked on the phone with Jack, threatening to leave town, but that didn't make her fear any less real.

Julia finished drying the dishes and checked on Beatriz. The bathroom door was closed, and she could hear the shower running. Julia went to the living room to inflate the air mattress. Cecilia had been cool about sharing her place, but the spare bedroom was barely big enough for Julia, and Beatriz still had no room of her own. Julia needed to find an apartment, but with the news about Jorge, it was scary enough living with Cecilia and her roommates. The thought of just the two of them, her and Beatriz, getting an apartment of their own in the same city as Jorge was beyond frightening. She'd talk to Cecilia in the morning about staying a little longer.

Julia unfolded the deflated air mattress and began her nightly search for the battery-powered air pump. It was Beatriz's job to deflate the mattress each morning before school, and she had yet to leave the pump in the same place twice.

A knock on the front door startled her. The thought of Jorge in town had her completely on edge, but she wondered if he would actually knock if he ever came for her. Probably not. Still, she stepped tentatively to the peephole, saw it was Theo, and opened the door.

"Jack asked me to swing by and check on you," he said.

"Oh, that was my bad. I guess he thought I was serious about leaving town."

"Serious was not the word. I believe he said 'freaked out.'"

"Yeah, I was a little freaked."

"But you're good now?"

"Yes."

"You're staying put?"

"Where would I go? And if Jorge followed me all the way from El Salvador, what good would it do to run from Miami?"

Theo nodded, seeming to follow her logic. "Okay, then. Glad you're all right."

"I'm sorry Jack made you come all the way over here."

"No problem. It's not far, really. Not too far, anyway. At least not in a *Star Wars* galaxy sense of the word."

It made her smile, but she knew his club was miles away in Coconut Grove, which made her feel bad about wasting his evening. "Would you like to come inside for a minute? I have some tea that was brewing in the sun all day. Have some with me."

He accepted with a smile. The air mattress and bedding on the floor was a little awkward, but they walked right past it on the way to the kitchen.

"Do you like herbal tea?"

"If it comes with bacon."

She assumed he was kidding and poured the tea into two ice-filled glasses. "Flor de Jamaica," she said. "Good for the liver and kidneys. Smart bartenders drink it every day."

"Smart bartenders don't own their own bar," said Theo. "Cheers."

Their glasses clicked, and Julia watched Theo's expression as the tea went down.

"Good stuff," he said.

"Liar," she said, and then she squeezed a shot of honey into each glass. "It's pretty nasty without it."

They shared a laugh, and then Julia turned serious. "Tell Jack I'm sorry I wigged out on him like that."

"He's used to it."

"I was cleaning a house over on Venetian Isle today. Lousy phone reception."

"Sorry about that."

Julia had almost forgotten that it was Theo who'd purchased the disposable phone for her when she got out of jail. "That's not your fault. But I was saying, it wasn't till I was riding home on the bus that I got the message from the school principal saying that the police talked to Beatriz. Then I called Jack, and he told me about Jorge and—well, that put me over the edge."

"Jack really thought you were gonna run off with that guy."

"What guy?"

"From the bakery at the church. Hugo."

"Oh, Hugo."

Theo added another shot of honey to his tea. A big one. "That was a pretty heavy 'oh' in the 'Oh, Hugo,'" he said.

Julia sighed. "There was a time when I thought Hugo was the answer to my prayers. And in a way he was. He made me feel safe. Or at least *safer* than I was without him. Hugo is the only man I've ever known who actually scared my husband."

"Was Hugo okay with you coming to Miami?"

"I didn't tell him I was leaving."

"Why not?"

"It's weird, but if you had asked me that question six months ago, my answer would have been 'I don't know.' It was just something I did. But now that time has passed, and especially after I saw him here in Miami, things have gotten clearer in my mind. I know exactly why I left the way I did it."

"Why?"

Her gaze leveled, and her voice dropped a bit. "Because Hugo was starting to scare me, too."

"Does Beatriz feel the same way?"

"Beatriz is living in the past. She wishes me and Hugo would get back together. There's an old photograph of us at the bakery from a couple of years ago. Beatriz and I have an ongoing tug-of-war over it."

"Tug-of-war?"

"Yeah. I keep putting it in the drawer, and Beatriz keeps putting it on my nightstand, as if that's going to rekindle something."

"So you and Hugo are not—"

"No, no. We are not a thing. I care for Hugo, but I don't need to go from a man whose mission in life is to destroy me to a man whose mission in life is to save me."

Theo added even more honey to his tea. "How is Beatriz doing after what happened at school today?"

"She's—" Julia stopped and checked the clock on the wall and listened. The bathroom and kitchen shared a common wall, and she could still hear the water running through the pipes. Beatriz had been in the shower for over an hour. "Excuse me one minute, Theo."

Julia pushed away from the table, walked down the hallway, and knocked on the bathroom door. "Beatriz?"

There was no answer, just the hiss of running water. Julia tried the knob, but the door was locked. She knocked again, harder this time, and waited. No reply.

"Beatriz," she said, louder. "Open the door, sweetie."

It was like white noise, the steady drone of an hour-long shower. Julia's pulse quickened, and her call became a shout.

"Beatriz! Open the door!"

Theo came up quickly behind her. "What's wrong?"

"She doesn't answer me. That shower's been running over an hour. We have five minutes' worth of hot water in this house, tops. She was so upset after what happened today and—oh, God, I'm afraid to think."

Theo tried the knob, which didn't turn.

"Beatriz!" Julia screamed.

Theo took a step back and kicked the door open on the first try. Julia hurried past him and screamed at the sight.

Beatriz was sitting on the tile floor, knees to her chest, huddled in her glass box, soaked to the bone from the falling water.

"Beatriz!" She flung open the shower door and turned off the water. It was freezing cold, but strangely Beatriz wasn't shivering. Julia wrapped her daughter in a towel and called for Theo's help. He rushed in from the hallway as Julia checked her pulse. The cold water had turned her skin a bluish purple, but her heart was beating.

"Take her to the bedroom," she told Theo.

Theo gathered her up in his arms, carried her across the hall, and laid her on the bed. Beatriz's eyes were open, and Julia was standing directly over her, calling to her—"Beatriz! Beatriz!"—but it was as if her daughter couldn't even see her.

Julia tapped her cheeks gently to revive her, but she drew only that vacant look.

"Could be hypothermia," said Theo. "I'll call nine-one-one."

"Hurry," said Julia, squeezing her daughter's cold hand. "Please, hurry."

CHAPTER 42

She wanted him. There was no doubt in his mind that she wanted him, bad. Julia was the master of mind games, always putting obstacles between them, forcing him to prove himself over and over again. How much did one man have to prove to a woman? Why should any man have to prove himself to his wife?

The Miami-Dade Metrobus stopped at the curb, and the doors opened. Jorge pitched his smoldering cigarette into the gutter and climbed aboard, exhaling his last lungful of smoke all over the bus driver as he passed.

"You mind, pal?"

In San Salvador, that kind of disrespect would land a bus driver facedown on the pavement in a pool of his own blood. But this was Miami, not El Salvador, and Jorge had more important things on his mind.

The bus rumbled forward as Jorge made his way down the aisle. There were plenty of empty seats, but Jorge chose to stand at the rail about halfway down, where the extra-long coach folded like an accordion to maneuver around tight corners. He watched through the window as the bus rolled past one residential cross street after another. The streets were dark, save for one, where the orange light of an ambulance swirled at the end of the block. The bus gathered speed, merging into traffic on the busy commercial boulevard on its way downtown. Jorge's gaze remained fixed on the orange beacon of the ambulance until a passing billboard blocked his view of the side street. Then he settled into the nearest seat.

Jorge had spent two hours on that street, casing the house since sundown. He'd gotten there around the time Julia's sister was leaving with her girlfriends and stayed until the ambulance arrived. Jorge had no idea who called 911 or why. Maybe Julia was choking on El Negro's dick. The irony was that if that ambulance hadn't shown up when it did, those two valentines would have needed one.

Jorge dug his new smartphone from his pocket. It wasn't technically his. He'd stolen it just that morning, and the true owner had canceled the phone service a few hours later, but the camera still worked, and it took excellent photos. Really excellent photos. He scrolled through the album he'd just created. El Negro pulls up to the house. Julia opens the front door. Julia invites him in. The kitchen light goes on.

Jorge had seen enough when the bedroom light went on. He didn't need to sneak up to the house, hold his camera up to the window, and video it. He knew.

Fucking slut.

Funny thing was, he'd gone there on Valentine's Day expecting to catch her in the act with Hugo. Hugo, the dumb shit who seemed to forget that Eighteen was not just in San Salvador, that its tentacles reached all the way to Miami. The unwritten code was that membership in Eighteen was a lifelong commitment. "Finding Jesus" was the only exception. Anyone who tried to fake "finding Jesus" was a dead man. Hugo was a fake. Convincing Eighteen that Hugo was a phony Bible banger had saved Jorge's life.

J orge was on his knees, his wrists bound so tightly behind has back that the cord had broken the skin. Rivulets of blood trickled down his fingers, the crimson drops collecting on the concrete floor of a dank garage that smelled of mildew. A spotlight shone down from the rafters, effectively blinding him. More than a dozen members of Eighteen had crammed into the abandoned building at midnight to witness Jorge's execution.

El Gusano, the drunken men called him. The worm.

The word in Soyapango was that Jorge had turned against Eighteen and was informing to the police. The *barrio* chief, a lunatic called El Demente—the Demented One—was minutes away from hacking him to pieces with a razor-sharp machete.

The side door to the garage opened, and El Demente entered to the cheers of his men. El Demente was naked from the waist up, except for the purple bandanna wrapped around his head. He had the ripped body of a gangbanger who'd spent most of his adult life in prison, with nothing to do but push-ups and sit-ups from sunup till sundown. A collage of multihued tattoos covered his body, including a rattlesnake that wound around his right arm, its gaping jaws and exposed fangs dripping with poison on the right side of his face. One of El Demente's disciples offered him a blow of meth, and the men went wild as he leaned over the workbench and sniffed a heaping, nearly lethal line of white powder up his nose and into his brain.

"El Demente! El Demente! El Demente!" the men chanted.

Sweat poured down Jorge's brow. He'd declined the offer of a blindfold, and he wished he hadn't. Jorge had witnessed the ritual before from the party side. This time he was the entertainment. The man of the hour always begged. It never worked. Not a marked man in the history of Eighteen had managed to talk his way out of a gang-ordered execution. At least not with El Demente in charge.

El Demente sorted through the tools on the workbench. A claw hammer. A hacksaw. A power drill. So hard to choose a favorite. He took the machete, "old reliable," and raised it over his head.

His men fell silent.

"Jorge likes to talk to the police," he shouted, which drew a chorus of boos from his men.

"It's bullshit!" Jorge shouted. "It's total bullshit, man!"

El Demente lowered the machete. He stepped toward the prisoner until he was within striking distance, but the machete remained at his side. He smiled sardonically and said, "You just called me a liar."

"No!" said Jorge, his voice quaking. "Not you. Hugo is the liar. Hugo put the lie on the street that I'm an informant."

Hugo had done no such thing, but Jorge was desperate for a scapegoat.

"Hugo has gone to Jesus," said El Demente. "Why would he lie about you?"

"Hugo is a fraud. He's fucking my wife!"

"We all fuck your wife!" one of the men shouted, and the others roared with laughter.

El Demente raised his machete, silencing them. It was highly unusual, even for a condemned man, to confess before Eighteen that his woman was unfaithful, at least if she was still alive. El Demente seemed intrigued.

"I don't believe you," he said.

"It's true. He fucked my wife and got her pregnant."

"When?"

"A while ago. He's been doing her ever since."

"Prove it."

Jorge struggled for a response, not sure how to prove such a thing. Then it came to him. "Talk to the doctor who did the abortion. I made her get one. It was a son. Would I make my wife abort my own son?"

El Demente was thinking it over. "Who was the doctor?"

"Vazquez. The one we always use."

A pregnant prostitute was a common problem in the Eighteen sex trade. Vazquez was the go-to problem solver, even if he hadn't actually graduated from medical school. El Demente had him on speed dial.

Jorge remained on his knees, sweat pouring from his body. The pressure was more than he could bear, as he and the other men watched El Demente make the call. It was quiet enough in the garage for him and everyone else to hear El Demente's side of the conversation, and his heart raced with the fear that Dr. Vazquez would have no memory of Julia. His only hope was that this procedure would stand out in his mind, the one that had gone terribly wrong, ending with all that bleeding that had nearly killed Julia and had landed her in the emergency room.

El Demente showed no emotion as he spoke into the phone, his expression cold as ice as he questioned Dr. Vazquez. Then he hung up.

"You are a lucky man, my friend."

Jorge nearly collapsed with relief. El Demente put away his phone and addressed his men.

"Hugo is a fake," he said in a booming voice. "What is the punishment for those who wiggled their way out of Eighteen by pretending to love Jesus?"

"Death," the men said.

El Demente stepped toward Jorge, stared down at him, and slapped his face lightly with the blunt side of the machete. "*You* will take care of Hugo."

It was a green light to eliminate one of Eighteen's only protected class of ex-members, and Jorge had waited years for it. Without El Demente's blessing, killing a gang member who had turned to Jesus would have been a capital offense.

"It will be my pleasure," said Jorge.

The bus stopped. Someone got on, but Jorge didn't even look up. His focus was entirely on his phone. He'd scrolled through all the evening's photos twice, and the best shot was the one of El Negro getting out of his car, before he'd gone to the front door. Jorge had snapped it from across the street, but this new camera had an amazing zoom. He enlarged the image on the screen to the max, cropped it so that he had a close-up of that black face, and then he hit "save." He stared down at that glowing image on the screen through the next two bus stops, memorizing that face, burning it into his mind.

He'd been commissioned to Miami for a specific purpose. But Hugo's execution could wait.

"You're next," he said, as he tucked his phone into his pocket. Then he smiled to himself, gazing out the bus window at the moonlit Miami skyline, soaking up the energy of "the capital of Latin America," knowing that El Negro had just fucked his last Latina.

CHAPTER 43

Miami's UM/Jackson Memorial Hospital was a two-minute drive from Jack's office, and he stopped by the ER on his way to work. The waiting room was filled with the typical array of morning patients, heavy on substance abusers who'd had a bad night and mothers with newborns who just wouldn't stop crying, not even with the sunrise. Theo was slouched in a chair under a ceiling-mounted television that was tuned to a Spanish-language broadcast. Jack took the seat next to him.

"How's Beatriz?" Jack asked.

"Spoke to Julia about an hour ago. She thinks the doctor's going to let her go home."

"When?"

"Who knows? Typical hospital bureaucracy. Like a glacier on Valium."

"Have you been here all night?"

"Yeah. Julia said I could go, but I didn't want her to be alone if something bad happened."

Sweet, thought Jack. It was Theo Knight's new handle. The whole world was turning upside down.

There was a commotion on the other side of the room. One of the substance abusers was getting tired of waiting, and another one was tired of his constant complaining about the wait. A couple of orderlies, one of them bigger than Theo, came out to calm the men down. It occurred to Jack that Miami could use more orderlies.

"I got an e-mail from the immigration court in Orlando this morning," said Jack.

"Don't tell me that the judge is sending her back to Macclenny."

"No. But he was serious about fast-tracking Julia's request for asylum. Judge Greely's calendar is full, so he transferred the case to the rocket docket down here in Miami. Her final hearing is specially set. We start two weeks from tomorrow."

"Rocket docket?"

"I made that up. The official name is the U.S. Immigration Circus Cannon. Judge P. T. Barnum packs it with Latinos and shoots them back over the border."

It made Theo laugh, and the depth of his laughter made it clear that he was getting punchy. "You should go home and get some sleep," said Jack.

The pneumatic door to the ER opened and Julia emerged. Jack and Theo rose to meet her halfway across the room. She looked frazzled.

"Everything okay with Beatriz?" asked Jack.

"She's awake and seems fine."

"Are they going to admit her to the hospital?"

"The doctor said no two hours ago. Dr. Nelson is her name. But now they tell me the doctor wants to talk to her alone and I have to wait out here."

"Let me see what's going on," said Jack. He went to the admissions window. The receptionist was on the telephone, and while he was waiting, the commotion resumed on the other side of the room. Two police officers had entered, and the gangbanger with a bloody hand took off like he'd seen a ghost, even though the cops didn't seem at all interested in him. The pneumatic doors opened, a doctor led the officers back to the patient bays, and the doors closed automatically.

Julia walked over to Jack and said, "That was Beatriz's doctor. Why are the police here?"

Jack was suspicious but didn't want to alarm her. "That doctor probably has twenty other patients. But let me check it out."

The receptionist finally got off the phone, but she was no help. "Are you having severe chest pain or the worst headache you've ever had in your life?" she asked.

"No," said Jack.

"Then please have a seat."

The pneumatic doors opened again. The police officers were back. So was Beatriz's doctor. "Julia Rodriguez?" one of the cops said in a voice that filled the waiting room.

Jack didn't like the feel of this situation. "I'm her lawyer," he said, stepping toward them. Julia and Theo went with him.

The female officer did the talking. "We'd like to talk in private to Ms. Rodriguez."

"What about?" asked Jack.

"Her daughter."

"Is she okay?" Julia asked, and Jack heard the panic in her voice.

"Yes," said Dr. Nelson. She was one of the younger-looking doctors on duty, but with the tired eyes of a resident in the twelfth hour of her ER shift. "Both the police and I have some questions for Ms. Rodriguez."

Theo waited in the lobby as Jack and Julia followed the doctor and police officers into an examination room down the hall. Dr. Nelson closed the door.

"I'm concerned about Beatriz's well-being," she said.

Jack glanced at the police officers. "My client is not answering any questions until I know exactly what your concern is, Doctor."

"Beatriz is a healthy teenage girl with no history of chronic illness reported. This is the second time she's presented to the emergency room in less than two weeks."

"We're going through a tough time," said Julia.

"Let's just listen," Jack told his client. "Doctor, why are you concerned about two visits to the ER?"

"I reviewed her medical record from her hospital stay. A complete battery of tests. Neuroradiology and neurophysiological examinations were negative. Electroencephalogram, magnetic resonance, computed tomography of the skull, and laboratory screenings were all unimpressive."

"I don't understand what she's saying," said Julia.

"They didn't find anything wrong with her," said Jack. "Which I think I can explain, Doctor. Have you ever heard of resignation syndrome?"

"No," she said without interest. "Have you ever heard of carfentanil?"

"No. Sounds like fentanyl."

"It's harder to detect that fentanyl, and tests can often miss it. Even autopsies are not foolproof. But we got lucky. It showed up in Beatriz's urine screening."

"Do you suspect drug use?" asked Jack.

"I asked her if she's a user," the doctor said. "She said no. I believe her. But what about you, Ms. Rodriguez? Are you a drug user?"

"Don't answer that," said Jack.

"No!" said Julia, ignoring her lawyer.

"Julia, I'm going to send you out to sit with Theo if you say another word," said Jack.

"This is my daughter, Jack!"

Jack gave her that much. "Exactly what is carfentanil, Doctor?"

"It's an animal tranquilizer that veterinarians use on elephants in zoos."

"Elephants?" said Julia.

"Julia, please," said Jack.

"No, Jack! I need to know what's happening here. What is this doctor saying?"

"Let me spell it out," said Dr. Nelson. "One of two things is going on here. Either Beatriz ingested a bad dose of a synthetic recreational drug, like fentanyl, which contained carfentanil. Or someone is trying to put Beatriz into a coma."

Jack narrowed his eyes, realizing what this show of police force was all about. "Munchausen by proxy. Is that what you think is going on here?"

"Factitious disorder," she said in a voice that made Jack feel old. "Nobody calls it Munchausen anymore. But yes, that's why I called the police."

Jack measured his words, responding in a calm tone. "I have one question for you, Doctor. Is there a medical reason to admit Beatriz to the hospital?"

The doctor didn't seem to like the question, but at least she was honest. "No. Medically speaking, we've done all that we need to do. This is a legal matter."

"Then we're leaving," said Jack. "And we're taking Beatriz with us."

The male police officer stepped in front of Jack, blocking his exit. Jack would never physically threaten a police officer, but a firm voice was in order. "Officer, unless you have a court order to keep my client away from her daughter, I suggest you step aside right now, or I will be filing a false imprisonment lawsuit against the Miami Police Department that will make you wish you'd never met me."

The officer glanced at the doctor, took her nonverbal direction, and then backed away.

"Just so you know, I do intend to report this to DCF," the doctor said.

Jack didn't know if Julia understood that DCF meant the Department of Children and Families, but she clearly grasped the gravity of the situation, and she started yelling in Spanish at the police officers in such an angry and hysterical voice that Jack couldn't even begin to comprehend. All Jack could do was whisk her out of the room before she said something that somebody more fluent could potentially use against her in a court of law.

"I'm not leaving Beatriz here!" Julia shouted as they exited through the pneumatic doors.

Jack handed her off to Theo in the waiting room. "Take her out," Jack told him.

"Huh?"

"Just take her to the car and wait," said Jack.

"What are you going to do?" Julia asked.

"I'm going to become one huge pain in the ass," said Jack, "until I walk out those doors with your daughter."

CHAPTER 44

Jack drove Julia home in his car. Theo drove Beatriz separately in his. Jack needed alone time with Julia to ask the hard question of his client.

"Did you give Beatriz that drug?"

"No!"

"Did you give her any drugs?"

"Absolutely not. I would never hurt Beatriz."

"Have you done anything to make it look like she has resignation syndrome?"

"Jack, I never heard of resignation syndrome until you told me about it."

Jack asked the same questions several different ways throughout the ride, and he got the same vehement denials.

They reached the house before eight a.m. Cecilia and her roommates had not yet left for work, so their cars were in the driveway. Jack pulled up behind Theo on the street. Beatriz jumped out of Theo's car and hurried up the walkway to the front door. Jack wasn't entirely fluent in the body language of teenage girls, but Beatriz was making a pretty obvious statement that she didn't want to talk.

"Mind if I come in for a minute?" Jack asked Julia. "I have a few questions for Beatriz."

"Sure."

Beatriz entered the house and closed the door as Jack and Julia climbed out of Jack's car.

"Good luck," said Julia.

Julia went to Theo and thanked him. Jack wasn't trying to listen to what she said to him, but he would have bet money that it included the word *sweet*. Theo drove away as Jack followed Julia into the house. Cecilia was in the kitchen making coffee. Beatriz marched to her aunt's room and slammed the door shut. Jack joined Julia in the kitchen.

"How is Beatriz?" Cecilia asked.

"Fine," Julia said sharply. "No thanks to you."

Cecilia set her coffee cup on the counter, as if taken aback. "I called you three times last night. You told me not to come to the hospital."

"That's not what I'm talking about, Cecilia. They found drugs in her urine."

"No way! Not Beatriz."

"Oh, don't act so shocked," said Julia. "And don't pretend like you don't know where she would get them. You're the only one in our family who ever did drugs, Cecilia."

Jack suddenly felt invisible, an unwitting witness to a previously unknown-to-him slice of history between sisters.

"Really?" Cecilia said, indignant. "You're putting this on *me*?"

"I was in jail the first time Beatriz had to go to the emergency room. Beatriz was staying with you and your party-girl roommates."

"My party-girl roommates and I have given you half our apartment, shared our kitchen and our bathroom and our food with you, given you our spare bedroom, and turned the living room into a bedroom for your daughter. We have been nothing but good to you. And this is how you thank us?"

"I don't owe a thank-you to anyone who turns my daughter onto drugs made out of elephant tranquilizers."

"Go to hell, Julia."

"No, you listen to me!"

"Stop!" Beatriz shouted. She was standing in the kitchen doorway. Heads turned in her direction, and they waited for Beatriz to speak.

"It wasn't Tía," said Beatriz.

Julia and Cecilia stood speechless. Jack spoke up as a neutral. "Where did you get it, Beatriz?"

"School," she said. "There's a boy who has an older brother."

Julia's gaze swung toward her sister, and she was about to apologize, but Cecilia walked out. Julia looked at Beatriz, but her daughter was even less receptive.

"Don't talk to me," said Beatriz. She left the room, headed down the hall, and just kept going—through the front door and out of the house.

"Let me talk to her," said Jack.

Julia nodded, and Jack left through the front door. He caught up with Beatriz at the end of the driveway. She was leaning against Jack's car, arms folded tightly, staring down the block.

"Hey," said Jack, leaning against the fender. He was at her side, and they shared a view of the morning commuters that zipped through residential streets in search of shortcuts to work.

"Hey, yourself," she said.

"Your mom was due for a blowup. I hope you know that. This is unbelievably stressful for any human being. And she's only human."

"She always blames Tía for everything. It's like she's jealous that Tía is the only one here legally."

Jack hadn't thought of that, and there could well have been something to it. But this conversation wasn't about the sisters.

"Why did you do it, Beatriz?"

She turned her head just enough to glance at Jack. "It wasn't my idea."

"Whose was it?"

"My friend at school. Vivien. I talk to her about what's going on. I told her what the judge said: that if I get better, my mom goes back to jail. She said her brother has this stuff that made him sleep for two days."

"Carfentanil?"

"She didn't say what it is. But it doesn't take much. Like one shake of salt is all you need."

Unless you're an elephant. "When did you take it?"

"Yesterday. After the cops talked to me, I felt like this was going bad. They think Mom and me have something to do with killing Mr. McBride. So I thought if I made myself sick again, then . . . I don't know what I was thinking. Stupid, I know. Just really stupid."

"When was the first time you took it?"

"That was the first time."

Jack paused, confused. "So that night I called nine-one-one and you ended up in the hospital, you're saying you didn't take any drugs?"

"No. Drugs had nothing to do with that."

Jack would have been more skeptical had Dr. Nelson not confirmed that the lab work from that first visit detected no toxins. "Then how did you get sick?"

"I wasn't sick."

"Were you faking it?"

"No. It's like I told you before. My mind and my body just went into this place, this trap, and I couldn't come out. I don't have a name for it. You did."

"Resignation syndrome."

"Is that real?" she asked.

"I don't know," said Jack. "Did it feel real to you?"

Beatriz nodded.

"Then I guess that's the answer," he said.

The front door opened, and Cecilia came out of the house. She was dressed for class and headed to her car.

"Why don't you go inside and give your mom a hug," Jack said. "I want to talk to your aunt."

Beatriz pushed herself away from the car reluctantly and headed for the house. Jack approached Cecilia as she opened the car door.

"Is everything okay between you and Julia?"

She stopped and gave Jack a serious look. "No. It's not okay, and it's not going to be."

"Look, Cecilia, your sister has been through—"

"No, please. Just stop right there. I don't want to hear more excuses. I've had enough, and my roommates have had more than enough. Beatriz can stay here if she wants, but Julia has to go."

"You're kicking her out?"

"She did it to herself."

"I'm sure she's sorry."

"I'm sure she is, too," said Cecilia. "She always is, and everybody always forgives sweet, pretty Julia because she's Julia—until they just can't take it anymore. Eventually, she drives everybody away. If you don't believe me, ask her husband."

Cecilia got into the car and closed the door. Jack watched as she backed out of the driveway and pulled away, wondering if Cecilia had spoken in anger.

Or if she'd meant it.

CHAPTER 45

On Monday Jack went on the legal offensive. He filed an emergency motion in criminal court to get to the bottom of the state attorney's decision to collect Beatriz's DNA not through a formal request to her mother but by ambushing her at school. Miami-Dade circuit judge Horatio Sloan set the motion for hearing at four o'clock. Assistant State Attorney Phillip Arnoff was on the other side of the courtroom to defend the actions of Detective Barnes and the Miami-Dade Police. Simone Jerrell from the Department of Homeland Security was at his side, which Jack did not take as a good sign.

"It didn't have to be done this way, Your Honor," Jack told the court.

"Just because it could have been done another way doesn't make it wrong," said Arnoff.

"I understand your position," the judge said. "But let me ask you this, Mr. Arnoff. Did Detective Barnes advise this child of her rights under Miranda before getting her consent to a DNA sample?"

"No. Under the law, Detective Barnes was required to issue a Miranda warning only if she was a suspect in the murder of Duncan McBride. She was not and is not a suspect."

"Judge, I'm not here to argue about Beatriz's rights as a suspect," said Jack.

"Glad to hear that," said the judge. "Personally I think the Supreme Court is off in la-la land when they say that a Miranda warning makes it okay to question a schoolkid without a parent in the room and with the school principal there to encourage her to tell the truth. The reality is that even as the police interrogator is telling them they have 'the right to remain silent,' most kids are texting about it or updating their Facebook status in real time."

Jack liked the way this was going. "Your Honor, this motion is filed on behalf of Beatriz and her mother, Julia Rodriguez. Part of the reason they fled El Salvador was the domestic violence inflicted by Beatriz's father. Until the body of Duncan McBride was found in their apartment here in Miami, my clients were under the impression that Jorge Rodriguez was still in El Salvador. For their own safety, they have a right to know if he is a suspect in the murder of Mr. McBride and is therefore in Miami."

"How does the DNA sample from Beatriz tie in with this?"

"We believe that MDPD has a DNA specimen from a suspect. They took a sample from Beatriz to see if there is a partial match that would identify the suspect as Beatriz's father."

The judge looked at the prosecutor. "Is that true, Mr. Arnoff?"

"Judge, the identity of the suspect is confidential information."

"Well, let's back up. First, do you have a DNA specimen from a suspect?"

"We have saliva from a cigarette butt that was found in the decedent's car. That saliva does not match the DNA of the victim."

"And you collected DNA from Beatriz Rodriguez for the purpose of making a comparison to the DNA from that saliva. Do I have that right?"

"Yes, sir."

"And you made that comparison not to see if there was a perfect match, but to see if there was a partial match, which would mean that the saliva is from someone who is related to Beatriz Rodriguez. Is that right?"

"Yes, Your Honor."

"And, Mr. Swyteck, all you want to know is did the comparison show a partial match, correct?"

"That's it," said Jack.

"So, how 'bout it, Mr. Arnoff. Did you get a partial match?"

The DHS lawyer rose. "May the Department of Homeland Security be heard on this point?" asked Jerrell.

"Certainly," the judge said.

"Your Honor, this intrusion into a homicide investigation isn't about domestic violence or the safety of Mr. Swyteck's clients. This motion is a completely improper end run around the immigration court. Mr. Swyteck seeks to gain a tactical advantage in an asylum hearing that is scheduled for a final hearing less than two weeks from now."

"What kind of tactical advantage?"

"The argument for asylum is that if Ms. Rodriguez is returned to El Salvador, she will continue to suffer abuse by her husband."

The judge seemed perplexed. "You can get asylum for that?"

"The attorney general's most recent opinion has made it difficult, I concede," said Jack. "But our position is that asylum can be appropriate if the government is unable or unwilling to protect a married woman from violence at the hands of her husband."

"Hmm," the judge said.

Jack took note. This judge seemed to be of the same mind-set as the Orlando immigration judge. The tone of the hearing had just shifted.

Jerrell continued. "There are so many reasons why this application for asylum should be and will be denied. But for today's purposes, DHS would only point out that Mr. Swyteck must prove that his client has a reasonable fear of continued abuse by her husband. No one has laid eyes on Mr. Rodriguez for months. Not in Miami, not in El Salvador, not anywhere on the planet."

"Is it DHS's position that Mr. Rodriguez is deceased?"

"It is indeed, Your Honor."

Jack fired back. "That's all the more reason to grant my motion, Judge. A partial match would prove that Mr. Rodriguez is alive and that the department's position is wrong."

"Mr. Swyteck's statement just shows how little he understands about DNA evidence," said Jerrell. "A partial match could show that the DNA from that saliva belongs to Beatriz's father *or her mother*. It would be the height of injustice to allow Julia Rodriguez to point to DNA from her own saliva to prove that her abusive husband is alive and well and therefore she should be granted asylum."

"Judge, that saliva does not belong to Julia Rodriguez. Julia was in detention in Macclenny, Florida, when Mr. McBride disappeared."

"She was not in detention when she worked with Mr. McBride at Café de Caribe. Her saliva could have survived on the cigarette for months."

"She was not riding around in Mr. McBride's car. He sexually harassed her at work."

"A mere allegation that Mr. McBride vehemently denied before he was found dead in Ms. Rodriguez's bathroom. And, Your Honor, I would also point out that Ms. Rodriguez had already been released from detention at the time Mr. McBride's vehicle was abandoned. That makes Ms. Rodriguez a viable suspect as an accessory after the fact."

Jack could hardly believe what he was hearing. "Judge, now they're just making stuff up. If Julia Rodriguez is now a suspect as an accessory after the fact, it's only to give the department one more reason to deport her at the hearing."

"It sounds like that would be a pretty good reason," the judge said.

"Thank you," said Jerrell.

"Mr. Swyteck, the court denies your motion. Best of luck to you and your client at the immigration hearing. We are adjourned," he said with a bang of the gavel.

Jerrell hurried out of the courtroom ahead of the prosecutor. Jack caught up with her in the hallway right outside the double exit doors. "Are these the kind of games I should expect at the asylum hearing?" he asked.

Jerrell stopped. "What you should expect is vigorous opposition to a frivolous request for asylum that would turn immigration court into family court. My job is already hard enough. I don't need lawyers like you making it even harder by inviting immigration judges to render terrible decisions. I'll see you next week." She turned and walked away.

The prosecutor emerged from the courtroom with a pen in his mouth and his arms full of loose expandable files as he hurried past Jack.

"Arnoff," Jack said, stopping him. "Look me in the eye and tell me Julia is really a suspect."

The prosecutor simply shrugged and continued down the hallway.

"That's what I thought," said Jack.

CHAPTER 46

Julia needed a place for her and Beatriz to live.

She'd apologized to her sister, and Cecilia probably would have forgiven her, eventually, if only because she liked having Beatriz around. Her roommates, however, wanted their privacy back. A weekend of apartment shopping turned into a crash course in why the Joint Center for Housing Studies at Harvard University consistently ranked South Florida the least affordable rental market in the nation. Anything within Julia's budget made the worst neighborhoods of San Salvador look safe. On Monday afternoon, Theo made her an offer she couldn't refuse.

"This is so nice of you," she said as they walked up the flight of metal stairs behind Cy's Place.

"I think you'll like it," said Theo.

Cy's Place was at one of the oldest addresses in Coconut Grove, a two-story brick structure that harked back to the Grove's bohemian roots of artists, musicians, hippies, and head shops. Condos in the massive glass towers overlooking the marina were the hot new properties, some selling for eight figures. The one-bedroom hovel directly above Cy's Place came with a prime view of the Dumpsters in the alley but was not without charm.

"Only one person has lived here since I opened the club," said Theo, as he unlocked the door.

"Who?"

He smiled. "Uncle Cy."

"You're kidding. There really was an Uncle Cy?"

"Still is. His old knees can't take the stairs no more. He hated to go, but moving in with his girlfriend made it a little sweeter."

Theo opened the door and showed her inside. The furnishings were simple, and the old wood floors creaked beneath her footfalls, but the walls were a treasure. Countless black-and-white photographs told a story of old Miami. Her gaze was drawn to the large framed poster that hung over the couch. It was weathered with age, but the young black woman in the picture looked radiant as ever. FIRST TIME IN MIAMI, the poster proclaimed. TICKETS $2 AT THE DOOR.

"Who is Nina Simone?" asked Julia.

Theo's mouth was agape, and she thought she'd offended him, but her question had merely excited him with the realization that she was a blank slate and he was Wikipedia. She watched and listened, fascinated as Theo took her around the apartment like a tour guide, sharing with her the mythic qualities of the historic village of Overtown and its once bustling music and entertainment district. He seemed especially proud of the photos of his uncle Cy playing "after-midnight" gigs with Ray Charles, Aretha Franklin, and other famous black entertainers who would finish their act at a Miami Beach hotel and then head across the causeway to jam with the brothers in Overtown, where their skin color didn't prevent them from getting a room for the night.

"Can we go there?" she asked.

He hesitated, and Julia was suddenly embarrassed.

"I'm sorry. That sounded like I was asking you to take me on a date, didn't it?"

"It's not that," he said. "These places are all gone. They built the interstate right through the heart of Overtown in the mid-sixties. Killed it. The Cotton Club, the Sir John Hotel, Harlem Square, the Knight Beat. All gone now."

"Knight Beat?" she said, checking out another old poster on the wall. "Isn't that your last name, with a *K*?"

"Yeah."

"Was the Knight Beat your uncle Cy's club?"

"No. But, knowing him, I'm sure he convinced many a young lady that it was."

They shared a laugh and then fell quiet. Julia checked out a few more photos on the wall, then glanced back at Theo, who had never looked away.

"What?" she asked.

"Nothing," he said, shaking it off. "So, you think you and Beatriz would be happy staying here?"

"I think we'd be really happy. How much is the rent?"

"Just pay me whatever you can afford."

"You have to give me a price."

"No, I don't. The place is sitting empty. I can't rent it out. Uncle Cy is practically deaf, so the noise from the club didn't bother him, but on Friday and Saturday nights you'll have to sleep with earplugs."

"Better than being awakened by gunshots twice a night," she said, thinking of her old neighborhood in San Salvador.

"Okay, then. It's yours."

"Shake on it?" she said, offering her hand.

He took it, and it seemed to disappear in his grasp. It occurred to her that as nice as Theo had been to her, this was the first time he'd laid a finger on her.

"It actually would be okay if you took me on a date," she said. "If you want."

"I'd like that."

"I mean, I don't know how much Jack has told you. I'm technically married, but I'm not married. The last man I kissed was Hugo, and that was three years ago."

"I got you beat there," he said.

"Really?"

"Yeah. I've never kissed a man."

It made her smile. He moved closer, and she wasn't sure if it was his idea or hers, but instinctively she rose up on her tippy-toes to meet him halfway. He kissed her lightly on the lips. They walked to the door, and he gave her the key.

"Welcome to Julia's Place," he said.

CHAPTER 47

O n the Friday before Julia's asylum hearing, Jack was in the immigration court on Miami Avenue for the final-status conference.

Julia's case had been officially transferred from Orlando, putting her about 250 miles farther away from Mickey Mouse, but if Orlando Immigration Court was an amusement park, Miami was a zoo. Forget the complexities of immigration law. The building itself was eight stories of confusion to anyone who tried to navigate it without a lawyer. More often than not, the notice of hearing told unrepresented immigrants to appear at room 700, which was the clerk's office on the seventh floor, which meant standing in line indefinitely, which probably meant that their hearings would start without them in one of the courtrooms on the fourth or fifth floor, which would end almost immediately with an order of deportation for "failure to appear." Anyone who stepped into the ICE offices on the lower floors for directions probably wasn't going to get much help, unless the directions sought were to Mexico.

"Good morning, all. I am the Honorable Patrick Kelly, and I am so pleased to be the new presiding immigration judge in this matter."

Wow. Way too sweet for Jack's legal palate. *And who refers to himself as "the Honorable"?*

"Fair warning," said the judge. "As you have probably heard, I recently announced my intention to retire."

That explained the cheeriness.

"After three decades, this honorable judge will no longer be the honorable anything."

Mystery number two solved.

"Ms. Rodriguez's claim for asylum will very likely be the last one I ever hear. So let's keep this proceeding as professional, as courteous, and as pleasant as possible. Can I have the agreement of counsel on that point?"

"Yes, Your Honor."

"'Your Honor,'" the judge said wistfully. "Gonna miss the sound of that. Maybe I can get the grandkids to pick that up. Anyway, enough about me. Mr. Swyteck?"

"Yes, Judge?" Jack almost said "Your Majesty."

"Let me just cut to the chase. "Does your client admit the government's allegation that she is an undocumented immigrant?"

"Yes."

"Very good," the judge said. "This hearing raises one issue: Can Ms. Rodriguez prove a valid legal defense to avoid deportation?"

"My client's defense is her claim for asylum under the federal Immigration and Nationality Act," said Jack.

"Got it," the judge said. "That's one I can recite in my sleep. And I say that not to brag, but to make sure that both sides confine their presentation of evidence to this issue: Does Ms. Rodriguez have a well-founded fear that, if she returns to El Salvador, she will be persecuted on account of her race, religion, nationality, membership in a particular social group, or political opinion? That's it, Counsel. That's what this hearing is about."

"If I may refine that a bit," said Jerrell.

"Please," the judge said. "This conference is your final opportunity to do so."

"Ms. Rodriguez is required to prove that she fears persecution *by the government* of El Salvador. What she fears is domestic violence, which is not government persecution. Judge Greely considered this issue, and his clear leaning was that fear of domestic violence provides no basis for asylum."

"Judge, I—"

"Save your breath, Mr. Swyteck. Ms. Jerrell, did you read the sign on the door on your way into this courtroom?"

"I'm not sure I did."

"Then read it on your way out. It says Kelly. The Honorable Judge Patrick Kelly. Not Greely. If that was Judge Greely's reading of the law, he's wrong. I know that some immigration judges have read the attorney general's opinion as a complete ban on asylum claims based on domestic violence. I don't. In this courtroom, if Ms. Rodriguez can prove that the government of El Salvador has either condoned the conduct or demonstrated an inability to protect her, she may be entitled to asylum."

"Thank you, Your Honor," said Jack.

"Don't thank me. You have a heck of a tough case, Mr. Swyteck."

"I understand," said Jack.

"Good. Then this has been a productive conference. Anybody got anything else on their mind?"

"There is one thing," said Jerrell.

"Make it quick."

"Judge Greely—"

"Kelly! The Honorable Judge Patrick Kelly."

"Sorry," said Jerrell. "I was about to say that the other judge—Judge You-Know-Who—left open the possibility that Ms. Rodriguez would be allowed to present evidence on something called resignation syndrome."

Jack didn't want to open the door to Beatriz's drug use. "We have abandoned the argument that asylum should be granted on that basis, Your Honor."

"Good call, unless your client wants to move to Sweden. So, to sum up: domestic violence, in; resignation syndrome, out. Anything else?"

"No, Your Honor," the lawyers said.

"Wonderful. After a hundred thousand cases, I finally got this down to a system. See y'all in this courtroom at nine a.m. Monday morning. Ms. Jerrell, that's the one that says Judge Kelly on the door. We clear?"

"Yes, sir."

"Perfect. Thank y'all. We're adjourned."

The proceeding ended with a bang of the gavel. Another team of lawyers stepped up, and Judge Kelly's ninth status conference of the morning began as Jack was leaving the courtroom. Simone Jerrell corralled him for a moment of justice, hallway style.

"You realize that's Judge Kelly's shtick, right? It's all an act."

"Maybe," said Jack. "I'd still be worried if I were you."

"I'm not. That's the way he operates. Kick the government in the teeth and then put the respondent on a one-way deportation flight."

Jack had seen it countless times in criminal court, an angry judge accusing the prosecutor of violating every rule in the book just before throwing the proverbial book at the defendant. "We'll see," said Jack.

"I'm authorized to offer your client voluntary departure. She agrees to leave the country in sixty days and she's eligible to apply for legal readmission in five years. Take it or leave it."

"Wow, tempting," Jack said dryly. "Throw in death by lethal injection and Julia might take it."

"Are you declining my offer?"

"I have to check with my client. It's her decision. But I will advise her to reject the offer."

"That's fine. I'll see you Monday."

"Yup," said Jack. "See you then."

CHAPTER 48

Jorge sat on the edge of the mattress, lit a cigarette, and took a long drag.

It was a habit he'd picked up at the age of eleven, back when he smoked anything he could bum or steal from the older boys. By thirteen he was a "runner" at street fights, reloading pistols for shooters in the heat of gang warfare and gathering up the weapons of those who had fallen dead. At fifteen he was a roadside extortionist collecting twenty dollars a month from each of the food trucks that rumbled through his district carrying chewing gum, sodas, and Bimbo bread. Every penny went to the district leaders, less the local allocation for weapons, including the 9 mm pistol he'd carried as an obedient soldier. Jorge was one of thousands of teenagers who made up the backbone of the gang economy, a grunt who risked his life to protect gang territory for no personal profit, only status and respect. By age nineteen, most of his friends were dead or in prison. He met a girl. She got pregnant. They got married. He promised to quit the gang. She nagged him to keep his promise. Julia nagged him day and night, and she refused to stop nagging him even when he beat the living shit out of her. "You're a father now," she'd tell him. "Do you want Beatriz to end up like one of Eighteen's girls?" Typical Julia: always putting people down, as if being pretty made her better than one of Eighteen's girls—as if the fact that Jorge *chose* to protect her meant she deserved his protection.

The bathroom door opened. A young, naked redhead named

Rosa sauntered across the room. He supposed the hair was a dye job, though that shaved pussy offered no basis for comparison.

"Yuck," she said, waving away the smoke. "I hate cigarettes."

Nag, nag, nag. Julia used to bitch the same way about cigarettes. He'd actually quit for two years, though it had nothing to do with Julia. An uncle with oral cancer, and seeing him with his tongue and upper lip removed, was probably the only thing that had truly scared Jorge in his entire life. He got over it.

Jorge exhaled a little longer than usual. "It's my only vice," he said.

She went to the bureau and removed a brush from her purse. Jorge watched in the mirror as she combed through the tangles in her long, wet hair. He'd slapped her ass so hard that she'd needed a cold shower to take down the swelling. Jorge grabbed her clothes from the foot of the bed and threw them at her.

"Time for you to get lost," he said.

She sorted through her clothing and pulled on her panties. "Aren't you forgetting something?"

"I paid you up front."

Rosa pulled her dress on over her head and fastened her stiletto heels. "Sorry, pal. I still got welts on my ass. That doubles the price."

That kind of premium would've emptied Duncan McBride's stolen wallet. "Your ass is not my problem."

Rosa glared from across the room, but he answered with a look so chilling that she immediately backed down. "Fine," she said, and she started toward the door. Jorge rolled across the bed and beat her to it, startling her as he jumped up and leaned his shoulder against the door to prevent her from leaving.

She smiled nervously. "You want to go again?"

He shook his head.

"Well, if you have any friends who—"

"I don't have any friends."

Rosa swallowed hard. "Okay. But if you change your mind, you know how to reach me."

Jorge grabbed her jaw tightly and forced her to look at him directly. "That's exactly right," he said, his expression deadly serious. "I know how to reach you. I know where to reach you. So if you walk out that door and send your pimp over here to collect 'double the price' just because I spanked your ass, I will hurt you. Understand?"

"Okay," she whimpered, barely able to talk. "Whatever you say."

He released the viselike grip on her jaw, unlocked the dead bolt, and opened the door. Rosa left with the haste of a freed hostage, and just as soon as she was gone, Jorge secured the door with both the chain and dead bolt.

It was time to get down to business.

He went to the nightstand and removed his .22-caliber pistol. It fit in the palm of his hand like a toy, a pretty good choice for killing varmints but, with such puny ballistics, the .22-caliber cartridge just wasn't of much use in a gunfight or as any form of self-defense. But it was *the* choice for close-contact, execution-style killings: barrel to the back of the head, the low-caliber bullet entering the cranium and ricocheting off the inside of the skull, no exit wound, turning the brain to scrambled eggs. A .38-caliber or 9 mm round at close range might go in one ear and out the other, so to speak. A target could survive the hit, albeit with brain damage.

Of course, all of this assumed that El Negro had a brain. Doubtful. Jorge had been watching him for days, and the guy was as predictable as clockwork. No changes to his routine, no extra look over his shoulder as he walked to the car he parked in the same spot in the same dark lot at the same time every night, no pistol in his belt or other show of firepower—none of the basic precautions that any man should take when having his way with another man's wife, let alone putting her up in an apartment.

Brainless.

Jorge crushed out his cigarette in the ashtray, leaned back against the headboard, and drew a mental map of one last trip to Cy's Place in Coconut Grove. A timid knock on the door interrupted his thoughts. Jorge grabbed his pistol, stood at the locked door, and peered through the peephole. It was the redhead.

"Now what?" he asked.

"I left my stuff in your bathroom. It's by the sink."

Stuff. Jorge assumed she meant meth, molly, or whatever else she blasted up her nose to do the things she did God only knew how many times a night. "Go buy some new stuff."

"Don't be a jerk! It'll take you two seconds. I'm already in a bad way. I *need* it. You want me to dial nine-one-one so the cops can find me in a coma outside your door with three to five years of jail time sitting on your bathroom counter?"

The fastest way to piss off Jorge was to threaten him. But with work to be done, the smart thing was to swallow his anger and just make her go away.

"All right, all right," he said, grumbling. "I'll get your stuff."

R osa stood outside the apartment door and waited.

Hugo was just a few feet away from her, his back to the wall, two steps away from the door to Jorge's apartment. It was a chilly enough night to wear a sweatshirt-style hoodie, and his hand was inside the pouch, finger on the trigger of his revolver. He hadn't told Rosa that he had a gun, and she seemed clueless as to his intentions. Poor thing. Maybe things were different in Miami, but a streetwalker that stupid wouldn't last long in San Salvador.

Hugo had worked every contact in Miami's Salvadoran community, real and virtual, to find Jorge. A conversation at a bar had led to a conversation at a chop shop, which led to a conversation with a small-time drug dealer, which led to a string of other conversations that finally led Hugo to the West Wind Apartments, a run-down joint that rented rooms by the month, the week, the day, or the hour, depending on the need. It was a typical three-story, vintage-seventies building, with external hallways that wrapped around the entire floor plan and apartments that opened to the outdoors. From the parking lot Hugo had staked out the corner apartment on the second floor. Twice in four days he'd watched the same redhead climb the external staircase to the second floor, enter apartment 201, and leave about an hour later. After the second gig he'd stopped her as she approached her car. She was walking with a limp, as if someone had just kicked her in the ass. She seemed in no mood for another job, but Hugo's proposition was different. He offered double her normal charge, and all she had to do was call him the next time Jorge used her services, leave a vial of powdered sugar in Jorge's bathroom when she finished, go back for it five minutes later, and let Hugo do the rest. Rosa took the deal.

"Okay, I got it," Jorge said through the door. "Back away so I can see you head to toe in the peephole."

Rosa took two steps back and dipped her knee like a cancan dancer. "How's that?"

She stayed put, waiting for Jorge's reply, but as she waited she did the one thing Hugo had coached her *not* to do: she glanced in Hugo's direction, as if seeking direction or approval. Her assignment was to act as if Hugo wasn't there. He hoped Jorge hadn't picked up on her slip.

"Hold one second," Jorge said through the door. "I got a phone call."

The obvious glance had not gone unnoticed. Jorge knew something was up—knew that the redhead had not come alone. He opened the vial that contained Rosa's "stuff." He sniffed it. Then he tasted it: powdered sugar. The whore had set him up. That was probably her pimp standing in the hallway outside his door, waiting to collect the premium that she charged men like Jorge who pushed it too far.

Son of a bitch.

Had Jorge been holding a 9 mm semiautomatic pistol, like the Glock he carried in San Salvador, he would have shot right through the closed door and sprayed Red with a good twelve rounds of copper bullets. But .22-caliber ammunition probably wouldn't even make it through the door, and even if it did, taking out Rosa that way would mean letting her pimp off the hook.

"Hel-*low*, I'm waiting," Rosa called in a singsong voice from outside the door.

"Just a sec."

The wheels turned quickly in Jorge's head. He knew Rosa was dumb as a stone, but her pimp was at least street-smart. He hurried to the bedroom, switched the camera phone to "selfie" mode, essentially turning the screen into a mirror, and went to the open window. He had the corner apartment, so if he could angle the camera just right from his west-facing window, he could see around the corner and get a look at whoever was standing near the north-facing door. He extended his arm out the window as far as possible, and the image appeared on his screen. As he'd suspected, someone had come with Rosa. He zoomed the image and caught a glimpse of the man's profile.

Hugo!

The rush of adrenaline was almost more than Jorge could contain. He had everything he needed to pull this off, his smartphone in one hand and the pistol in the other. He set the alarm on his phone to blare with the sound of an old car horn in thirty seconds, and he left the phone on the windowsill. He counted the Spanish-language version of "one-Mississippi" in his head—*un maldito segundo, dos maldito segundos*—as he walked back to the front door.

"Okay, Rosa," he said as he removed the chain.

Veinte y cinco maldito segundos. Twenty-five damn seconds.

"Got your stuff."

Veinte y siete maldito segundos.

The alarm blared as he yanked the door open, Hugo's head jerked in response to the alarm, and that split second of distraction was all the advantage that Jorge needed. He led with his pistol, pressed the end of the barrel to the base of Hugo's skull, and squeezed the trigger.

The hot spray of crimson blowback on Jorge's hand was the first sign of success, as the little bullet bounced around inside Hugo's brain like a hyperactive pinball, ricocheting off the inside of his skull in all directions until the gray matter between his ears was reduced to mush. Rosa screamed and ran as Hugo fell to the concrete in a lifeless heap.

Jorge grabbed Hugo's gun, ran around the corner to grab his phone, and kept on running, leaving behind the few possessions he'd brought with him from El Salvador, leaving behind the piece-of-shit excuse for a human being who'd followed him from El Salvador.

CHAPTER 49

The Saturday before Monday's hearing was a workday at the
Law Offices of Jack Swyteck, P.A. Jack needed to prepare his
client for both her direct testimony and cross-examination,
but before that, he met with both Julia and Beatriz.

"With resignation syndrome out of the case, there's less need for
Beatriz to testify at the hearing," said Jack.

They were in the sitting area of Jack's oversized office, with Jack
in the armchair and mother and daughter on the camelback couch.

"Why is there any need at all?" asked Julia.

"Proving that you're afraid to go back to El Salvador is a lot
easier if you were a victim of domestic violence in the past. Simone
Jerrell is not going to concede that point. We have to prove it. We
don't have any photographs of you with bruises, no police reports,
no recorded phone calls to nine-one-one. All we have is your testimony. Unless Beatriz corroborates it."

"You want that psychiatrist to hypnotize Beatriz in court?"

"No. I don't want to put Beatriz on the witness stand at all. At
most, I would ask the judge to let us call Dr. Moore as a witness
and play the tape recording of her session, where Beatriz referenced
her father's attack on you."

Julia glanced at her daughter, considering it. "I guess that would
be okay."

"There's a downside," said Jack. "If Dr. Moore testifies about her
session with Beatriz, Simone Jerrell would likely call Beatriz to
cross-examine her."

"We can't let that happen," said Julia.

"I can't promise you it won't if we call Dr. Moore as a witness."

Julia looked at her daughter, and the answer was plain to see in Beatriz's expression.

"Then the only witness will be me," said Julia.

"I can't say I disagree with the decision," said Jack. "I just want to make sure that we all understand what one witness means: if the judge doesn't believe you, or as a practical matter even if he has his doubts, the case is over. You lose."

Julia seemed to understand the mountain she had to climb—alone. "I'm okay with that," she said.

"Beatriz, it looks like you can go home," said Jack.

"There's one other thing that the three of us should talk about," said Julia. "What happens to Beatriz if I lose?"

"Mom, no, I—"

"We need to have a plan," said Julia. "Jack, I heard about this special-status program for children. Do you know what I'm talking about?"

"It's called Special Immigrant Juvenile Status," said Jack. "I've been thinking about a backup plan, too, and this is one thing to consider."

"How does it work?" asked Julia.

"We would file a petition in family court on behalf of Beatriz. We'd have to prove that she was abused, neglected, or abandoned by her parents."

"Is it abandonment if I get deported?" asked Julia.

"That's the argument I would make to the judge."

"Abandonment?" said Beatriz, her eyes wide with fear. "You can't abandon me."

"Of course not," said Julia. "You would stay with Tía."

"No. *No!*"

"We don't have to decide this now," said Jack.

"I think we should," said Julia. "We have an offer from Ms. Jerrell."

"Voluntary deportation," said Jack.

"Right. What if you tell her we'll take that offer; I'll go voluntarily, if the department will give Special Immigrant Juvenile Status to Beatriz?"

"No, Mom! I don't want that!"

Julia's proposal was a creative one, at least when viewed through a lawyer's lens. But it was going to be a tough sell to her daughter.

"If you get deported, I'm going with you!" said Beatriz.

Jack rose. "Would it be a good idea if I left you two alone to talk for a minute?"

"No," said Julia, rising. "I think *I* should leave Beatriz with you for a minute. This is her future. She should hear from someone other than her mother."

Julia left the room and closed the door.

Jack's mouth opened, but he had no idea what to say. It was strange how the mind worked, but Jack suddenly recalled the day Righley was born, when Jack had spent the night in the hospital room with Andie, only to be awakened at two a.m. by an elderly night nurse, who switched on the light, wheeled in the bassinet, and, borrowing Ed McMahon's classic introduction of Johnny Carson on the *Tonight Show*, announced, *"Heeere's* your baby!" The nurse disappeared without another word, leaving the three of them—the *three* of them—alone for the first time and for the rest of their lives.

With Julia out of the room and an angry teenager glaring at him, her arms folded tightly, Jack got that same "Shit, now what?" feeling.

"Is that your friend?" asked Beatriz.

"I'm sorry, what?"

"Up there on the wall. Theo. That's him, right?"

Her gaze was fixed on the framed newspaper article near the window, with the eye-catching headline, "Groundbreaking DNA Evidence Proves Death Row Inmate Innocent." The story was so much a part of Jack's personal and professional life that his mere glance at the old newspaper seemed to bring the printed words to life: "After four years in Florida State Prison for a murder he did not commit, twenty-year-old Theo Knight—once the youngest inmate on Florida's death row—is coming home to Miami today."

"Yeah, that's Theo," said Jack.

"I think my mom likes him. Tía says she always goes for the bad boys and then acts surprised when they turn out to be bad."

Jack's first instinct was to jump to his friend's defense and point out that there was no comparison between Theo and Beatriz's father. But Jack understood Beatriz's anger toward her mother more than Beatriz would ever know. If he wanted to get self-analytical about it, how logical was his own childhood resentment toward his mother for dying before he'd gotten the chance to remember her?

"Your mom loves you, Beatriz. That's why she left us alone to talk about what's best for you."

"How could being away from my mother be the best thing for me?"

It was suddenly clear why Julia had left the room, and it was equally clear who had planted the seed in Julia's head about a better life for Beatriz without her mother. This time, when Jack opened his mouth, the words came.

"Let me tell you a story," he said.

And tell it Jack did, even though it had been so long since he'd told anyone the story of his own roots as the child of an immigrant. He told her how Abuela had faced the same decision when Jack's mother was a teenager, when Fidel Castro had come to power. He told her how most Cubans had rejoiced at the fall of the U.S.-backed dictator Fulgencio Batista, until anyone who disagreed with the new despot was given two choices: prison or the firing squad. He told her how thousands of parents had made the painful decision to spirit away their children, and specifically how Abuela had stayed behind in Cuba to live under Castro and had put her own daughter on one of the last planes out of Havana so that her daughter could live a better life in Miami.

Beatriz listened, and Jack talked. And for the first time in his

life, despite all the jokes about his bad Spanish, and despite the
"C+" his grandmother had given him on their trips to the grocery
store and other lessons in Cuban culture, Jack felt Cuban American. Best of all, Beatriz seemed to get it.

"Thanks for that," she said.

"De nada," said Jack.

Jack's cell phone rang, and a warm moment soon flooded with
concern. The call was from Detective Barnes in the MDPD Homicide Unit. Jack excused himself and stepped to the other side of
his office, away from Beatriz. Jack assumed the call was about the
McBride homicide investigation.

"Nope," said Barnes. "Got another body. Hispanic male, early
thirties."

Jack listened, but he could draw no connection between his client and the execution-style murder at the West Wind Apartments
that Barnes described.

"I'm not sure how I can help you," Jack said into his phone.

"You could start by bringing your client down to the medical
examiner's office. I'm here now. We need someone to ID the body."

"What makes you think Julia knows him?"

"We checked the victim's smartphone. Her photograph is in it."

Jack felt his plans for the weekend crumble. "We can be there in
half an hour."

They left Beatriz with Jack's assistant, and a minute later Jack
and Julia were making the short drive across the river to meet with
Detective Barnes.

"It's either Hugo or Jorge," Julia said, as they crossed the draw-
bridge.

Jack chose not to weigh in with a guess as to which of the two
would survive a confrontation.

The county medical examiner's office was in the Joseph H. Davis
Center for Forensic Pathology, a three-building complex on the
perimeter of the University of Miami Medical Center/Jackson
Memorial Hospital campus. Even on a Saturday the campus was

bustling with activity—people headed to the spine institute, the eye institute, and other world-class specialists. A guard buzzed them through at the main entrance, and the receptionist took them straight back to see Detective Barnes.

"Victim had no wallet, no identification," said Barnes.

"What about the cell phone with Julia's picture?" asked Jack. "Was there a service agreement attached to it?"

"Yeah, but it's in the name of a seventy-three-year-old woman in North Carolina who obviously never reads her monthly bill. Happens all the time."

An assistant medical examiner met them at the end of the hall and took them around the corner. A wall of stainless steel drawers was before them. One to the right, three drawers from the bottom, was open. The examiner led Julia to it and pulled the drawer farther from the wall, drawing the sheet-covered body into the room.

"I should warn you that there is a wound in the back of the head. The skull has multiple internal fractures from the movement of the bullet. There is no exit wound, but the face is bloated and distorted."

Jack held his breath. With a nod from Julia, the examiner lifted the white sheet. Julia closed her eyes slowly, as if she, too, had known that it wouldn't be Jorge.

"His name is Hugo," said Julia.

The examiner draped the white sheet back over the face.

"Ms. Rodriguez, can you tell me more about him?" asked Barnes.

"Would it be okay if I have a minute alone with him first?"

Barnes allowed it. Jack walked around the corner with him to talk on his client's behalf.

"Do you know who did this?" Jack asked.

"Not yet. But I think your client knows."

"Can I see the cell-phone photo you mentioned?"

Barnes brought it up on his tablet. It was a woman standing on the steps outside a church. "That's St. Jude on Brickell," said Barnes, as he zoomed in.

Jack couldn't deny that it was Julia. "She already told you she knows the victim. Not surprising that he'd have a picture of her on his phone."

"Shooting was right outside apartment two-oh-one. Tenant hasn't been seen since the neighbors heard the gunshot. Landlord has no idea who he is. Said he paid the rent in cash and lived alone."

"He definitely sounds like someone you'd want to talk to," Jack said, offering nothing.

"Fingerprints from inside the apartment match the fingerprints we found in Duncan McBride's car. I'm betting that the DNA we gathered from the toothbrush inside the apartment will also give us a match to the saliva secretions from the cigarette in McBride's car."

"Good work," said Jack, still offering nothing. "Let me know if there's anything more we can do to help."

"We also have footprints inside and outside the apartment. They're from a woman's shoe."

Jack showed no reaction. "Is that so?"

"Yup," said Barnes, as he put away his tablet. "So tell me something, Swyteck: How good is your client's alibi for Friday night?"

"I'll ask her."

"You do that," said Barnes. "If I were you, I'd ask her two or three times and make sure her story is rock solid from top to bottom. 'Cause I think the tenant who's gone missing is her husband. And I think the footprints are hers."

Jack was in no position to counterpunch. "Like I said, I'll ask her."

CHAPTER 50

J orge woke at Rosa's apartment.

No one ran faster than Jorge after a gang-style hit. He'd caught up with Rosa just as she was getting into her car at the West Wind Apartments. She'd begged him to let her go, but that wasn't going to happen. At gunpoint—Hugo's gun—she'd driven Jorge to her apartment.

It was much nicer than expected, a spacious and practically brand-new one-bedroom unit in Downtown Dadeland, a mixed-use development for young professionals. Rosa talked, talked, talked when she wasn't sucking cock, so Jorge had heard the whole story. Her parents up in Indiana thought she was still a college student, which meant that the rent was prepaid by Mommy and Daddy through July. The landlord would be pretty upset come August to find out that Rosa had sold the refrigerator, the stove, the dishwasher, and virtually every stick of furniture except the bed. It was amazing how low a young woman could go and how fast she could get there when addicted to opioids.

"What are you going to do with me?" asked Rosa. She was sitting on the carpet, chained to the bed, where Jorge had left her for the night. The handcuffs she carried in her bag of sex toys had proved useful.

"I don't know yet," he said.

Jorge peeked through the mini-blinds from the third-story window. Downtown Dadeland was one of Florida's many Disneyesque incarnations of the quaint urban village. Narrow streets of cobblestone encouraged pedestrian traffic. Each building was painted a different color and was a little taller or a little shorter than its neighbor, all designed to create the false impression that the community had grown over a period of years, not weeks. Residences on the upper floors had balconies that overlooked the town square, while the street level was loaded with shops and canopied cafés. Jorge was trying to decide which of the many restaurants looked good for lunch. Everything from pizza and burgers to sushi and dim sum made it hard to decide. The liquid option at World of Beer was also tempting.

"You hungry?" he asked.

"Yeah."

"What do you do when you get hungry? Call your OxyContin supplier and ask him what looks good in the fridge you sold on eBay in order to pay him?"

"Not funny."

"Your life is pretty fucked up, isn't it?"

"Like yours isn't?"

He smiled a little, not at all friendly, smile. "That guy I shot last night. He came to my apartment to kill me."

"He didn't tell me that. He said you owed him money and he needed me to literally help him get his foot in the door. I would never have done it if I thought there was going to be a gunfight."

"For a lot of reasons, he got what he deserved."

"I don't care what he deserved, and I don't want to know your reasons. I just want you to leave."

Jorge stepped away from the window. "It's not that simple. If I turn you loose, the first thing you'll do is call the police and tell them what I look like, tell them everything you know about me."

"Your neighbors will tell the police what you look like."

"My neighbors didn't see me put a bullet in Hugo's head."

She thought for a moment. "Neither did I," she said, seemingly pleased with the clever response she'd come up with.

"Nice try, Red."

"Seriously, I'm not going to turn you in. I promise."

"I don't believe you."

"I'm not a liar."

Jorge's gaze swept the shiny new but empty apartment. "You're living a lie, sweetie."

Rosa didn't answer.

Jorge scratched his head, as if bringing an idea to fruition. "There is one way you could convince me that you won't go to the police."

She looked up eagerly from her seat on the floor. "What?"

"You have to be as dirty as I am."

"I'm a drug addict and a prostitute. How much dirtier do you want me?"

"That's petty bullshit. You have to get in big-time."

"Meaning what?"

Jorge sat on the edge of the bed and took the pistol from the nightstand. "There's one more bullet I need to deliver before I go back to El Salvador. But I got a big problem now. You made a good point: my neighbors will tell the cops what I look like. This whole city will be crawling with cops out on the street looking for me, which makes it pretty hard for me to deliver this bullet all by myself."

"Are you saying—" Rosa was silent for a moment, as if she didn't want to get his drift. "Are you asking me to help you kill someone?"

Jorge held the pistol loosely in his hand, casually pointing the barrel in Rosa's direction, not really aiming, but threatening her all the same. Then he leaned closer, his expression deadly serious.

"No, honey," he said in a deep, coarse whisper. "I want you to save yourself."

CHAPTER 51

I was with Theo Friday night," said Julia.

"*My* Theo?" asked Jack.

"How many Theos do you know?"

Thankfully, there was just the one.

When it came to alibis, Jack had heard them all. I was with a prostitute. With *two* prostitutes. With my husband's brother who, by the way, is a priest. With Elvis. "With Theo" wasn't the alibi Jack would have scripted, but it was enough at this point. The investigation into Hugo's homicide would run its course in due time. It was Jack's job to keep his client focused on the asylum hearing, which was less than forty-eight hours away.

They finished the prep session around six p.m. Before heading home, Jack drove to Cy's Place to get the details that he'd chosen not to pursue in his meeting with Julia.

"What does 'with' mean?"

"We just talked," said Theo.

"You talked?"

"Yeah. Julia came downstairs after Beatriz went to bed. She sat right on the stool you're sitting in now. We talked till about midnight. Then I turned the bar over to Sandy. Me and Julia moved to that table over there," he said, pointing with a nod, "and talked till about two. Then she went home."

Jack smiled to himself. It was at one of those tables, just big enough for two pairs of elbows, that Jack had proposed to Andie.

"That's so—"

"Weird?" Theo suggested.

Sweet was the word that echoed in Jack's mind, but Jack didn't dare repeat it. "Let's go with weird."

Theo poured him a draft and set the tall beer glass in front of him. Jack watched the amber bubbles rise, seemingly out of nowhere, and disappear into a perfect head of foam.

"You know, I'd be happy for you and Julia," said Jack, "under normal circumstances."

"What's normal?"

Good question. It was like justice: easier to say what it was not. "Getting involved with a woman whose insanely abusive husband is probably behind two of Miami's most recent homicides is not normal."

"Being her lawyer *is* normal?"

Jack drank from his beer. "Now you sound like Andie."

"Julia and me are friends, Jack. I have friends in prison, friends who used to be in prison, and a few friends who probably should be in prison. My brother and my best friends growing up would be in prison right now if they weren't dead. I'm not going to stop being Julia's friend because you think it's not normal."

It was hard to push back against that kind of reasoning. "She's scared," said Jack. "You know that, right?"

"I know she is."

"I mean *really* scared. Julia has to walk into that courtroom on Monday morning and tell a judge that her husband sexually assaulted her. She *has* to say it in explicit fashion if we are going to get to square one on her claim for asylum. After what happened to Duncan McBride and now Hugo, I'm not sure she'll find the courage to testify about all the things her husband did to her."

"You want me to talk to her?"

"I don't see how that would help."

"It can't hurt for her to know that she doesn't have to be afraid to tell the truth."

Jack gave him a sobering look. "Her husband is a murderer, a rapist, a gang member, and domestic abuser. And he's probably in Miami. You can't guarantee her safety."

"I can guarantee that I'll do everything I can to keep her safe."

"Why would you do that?"

"Because she's my friend, Jack."

Jack thought about it. There was a depth of clarity and purity to Theo's commitment that Jack envied, a complete absence of the "What's in it for me?" mentality that governed so many relationships. "That's a good reason," said Jack.

"Hopefully, we'll stay friends. There's only one major issue I see so far."

"What?"

"Toilet seat."

"Ah, that one."

"I'm right, ain't I? Women always leave the damn thing down. They refuse to put it up the way it belongs when they're finished."

Jack gave him the benefit of the doubt: a guy who lived for four years with an open toilet in his own cell at Florida State Prison was definitely challenged in the ways of women in shared bathrooms. But it was an interesting twist on the immutable premise underlying an age-old argument.

"You'll never win that one, dude," said Jack, and then he finished his beer. "Trust me. *Never.*"

CHAPTER 52

Monday morning came quickly. The final hearing on Julia's claim for asylum began at nine a.m. Jack and his client were seated side by side in the courtroom of the Honorable Patrick Kelly. Cecilia sat behind them in the first row of public seating. It didn't hurt to let the judge know that Julia had family in Miami. Beatriz was at school, it being the collective judgment that Julia's daughter didn't need to hear Julia testify about the violence in her marriage.

"Would counsel announce their appearances for the record," Judge Kelly said.

Simone Jerrell was not alone this time. With her was a young lawyer from the Department of Homeland Security. His name was Jesús Padron, he was a first-generation Hispanic American, and when Jerrell allowed him to introduce himself to the judge, he spoke with an accent so affected that he made Jack's client sound like the president of the Daughters of the American Revolution. Jack saw through the stunt immediately. Fortunately, so did Judge Kelly.

"Well, how nice," said the judge. "Hispanic equilibrium between petitioner and respondent."

Neither government lawyer knew what to say. Jack saw it as a good start, though a seasoned, if not jaded, jurist on the brink of retirement presiding over his final hearing was bound to sling arrows in both directions.

"Normally I begin this type of proceeding with opening statements," the judge said.

Jerrell rose, ready to deliver hers on behalf of the department.

"But at this point in my career, I pretty much know what you're going to say, so, Ms. Jerrell, take a seat. I'll deliver yours: 'Judge, it's the duty of this court to uphold the immigration laws of the United States and to safeguard a lawful immigration process that protects Americans, secures the homeland, and honors our nation's values.' Mr. Swyteck, here's one for you: 'Your Honor, as the United States Supreme Court recognized almost a hundred years ago in the case of *Ng Fung Ho versus White*, an immigrant facing deportation stands to lose "life and property" and "all that makes life worth living."' Thank you very much, Counsel. I apologize for my failure to include biblical references in your opening statements, but we're short on time. Now let's get to the evidence. Mr. Swyteck, call your first witness."

Not an arrow, but the judge had definitely flung a curveball in Jack's direction. Jack could roll with it, but Julia surely would have liked a little time to warm up to the process before taking the witness stand. Jack touched her hand, a little nonverbal reassurance to let her know that showtime had arrived much sooner than expected.

"Our first witness is the petitioner," said Jack, "Julia Rodriguez."

Julia rose, obviously nervous as she walked to the witness stand, swore the familiar oath, and settled into the oak chair.

"Good morning, Ms. Rodriguez," said Jack.

"Good—" she said, and her voice cracked, as if to confirm that she'd had much better mornings. She cleared her throat and tried again. "Good morning."

There was no jury in immigration court, so Julia directed her answers to the judge, who would play the role of judge and jury. He alone would decide what Julia would be allowed to say; he alone would determine if Julia was telling the truth.

"Let's start by telling Judge Kelly a little about yourself," said Jack, and for as long as it would take for Julia to get comfortable, and for as long as Judge Kelly would allow, Jack guided Julia through her life story with simple questions. She pointed out her sister in the first row. She even smiled as she told the judge about her daughter. Then Jack asked about her marriage, and the mood noticeably darkened, as a story of ever-escalating violence unfolded.

"Tell me about the first time your husband hit you," said Jack.

She took a breath before answering, took another breath before telling the judge about the second beating, and took even deeper breaths before describing the next one and the one after that.

"Would you please raise your hair up over your head and show Judge Kelly the back of your neck?" asked Jack.

She did, revealing a four-inch scar that ran along the base of her hairline. The judge leaned over the bench for a closer inspection.

"Looks a little faded," the judge said. "How old is that scar?"

"It's from about six years ago."

"Okay. Proceed, Mr. Swyteck."

"Ms. Rodriguez, how did you get that wound?" asked Jack.

"My husband. He burned me."

"With what?"

"A chain," she said, and then her voice lowered. "A dog chain."

"You mean a choker chain that's used to restrain an animal?"

She nodded. "Yes."

"Was the chain hot?"

"Yes. With his cigarette lighter, he made it hot. It's how they do it."

"When you say 'they,' who do you mean?"

"Eighteen. It's a gang in El Salvador. This is one of the things they do. Make the chain glowing hot in the fire and put it around the neck."

"Put it around whose neck?"

"Women who disobey."

"Wives? Girlfriends?"

"Property," she said.

Jack paused, and not only because Julia needed it. To elevate his client from an abused spouse to a member of a persecuted group under U.S. immigration law, Jack needed to impress upon Judge Kelly that Jorge was only a part of Julia's fears.

"Is your husband a member of the gang known as Eighteen?"

"Yes."

"And he did this to you? He put a glowing-hot dog chain around your neck?"

She nodded.

"You have to answer audibly," the judge said.

"Yes. He did this while he was—"

Julia's voice trailed off. Jack gave her a moment.

"Your husband did this while what?" asked Jack.

"While he raped me." A tear rolled down her cheek. She pulled a tissue from her pocket and wiped it away.

"Do you need a break?" asked Jack.

"No," she said, sniffling. "I would rather get this over with."

Julia was openly distraught, and Jack allowed her to recover, but he may have paused too long. The judge broke the silence.

"I'm sorry, Ms. Rodriguez. Could you back up a second? I didn't hear you say what triggered this violent episode. The burning, the assault."

"I'm not sure I understand the question."

"Let me just ask you, then," the judge said. "Why did your husband do that?"

It was the question Jack had not planned to ask, but a judge had the absolute right to question the witness, whether Jack liked it or not.

Julia swallowed hard. "He accused me of being with another man."

"That you'd been *intimate* with another man?" the judge asked pointedly.

"Yes."

Jack had the sinking feeling that all trial lawyers dread, the feeling that the judge was on a roll and the roll was in the wrong direction.

"Had you in fact been intimate with another man?" the judge asked.

Julia lowered her eyes, answering in a voice that was barely audible. "Yes."

"Was that the first time you had been intimate with another man?"

"You mean while I was married to Jorge?"

"Yes," the judge said, "while you were married."

"No."

"No, it was not the first time?" the judge asked in an accusatory tone.

"I'm sorry, I misunderstood you. Yes, it was the first time."

The judge didn't seem to believe that she'd misunderstood, or at least that was Jack's impression. Jack would have liked to point out that in some places women were still stoned to death for being an accused adulteress, but that didn't justify Jorge's actions.

"Very well," the judge said, as he settled back into his leather chair. "You may proceed, Mr. Swyteck."

Jerrell rose. "Judge, would it be appropriate to ask *who* Ms. Rodriguez was sleeping with?"

"No," Jack fired back, "it's certainly not appropriate now, during my examination. Nor will it be appropriate after I've finished and Ms. Jerrell has her right to cross-examination."

"Perhaps my question was too broad," said Jerrell. "As the court may be aware, a man named Hugo Martinez was murdered this past Friday night here in Miami. Ms. Rodriguez's photo was found on his cell phone. I think it's appropriate to ask if Ms. Rodriguez's lover was Hugo Martinez."

"This isn't cross-examination," said Jack.

"Technically, you're right, Mr. Swyteck. Ms. Jerrell, sit tight until it's your turn. But, seeing that we've already gone this far down the road, let me ask the question. Ms. Rodriguez, did your husband do these things you just described because you were having an affair with this man, Hugo Martinez?"

Jack didn't like the way the judge had phrased the question, as if it were Julia's fault, but an objection would only have aggravated the situation.

Julia swallowed her response, but the microphone picked it up. "I believe so."

"Got it," said the judge. "Mr. Swyteck, do you have any more questions?"

"Yes," said Jack. "Many more."

"Okay, proceed."

Jack moved on from the sexual assault, and the questions wouldn't get any easier for Julia to answer. There was the forced abortion that had nearly killed her, the futility of reporting domestic violence to the police, Jorge's threat to kill Beatriz if she ever divorced him, and all the other things that had led to her decision to risk her life and that of her daughter to flee San Salvador. Jack would spend the rest of the morning bringing it all out on direct examination, but he had one overarching concern.

He wasn't sure that the Honorable Judge Patrick Kelly was even listening.

CHAPTER 53

Detective Barnes left the Criminal Justice Center with a search warrant in hand. His partner, Damien Reyes, rode with him to the Downtown Dadeland Apartments. They were hoping to find a pair of women's shoes in Rosa Fields' apartment. The home run would be a match to the footprints in the blood-sprayed concrete outside apartment 201 at the West Wind Apartments.

"How'd you connect the girl?" Reyes asked.

"Luck," said Barnes. The property manager at West Wind Apartments had a nice kickback arrangement with the towing company that removed illegally parked cars, so he made it his practice to walk the parking lot every now and then to write down tag numbers. The fact that one of twenty-odd tags on the property manager's list belonged to Rosa Fields didn't mean much by itself. The fact that she had a misdemeanor conviction on her criminal record for trading sex for drugs made her a person of interest.

"I'm thinking a threesome gone wrong," said Barnes.

"Not easy to get a hooker to talk about a john, let alone two johns," said Reyes.

Barnes tucked the warrant into his coat pocket. "A footprint that puts her at the scene of a homicide should be all the leverage we need."

The ride to Downtown Dadeland Apartments took half an hour. A pair of officers in the taupe-and-brown uniforms of the MDPD met the detectives outside the rental office. Barnes entered and found the manager behind her desk eating lunch. She took one more bite of her foot-long sub and stepped around her desk to inquire.

"Diana Stokes," she said, still chewing. "Can I help you?"

Barnes showed her the papers. The manager wiped her hands with a napkin and inspected the warrant.

"I run a first-class operation here," said Stokes. "Pretty picky about my tenants. You mind telling me what this is about?"

"Police business."

"I just ask because Rosa seemed like a nice kid when she moved in. She's a student at Miami-Dade. Her parents came in the first week of classes and paid the rent for a whole year. From Indiana. You know what I'm saying?"

"I think you're saying they're from Indiana."

"They're good people, is what I'm saying. These New Yorkers sign as guarantors for their kids and claim they're worth a million bucks, which means they got nothing in the bank but two million in debt. Parents from Indiana say they're worth a million, it means they got two million in the bank, but they discount it to a million just in case the Apocalypse hits tomorrow and the financial world crumbles. That's the kind of family this girl is from. But, come to think of it, I have been getting some complaints from her neighbors lately."

"What kind of complaints?"

"Sketchy men coming and going from her apartment. It's mostly students and young professionals here."

"You might call Rosa a professional," said Reyes, offering up a little cop humor.

The manager seemed to take some of his meaning. "She's not mixed up with drugs, is she? Pretty girl like her, that'd be a cryin' shame."

Barnes didn't even want to get started on the number of cryin' shames he'd seen. "Can you take us up, please? We didn't get a no-knock warrant."

The manager grabbed her master passkey from her desk. "Follow me."

Barnes and his partner followed her out of the rental office, and the two MDPD officers rode up with them in the elevator. Rosa's apartment was at the end of the hall. The manager knocked and, getting no answer, used her passkey to open the door. The MDPD officers stood guard outside the door as the detectives entered.

"Miami-Dade Police," Barnes announced, stopping just inside the doorway. There was no response. He could see the living room and kitchen from where he stood.

The manager was right behind him. "Oh, my God! This is a furnished apartment. It's all gone."

"Sold it for drugs, I'm guessing," said Barnes.

The manager went to the kitchen. "The appliances, too!"

Detective Reyes walked to the bedroom. "Nobody here," he said.

Barnes went down the hall, past the bedroom, the only furnished room, and then to the bathroom. The light was on. Used towels hung on the rack. The sink area was a mess. Shaving cream was splattered in the basin and on the faucet.

"Looks to me like a man was here," said Barnes.

"There's no rule against overnight guests," said the manager. "Unless it's more than five consecutive nights."

Reyes emerged from the bedroom with a look of disappointment. "No shoes matching the description in the warrant."

"If she stepped in blood, she probably tossed them," said Barnes.

"Stepped in blood?" the manager asked with concern.

"You mind if we check your trash chute and Dumpster?" asked Barnes.

"Does your warrant cover that?"

"I don't need a warrant to search through trash."

"Then be my guest. But I don't like the sound of this. What blood are you talking about?"

Barnes didn't answer. He shone his penlight on the shaving cream and took a closer look. A few whiskers were visible. Had Rosa's apartment been a designated crime scene, he would have bagged the whiskers for the lab, but this was the execution of a search warrant, and he could collect only the items specified in the warrant.

The detective's gaze followed the sweep of his flashlight across the bathroom. It came to rest on the silver chain hanging on a hook behind the door.

"Is that a dog choker?" he asked.

"Looks like it," said the manager.

"Do you allow pets in this building?" asked Barnes.

"Absolutely not."

"In this town a prostitute with a dog chain barely qualifies as kinky."

"Oh, my God," said the manager. "This girl's a hot mess."

Barnes glanced over his shoulder, toward a living room with no furniture, toward a kitchen with no oven and no refrigerator, just empty spaces where appliances used to be.

"Do you have security cameras in this building?" asked Barnes.

"Yes," said the manager. "At the main entrance and in the parking garage."

"I'd like to see if Rosa came or went with anyone since Friday night."

"It's not continuous video, but I'll share what I have. Do you have a picture of the guy you're looking for?"

Barnes switched off his penlight. He'd put that exact request to Julia Rodriguez but, according to her lawyer, she'd turned a page in her life and left every photograph of her estranged husband in El Salvador.

"That's what I'm hoping your surveillance cameras can give us," said Barnes.

CHAPTER 54

I n Miami-Dade circuit court, where Jack tried the occasional civil case, a wall plaque in each courtroom proclaimed: WE WHO LABOR HERE SEEK ONLY TRUTH. There was nothing similar in the Criminal Justice Center, where Jack did most of his trial work. Those words were also notably absent in the Miami Immigration Court. Jack wondered if the judicial gods were trying to tell him something.

"Ms. Jerrell, you may cross-examine," said Judge Kelly.

Jack's direct examination of his client had taken the full morning, and the judge had ordered everyone back by one o'clock. They'd gone to lunch, but Julia had returned with an empty stomach, having eaten almost nothing. She seemed to know, without Jack having to tell her, that the hard part was yet to come.

"Thank you, Your Honor." Jerrell gathered her notebook and stepped to the podium, facing the witness. She dispensed with the "good afternoon" and went straight into attack mode.

"Ms. Rodriguez, in response to a question from your lawyer, you testified that you were afraid of your husband, correct?"

Jack had prepared her for that precise question, but it still seemed to jar her, especially right out of the gate. "Yes."

"In fact, you said you were so afraid of retaliation by your husband that you were afraid to testify in court today."

"Yes."

"Here in Miami."

The geographic reference seemed to perplex her. "Yes. This courtroom. In Miami."

"And that's because your husband is here in Miami, correct?"

"Objection," said Jack, rising. "There's been no evidence to establish that point."

"Overruled. The witness may answer."

Julia paused, but she took Jack's cue. "I don't know where my husband is."

"Precisely," said Jerrell, her voice rising. "You don't know if he's here in Miami, back in El Salvador, or on the planet Mars, do you?"

"Well, I know he's not on Mars."

Jerrell skated right over the remark, her voice taking on an even icier edge. "Ms. Rodriguez, you had a lover by the name of Hugo Martinez, correct?"

"I wouldn't call him my lover. Hugo was a good friend, and for a short time, it was more than that. I ended it, and we stayed friends."

"You were intimate with Mr. Martinez while you were married to Jorge Rodriguez, were you not?"

"Yes," Julia said softly.

"Is it fair to say that you ended the sexual relationship with Mr. Martinez out of fear of your husband?"

"That was part of it," Julia said, clearly uncomfortable. "I also knew it was a sin. But I told my priest what my life was like with my husband, and even he said God would forgive—" She stopped, choked with emotion.

While Jack had never thought of Julia as "cheating" on her husband, it was clear that even after all she'd endured, the breach of a marriage vow, even to a monster like Jorge, was something that Julia had not yet reconciled with her faith.

Jack needed to speak up. "Your Honor, this is an asylum hearing, not a scarlet letter inquisition. Ms. Rodriguez befriended a coworker in the church bakery who made her feel safe from a husband who abused her, raped her, and threatened to kill their daughter if she divorced him."

"Mr. Swyteck, I detest speaking objections from counsel, espe-

cially when your client is on the stand. But just this once, I'm going
to let you get away with it. Ms. Jerrell, please pursue an appropriate
line of inquiry with this witness."

"Glad to, Your Honor. Ms. Rodriguez, let's keep this simple:
You know that Hugo Martinez was murdered, correct?"

"I know he was shot."

"He was shot at close range in the back of the head. Does that
sound like a suicide or an accident to you?"

"Objection," said Jack.

"Sustained. Let's not argue with the witness," the judge said.

"My apologies. Ms. Rodriguez, the shooting was here in Miami,
correct?"

"Yes."

"Now, I'm going to ask you something, and I want you to be as
honest as you possibly can be: Do you believe that Hugo Martinez
was shot by your husband?"

Jack was on his feet again. "Objection, Judge. My client isn't
privy to the homicide investigation. Her speculation is irrelevant."

"Judge, her state of mind certainly is relevant. In order to be
granted asylum under U.S. law, Ms. Rodriguez must show that she
has a reasonable fear of returning to her country. If her husband is
here in Miami, she has nothing to fear about being deported and
sent back to El Salvador."

"That's a complete distortion of the law and facts," said Jack.

"Overruled. I'll allow the question for the limited purpose of
determining whether the witness's alleged fear of returning to El
Salvador is reasonable. Ms. Rodriguez, please answer the question."

Julia was smart enough to see the trap that Jerrell was setting,
but the judge had left her little wiggle room. "I don't know how to
answer that question. I don't know who killed Hugo."

"Let me ask it this way," said Jerrell. "True or false, Ms. Rodriguez? If your husband is here in Miami, it's safer for you to be in El
Salvador than to be in Miami."

"Objection."

The judge shot an angry glare in Jack's direction. "Mr. Swyteck, I've already ruled. The witness can answer."

Julia was struggling. "Maybe. I don't know."

"Judge, I would ask the court to direct the witness to answer the question," said Jerrell.

"She's answered to the best of her ability," said Jack.

"Mr. Swyteck, I've warned you," the judge said. "Stop coaching your witness with speaking objections. It's one of my pet peeves."

"Thank you, Judge," said Jerrell.

"Don't thank me!" the judge snapped. "That's my other pet peeve. I hate when lawyers thank me for a ruling."

"My apologies," said Jerrell. "I would simply like an answer to my question."

"Your question has made its point in spades," the judge said. "I get what you're saying: Ms. Rodriguez has no reasonable fear of being sent back to El Salvador."

Jack had to jump in. "Excuse me, Your Honor, but that was not her testimony. Ms. Rodriguez's husband is a member of the gang Eighteen, which, along with MS-Thirteen, rules San Salvador, and which persecutes 'disobedient' women through torture and sexual assault while the government of El Salvador is either unable or unwilling to do anything about it."

The judge looked as if he might overheat on the spot. "Mr. Swyteck, this is your last warning. Stop testifying for your client."

"I'm only trying to make the record clear," said Jack.

"Not another word, Counsel," the judge said. "Let's move on."

The cross-examination continued for another thirty minutes, but it couldn't be said that Jerrell was following the judge's direction to "move on." It was a relentless theme, and it was clear to Jack that the Department of Homeland Security had made a strategic decision to avoid setting a bad legal precedent: DHS did not want to take the risk that an immigration judge on the brink of retirement might issue a ruling that chipped away at the attorney general's very narrow view of asylum based on government failure to protect women from domestic violence. Jerrell's strategy was to send Julia back to El Salvador on the strength of the much simpler argument that the instrument of persecution—her husband—was no longer there.

By two o'clock, Julia had reached her limit, and Jack spoke up. "Your Honor, could we have a break, please?"

"Does the witness need a break?" the judge asked.

"I didn't eat lunch or breakfast," said Julia. "My stomach is empty, but I honestly feel like I'm going to throw up."

"Welcome to my world," the judge said.

"Judge, I truly have just one last question, and it calls for a simple yes-or-no answer. And then I'm finished."

"Counsel, I'm going to hold you to that representation. Ms. Rodriguez, if you can handle one question—just *one*, Ms. Jerrell— we can wrap this up."

"Judge, the witness requested a break," said Jack.

"I heard her, Mr. Swyteck. But you know how these things work. Right now, Ms. Jerrell has one last question, and that's all I'm going to allow. If we take a five-minute break, she'll come back into this courtroom with her legal pad all marked up with a list of fifty more questions that she wants to ask, and I'll let her ask them. It's your choice."

"I can do it," said Julia. "I can answer one question."

"Good decision," the judge said. "Ms. Jerrell, your one question, please."

Jerrell closed her notebook, as if to double down on her assertion that this was her last question. "Ms. Rodriguez, yes or no: Does your husband smoke cigarettes?"

"No."

Jerrell's expression fell. "But—"

"No buts!" said the judge. "That's it. That's your one question."

He glanced at the clock in the back of the courtroom. "Counsel, it is now almost two thirty, and I have at least three hours of work on my other cases before I can go home tonight. Ms. Rodriguez, take the afternoon off and eat something between now and tomorrow morning. I'll see you at nine a.m. in my courtroom. Ms. Jerrell, which courtroom would that be?"

"The one with your name on the door," she said begrudgingly.

"Very good. We're adjourned."

CHAPTER 55

It was a busy afternoon for Jorge and Rosa.

First stop was "the gun shop," which wasn't a shop at all, just a nickname for a three-hundred-pound thug named Felipe who called himself "the gun shop" and fenced stolen firearms to other thugs like Jorge—serial numbers rat-filed away, no extra charge. It was legal in Florida to buy a suppressor, and Jorge had actually walked into a legitimate gun store with Rosa and tried to buy one under her name. But the federal paperwork to buy a suppressor made immigration forms look easy, and Jorge couldn't wait the eight to twelve months it would take to get the approval from the bureaucrats in Washington. Fatso Felipe charged double the price for his stolen goods, but an untraceable suppressor was probably worth the extra money anyway. It was one thing to purchase a suppressor so that the crack of a hunting rifle didn't scare away the animals. Jorge had something else in mind.

The deal with Felipe done, Jorge pulled out of the parking lot. They were stopped at the traffic light when Rosa got the lifesaving call on her cell phone—lifesaving for Jorge.

"It's the rental office from my apartment," she said, checking the display on her caller ID.

"Take it on speaker," said Jorge. "If you even hint that you're with me, you know what will happen to you."

Rosa answered. If it made the manager angry to tell her tenant that the police had been to Rosa's apartment to execute a search warrant, it made Jorge even angrier to hear it.

"I want you out by morning," said the manager. "And I'm keeping your security deposit. Let your parents know that I'm coming after them as guarantors for the cost of the missing furniture."

"Yes, ma'am," she said, and the call was over.

"Shit!" Jorge shouted, as he pounded the steering wheel.

"You have to take me back there."

"We're not going back there!"

"But I have to get my stuff."

"Forget your stuff."

"What are you going to do with me?"

Jorge was too deep in thought to hear the question. If the police had searched Rosa's apartment, they would be looking for her car. He needed to stay one step ahead of them. He quickly pulled a U-turn and drove back to the parking lot they'd just left. Felipe "the gun shop" was still there in his truck. Rosa's car skidded to a screeching stop beside him, and Felipe rolled down the driver's-side window.

"Gun shop is closed," he said. "No returns."

"I'm not looking to return anything. I need a car."

"You trading that one?"

"Yeah."

"How soon?"

"Right now. Can you help?"

"*No problema*," Felipe said, his gold caps flashing in the sunlight. "Welcome to Felipe's chop shop."

C y's Place was quiet on Monday night. Beatriz was alone in a booth near the front window, headphones on, doing her homework. Julia was at the bar drinking an iced tea.

"What's wrong?" asked Theo.

Julia drew a breath, as if the world's problems were weighing on her. "I may have lied in court today."

Theo leaned on the bar, shifting into listening mode. "Tell me what happened."

"It was at the end of my testimony. The judge gave the DHS lawyer one last question. Just one."

"What was the question?"

"Does Jorge smoke cigarettes."

"Why does that even matter?"

"Jack said the Department of Homeland Security is trying to prove that it's safe to send me back to El Salvador because Jorge is here in Miami. We know that MDPD found some DNA on a cigarette. Jack says the lab work must not be completely clean. He thinks there might be some question whether the DNA belongs to Jorge, so the lawyer wanted me to admit that he smokes cigarettes."

"Does he?"

"He did for the first five years I knew him. But honestly, the last year we were together, I never saw him touch a cigarette. So I said no."

"Atta girl! You jammed that mean ol' lawyer!" Theo smiled and reached across the bar, trying to draw a fist bump from her. But Julia didn't feel like it.

"You don't think I told a lie?" she asked.

"Not at all. As far as you know, the man doesn't smoke cigarettes. Right?"

"I didn't say 'as far as I know.' I said no."

"And let me guess. The smarty-pants government lawyer got right up in your face like this," he said, playing lawyer. Then he took on the voice of the Wicked Witch of the West: "It's a simple question, Dorothy! Does Toto smoke cigarettes? Yes or no!?"

Julia smiled. "Well, it didn't go exactly like that. But kind of."

"Then you did the right thing."

"You think so?"

"I know so."

Julia reached across the bar and took his hand. "I really like you, Theo."

"I like me, too."

• • •

Flagler was one of Miami's oldest and busiest streets, and the Fla-mingo Motel was at its western end, midway between Miami's Little Havana and the Florida Everglades. Jorge chose it on the recommendation of Felipe, "the gun shop/chop shop."

Most of the old motels in this once-vibrant area were in de-cline and slated for demolition, but Jorge had seen much worse in Soyapango. The two-story building was typical of Miami in the 1970s. Rooms faced the parking lot and opened to the outdoors. Noisy climate-control units protruded from below the front win-dow. The neon letters on the roadside marquee were partially burned out, leaving the VACANCY sign to proclaim VACA, which Jorge read in his native tongue: *cow*. He smiled, wondering if there were sheep and goats, too. He found a parking space near the marquee.

"Sit tight," he told Rosa.

He got out of the car and walked across the parking lot to the manager's office. The glass door was locked, a reasonable precau-tion in this neighborhood, but Jorge could see a woman seated be-hind the reception counter. She laid her cigarette in the ashtray and, with the press of a button, her gravelly voice crackled over the speaker.

"Can I help you?"

"I need a room," said Jorge.

"I'll buzz you in. And fair warning, mister: I have a gun, I've used it before, and I don't miss."

The buzzer sounded and Jorge entered the small reception area, positioning himself by the glass so that he could keep an eye on Rosa in the car. The elderly woman behind the counter said noth-ing, but the name tag that was pinned to her blouse told him plenty: HELLO, MY NAME IS A. BITCH.

"How much a night?" he asked.

"Eighty."

Jorge could afford it. His "new" Chevy was priced at less than half the chopped value of Rosa's two-year-old Toyota, and Felipe had paid him the difference in cash. But Jorge didn't need to see the room to know the rate was too high.

Jorge laid a fifty on the counter. "No names, no receipts. That'll cover it."

She took a drag from her cigarette, her eyes narrowing on the inhale, which brought out a whole new pattern of smoke-hardened wrinkles. "No problem."

She gave him a key to room 115. "It's on the south side of the complex. You'll want to drive around to the back and park along the fence facing the gas station."

Jorge took the key and headed for the door, but she didn't buzz it open.

"That redhead in the car out there," she said. "She with you?"

Jorge knew exactly what she was up to. A. Bitch was a smart one, and she was going to get her eighty bucks a night if it killed her. He walked back and laid more cash on the counter. "Forget you saw her."

"Saw who?" She put the money in a drawer.

The buzzer sounded, Jorge stepped out, and he returned to his car. Rosa was seated obediently in the passenger seat.

"Good decision," he said.

"What?"

"Not to run," he said, as he pulled her long hair away from her neck. "Lemme see."

She turned her head and showed him the back of her neck. The three-inch burn from the red-hot choker chain was starting to ooze.

"Looks a little better," he lied. "Shouldn't get any worse. Unless you try to run. You're not going to run, are you, Red?"

Rosa was afraid even to look at him, but look at him she did, if only because she'd been trained to do so whenever he asked her a question. "No," she said softly.

"No what?"

"No, I won't run."

"Good girl," he said.

Jorge started the car, backed out of the parking space, and drove around the rental office to their new home in room 115.

CHAPTER 56

Julia's asylum hearing resumed Tuesday morning. It was the usual cast, with the addition of Assistant State Attorney Phillip Arnoff, who stood with the DHS lawyers on the other side of Judge Kelly's courtroom. Jack had subpoenaed Detective Barnes to testify at nine a.m. The assistant state attorney was there to explain why the detective wasn't.

"Detective Barnes is testifying before the grand jury in another matter," said Arnoff.

"When can he be here?" the judge asked.

"Possibly this afternoon."

"That's soon enough. Mr. Swyteck, call a different witness."

Jack rose. "Judge, we have presented the testimony of several other witnesses through affidavits filed with the court. Other than Detective Barnes, the only live witnesses I would like to call are Israel Tovar and Gabriel Santos."

"Who are they?"

"Mr. Tovar prosecuted Ms. Rodriguez under Article One-Thirty-Three of the Salvadoran penal code, and Mr. Santos was her defense counsel. Their testimony will corroborate my client's testimony that her husband forced her to have an abortion against her will. These lawyers can also confirm that it is futile for a married woman in El Salvador to complain to the police about a sexual assault and other forms of domestic violence because, as a practical matter, nothing will be done about it."

"These witnesses are outside the subpoena power of this court," the judge said. "How do you plan to get them to testify live in this courtroom?"

"I've been trying to convince them to appear voluntarily via videoconference."

"How's that going?"

"Not well. I have not yet been able to secure their agreement to testify."

"Then call another witness."

Jack glanced at his client. The only other witness they'd discussed was Beatriz, and a shake of Julia's head told him that her position was unchanged.

"At this time, I don't have another witness," said Jack.

"Very well. I won't force the respondent to rest her case, since we have Detective Barnes this afternoon. But I'm not going to sit here and twiddle my thumbs till then. We'll proceed out of order. Ms. Jerrell, call your first witness."

Jerrell rose and said, "The Department of Homeland Security calls Cecilia Varga."

Jack forced himself not to show any reaction. Julia was not nearly as stoic as her sister rose from the first row of public seating, came forward, and swore the oath.

Jack's decision *not* to call Cecilia as a witness for Julia had been an easy one. He hadn't forgotten his talk with Cecilia after Julia's arrest, the two of them seated on lawn chairs outside Cecilia's front door. Cecilia's take on whether Julia had been raped was less than helpful. Jack had warned her that the prosecutor might call her to the witness stand, and he'd given her the standard lawyer's lecture on how to be truthful without being hurtful. Jack hoped she was ready.

"Ms. Varga, you just swore an oath to tell the truth, did you not?" asked Jerrell.

The aggressive tone seemed to catch Cecilia off guard, but even though Jerrell had called her as a witness for the government, this was cross-examination. "I did."

"You understand that lying under oath is perjury?"

"Yes."

"Are you aware that perjury is a crime of moral turpitude under the Immigration and Naturalization Act?"

"Objection," said Jack. "Moral turpitude? What is this, a bar exam?"

"I'm just asking if she knows," said Jerrell.

The judge was leaning way back in his chair, staring at the ceiling. "Overruled. Ms. Varga, just tell her if you know or don't know."

"I didn't know that," said Cecilia.

"Did you know that any alien who commits a crime of moral turpitude, such as perjury, is no longer eligible for a visa?"

"Objection."

"Sustained. Ms. Jerrell, the witness has sworn to tell the truth. You don't have to threaten her. Move on, please."

"Yes, Your Honor. Ms. Varga, have you ever met the respondent's husband, Jorge Rodriguez?"

"Of course."

"Has he ever hit you?"

Again the question caught her off guard. "No."

"Has he ever threatened you in any way?"

"No."

"Have you ever seen him abuse his daughter, Beatriz, in any way?"

"No. I mean, he's not much of a father."

Jerrell's tone sharpened. "So the answer to my question is no. You've never seen Jorge Rodriguez abuse his daughter in any way."

"No."

"Have you ever seen him and your sister together?"

"Sure. Many times."

"Did you ever see him hit your sister?"

"No."

"Did you ever see him burn your sister?"

"Physically burn her? Like with fire?"

"Fire, hot metal, laser beam, molten lava—anything at all. Have you ever seen him burn any part of your sister's body?"

"No."

"Did you ever see him place a dog-choker chain around your sister's neck?"

"No."

Jerrell checked her notes, then continued. "Yesterday, your sister showed Judge Kelly a scar on the back of her neck. Have you seen that before?"

"Yes."

"Did your sister ever tell you how she got it?"

Her voiced softened. "She did."

"What did she tell you?"

Her voice dropped even lower. "She said it was from the zip line."

"What's the zip line?"

"There's a place to cross the river outside San Salvador. A cable runs from one side to the other and there's a swing attached to it about twenty feet in the air. Julia said she scraped her neck on the cable when she was zipping across the river."

Jerrell turned the page in her notebook. Cecilia wrung her hands as she waited for the next series of questions.

"Ms. Varga, your sister had an abortion in El Salvador, correct?"

"Yes."

"At any time prior to having an abortion, did your sister tell you she'd been raped?"

"Before the abortion, no."

"You're aware that your sister was later charged with a crime in El Salvador for having an abortion, are you not?"

"Yes."

"At any time before she was criminally charged, did your sister tell you that she had been raped?"

"I believe she told me after the case was over."

"So the first time that your sister ever mentioned to you that she'd been raped was after she'd been charged and after she'd talked to a lawyer, correct?"

"Right. After the case was over."

Jerrell stepped out from behind the lectern, leaving nothing between her and the witness. "Now, I'm going to ask you a little different question," said Jerrell. "When was the first time your sister told you that the man who'd raped her was her husband, Jorge Rodriguez?"

Cecilia paused. The silence lingered.

The judge sat up. "Ms. Varga, do you understand the question?"

"Yes. I'm trying to think."

"Let me ask it again," said Jerrell. She did.

Cecilia blinked hard, then answered. "I don't think Julia ever told me that. That's just something I've heard."

"But you've never heard it from your sister, is that correct?"

"Julia's a lot older than me," said Cecilia. "I was just a girl when all this happened."

"Excuse me," said Jerrell, using the same tone that had backfired at the close of Julia's testimony. "It's a yes-or-no question. Have you *ever* heard your sister say that she was raped by her husband?"

"Well, I was here in the courtroom yesterday. I heard her say it then."

"That's the first time you've ever heard her say it? In court, yesterday?"

"I believe so."

Jerrell returned to the lectern and gathered her notebook. "Thank you, Ms. Varga. Your Honor, I have no further questions."

"Mr. Swyteck?" said the judge. "Any questions for the witness?"

Before Jack could answer, the assistant state attorney spoke up. "Judge, I'm told that Detective Barnes has just arrived and is in the hallway."

"Can he wait until after Mr. Swyteck has finished with this witness?"

"Actually, he can't," said the prosecutor. He must attend an autopsy at noon, which cannot be rescheduled. This is his only availability."

Jack was a long way from Denmark, but something definitely smelled rotten. It had all seemed far too convenient: Barnes' unavailability, testimony from Julia's own sister that cried out for serious damage control, followed by Barnes' sudden availability, which would delay Jack's rehabilitation of Cecilia as witness.

"I can be quick with my examination," said Jack.

"Yeah, I've heard that one before," said the judge. "This isn't a jury trial. I understand your sense of urgency, Mr. Swyteck, given the substance of this witness's testimony, but there's no rule that says you have the right to rehabilitate Ms. Varga this very minute. I'm not going to make Mr. Barnes sit in the hallway waiting and miss an autopsy, which would not only inconvenience the medical examiner's office but could also delay and prejudice a homicide investigation. So it's your choice: question Detective Barnes now, while he's available, or I will enter an order releasing Mr. Barnes from his subpoena, and you can forfeit your right to question him at all."

"Thank you, Judge," said Jerrell.

The judge smacked his gavel with anger. "I told you not to thank me for my rulings, Ms. Jerrell!"

Jerrell couldn't hide her smile, and Jack couldn't help noticing it. Judge Kelly had left him and his client no choice, and despite the judge's professed pet peeves, Jerrell's "thank you" should have been delivered in fountain pen ink on letterpress stationery.

"We'll proceed with Detective Barnes," said Jack.

Judge Kelly excused the witness, and the assistant state attorney stepped out of the courtroom to bring in the detective.

"Up until this point we have not invoked the rule," said Jerrell, meaning the unwritten rule that no witness should be in the courtroom to hear the testimony of other witnesses. "But, seeing how Ms. Varga is in the middle of her testimony, the department would ask that she wait outside."

"That's fine," said the judge. "Ms. Varga, there's a nice bench in the hallway with your name on it. Please wait there, and do not discuss your testimony with anyone."

Cecilia acknowledged that she understood and started toward the rail. She glanced in Julia's direction, as if to offer a silent apology, but she didn't look at Jack, and Jack noticed something as she passed that he hadn't noticed before.

Cecilia smelled of cigarette smoke.

CHAPTER 57

Jack took his time as he rose to examine the next witness. His mind was awhirl with what he'd just heard from Cecilia on the witness stand, what he'd heard from Cecilia since Julia's arrest, and what he'd just smelled as Cecilia walked past him.

"Mr. Swyteck, you may question the witness," the judge said, nudging him along.

Detective Barnes sat comfortably in a wood chair that so many witnesses before him had found unbearably uncomfortable. Immigration court was not his usual venue, but he was no stranger to courtrooms, and he'd seen virtually every trick in the trial lawyer's book. Jack's slow-motion gait, however, seemed to confuse even the seasoned detective.

"Mr. Swyteck," the judge said in a firmer voice, "your witness."

Jack had prepared thoroughly for Barnes. He'd thought about this showdown in his office, in the shower, and on the drive home. His questions and their possible answers had played out in his mind countless times. The watershed moment in the hearing had been Jerrell's asking Julia if her husband was a smoker: it told Jack that the DNA evidence connecting Jorge to the cigarette in McBride's car was less than conclusive. But Jack didn't know where that ambiguity took him. He'd been in similar predicaments in the courtroom before, and experience taught him to ditch the prepared outline and follow his instincts.

"Detective Barnes, you are the lead detective in the investigation into the death of Duncan McBride, correct?"

The assistant state attorney was in the courtroom, and a quick glance from Barnes brought him immediately to his feet. "Your Honor, I object," said Arnoff.

"You can't object," said the judge. "This is immigration court. Not your turf."

"Then I'll object for him," said Jerrell. "And to pick up on Your Honor's point, immigration court is no place to put an active homicide investigation on public display."

"Your Honor, my questions will focus on an issue that Ms. Jerrell has put front and center in this proceeding: the whereabouts of Ms. Rodriguez's husband."

"All right," said the judge. "But I'm going to keep a tight rein on this."

"Understood," said Jack.

Jack spent the next few minutes exploring the detective's two decades of experience, focusing in particular on his knowledge of DNA evidence. Barnes wasn't a scientist, but this wasn't a murder trial, so Jack didn't need a DNA analyst from the Florida Department of Law Enforcement to explain the complexities of deoxyribonucleic acid. All he needed was an admission from the lead detective on the investigation.

"Detective, you know from your own experience in law enforcement that, except for identical twins, no two people have the same DNA."

"That is my understanding."

"You, personally, have collected DNA evidence from crime scenes before?"

"Yes. Many times."

"Dried saliva on a cigarette butt can be a source of DNA, correct?"

"Not always, but it can be."

Jack made a mental note of the "not always" qualification, then moved on. "In the McBride homicide investigation, you, personally, collected a cigarette butt from the ashtray of the victim's vehicle, did you not?"

"I did."

"And the lab was able to extract DNA from the saliva on that cigarette butt, correct?"

"Yes."

"Now, speaking more generally, sometimes an investigator collects DNA evidence from a crime scene and the lab compares the sample to the DNA of a known suspect or person of interest, correct?"

"Yeah, if you have a suspect or a person of interest."

"Fair point," said Jack. "Is it correct to say that you had no suspect or person of interest at the time you collected the DNA sample from Mr. McBride's car?"

"No, that's not correct. Julia Rodriguez was a person of interest."

Jack did a double take. It was not the answer he'd expected, which put him in the exact position no trial lawyer wanted to be in: deep into cross-examination and having no idea of the answer to the next question. The judge asked the question that Jack didn't want to ask.

"So, Detective, did you compare the DNA sample from the cigarette to DNA from Julia Rodriguez?"

"The lab did. During her INS detention, Ms. Rodriguez was held in Baker County Facility, which collects cheek swabs from all detainees. It's done to help solve unsolved crimes, and, consistent with that purpose, we made the comparison in our investigation."

Jack hesitated, but if they made a comparison and didn't revoke Julia's release on bond, Jack could guess the answer to the next question. So he asked it.

"You didn't get a match, did you, Detective Barnes?"

"No match."

"Am I correct in saying that Julia Rodriguez is no longer a person of interest in your investigation?"

"She's not," said Barnes. "But her husband is."

The detective's answer was clearly intended to jam the lawyer, but Jack kept his composure. "We'll get to that," said Jack. "But I want to stick to the DNA. After the DNA comparison to Julia Rodriguez returned no match, you collected DNA from her daughter, Beatriz, correct?"

"She consented to a cheek swab, yes."

The issue of a high school student's "consent" was debatable, but this wasn't the time. "You compared Beatriz's DNA to the DNA collected from the saliva, correct?"

"The lab did."

"You didn't get a complete match, did you?"

"We got a partial match."

"By 'partial match' you mean what?"

"A complete match would mean that it was Beatriz's DNA on the cigarette butt. We didn't have that. But there was enough common DNA between the two samples to tell us that the person who left that saliva on the cigarette butt was related to Beatriz."

"You knew from the earlier lab work that the relative wasn't Beatriz's mother. Correct?"

"That's correct. The comparison to Ms. Rodriguez showed no match."

"One theory is that the DNA belongs to Beatriz's father. Is that right?"

"Yes."

"But you don't know for sure, do you?"

"It's a complicated DNA analysis that's beyond me."

"Let's keep it simple," said Jack. "There's enough common DNA that it could be Beatriz's father, right?"

"Right."

Jack paused, feeling like a pitcher one out away from a no-hitter. "There's enough common DNA that it could also be Beatriz's aunt. Isn't that true, Detective?"

Barnes glared at him coldly, but he was too experienced to dig himself into a hole by trying to evade the inevitable outcome. He simply answered, "Yes."

Jack wasn't certain, but he was sure enough that MDPD had yet to collect a DNA sample from Cecilia. "You have not compared the DNA from the cigarette butt to the DNA of Cecilia Varga, have you?"

"No."

"It would be logical to run that comparison, would it not?"

"It would be something to consider."

"Were you waiting to make that comparison until after Ms. Rodriguez was deported?"

"Objection."

"Overruled."

Barnes shifted in his chair, looking nowhere near as comfortable as he had just minutes earlier. "I don't understand your question."

"Let me restate it," said Jack. "Did Ms. Jerrell ask you to hold off on comparing the cigarette DNA to Cecilia Varga's DNA until *after* Ms. Jerrell 'proved' that Jorge Rodriguez is here in Miami, until *after* this hearing was over, until *after* this court ordered my client deported, and until *after* her deportation flight touched down in San Salvador?"

"This is outrageous!" Jerrell shouted, with a heavy dose of indignation.

Jack's gaze remained fixed on the witness, and everything about the detective's body language told Jack that he was spot-on.

Jerrell's indignation only heightened. "Your Honor, I strongly object to Mr. Swyteck's insinuation and the attack on my professional integrity."

"Sustained."

It was a punch to the chest—the proverbial infield hit with two outs in the bottom of the ninth to end the no-hitter. *Sustained?*

"Judge—"

"I sustained the objection, Mr. Swyteck. I'm not going to turn a deportation hearing into a mudslinging contest."

Jack could see the writing on the wall. "Technically it's an asylum hearing, Your Honor. Not a deportation hearing."

"Call it what you like. Do you have any more questions for the witness, or can we let him return to his job?"

"I have one more," said Jack. "Detective Barnes, is Cecilia Varga a person of interest in your investigation?"

"She is a person of interest as a possible accessory after the fact in connection with the disposal of Mr. McBride's vehicle. Not in the murder."

"Thank you," said Jack. "Nothing further."

"All right," the judge said. "It seems we have a bit of a situation here. I told Ms. Varga to wait out in the hall until we finished with Detective Barnes."

"Judge, I have no questions for Detective Barnes," said Jerrell. "Notwithstanding Mr. Swyteck's personal attack on the detective's professionalism and mine, the criminal investigation into the death of Mr. McBride should remain confidential, and I have no desire to jeopardize that investigation by subjecting Detective Barnes to more of whatever it is that Mr. Swyteck is trying to accomplish."

"That's very professional of you, Ms. Jerrell," the judge said, but he was looking at Jack, as if he wished Jack were more like her. "That still leaves us a situation, as I called it," he continued. "Accessory after the fact to murder is a serious crime. Since Detective Barnes has identified Ms. Varga as a person of interest, this court is compelled to allow Ms. Varga the opportunity to consult with counsel before subjecting her to cross-examination in this proceeding. She may have a Fifth Amendment right she would like to assert. Mr. Swyteck, as a criminal defense lawyer, I assume you understand where I'm coming from."

"I do, Your Honor."

"All right, then," the judge said, again looking at Jack. "If someone could bring Ms. Varga into the courtroom, I'll let her know that we will adjourn for the day, and that I will expect an answer from her by nine o'clock tomorrow morning as to whether she will testify or assert her rights."

"I'll go," Jack and Julia said in unison.

Jack was about to tell Julia to stay, but she bolted from the table, hurried down the center aisle, and exited the courtroom through the double doors in the rear. Jack rushed after her and caught up with her in the hallway.

"Where is she?" asked Julia.

Benches lined the walls on both sides of the hallway outside the courtroom. Jack didn't see Cecilia.

"The judge told her to wait," Julia said, her voice rising with anger. "Where *is* she?"

Jack checked again, looking one way and then the other. The answer was clear.

"She left," said Jack.

CHAPTER 58

J ack got a phone call from the assistant state attorney later that afternoon. Arnoff wanted a face-to-face meeting with Jack, his client, and Detective Barnes. The drive to the Graham Building near the Criminal Justice Center was against rush-hour traffic, and Jack arrived in less than twenty minutes. Julia took the bus and met him in the lobby.

"Any word from Cecilia?" Jack asked.

"No. Could that be what they want to meet with us about?"

"We'll find out," said Jack.

They rode the elevator together to the eighth floor. Jack wanted details before bringing his client into a room with a prosecutor and a detective. He told Julia to wait in the reception area while he had a pre-meeting without her in Arnoff's office.

"You went too far in court today," said the prosecutor.

Arnoff was seated at his desk with the window behind him. In the distance was a sunset over the Everglades, an orange-pink blast enhanced by clouds of smoke rising from the spring brush fires that were so typical of South Florida's dry season. Two armchairs normally faced the prosecutor's desk, but Barnes had moved his around to face Jack and align himself with the assistant state attorney.

"Seriously?" said Jack. "Is that what this meeting is about? My cross-examination tactics?"

"You implied that MDPD is conducting a homicide investigation in a way that works to the advantage of the DHS in a deportation hearing."

"Miami is not a sanctuary city. As a matter of policy, local law enforcement coordinates with federal immigration authorities. I'm entitled to pick and probe to uncover the extent of that coordination."

"MDPD doesn't compromise homicide investigations to help the feds win deportation hearings," said Arnoff.

"All I did was point out the truth," said Jack. "Your DNA evidence didn't connect Jorge Rodriguez to the murder of Duncan McBride. My only intent was to help my client, not to hurt your investigation."

Detective Barnes could sit quietly no longer. "Forget the DNA evidence, Swyteck. What if I told you MDPD has other evidence that Jorge Rodriguez is in Miami?"

"I'd say I haven't seen it."

Barnes opened the manila file folder in his lap, removed a one-page document, and laid it on the corner of the prosecutor's desk. "Here's a draft BOLO," said Barnes, referring to a "be on the lookout" notice. "How's that hit you?"

Jack took it. The BOLO warned that "the subject should be considered armed and dangerous." It included a grainy photograph, typical of security-camera images, with the caption: "Last seen at Downtown Dadeland Apartments."

"When did you get this picture?" asked Jack.

"This afternoon. It took time to review the security-camera video from Downtown Dadeland and find a good image."

Jack looked at the photograph again. He'd met plenty of murderers behind bars. Nothing had quite the impact of the photo of a murderer on the loose. "Has this been issued?"

Barnes and the prosecutor exchanged glances, seeming to agree that Arnoff should be the one to explain.

"Look, Jack," he said in a civil tone. "I hear you're a straight shooter. If I tell you something, I need your agreement that it doesn't leave this room. Can I have your word on that?"

Jack glanced at Barnes, who still seemed angry. But Arnoff appeared to be on the level. "Sure. You have my word."

"We don't have enough evidence to arrest anyone on murder charges. Not yet. But the guy in that security video left the Downtown Dadeland Apartments with a twenty-year-old woman who has an apartment there. He stayed with her for at least a couple of nights after the murder of Hugo Martinez. We don't know if this young woman left the apartment with him of her own free will or if he forced her to go with him. We don't know if the guy is dangerous or just a friend."

"You don't consider Jorge Rodriguez dangerous?" Jack asked with surprise.

"There's the rub," said Arnoff. "If we knew this was Jorge Rodriguez, we'd issue a missing-person's BOLO for the safety and welfare of this young woman."

Jack double-checked the BOLO. "So you're not sure this is Jorge Rodriguez?"

"We have nothing to compare this image to. We've never seen his picture."

"Neither have I," said Jack. "Julia left everything to do with him back in El Salvador. But surely you can get something through law enforcement channels. Mug shot, driver's license, passport."

"We tried," said Arnoff. "The response we've gotten so far is that he's an informant in their witness protection program. Eventually, we'll get through the red tape, but at the moment we have nothing."

Jack's thoughts turned back to safety. "The woman who has the apartment at Downtown Dadeland. Who is she?"

"Rosa Fields. A college kid who messed up her life. Drugs. Prostitution. Her neighbors say it's normal for her to disappear for days at a time, and no one has filed a missing-person report. But like I said, if we knew for certain that the guy she left with is a badass like Jorge Rodriguez, we'd issue a missing-person BOLO for her safety."

"You think she . . ."

"We don't know," said the detective.

"Which brings us back to the purpose of this meeting," said Arnoff. "We need someone to confirm that the man in this security video is Jorge Rodriguez."

"By 'someone,' you mean my client," said Jack.

"To be blunt," Barnes added, "if that guy in the picture is Jorge Rodriguez, and your client keeps it to herself, how's she going to feel if he kills again? What if that woman with the apartment at Downtown Dadeland didn't leave with him by choice?"

Of course Jack had already considered that possibility, but the fact that Barnes would spell it out so clearly gave him pause.

"That would be a horrible thing, wouldn't it?" said Jack.

"Yes, it would," said Barnes.

Jack held his response, partly because he wanted to be sure to say everything that needed to be said, but also because he couldn't believe the game that was being played. As the silence lingered, the sincerity seemed to drain from the prosecutor's expression. Neither man looked sincere. They were flat-out smug.

"You had me going for a minute there," said Jack.

"Excuse me?" said Arnoff.

"That line about not being able to get so much as a driver's license photo from El Salvador? Nice try. But who do you think you're dealing with, a first-year law student? The police don't have to link a name to a face in order to issue a BOLO. And you sure as hell can issue a BOLO before you have enough evidence to arrest someone. I'm betting you've already issued this BOLO."

"Why would we call you in here if we already issued it?" asked Arnoff.

"I don't know," said Jack. "Maybe ICE sees this case as an important precedent and wants to win at all costs. Maybe I pissed off the wrong government lawyer ten years ago and now it's finally coming back to hurt one of my clients. But this phony ask for Julia's help to attach her husband's name to this photo has Simone Jerrell's fingerprints all over it."

Barnes scoffed. "There you go again with your government conspiracy theories, Swyteck."

"The department is trying to convince Judge Kelly that it's safe to deport my client back to El Salvador because her husband is here in Miami. Jerrell hasn't proven where Jorge Rodriguez is. But if you can get Julia to confirm that the man in this photograph is her husband, that's an admission right from her own lips. Slam dunk. Case over."

"Everything has unintended consequences," said Barnes.

"*Un*intended?" said Jack, incredulous. "This isn't about getting the information you need to issue a BOLO. You're asking my client to sign her own deportation order."

"If it makes it any easier," said the prosecutor, "I'd be happy to submit a letter to Judge Kelly letting him know that she cooperated in our investigation."

"I'm sure that would look very nice in a frame hanging on the wall in her apartment in San Salvador," said Jack.

Barnes sharpened his tone. "You think you're pretty smart, don't you, Swyteck? But I can tell you how this is going to play out if something happens to that young woman from Downtown Dadeland. Does your client really want to be the illegal who refused to help MDPD save the life of a college girl from Indiana? Do you want to be the lawyer for that illegal?"

Jack rose without responding.

The prosecutor rose with him. "Jack, let's get real. You know her husband is here. Your client knows he's here. Simone Jerrell dropped the ball and failed to prove it. But haven't you won enough cases on technicalities in your career?"

Jack folded the draft BOLO and tucked it into his coat pocket. He would never accept that forcing the government to prove its case was a "technicality," but the thought of a young woman who may or may not have left her apartment "by choice" had gotten to him. Deep down, he knew he was right—that the BOLO had already been issued and that this meeting was a stunt.

But he wasn't willing to bet someone else's life on it.

"I'll speak to my client," said Jack.

CHAPTER 59

Jorge parked the car on Main Highway, which he found confusing, since it wasn't a highway at all. It was the main street through Coconut Grove, where vehicles moved only slightly faster than the pedestrians who strolled past sidewalk cafés and open-air bars that catered to a casual clientele. Rosa was in the passenger seat. Outside her window, across the sidewalk by the old stone wall, was a brass plaque of the National Register of Historic Places. They were near the Barnacle, Miami's oldest house, built before Coconut Grove had streets, highways, or even motorized vehicles. More important, they were a half block away from Cy's Place.

"I can't do this," said Rosa.

Her constant chatter and restlessness were making Jorge crazy. Not even the threat of the choke-chain collar could keep her in line. An addict in need of a fix responded to one thing only. Jorge pulled a foil packet from his pocket and dangled it before her eyes. She lit up like a child on Christmas morning.

"Oh, my God. Is that—"

"Yup. How long's it been, Rosa?"

She nearly doubled over, rocking back and forth in her car seat, as if it hurt just to think about it. "I don't know. Too long."

Jorge lowered the driver's-side window. "I could just throw it away."

"No, no!"

"If you can't help me with one little thing, why should I reward you with this?"

Rosa fell back into her seat, breathing out her frustration. "How do you know she's even going to be there?"

Jorge pulled up a photograph on his cell phone and showed her the fruits of his informal surveillance of Cy's Place. "This is Beatriz's routine," he said. "She sits at the table in the front by the window and does her homework every school night."

Rosa checked out the image on his screen. "Cute girl."

It was just her honest reaction, but Jorge took it as an opportunity to work a little psychology on Rosa. "Yeah," he said in the sincerest tone he could muster. "I really miss her."

Rosa looked at him curiously. "No offense, but you don't seem like the loving-father type."

He looked at her with sad eyes. "You don't know me. Why do you think I act the way I act?"

"I have no idea."

"Beatriz was my whole life in El Salvador. She's my only child. I almost had a second, but you know what happened?"

"No."

"My wife got a boyfriend, and he made her have an abortion. He didn't want my kid in her life."

"That's terrible."

"I know, right? But that's not all. Then she and her boyfriend stole my little girl and took her to Miami."

"That's so—" She stopped herself, flashing a quizzical expression. "Wait a minute. If the boyfriend made your wife get an abortion because he didn't want your kid in his life, why did they steal your daughter?"

Jorge's lie was quickly falling apart. "Just to spite me, I guess. They're bad people."

"So mean."

"Yeah, it is. That's why I say her boyfriend got what he deserved."

"Was that the guy you shot?"

"Yeah."

Rosa seemed to accept it, but she was rocking back and forth in the car seat again, her thoughts consumed by what really mattered to an addict. "I can have that packet if I help you, right?"

"Absolutely."

"I'm not going to help you steal your daughter back. You can put that dog collar on me all you want. I won't do it."

"I'm not saying you have to do anything like that. This is very simple. I just need to know where my daughter is."

Rosa folded her arms tightly, still rocking, trying to stop her hands from shaking. "You know where she is. You just said she's in Cy's Place doing her homework."

"I need to know where she is *all the time*."

"How can you do that?"

Jorge opened the console and removed the bag from the pet store. Rosa recoiled, as if expecting a dog chain. But they sold all kinds of gadgets at the pet store.

"This is a little GPS tracker," Jorge said, showing her the package. "It attaches to a dog collar. The app on your cell phone tells you where the dog is, wherever he goes."

"Doesn't the battery run out?"

Rosa asked way too many questions. "That's not your problem. It lasts a week without recharging it. That's long enough for me to track Beatriz."

"So you want me to ask her to wear it?"

She was truly annoying. "No, she doesn't have to *wear* it. Beatriz carries her backpack with her wherever she goes. I want you to go into Cy's Place, strike up a conversation with her about any bullshit that interests a teenage girl. Do whatever you need to do to get next to her. And when you get the chance, just slip this into one of the five hundred little pockets in her backpack."

"What if I don't get the chance?"

Her dumbest question yet. "Then instead of this," he said,

showing her the foil packet, "you get this," he said, pulling the dog chain from his coat pocket.

Rosa crossed her arms tightly again, as if hugging herself, trying to stop the trembles. "Okay," she said. "I'll get it done."

He handed her the transmitter. "Make sure you do," he said in a very serious voice.

CHAPTER 60

J ulia did the right thing.

Jack had laid out the options. Her best case for an asylum claim was to keep quiet and force Simone Jerrell to live with the record she'd created—to leave it "inconclusive" as to whether Jorge Rodriguez was in Miami or in El Salvador. Jack was "99.9 percent certain" that MDPD had already issued the BOLO and that the sole purpose of showing Julia the security-camera photo was to force Julia to admit, conclusively, that her husband was in Miami. For Julia, the one-tenth of 1 percent chance that she held another woman's safety in her hands was enough.

"It's him," Julia had told Detective Barnes. "That's my husband."

Jack attached similar odds—99.9 percent—to the likelihood that Judge Kelly would order her deported.

Julia caught the bus but didn't go home. She rode to Cecilia's house, took a seat on one of the lawn chairs on the front stoop, and waited in the darkness. She knew her sister would return home eventually. An hour passed, the night air turned chilly, but Julia's anger didn't cool. A bus stopped across the street and pulled away. Cecilia was left standing on the sidewalk.

Julia rose, and their eyes met. Darkness stretched in the fifty feet between them, but Cecilia was bathed in the glow of the streetlamp, and Julia was in the yellower glow of the porch light. Julia tightened her glare, as if to tell her younger sister, Don't you dare walk away from me.

Cecilia crossed the street and stopped halfway up the sidewalk. Julia stepped toward her and stopped.

"You want to explain yourself?" asked Julia.

Cecilia said nothing. From her puffy eyes it was clear that she'd been crying, but any Salvadoran girl who'd ever set foot in a Catholic church knew that Judas had also wept.

"I'm sorry," said Cecilia. "It's not the way you think."

"Jack told me what 'accessory after the fact' means. Jorge killed Duncan McBride. You helped him ditch the car."

"That's not what happened," said Cecilia.

"It's *your* DNA on the cigarette butt, isn't it?"

"Yes. But listen to me, will you, please? Just once, hear my side of it?"

Julia swallowed her anger. "All right. Talk."

"You were in jail. Beatriz was staying with me and turning numb before my eyes with that resignation syndrome or whatever it was. Then, to make it even worse, this McBride bastard threatened her on the bus on her way to school."

Julia knew that much was true; Beatriz had told her about the bus. "What does that have to do with Jorge?"

"The night you got out of jail, Jorge came here to see me. I told him to go away, but he wouldn't leave. He said he had to talk to me. I didn't want to make a scene in front of my roommates, so I agreed to go for a ride with him."

"In Duncan McBride's car?"

"I thought it was Jorge's car. He offered me a cigarette, and I smoked it. He told me Beatriz didn't have to worry about McBride anymore."

"Yeah, because he killed him," Julia snapped.

"I didn't know that! I had no idea what that meant. Nobody knew McBride was dead at that point. Jorge dropped me off. I left the cigarette butt in the ashtray. That was it. I swear."

Julia studied her sister's expression. It could have been true. Probably was true. But Julia sensed that she was leaving something out.

"How did Jorge even know that McBride threatened Beatriz on the bus?"

Cecilia was silent.

"Cecilia? How did he know?"

Tears welled in Cecilia's eyes.

"You told him, didn't you? Be honest with me, Cecilia. How long have you known Jorge is in Miami?"

"A while," she said softly.

"How long have you been in touch with him?"

Cecilia started to tremble. "Jorge is not the guilty person you say he is, Julia."

"He raped me and choked me with a dog chain!"

"You said you got that burn mark on your neck from the zip line."

"Yeah, just like I said the black eye was from walking into a door. And the sprained wrist was when I tripped while running. Do I have to go on and on? Do you think I'm the first victim of domestic violence to make excuses for her husband?"

"I didn't lie on the witness stand. I never saw him hit you."

"I didn't say you lied. But that doesn't excuse what you just said. How can you stand there and tell me to my face that Jorge is not the guilty person I say he is? Forget what he did to me. He killed two people just in the short time he's been in Miami."

"I didn't mean he's a good guy. I meant . . . he's not the only one to blame."

"Blame for what?"

Cecilia hesitated, then just blurted it out. "For what Beatriz has had to live through."

"Then who is to blame?" Julia asked, her anger rising.

"There are two sides to this story, Julia. Yes, Jorge did things to you that a man should never do to his wife. But you cheated on him. You fell in love with Hugo. And when you found out the baby wasn't Hugo's, you got an abortion. *That's* what I'm talking about!"

Julia stood in stunned silence. The accusation was so outrageous that she could barely muster a response. "Who told you I had an abortion because it wasn't Hugo's child? Jorge?"

"No! Hugo!"

It was like a punch to the gut, but Julia wasn't completely shocked. Jorge's abuse was in a class by itself, but Hugo had his own brand of machismo. She'd tried to tell Hugo that she'd been raped. She'd tried to tell him that Jorge had forced her to have an abortion. But after hearing the word *abortion*, the self-centeredness that seemed embedded in the Y chromosome kicked in, and there was only one thing Hugo cared about: *Was the baby mine?*

She'd told Hugo what he wanted to hear and suffered alone.

"You believe everybody but me, your own sister," said Julia.

"I believe that Beatriz deserves better."

Almost immediately, Cecilia seemed to want the words back, and Julia wished she hadn't heard them. But they were out there, the unspoken feelings that a sister should never say to the mother of her niece.

"I'm sorry, I didn't mean—"

"Yes, you did," Julia said in the calmest voice she could muster. "You're entitled to your beliefs."

The eye contact lasted a moment longer, and then Julia looked away. Neither woman spoke as Julia walked past her sister. She crossed the street but didn't even slow down at the bus stop, never looking back as she continued down the sidewalk to wait for the bus on another block.

CHAPTER 61

Rosa was asleep on the bed in their room at the Flamingo Motel. She lay on her side in a deep state of unconsciousness, her arm dangling over the edge of the mattress. She looked almost lifeless, but Jorge could see the subtle rise of her rib cage with each silent breath. The syringe, metal spoon, water bottle, and Jorge's cigarette lighter were on the nightstand, beside the open foil package of heroin.

Rosa had successfully planted the GPS tracker in Beatriz's backpack. The app on Jorge's cell verified that much, allowing him to monitor Beatriz's movement every three minutes. Hard work had its rewards, and he'd delivered the promised packet upon their return to the motel. Rosa was shaking with anticipation, and he'd offered to cook it for her, but when the going gets tough, the addicted get going. Red was a self-injection machine, heating it in the spoon, filling the syringe, and dispensing the drug into the overused vein in her forearm with the determination of a wounded soldier on a final lifesaving mission.

On the other side of the dimly lit room, one of the last remaining tube televisions in Miami was tuned to ESPN *deportes*. Real Madrid was delivering a serious ass-kicking to a lesser *club de fútbol*, but Jorge wasn't watching. His gaze was fixed on the image displayed on his cell phone. *His* image.

Social media is an effective tool for law enforcement, and the South Florida Homicide clearinghouse puts it to good use. A BOLO issued by the Miami-Dade Police Department's Homicide Unit spreads quickly, not only to law enforcement but to the community at large. Any citizen with Web access can easily find out if police are looking for someone in the neighborhood just by checking the MDPD Facebook page and links to local watch groups.

It worked equally well for a criminal who wanted to know whether the police were actively looking for him.

"Shit!" Jorge shouted, as he kicked the plastic trash can across the room. Rosa didn't stir.

There were two BOLOs from MDPD. The first was for Rosa's car, which didn't concern him. It had long since been chopped, and the parts were probably on a freighter to the Caribbean or South America. The second BOLO was the problem. Jorge's face was clearly visible in the grainy freeze-frame from surveillance video at Rosa's apartment building. It even had his name below the photo. And Jorge knew who to blame.

"Damn you, Julia!"

Jorge went to the closet and sifted through his weapons bag. He'd discarded the .22-caliber he'd used to off Hugo, but the semiautomatic 9 mm pistol from Hugo was a keeper. The extra ammunition clips would come in handy later. He grabbed the titanium diver's knife with the mixed serrated and nonserrated edges and went into the bathroom. The smooth side of the blade made quick work of his medium-length hair, and he pitched fistful after fistful into the toilet before flushing it away. When he was down to a patchwork of stubble, he soaped up and shaved his head clean with the razor. A shaved head had been his regular look as a teenager, and he'd almost forgotten about the "18" tattoo on his scalp behind his left ear. It made him smile to see it again.

Jorge gathered up the toiletries and the knife, went back to the closet, and stuffed them into the weapons bag, along with his shoes, clothes, extra cash, and everything else worth taking. He turned around and took a look at Rosa. She was still out cold, floating along somewhere with Lucy in the Sky with Diamonds.

Jorge had strongly suspected that the police might be on his tail, which was why he'd chosen to lie low, put off his plans for Theo Knight, and monitor Julia's movements via the GPS transmitter in Beatriz's backpack. But the BOLO made it impossible for him to stay another minute at the Flamingo Motel. A. Bitch at reception had promised not to say anything to anyone, but she'd seen his face, she'd pointed out "the redhead" waiting in his car, and she could not be trusted. Nor could he be seen carrying Rosa like a corpse out of the motel room to the car. He had to do what he had to do.

Jorge put down his bag and took a seat on the edge of the mattress near the nightstand. Rosa had carefully measured out her dosage, having left enough heroin in the foil packet for another five injections. Jorge emptied the entire package into the spoon, added a few drops of water, and fired it up into an injectable liquid with his lighter. The vinegary odor told him that this batch wasn't particularly pure, but it didn't matter. He drew every bit of solution into the syringe. He tied Rosa's arm with the tourniquet, found a vein, and inserted the hollow hypodermic needle at an acute angle.

Rosa just lay there, making not a flinch, not even as he pushed the plunger slowly and injected the deadly dosage in the direction of her blood flow, toward the heart.

"Night, night," he said, as he tossed the syringe aside and removed the tourniquet.

Jorge rose, grabbed his bag from the floor, and opened the door. He glanced back at Rosa on his way out. She'd been pretty good to him, but he managed to feel just fine about himself and how things had turned out.

Unlike so many others, Rosa would die a happy girl.

Jorge closed the door and headed to the car, checking the app on his cell for Beatriz's latest location.

CHAPTER 62

On Wednesday morning Jack was in court for the final day of Julia's asylum hearing—alone.

"Are you stag today, Mr. Swyteck?" the judge asked.

Julia had called to tell him she wasn't coming, to which his initial reaction was, "You need to be there." But after hearing her out, Julia's explanation had made sense. Jack put his best spin on it for the court, recounting the meeting with Detective Barnes and the assistant state attorney that confirmed the identity of Jorge Rodriguez.

"Your Honor, the fact of the matter is that my client is afraid to step out of her apartment. She recognizes the importance of this hearing, but she is especially fearful coming to this court-house when her exact destination and precise time of arrival are matters of public record. Retaliation by her husband is a very real possibility."

"It's her choice," the judge said. "She doesn't have to be here if she's represented by counsel. May I see the BOLO, please?"

"I have it," said Jerrell, and she happily handed it up to the judge. "It was just upgraded to a probable-cause-to-arrest BOLO. The image in that BOLO is from a surveillance video of Mr. Rodriguez leaving the apartment of a college student named Rosa Fields. Ms. Fields was found dead this morning in a motel room. The manager confirmed that she was staying with Mr. Rodriguez."

The news hit Jack hard, but not as hard as the judge's glare. "Were you aware of that, Mr. Swyteck?" the judge asked, as if the actions of Julia's husband were his wife's fault.

"I was not, Your Honor. But I did want to share with the court a letter from Assistant State Attorney Phillip Arnoff acknowledging my client's assistance in the investigation. Her identification of Mr. Rodriguez in the video was extremely helpful."

Jack handed up the letter, which Arnoff had delivered in keeping with his promise. The judge read it quickly.

"Nice letter," the judge said. "But I don't see how the respondent's cooperation with law enforcement is relevant to her claim for asylum."

"Not to beat a dead horse," said Jerrell, "but the letter actually supports the department's position that Ms. Rodriguez's claim for asylum is conclusively foreclosed by her admission that Jorge Rodriguez is here in Miami. She has no reason to fear anything by returning to El Salvador."

"Understood," the judge said. "Does that conclude the parties' submission of evidence?"

The lawyers acknowledged that it did.

"Thank you, Counsel," the judge said. "I have an extremely crowded calendar again today, so I've decided to receive closing arguments by written submission. Have them delivered to my chambers by the end of the day."

"Is there a page limit?" asked Jerrell.

"Technically, no. But I'm a firm believer in the old adage 'If I had more time, I would have written a shorter letter,' which is to say, I stop reading at twenty pages, so I suggest you not go any longer than that. Anything else?"

"When can we expect a ruling?" asked Jerrell.

It was the question that most lawyers never asked a judge—ill-advised, at best; impertinent in some courtrooms—but it was a sure sign of the department's supreme confidence in the outcome.

"I would not expect a ruling anytime before I'm ready to issue it," the judge said flatly. "Are there any *intelligent* questions?"

Silence.

"Then we are adjourned."

With the pistol-shot crack of a gavel, Julia's hearing on her claim for asylum was over.

Jack gathered his files and headed for the exit to call his client. The hallway was bustling with scores of undocumented immigrants and their families, some with lawyers and some without, some who still had hope and others who'd lost it. Jack found a relatively quiet place at the end of the hallway by the fire exit and dialed Julia on her cell.

"Did the judge deport me?" she asked.

Jack didn't want to say no for fear that she'd misunderstand. "He hasn't ruled yet."

"What do you think is going to happen?" she asked—or at least that's what Jack thought he heard. The background noise on Julia's end was terrible.

"It's kind of hard to hear you, Julia. Where are you?"

"I'm outside," she said. "I don't want Beatriz to hear me. Tell me the truth. What do you think will happen?"

Jack took a breath and delivered it to her straight. "I think we are going to have to take this to the Board of Immigration Appeals."

"How long does that take?"

"In a way, that's the good news. An appeal can buy you months of time. Maybe more than a year."

"Another year of looking over my shoulder for my crazy husband."

"His days are numbered. MDPD upgraded the BOLO to include probable cause to arrest. They found a—"

"I know," she said. "Theo showed me the article online. It said possible drug overdose, but I don't believe anything is accidental when it comes to Jorge."

"The police would probably agree with you," said Jack. "But I do think they'll catch him soon, which means you and Beatriz won't have to worry about him."

"So I take a year or more setting up a life for Beatriz and me in Miami," she said. "And then I lose the appeal. What happens?"

"You would be deported."

She didn't say anything. Jack heard only the clatter of background noise.

"Julia?"

"I think I get the picture, Jack."

"I know this is not what you were hoping to hear. After the judge rules and I read the actual written order, I'll have a better sense of your chances on appeal. In the meantime, we can talk whenever you need to. Just call."

"Thanks, Jack. Thank you for everything you've done for us."

Jack said good-bye, but she didn't. The noise in the background ceased, and the phone call was over. Julia was gone.

Julia put her phone away in her purse. Beatriz, seated across from her at an outdoor table, took a bite of her onion ring. A spring breeze snatched Theo's hamburger wrapper and sent it flying across the parking lot. Theo chased it down before it sailed over the railing and landed somewhere in the ten lanes of interstate fifty feet below them.

The Varsity, the largest and arguably the most famous drive-in fast-food joint in the South, was perched on a concrete ledge overlooking one of the busiest stretches of interstate in America, Atlanta's Downtown Connector near Georgia Tech. It was their first stop, other than bathroom breaks, since leaving Coconut Grove the night before. Theo had loaded up his car with bar food, Julia packed their belongings, and, without a word to Jack, Cecilia, or anyone else, they'd taken to the road.

"How 'bout those rings?" Theo asked, as he returned to the table.

"Good," said Beatriz.

"Did you know they're made with kale?" asked Theo.

"Seriously?"

"*No*," said Theo, in his "get real" voice. "One thing I know for sure is that the deep-fry vats of the Varsity will never be polluted with kale."

Beatriz laughed, but Julia was in a serious mood.

"Not good news from Jack?" asked Theo.

She shook her head.

They'd talked about it at length before leaving. Julia had expected bad news from the immigration court, and she'd been talking to Theo about plan B for days. The fact that her husband was in Miami made it easier to put plan B into action sooner than she might have, even before the judge issued the ruling that they all expected.

"Sounds like we're doing the right thing," said Theo.

Beatriz checked Google Maps on Theo's cell. "Can anyone tell me why we're going through Atlanta? The map says we should go straight up I-95 through South Carolina, North Carolina, and all the way up."

"There are two good reasons," said Theo.

"I hope they're good," said Beatriz. "It adds two hundred miles to the trip."

"Number one, your mother is not supposed to leave Miami-Dade County. I'm not saying they're going to come looking for her, but I'd rather not make a trail of credit card charges and other shit that makes it easy for ICE to figure out that the two of you are making a run to the Canadian border."

Canada: plan B.

"That makes sense," said Beatriz. "What's the other reason?"

Theo took a huge bite of his hamburger and swallowed. "We get to eat at the world-famous Varsity. That good enough for you?"

Beatriz smiled, and her mother smiled with her. "Good enough," said Beatriz.

"We should get going," said Julia.

Theo gathered up the trash and threw it away. Julia grabbed her purse. Beatriz slung her backpack over her shoulder, and the three of them walked to Theo's car.

CHAPTER 63

J ack drove to Coconut Grove for lunch.

The phone call with Julia had left him with an empty feeling, and twice he'd tried to follow up with her. She didn't answer, and he totally understood her need to be left alone. He'd called and texted Theo to make sure she was okay, and it wasn't like Theo to ignore him. Jack was getting a strange vibe.

He entered Cy Place's a little before noon and found none other than Uncle Cy himself behind the bar. He was technically Theo's great-uncle Cyrus, and Theo just called him Cy, but to Jack he'd always be an uncle.

"Well, look what the cat dragged in."

It was an expression no one had ever heard Uncle Cy use until he turned eighty, which made Jack wonder if there was some form of dormant nucleic acid in the human body that kicked in on the eightieth birthday and made people say the things that octogenarians have been saying since the beginning of time.

"Where's your nephew?" Jack asked as he settled into the barstool.

"Yeah, it is a nice day, isn't it?" Cy said in a cheery voice.

Jack didn't know what to make of the apparent disconnect. Hearing loss was common among old musicians, especially nightclub stars like Cy, who'd spent countless nights blowing a saxophone until the wee hours of the morning, powered by gin, cigarettes, and God only knew what else. But this seemed more like a change of subject than an auditory issue.

"I asked, where's Theo," said Jack.

"I heard you the first time," said Cy. "I swore not to tell you."

Jack was getting somewhere. "Okay, let's stop the dance. What's Theo up to?"

The old man shot him one of those lonely hound-dog looks. Cy was tall and thin as a reed, and he had a sax player's stoop even when he wasn't playing, as if his chin were glued to his sternum. He could cut to the soul when he looked at you, head down, through the tops of those sad eyes. The man just didn't play fair.

"Don't give me that look," said Jack. "Seriously, what's going on?"

"They left last night," said Cy.

"Who left?"

Cy told him, and Jack felt both betrayed and stupid. "Call him," said Jack.

"You call him."

"He won't answer my calls. Call him and hand me your phone."

Cy dug an old flip phone from his pocket, punched out ten numbers with all deliberate speed, and handed the phone to Jack.

"What's up, Cy?" asked Theo.

"Canada is a really dumb idea," Jack said.

"Tell Cy he's fired," said Theo, not missing a beat.

"I'm serious, Theo. Julia can't seek asylum in the United States, see how it goes, and then run to Canada. There's a treaty between the United States and Canada that prevents that. The minute Julia shows up at the border, the Canadians will notify ICE and send her right back."

"There's more to our plan than that."

Jack drew a breath. Theo's "plans" were legendary. "Here's my advice. Turn around right now, come back to Miami, and hopefully ICE will never know that Julia left Miami-Dade County. Because if they find out, she will be deported immediately."

"We have a better plan, Jack."

"How is it better?"

"Asylum in the United States is a lost cause. I heard it in your voice. Shit, Jack. You sounded more optimistic about my chances on death row even after they shaved my head and served me a last meal."

He had a point. "Canada is not the answer."

"It's the best shot she's got. We checked this out. I know about that treaty you mentioned. It only applies if you enter Canada legally."

Jack's response caught in his throat. "Are you saying what I think you're saying?"

"I think you get it," said Theo.

"Theo, do not get involved in an illegal border crossing. Julia will end up deported to El Salvador, and if you're not careful, you could be charged with human trafficking."

"Don't worry about that. We found a loophole."

Jack groaned. "Oh, my God, Theo. You found a loophole in an immigration treaty? Do you have any idea how complicated immigration law is? This is not the time to be playing jailhouse lawyer."

"Fuck you, Jack."

"Sorry, I didn't mean it the way it sounded."

"Yeah, you did. You just shit all over this before you even know what it's about. I gotta get back in the car. If you want to learn something, ask any immigration lawyer about Roxham Road."

"Where's that?"

"I'll call you when we get there. If I can figure out how to use my phone. It's pretty fucking complicated."

He hung up. Jack closed the flip phone and laid it on the bar.

"Did that go as bad as it sounded?" asked Cy.

"Worse," said Jack. "I think we've both been fired."

CHAPTER 64

It was Jorge's first trip to Georgia. He was happy to blow right through it.

Around midnight he'd checked the MDPD website and noticed the update on the BOLO. The words PROBABLE CAUSE TO ARREST appeared in bold red letters above his photograph. Apparently, the cops weren't buying his suggestion that Rosa had died of an accidental drug overdose. He'd overstayed his welcome in Miami, and it was time to move on. A check of the GPS tracking app—*Thank you, Rosa*—had told him that Julia, too, had taken to the highway. Jorge had seen it as no mere coincidence. It was a sign. No, not a sign. A signal—from her to him.

Julia *wanted* him to follow her.

Atlanta was behind him, and Jorge was heading northeast on I-85 toward Charlotte. He checked the app on his phone again. The transmitter in Beatriz's backpack put them in Virginia on I-77 northbound. They were a good two hours ahead of him, but, like him, Julia was minding the speed limit to avoid getting stopped by a state trooper. She wasn't pulling away from him, and as long as the battery lasted, he'd know exactly where she was. A dog tracker was something he should have purchased years earlier. A nice accessory to the choke chain.

Jorge exited the interstate and made a quick stop for gas. A dozen other cars were refueling ahead of him, the black dispensing hoses hanging from the metal canopy like vines in a Salvadoran jungle. Jorge pulled into the last open slot and jumped out. The morning sun had dissolved into overcast skies somewhere north of Atlanta, and he'd been inside the car since Florida, so the late-winter chill of North Carolina was a shock. He would need to buy a coat if Julia kept tracking north.

The pump display screen told him to pay in advance. He checked his wallet. Paying with Rosa's credit card would leave a digital footprint for MDPD to follow. A terrible idea. He used another stolen card.

His thoughts churned to the sound of gasoline flowing into the tank. He wondered if Julia and Beatriz were alone. They'd made the trip from El Salvador to Miami that way, just the two of them, but that wasn't the Julia he knew. Life with Julia was more like a constant game of whack-a-mole: take out Hugo, the black guy pops up.

It was easy enough to confirm his suspicions. Jorge got the number from directory assistance and dialed Cy's Place. The man who answered sounded about ninety.

"Cy speaking."

"Is Theo there?"

"No," the old man said. "He ain't here today."

Just as Jorge had suspected. "When will he be back?"

"Oh, a couple days, I would think. He didn't say exactly. Try his cell."

"What's that number?"

"Who is this?"

"Just a friend."

"Yeah? Well, if you was a friend, you'd have his cell."

"Blow me, old man," he said, and ended the call.

The pump clicked off and the gas stopped flowing. Jorge didn't wait for the receipt to print. He finished up quickly, climbed behind the wheel, and checked the tracking app. Julia was making better time, passing Roanoke already. Theo must have been driving. No way would Julia risk a stop for speeding.

Jorge started the engine and steered back onto the interstate. He had some serious catching up to do.

• • •

Jack submitted his closing argument in written form to Judge
Kelly's chambers and joined Andie and Righley for dinner at
the pancake house near the airport. Righley was on a breakfast-
for-dinner kick, which suited Jack just fine. His flight to Albany
didn't leave until 7:09 p.m., which would put him at his motel in
Plattsburgh sometime after midnight.

"What the heck is in Plattsburgh?" asked Andie.

Jack had taken Theo's advice, called a friend who was a "real"
immigration lawyer, and learned all about Roxham Road. It made
him only more worried for his client and her daughter. He tried to
tell himself that he didn't give a rat's ass about Theo, but he knew
that wasn't true. Jack was on a mission to save Theo from himself.

"It's kind of a cool place," said Jack. "Before the Civil War, it
was the last stop on the Underground Railroad for runaway slaves.
There was a pathway straight into Canada. The very end of that
path is now called Roxham Road."

Andie smeared a pad of butter on Righley's pancake. "That's an
interesting history lesson, but I don't see why you have to go there."

Jack and Andie had been in this situation before, where the FBI
agent couldn't tell the criminal defense lawyer what she was working on, or the lawyer couldn't tell the law enforcement officer what
he was up to. It required a high level of trust, even more than most
marriages, but it was "the deal" that made their relationship work.

"You're not going to tell me why, are you?" she asked.

Jack smiled flatly and shook his head.

Andie cut her daughter's pancakes into bite-size squares.
"Righley?"

"What, Mommy?"

"Never marry a lawyer." She cut her eyes at Jack and added, "Or
an FBI agent."

CHAPTER 65

Jack preferred March in Miami, but the beauty of an old red barn on a snow-covered pasture at sunrise could not be denied.

A barn with a tin roof and double silos was all there was at the south end of Roxham Road, which jutted out of North Star Road to form an inverted T. The pavement stretched north for about a half mile and then just stopped for no readily apparent reason. One step beyond was Canada.

Jack parked his rental car at the end of the road. He counted five taxis and a shuttle van that had arrived before him. According to his immigration lawyer friend in Miami, a cluster of cabs was part of a typical morning on Roxham Road. Migrants from Central America, the Caribbean, Nigeria, Syria, and elsewhere found their way to Clinton County by overnight bus. They came from Philadelphia, New Jersey, Chicago, and other American cities. Taxis waited for them at the gas station in Plattsburgh, which also served as the town's bus station. The journey for some spanned oceans and continents, and the final leg was a thirty-minute cab ride to Roxham Road, for which they might get tagged with a three-hundred-dollar fare—one final rip-off before they set foot on Canadian soil.

Jack got out of the car and zipped his jacket. The morning wasn't as cold as he'd expected, but it was too cold and damp to be wheeling an overpacked suitcase across icy pavement, which was what a Haitian mother and her three children were doing right in front of him. They joined about a dozen other migrants who were gathering at the end of Roxham Road, less than ten yards from the imaginary line that separated one country from another. Up the small hill, just beyond a little knee-high sign that read UNITED STATES on one side and CANADA on the other, was a cluster of white tents.

The border between Canada and the lower forty-eight states stretches 3,987 miles, most of it unpatrolled. The official border crossing nearest to Roxham Road was a few miles east at Champlain. The white tents staffed by the Royal Canadian Mounted Police were the Canadian government's response to a dramatic rise in illegal crossings at Roxham Road, from a handful each month to thousands. When Jack first heard about the tents and the RCMP response to the illegal crossings, the seeming absurdity of it reminded him of the scene in the classic Mel Brooks comedy *Blazing Saddles*, in which a tollbooth springs up out of nowhere in the Old West, and cowboys on horseback must stop in the middle of a chase, wait in line, and search their bags for correct change.

A sentry wearing the RCMP uniform and a black Kevlar vest emerged from one of the tents and, from the Canadian side of a temporary crowd-control fence, addressed the forlorn group of migrants across the border.

"This is not a legal point of entry," she said in a loud voice. "This is an *illegal* point. Do you understand?"

"Yes, we know," they answered in a mix of accents—Nigerian, Mexican, and everything in between.

The sentry's morning announcement continued. "Does anyone have a valid visa from the United States?"

Most nodded and said they did; others were silent, perhaps because they didn't understand English.

The sentry continued, "Are you aware that as soon as you cross this border, your status in the United States is nullified and there is no guarantee that you will receive asylum in Canada?"

"Yes, yes," they answered in desperate voices. "We want to come in."

The immigration drama played out as Jack had been told it

would. The sentry warned all of the migrants, as she warned hundreds of others every week, that they would be immediately arrested upon crossing at this illegal point. Therein was the loophole that Theo had discovered by surfing the Internet, the same way these people had found it. If they crossed at a legal point of entry, a treaty between the United States and Canada required the RCMP to return them to the States, where they would be immediately deported to their home country. But if they crossed at an illegal point of entry, like Roxham Road, the treaty didn't apply. They could apply for asylum in Canada.

These migrants *wanted* to be arrested at the illegal point of entry.

For Jack, it made about as much sense as the other immigration hoops his client had jumped through. Or the tollbooth in the Mel Brooks movie.

"What are you doing here, pal?" a man asked him.

Jack turned. He was still on U.S. soil, and he was looking into the eyes of a U.S. immigration officer.

"Is this not the line for Maple Leaf tickets?" asked Jack.

"Funny," the officer said without humor.

One of the Syrian migrants was fed up with waiting. He wheeled his suitcase across the thirty feet of frozen no-man's-land between the end of Roxham Road and the white immigration tents, stepped past the sentry at the temporary gate, and surrendered himself to the RCMP. As he disappeared into the tent for processing, others followed.

"You with the media?" the U.S. border patrol officer asked Jack.

He seemed friendly enough. Jack decided to pick his brain. "No, I'm not media. But do you mind if I ask you a question?"

"Shoot."

"You're border patrol, but you just stand here and watch. I don't get it."

"I can't stop anybody from leaving the U.S. if they want to leave. Unless they're here unlawfully."

Unless they're here unlawfully. "So that's why the sentry warns them that their U.S. visa will be nullified? These people are in the U.S. lawfully?"

"Most of them."

"What if they're illegal?" asked Jack. "You can arrest them?"

"We can, and we do. Clinton County jail is full of undocumented migrants we picked up on their way to Roxham Road."

Undocumented—like Julia and Beatriz. "Got it," said Jack. "Have a good day."

Jack went back to his rental car, started the engine, and blasted the heat while speed-dialing Theo's cell. His friend answered, and Jack told him where he was.

"Cool. We spent the night in Plattsburgh and were just going down to the breakfast buffet. Free and all you can eat. My kind of place. We'll be right where you are in about an hour."

"Just stay where you are until I get there."

"Why?"

"I looked into that loophole you found in the immigration treaty."

"It works, right?"

"Sort of," said Jack. "But there's a really nasty footnote."

CHAPTER 66

Jorge didn't reach Plattsburgh until dawn.

He'd been losing ground since Pennsylvania, where he just couldn't drive any farther without sleep and had to pull over for a nap. Julia had the advantage of being able to split the driving time with Theo, coupled with Theo's lack of concern for the speed limit when he was behind the wheel. By the time Jorge woke from his roadside slumber, he'd fallen at least six hours behind them. And he could see where they were headed: Canada. If he didn't catch them before they crossed the border, Julia would be out of his grasp forever. Jorge was a Salvadoran first and a Miamian second. If for climate reasons only, "Canadian" landed somewhere in the bottom third of his personal comfort zone.

An orange sliver of the morning sun rose over the snowy hilltop. Swirling blue lights appeared in his rearview mirror.

"*Puchica!*" he shouted, pounding the steering wheel with his fist.

The drive from Miami to Plattsburgh via Atlanta was over eighteen hundred miles. Jorge had gone the entire distance without being stopped by the cops—until he reached Plattsburgh and its twenty-five-mile-per-hour speed limits. Welcome to small-town U.S.A.

Jorge chose not to run for it; where would he go? He pulled off to the side of the road, the snow crunching beneath the tires until he came to a stop. The Clinton County squad car pulled up behind him, beacons flashing. Jorge left the motor running and waited.

This was not going to end well. Jorge fully understood that. A local cop. A Salvadoran driver. A stolen Florida tag. A BOLO issued in his name.

Jorge reached inside the console for his pistol and placed it between his thighs. He watched through the rearview mirror and considered his options. His only good one depended on the cop getting out of the car. If the cop waited for backup, Jorge was in trouble.

"Get out of the car," he said under his breath in Spanish, willing it to happen, staring into the rearview mirror.

A car passed heading in the opposite direction, but Jorge's gaze remained fixed on the squad car in the mirror. The driver's door opened, and Jorge's heart raced. The cop stepped out of the car, checked for traffic, and started walking toward Jorge's vehicle.

"That's it, you dumb fuck."

Experience had taught Jorge that you didn't wait for the cop to get all the way to the driver's-side window. An alert officer was way too on guard at that point. A seventeen-year-old gangbanger in Soyapango had educated Jorge on the proper technique when he was just fourteen. Jorge was riding in the passenger seat. The older boy—a kid named Pablo who'd eventually ended up facedown in a cane field with a machete in the back of his head—had walked Jorge through it, step by step.

You watch in the side mirror until he reaches the taillight.

Then what?

Then you make your move.

What do you want me to do?

Lean forward and put your head between your knees like you're trying to suck your own dick. Because bullets will fly.

Jorge flung the door open with his left hand, rolled out of his seat to the ground, keeping much lower than the cop's anticipated line of fire, turning his body as he swung the semiautomatic pistol around and squeezed off round after round after round—*pop, pop, pop!*

The cop dropped to the cold pavement like a sack of concrete. He didn't move.

Jorge leaped to his feet and checked him out. Eyes open. No pulse. Two slugs to the chest, but the kill shot was probably the messy one to the forehead with the angled exit wound that had blown the hat right off his head. Jorge took the dead officer's weapon and left him where he lay. Only one car had passed in the five minutes he'd been there, but the next one could come any second. He jumped back in the car, put the car in drive, and hit the gas. The tires spun in the snow, and the car jerked to the right, deeper into the pile of slop left behind by snowplows. He tried backing up and then rocking it forward, but driving in the snow was not something he'd learned in El Salvador, and the tires only sank deeper. At this rate, he'd be lucky to get out by spring. His car was worthless, and walking all the way into town would have been just plain stupid, which left only one alternative.

He jumped out of the car, grabbed the keys from the dead cop, and climbed into the Clinton County Sheriff's squad car. The engine started. He had no idea how to turn off the flashing beacons, so he left them on, nearly driving over the cop's body as he pulled onto the highway and headed toward town.

Jorge glanced in the mirror and, as the mess he'd left behind got smaller, he knew his problems had just grown exponentially. A dead cop and a stolen squad car were a death sentence anywhere, from San Salvador to Plattsburgh. Law enforcement and immigration would soon be all over him, and there was only one way out of this alive.

He checked the tracking app on his phone. Beatriz was at the Plattsburgh Inn, just two miles away.

Jorge needed a hostage. And he knew exactly where to get one.

CHAPTER 67

The breakfast bar at the Plattsburgh motel smelled of scrambled eggs and bacon. Jack found Theo and Julia together, alone, at a table near the toasters and waffle makers. They were seated opposite each other, and Julia's hand was in Theo's, their fingers interlaced on the tabletop. Julia retracted her hand and wiped away a tear with a napkin as Jack approached. He'd walked right into their good-bye.

"You guys okay?" asked Jack.

"Fine," she said with a sniffle. Another tear rolled down her cheek, which seemed to embarrass her. She excused herself for a moment, headed to the ladies' room, and left Jack with Theo at the table.

"Where's Beatriz?" asked Jack.

"Still in the room. She didn't want to come down. Kind of a shitty morning. I think it finally dawned on us that this was the end of the road. Literally."

Theo picked at his eggs. It was the first time Jack had ever seen Theo touch food with a fork and not put it in his mouth.

"You really like Julia, huh?"

Theo shrugged. "Doesn't really matter now, does it?"

"You shouldn't take her to Roxham Road," said Jack.

"That's not up for discussion. Julia made up her mind. She has to do what's best for Beatriz and her. Sitting around waiting for that judge in Miami to deport her doesn't make no sense."

"Listen to me," said Jack. "The first thing the Canadians will do when they take Julia into one of those immigration tents at the border is run a computer check on Julia's status in the States. The minute they see she has a pending asylum claim in the United States, that's it. They will kick her back. The loophole in the treaty that's drawing all these migrants to Roxham Road won't work for someone like Julia."

"Are you sure?"

"Yes. The best thing for Julia and Beatriz is to go back to Miami, hope ICE never finds out she violated the conditions of her release by leaving, and let me take Judge Kelly's order up to the Board of Immigration Appeals."

"You're that certain the judge is going to deport her?" asked Theo.

"I'm that certain," said Jack.

"The problem is she's afraid to go back to Miami if her husband is there. I'm not too cool with it, either. I'm already packing a pistol wherever I go."

Jack lowered his voice. "Do you have a gun with you?"

"Wouldn't you?"

"Theo, you don't have a license to carry a concealed firearm in New York or any of the other states you drove through. That's a felony."

"It's not *on* me. It's locked in the trunk of the car."

"That doesn't matter."

Julia reappeared at the table. The tears were gone, and her hair was brushed. "Where's Beatriz? Didn't she come down for breakfast?"

"We haven't seen her," said Theo.

Julia's sadness turned to concern. "She's not in the room."

CHAPTER 68

S now was falling as Beatriz wheeled her roller board toward the motel parking lot. She'd seen snow for the first time in her life on the drive through Pennsylvania, which was exciting. By New York, though, she'd had enough of it. She was having serious doubts about Canada.

Beatriz retrieved a knit cap from her backpack, pulled it on, and kept walking.

Her mom must have known that she'd lain awake all night. Beatriz was in bed but with eyes wide open when her mother had kissed her on the forehead, told her to try to get a little sleep, and quietly gone down to breakfast with Theo. It wasn't that Beatriz couldn't fall asleep. She was afraid that, if she allowed her eyes to close, she might slip into that strange place she'd landed before, trapped in her own fears, sealed off from the rest of the world, encased in a glass box.

"Good morning," a hotel worker said to her. The snow was falling faster than the old man could shovel it from the walkway, which meant that it really wasn't a "good morning" for him or Beatriz.

"Bonjour," she said, but she immediately felt silly, not sure if New York actually bordered a French-speaking province. Maybe it did. Maybe it didn't. Why should it even matter to a girl from El Salvador?

Beatriz continued past the carport at the motel entrance, the tight squeak of new-fallen snow punctuating each footfall. A whip of wind brushed her face like an icy wisp of hair. A flake as big as a dragonfly hit her in the eye and immediately started to melt, soaking what was left of her eyelashes. All night long, in her fight against sleep, she'd refused to let her eyes close, and when her eyelids grew heavy, she'd tug on her eyelashes to snap herself awake. It was a bad habit she'd started as a little girl, when the sound of her father shouting and her mother screaming made her afraid to go to sleep at night. She was angry at herself for acting so weird, but losing a couple of eyelashes was worth it if she could avoid sinking back to that place. Mom wouldn't be happy when she got a good look in the daylight and saw that Beatriz had been plucking again. Rather than go down to the breakfast bar and face the music, Beatriz had packed up her things and headed down to load them in Theo's car. Maybe she could convince her mom that she hadn't been pulling on her lashes again, that they'd frozen in the wind and broken off.

Not my fault, Mom.

Theo's car was parked beside a snow-covered pickup truck at the end of the row. It was locked, but like a lot of people who'd been locked out of a car, Theo kept a spare key in a small magnetic box that attached to the frame near the front driver's-side wheel well. Beatriz retrieved the key and opened the trunk. The other bags were still in the motel room, so everything Theo had left overnight in the trunk was in plain view. The tire and the tool kit were no surprise. The same could not be said for the pistol, which was tucked into the side-panel pouch made of cargo netting. Beatriz had had no idea it was there, but it did explain why Theo had told her to stay out of the trunk—which, to a teenager, was as good as a direct order to open it.

Beatriz slid her backpack off her shoulder and placed it next to the spare tire. As she turned to lift her suitcase, the swirling blue beacons caught her eye through the falling snow. A police car entered from the highway and was speeding across the parking lot. Beatriz froze. It felt like the day they'd come to her house in Miami to take her mother.

The squad car was heading straight toward her.

• • •

The roads of Plattsburgh had been salted, but the motel parking lot hadn't. Jorge gripped the steering wheel tightly as the Clinton County squad car transitioned from the wet highway to snow-covered asphalt. His cell phone was resting on the dash, and the blinking GPS signal on the screen was drawing him just ahead, toward the girl who was standing behind the car with the open trunk. Definitely the black guy's car.

He'd found them.

Jorge was just a few car lengths away from the prize, the hostage he would need in order to bargain his way out of trouble with the police. Beatriz had the classic deer-in-the-headlamps expression, her gaze locked onto the swirling lights. It was a little unnerving, causing Jorge to freeze up for a moment—just long enough to make him hit the brake pedal a second too late, which sent the squad car sliding across the snow. Jorge slammed the brake even harder, which was exactly the wrong thing to do. He'd lost control, but it was as if everything were in slow motion. The front end spun around gradually, until Jorge was looking through the windshield at where he'd just been. The back of the car was now the front, the red taillights leading an unstoppable slide that Jorge knew wasn't going to end well.

The squad car slammed into the rear of the pickup truck that was parked beside Theo's car. Jorge's head snapped back against the headrest as the car came to a sudden stop. Jorge didn't even check to see if he was okay. He grabbed the dead cop's pistol, jumped out of the car, and stood in the blue swirl of authority as the snow continued to fall. From the driver's side of the squad car, his gaze cut like a laser over the hood of the vehicle, locking onto Beatriz.

"Get in the car!" he shouted. "Now!"

CHAPTER 69

Beatriz!" the man shouted. "Get in the damn car!"

He was speaking in Spanish, but it was the familiar voice, not the language, that threw her. Beatriz had expected a police officer and had gotten the furthest thing from it: the chilling voice that had never failed to make her freeze up with fear.

"Beatriz! Get in!"

The back of her neck tingled with a surge of horrible memories, and Beatriz dug deep for the strength to fight off the emotional paralysis that was overtaking her body like the shadow of a solar eclipse. The police beacon continued to swirl in silence, lending a strange blue hue to the anger on her father's face. He'd run out of patience, but as he hurried around the front of the squad car to grab her, he lost his footing on a patch of ice. The soles of his shoes were suddenly pointing at the sky, and he landed with a thud flat on his back.

Beatriz sprang into action. Instinct told her to simply run for her life, but the gun was right there, within easy reach. She swallowed her fear and went for it so quickly and with so much determination that she ripped the entire cargo-net pouch from the Velcro fasteners on the side panel—and sent the gun flying through the air. She watched it spin through the falling snowflakes, bounce on the ice, and skid right under the squad car.

"No!" she shouted, but there was nothing else to do. She ran.

Toward the motel would have been her first choice, but that would have been running straight into her father's arms. She raced toward the highway, her body flushed with adrenaline, arms pumping and legs moving like an Olympic sprinter's.

J orge lay flat on the sinister patch of ice, stunned and breathless from a fall unlike any he'd suffered before. It took a moment, and by the time he could breathe again and climb to his feet, Beatriz was already across the street and still running. An old man with a snow shovel was fifty feet away and hobbling toward him.

Jorge considered getting back in the squad car but noticed the rear tire resting on the pavement at a much-less-than-perfect angle. Victory in the collision had gone to the pickup truck, leaving the squad car with a bent rim, if not a broken axle.

"Are you okay, Officer?" the old man shouted.

Jorge didn't wait for the man to get close enough to see that Jorge wasn't actually the police. He turned and ran after Beatriz, more careful with his footing this time, and making sure that his gun was secure in his coat pocket.

J ack heard the crash in the parking lot. He and Theo jumped up from the breakfast table, and Julia joined them as they raced through the lobby and through the pneumatic entrance doors. They stopped beneath the carport to see what was going on. The swirling police beacons caught Jack's attention, but Theo seemed more focused on his own vehicle.

"Somebody broke into my car," he said.

Jack ran straight down the row of parked cars toward the accident. Theo and Julia followed, all oblivious to the fact that it was way too cold to be outside without a jacket. They quickly caught up with the old man holding the snow shovel.

"What just happened?" asked Jack.

"Cop came in from the highway like a rocket and slammed into the pickup truck. Wanted the girl to get in the car with him."

"That's Beatriz's suitcase!" said Julia.

"And her backpack," said Theo, as he removed it from the trunk.

"Where's the cop?" asked Jack.

"Went running after her. More I think of it, I'm not sure he was a cop. Wasn't wearing a uniform."

"I'm calling nine-one-one," said Julia, as she pulled her phone from her purse.

Jack was on the same wavelength. "Which way did they run?" he asked the old man.

"My gun's gone," said Theo, showing Jack an empty cargo pouch.

"Yes," Julia said into her phone, speaking to the 911 operator, "my daughter was just taken from the Plattsburgh Inn parking lot."

"Across the street and then up the hill," the old man said. "There's a fork in the road 'bout a quarter mile from here. One way takes you into town. Other way there's nothing but a gas station."

"She's five feet tall," Julia told the operator.

Theo dug his car keys from his pocket. "Let's go!"

They jumped into the car with Theo at the wheel and Jack shotgun. Julia was in the back seat, still on the phone with the 911 dispatcher, as Theo drove way too fast out of the parking lot—as fast as Jack would have driven had someone been chasing Righley. The car fishtailed, but Theo recovered as they started up the highway. The *whump-whump* of the windshield wipers and the hiss of speeding tires on wet pavement stayed with them all the way to the fork in the road.

"Straight or left?"

"I don't know!" said Jack.

"What's your gut tell you?"

Jack didn't have a gut on this one. "Straight!"

"Left it is," said Theo, and so they went.

CHAPTER 70

The snow was falling harder. Beatriz kept running. And her father was gaining ground.

Beatriz had done an all-out sprint up the hill, hoping that on the other side she'd find a bustling city center filled with helpful people and, most of all, police cars with actual police officers. She found none of that. It made her heart sink to see nothing but snow-covered pastures that went on and on, all the way to the forest-covered hills in the distance. She wished she'd gone the other way at the fork in the road. But she couldn't turn back now. Her thighs burned, and she felt a side stitch coming on; her father was still charging up the hill behind her. All she could do was continue down the long stretch of salted wet highway lined with barbed-wire fences and previously plowed snowfall.

"Beatriz! Stop!"

The sound of his voice only propelled her, and gravity pulled her down the hill almost faster than she could move her legs and feet. The road curved at the bottom of the hill, and a ray of hope arrived through the snowstorm in the form of oncoming headlights. Beatriz continued down the hill, running, jumping, and waving her arms to get the driver's attention. He zipped right past her, never slowing down and spraying her with salty snowmelt.

"No!" she cried.

"Beatriz!" her father shouted.

She glanced back. He'd reached the crown of the hill. It gave her heart to see him hunched over, hands just above his knees, as he paused to catch his breath. Each step she took while he rested was another yard gained in the footrace to—where?

A faint glow of light reappeared in the distance. This time, if she had to, she would throw her body onto the highway in front of the oncoming car. She wiped the snow from her eyes—lashes really did serve a purpose—and saw that the fuzzy glow in the snowstorm wasn't a pair of headlamps. The light was from a gas station. Beatriz dug inside herself, found another gear, and made a dash for what seemed like the last outpost of civilization between her and the Canadian border. The yellow signage got bigger and brighter with her every step. Soon the pumps came into view, but it worried her that she was less than a hundred yards away and hadn't spotted a single vehicle.

"Please be open, please be open," she said over and over, still running, still closing in on this oasis, as if the mantra kept her going.

It was one of the newer-style mini-stations: no service garage, no car wash; just a cashier's booth in the middle, a row of pumps on each side, and a flat canopy-style roof to cover the whole operation. But Beatriz had been wrong about no vehicles. A covered jeep was parked by the air hose behind the station. Inside the booth the lights were on. The cashier was seated behind the window. Her prayers were answered, but Beatriz was figuratively out of gas. The test of endurance had pushed her to the limit, and like the ancient Greek Pheidippides on his fatal run from Marathon to Athens, she stumbled and collapsed ten yards from the mini-station. She tried to pick herself up from the pavement but couldn't find the strength. She checked behind her, and though her father was a silhouette, it was enough to make her find the breath to cry for help.

The door opened. The cashier emerged from the booth.

"Help!" she said in a stronger voice.

The cashier hurried over, and Beatriz grabbed onto the sleeve of his flannel shirt as he helped her up.

"Are you okay, girl?"

"Hide me!" she said.

"From what?"

"My father," she said, pointing. He was just twenty yards away and closing. "He's going to kill me!"

The cashier smiled, as if he knew better. "Dads get mad sometimes, sweetie. He ain't gonna kill ya."

"No, you don't understand. He beats my mom. He killed two people in Miami. The police are after him!"

The cashier's smile vanished. "Get in the booth. The glass is bulletproof."

Her legs were like rubber, but the cashier was one of those Paul Bunyan–type men who wasn't particularly buff, just big and strong as an ox. He practically carried her to the booth, yanked open the door, and took her inside. It was tiny, barely big enough for the stool at the counter, the cash drawer, and one person, let alone two. The cashier closed the door, shutting out the weather and worse, and locked it. Then he picked up the landline and dialed 911.

Beatriz noticed his cell phone charging on the counter. "Can I call my mom?" she asked, but he was too busy with 911 to answer her.

Beatriz dialed her mother's number, praying that she would answer, hoping that the glass between her and her father really was bulletproof.

CHAPTER 71

Jorge thought he heard sirens. He stopped and listened over the sound of his own breathing. Definitely sirens, and they were getting louder. A dead cop by the side of the road. A wrecked squad car in the motel parking lot. It was only a matter of time before the cops were all over him.

Need a hostage.

Jorge's hands were so wet and cold they were shaking. He rubbed his palms together briskly and blew into his fists. It helped a little, bringing back enough feeling for him to check his new weapon. The deputy sheriff's Glock .22 was a serious sidearm. Jorge had witnessed firsthand the stopping power of .40-caliber ammunition, which was at least as good as 9 mm, and when it came to shooting through a car door or a bathroom wall to take out a rival gangster, a .40-caliber was in his experience better than a 9 mm or even a .45 ACP. A semiautomatic pistol with a fifteen-round magazine and two extra magazines in his pocket made Jorge a veritable one-man army, and this soldier was about to deploy. He'd seen Beatriz take a hard fall by the gas pumps and the cashier who was stupid enough to help her inside. Jorge didn't need two hostages with him in that bulletproof box for a standoff with police. One was enough.

Either one.

Jorge racked the slide to load the first round into the chamber, drew a breath of cold air, and started toward the mini-station, Glock in hand.

. . .

Julia didn't recognize the incoming number on her cell phone but she was glad she answered.

"Mom, it's me!"

Julia's heart leaped into her throat. "Beatriz! Where are you?"

Beatriz told her, and Julia told Theo, who immediately pulled a U-turn that sent them heading back toward the fork in the road. Nobody pointed any fingers about the previous debate over straight versus left.

"She's with the cashier inside the booth," said Julia.

"Tell her to stay in there," said Jack. "The glass on those booths is bulletproof."

"To a point," said Theo.

"What do you mean by that?" Julia asked with concern.

"Depends on what you're shooting and how many rounds."

It wasn't what Julia wanted to hear, but at that moment all she really needed was the sound of her daughter's voice.

"Tell the cashier to call the police."

"He's doing that now."

"Good. Then just stay there and wait. I love you, sweetie."

"He's coming, Mom! He's coming!"

Julia had never doubted it was Jorge, though the panic in Beatriz's voice made a positive identification all the more distressing. "Stay on the line with me, Beatriz. We're on our way."

CHAPTER 72

B eatriz backed as far away from the glass as she could, which wasn't very far at all. Right behind her was a floor-to-ceiling display rack for cigarettes, chewing gum, mints, candy bars, and all the other junk that customers couldn't seem to get enough of when filling their gas tanks. The electric space heater on the counter was no match for the blast of winter they'd dragged in from the cold. Beatriz was still shivering, too frightened to sit and too tired to stand, so she leaned against the door, watching and waiting for the police to get there.

"Tell them to hurry up!" said Beatriz.

"It's going to be okay," her mother said over the cell phone, but Beatriz was talking to the cashier, who was still on the landline with the 911 dispatcher.

He covered the speaker and said, "Police are on their way."

"He's right there!" Beatriz said, pointing.

"Get down on the floor!" her mother told her.

Beatriz cowered into the corner near the side door, but the cashier leaned closer to the glass, trying to get a better look at the man who was still a blur in the falling snow. He was coming toward them but still beyond any protection from the weather afforded by the canopy that extended out over the pumps.

"Are you sure he has a gun?" the cashier asked.

"Yes! Don't you see it?"

"See what?" her mother asked, but Beatriz wasn't listening anymore.

The cashier narrowed his eyes, trying hard to see. But it wasn't until the blur emerged from the snowstorm and stepped into the relative calm beneath the canopy that the cashier's inquisitiveness turned to fear.

"The man's definitely got a gun!" he said into the landline.

Beatriz screamed as her father rushed toward the glass.

"Beatriz, what just happened?" her mother asked, but Beatriz dropped the phone.

His head covered with snow and ice, his face red from the cold, her father looked scarier than ever. He stopped just three feet away from the glass and aimed his pistol straight at the clerk.

"We'll be okay," the clerk said, swallowing the lump in his throat. "It's bulletproof."

Beatriz didn't care what the cashier said. She knew glass could break. She'd seen it happen with her mind's eye, trapped inside her glass box.

"Beatriz, answer me!" her mother said, but the cell was on the floor, and the faint voice was just noise in the background. As Beatriz cowered in the corner, her father opened his mouth to speak.

"Open the door," he said, his voice carrying through the mouthpiece in the glass, his gun still aimed at the cashier.

"The police are on their way!" the clerk shouted back. "Put the gun down!"

Beatriz heard sirens in the distance. Way in the distance. *What's taking them so long?*

"Sir, just calm down, okay?" the clerk said. "Please, put the gun down!"

The crack of a single gunshot was Jorge's reply. The bulletproof glass absorbed it with the pop of a catcher's mitt, sending spiderlike cracks in all directions from the point of impact. The clerk ducked behind the counter and huddled beside Beatriz.

"Your dad's nuts!"

Jorge's face was suddenly right on the other side of the glass, so close that his breath steamed the cracks. "Open the door!"

The police sirens drew closer, but to Beatriz they still sounded too far away.

"Go away!" the clerk shouted.

Jorge raised the gun muzzle to the exact point of impact and squeezed off five, six, seven quick shots—Beatriz lost count—and then two or three more. The loud burst of semiautomatic gunfire smothered her screams. The cashier made a strange noise and then dropped to the floor.

"Open the door!"

Beatriz froze, stunned by the dead weight of the clerk at her feet and the crimson pool of blood on the floor. She couldn't speak, couldn't scream, couldn't even move her lips to attempt an answer.

"Open it, Beatriz!"

She couldn't lift her gaze up toward the glass. She didn't want to see the cracks in her protected space, and she couldn't even begin to deal with the danger that might pour into her box and smother her in an instant. But the blood at her feet was even more terrifying, so she looked straight ahead at the space below the cash drawer, and her gaze fixed on the middle shelf. And then she saw it.

"Beatriz, I'm giving you five seconds to open that door!"

She heard him, but she didn't move. Beatriz's entire focus was on the handgun right before her eyes.

CHAPTER 73

Theo's windshield wipers weren't moving fast enough. One after another, in kamikaze fashion, huge, wet flakes splattered on the glass like cold slush from a fire hose.

"I can't see shit," said Theo.

Jack didn't want to tell him to slow down, not with Julia's daughter in danger, but he didn't want to die in a blinding snowstorm, either. Then, out of the gray-and-white vista emerged a glowing yellow dot of signage.

"That's it!" said Jack. "That's the gas station."

"Oh, my God, I just heard gunshots!" said Julia, and then she shouted into the phone. "Beatriz! Beatriz, answer me!"

They were already barreling down the highway at a reckless speed for these conditions, but Theo took it up another notch.

"Say a prayer and hold on to your ass, Jack."

It wasn't the first time he'd heard that from Theo. But this time he sounded like he really meant it.

"I will," said Jack, as the mini-station came clearer.

Beatriz was sure he was dead. She couldn't bring herself to look at the clerk's face, so she didn't know if there were any shots to the head, but she'd counted at least six to the chest. No one survived that many gunshots. He showed no sign of breathing, made not a sound, and hadn't moved a muscle since slumping to the floor. Most telling of all, the pool of blood had ceased to grow. Beatriz knew that the dead didn't bleed; the heart stopped pumping. She'd seen gunshot victims before. One had lain outside her house in San Salvador for almost eleven hours before it was safe for the police and the medical examiner to come into the neighborhood and get him.

Just to make sure, she grabbed the cashier's wrist and checked his pulse. Nothing. She dropped his hand, and it slapped lifelessly onto the floor. It could have easily sent her into a tailspin of panic, but Beatriz fought it off. She forced herself to think of his body as nothing more than an object that lay between her and the gun— something that she had to get around. She didn't dare stand, where her father could see her. She'd have to stay low and crawl right over the clerk's body.

"Beatriz!"

Beatriz was no stranger to guns. They'd always been around the house, at least when her father was there. Pistols, revolvers, and more—you name it, and at one point or another, her father had owned it or stolen it. He rarely left the house without a gun. The nights he stayed home, a gun was never farther away than the nightstand. Sometimes he slept with a gun under his pillow. His firearm of choice changed from time to time. Beatriz knew where he kept the ones that fell into disuse. Her father stored them in a footlocker inside the closet in the master bedroom. She'd first found the footlocker when she was barely eight years old, a frightened-to-death child who was hiding in the closet. Not until she was twelve years old did Beatriz go back to that place. She took a boy named Antonio with her to help select the right weapon. Her body was changing. The gangs were taking notice. She didn't feel safe. She wanted to learn how to use a gun, just in case. Antonio taught her. Her mother caught the two of them shooting bottles in the backyard. Beatriz didn't know it, but Antonio was himself a gangbanger. It was one more reason they'd left El Salvador.

Outside the booth, the wind whistled. A shot of winter funneled in through the bullet hole in the glass. It made Beatriz shiver, not from the cold, but from the way it reminded her of that dreamlike image and her subconscious fear of frigid water pouring through the cracks in her glass box.

Beatriz drew a breath and made her move, taking care to avoid the blood as she maneuvered past the clerk and inched toward the shelf.

Jorge glanced down the highway in each direction, and he could see that time was running out. To the east was a pair of headlights, and they were approaching way too quickly in this weather to be anything other than help on the way. To the west was the blue swirl of what had to be one of the drivable squad cars from the Clinton County Sheriff's Department.

Jorge had two backup magazines in his pocket, leaving him more than enough .40-caliber rounds to shoot through the glass. But the glass would be his protection in a standoff with police, and a hostage was his ticket out of this mess. Shooting the lock off the door was the better plan. He hurried around to the side of the booth and jiggled the handle to see if in a stroke of luck it would open. Locked.

"Beatriz, get away from the door!"

She didn't answer.

"Beatriz, I'm going to shoot the lock off. Get back!"

He put his ear to the door to listen for her answer, or at least for the sound of her movement away from the door. But the only sound was from the highway. Police sirens were closing in.

Jorge aimed his pistol at the lock and squeezed the trigger.

CHAPTER 74

B eatriz screamed at the crack of a gunshot.

It should have been a call to action, but she froze, expecting the door to fly open. It didn't. The door, like the glass, must have been reinforced—to a point.

"Get back!" her father shouted.

Beatriz scurried across the floor, deeper into the corner, as far away from the door as she could possibly get. With her back to the wall, she drew her knees up to her chin and braced herself for a barrage of gunfire. It came, one crack after another, as loud and as terrifying as the hell that had rained down from the hole in the glass and killed the clerk.

"Stop!" she shouted, but she couldn't even hear her own voice.

The heel of a boot slammed against the door, and it burst open. A blast of snow and winter wind carried the scream of approaching sirens into the booth. Beatriz's father stood in the doorway, glaring down at her.

Beatriz snatched the gun from under the counter. It took more courage than she thought she had, but with a two-handed grip she somehow managed to steady the gun and fix the front sight right on him, her whole body trembling as the tears streamed down her face.

But she didn't pull the trigger.

"I'll shoot you!" she said, her voice quaking.

Her father stayed where he was, straddling the threshold, one foot in and one foot out of the booth. His eyes narrowed, and with a glint of amusement he slowly raised his pistol and took aim at Beatriz's forehead. "No, you won't," he said.

The sirens grew louder, but Beatriz knew they were too late, if only by a minute. "I will!" she shouted. "I'll shoot you!"

Beatriz wished she could—wished it with the aching heart of an eight-year-old girl trapped in a bedroom closet, listening to her mother's screams but powerless to do anything about them.

"I'm afraid this is not going to end well for you, Beatriz," her father said in a voice that chilled her. "Not well at all."

CHAPTER 75

Through the windshield Jack saw the oncoming squad car with beacons flashing. As the two vehicles sped toward each other from opposite directions, the wet highway glistened in a joust-like battle of headlights on a collision course. By a split second Theo won the race. His car jumped the culvert like a snowmobile as they turned into the station and skidded to a stop near the first set of pumps, a reasonably safe distance from the booth.

"Stay low!" Theo told his passengers.

The squad car pulled up on the other side of the booth as Julia pushed open the rear door and jumped out of the back seat.

"I said stay low!" Theo shouted.

Before Julia could take a step, they were met by the sound none of them wanted to hear: a gunshot echoed from inside the booth, and another immediately followed.

"Beatriz!" she shouted.

"Stop right there!" the officer shouted at Julia. He was in the isosceles stance with weapon drawn, his feet planted at shoulders' width, and his elbows locked. His gunsight was trained on Julia.

"That's my daughter in there!"

Julia took one step toward the booth, and another shot rang out—this one from the cop. Jack flung open the car door, launched himself from the passenger seat, and pulled Julia to the pavement. Theo's car and a set of gas pumps stood between them and a confused cop who was shooting at the wrong people. Theo had the good sense to get down on the floor. Jack hoped the cop had the good sense not to send another stray bullet whizzing past gasoline pumps.

"Don't shoot!" Jack shouted from behind the cover of Theo's car. "We're unarmed!"

Another squad car pulled into the station and stopped on the passenger's side of Theo's car. On Jack's lead, he, Julia, and Theo dropped to their knees and raised their hands into the air.

"Smart money says the black guy gets it," Theo said under his breath.

"Freeze—all of you!" the cop shouted. He approached cautiously with weapon drawn. The other officer came around the back of Theo's car to assist.

"My daughter's in that booth!" Julia shouted. "We're here to help!"

The cops exchanged glances. "Check it out, Caldwell," the second officer said.

"You sure you got this, Willie?"

"Yeah," he said. "Check it out!"

Officer Caldwell led with his weapon as he walked around the front of Theo's car and started toward the booth. He stepped carefully, slowly, and as Jack heard each footfall, one in front of the other, he was struck by what he didn't hear: Not a sound was coming from inside the cashier's booth.

CHAPTER 76

Bring the mother over here!"

Julia was still on her knees, alongside Jack and Theo, and all three heads turned at the sound of Officer Caldwell calling out from inside the cashier's booth.

"You two, on your bellies," the cop told Jack and Theo. It was like cuddling up with a block of ice, but they complied. Then the officer told Julia to stand up slowly. She did.

"Keep your hands in the air!" he shouted, and she jerked them back up.

The cop did a quick pat-down of Jack and Theo to make sure they weren't going to pull a weapon and shoot him in the back. "Do not move," he told them.

He grabbed a fistful of the back of Julia's jacket and led her toward the booth. She kept her hands in the air, which only seemed to tighten the knot in her stomach.

Bring the mother over here—what did that mean? Good news? Bad news? The cop was moving way too slowly to satisfy Julia's need to know.

"Beatriz?" she said with trepidation, as they drew closer to the booth. But there was no reply. They were close enough to see the cracks in the bulletproof glass, which drew an involuntary "Oh, my God" from Julia's lips.

The officer led her past the glass, which had fogged from the weather, making it impossible for Julia to see inside. The door was open on the other side of the booth. The officer glanced back toward Jack and Theo, who were still facedown on the frozen pavement.

"Beatriz?" Julia said again, her voice shaking. They rounded the corner and stopped in the open doorway. And Julia gasped.

Jorge lay on his side in a pool of blood, a crimson dot on his forehead and a second wound to his chest. The cashier's body lay beside his. Officer Caldwell was on one knee at Beatriz's side, holding the weapon of self-defense.

Beatriz looked up at her mother, no sign of regret in her expression, just utter disbelief.

"I shot him, Mom."

Julia rushed inside, hugged her daughter with every fiber in her body, and kissed her face repeatedly.

"Good girl," was all she could say.

CHAPTER 77

You two can get up," said the officer.

In the time it had taken the Clinton County Sheriff's Department to check out Jack's story, three more squad cars had arrived at the mini-station and nearly an inch of new snow had fallen on Jack's back. He and Theo rose from the frozen pavement, shook off the snow, and stepped beneath the cover of the canopy. They were just in time to see a pair of border patrol officers putting Julia into the back of an ICE van.

"You gotta be kidding me," Jack said to Theo.

About a mile down the road from the service station, a stone's throw away from Big Sal's Pizzeria, was the Clinton County Sheriff's Office. The complex sat on several acres and included a state-of-the-art jail that housed three hundred inmates and employed ninety-six corrections officers. Corrections was by far the largest division, more than three times bigger than the law enforcement division, due in no small measure to the fact that the jail also served as the Buffalo Field Office for U.S. Immigration and Customs Enforcement. On any given day, ICE relied on Clinton County to hold dozens of undocumented immigrants who didn't quite make it to Canada.

Jack battled the ICE bureaucracy by phone while Julia was booked and processed. Beatriz changed out of her bloodstained clothes and then sat in the visitors' waiting room with Theo. By midafternoon Julia was officially Clinton County Inmate No. 19-10681. She was dressed in the familiar orange jumpsuit for the meeting with Jack. They were seated on opposite sides of a small table.

"Did you talk to immigration?" Julia asked.

"It took a while, but I finally got through to the DHS lawyer on your asylum case."

"What's going to happen?"

Jack didn't sugarcoat it. "Our strongest argument for asylum was that the government of El Salvador has demonstrated an unwillingness or inability to protect you from domestic violence. DHS will notify the judge that Jorge is dead. It's the department's position that the factual basis for your claim for asylum has evaporated. You can't have domestic violence when your domestic partner is dead."

"Will the judge agree with that?"

"Judge Kelly was going to rule against you even before this happened. This just makes our appeal tougher."

"But we still have an appeal, right? You said that could take more than a year."

"Yes, but that's going to be a little different now."

"How do you mean?"

"Before this happened, the judge would have let you stay out of detention until the Board of Immigration Appeals decided your case. Now DHS is going to oppose your release because you left Miami-Dade County."

"Will the judge do that to me?"

"I think he probably will," said Jack. "You were released on the condition that you wouldn't leave Miami-Dade County. You violated that condition."

Julia's eyes welled with tears, but she sucked them back. "What about Beatriz? What will happen to her?"

"Obviously, she's in no trouble for the shooting. Even if Jorge hadn't killed the gas station attendant, it would have been a clear case of self-defense."

"I meant, where will she live."

"Can she stay with your sister?"

"I suppose. But if Beatriz is in Miami and I'm up here, how will she visit me?"

Again, Jack didn't want to give false hope. "I can file a motion to see if we can get you transferred to a closer facility."

"Can we get that?"

Jack went as far as he could. "We can try."

Jack sat beside Theo in the waiting room while Beatriz went in to see her mother. The windowless room had three rows of fixed seating, all facing in one direction toward a pointless infomercial playing on the flat-screen television mounted on the wall. A half dozen visitors stared at it blankly, having nothing better to do while waiting to see a loved one behind bars.

"This just sucks," said Theo.

"Yeah, it does," said Jack.

"Do you think they'll move Julia to a jail in Miami?"

"Not a chance. The per diem from ICE is what makes these local jails profitable. Clinton County will cling to Julia like a cash cow."

"So she sits here in New York for another year until the appeals board says she has to go back to El Salvador. Do I have that right?"

"Hate to say it, but that's the most likely outcome."

"Shit, Jack. There has to be some way to fix this."

Jack was out of ideas. They sat in silence, arms folded and eyes straight ahead. The infomercial rolled on, and Jack wondered why anyone would ever need to cut a soda can in half.

"I guess I could marry her," said Theo.

Jack snickered. "Yeah, right."

Theo cut him a sideways glance. He wasn't laughing.

"*Marry* her?" asked Jack.

Theo shrugged. "I could."

Jack turned his attention back to the beefsteak tomatoes sliced paper thin. "Yeah. I guess you could."

ACKNOWLEDGMENTS

I'm grateful, as always, to the talented team of friends and professionals who help make me a better writer. "Thank you" to my editors, Carolyn Marino and Hannah Robinson; my agent, Richard Pine; and all those at HarperCollins Publishers who have a hand in the amazing journey of creating a book. Special thanks to my beta readers, Janis Koch and Gloria Villa, who remind me that "grammar matters" (the errors that remain are all mine).

Most of all, thank you to my wife of twenty-five years, Tiffany, who makes it all worthwhile.

ABOUT THE AUTHOR

JAMES GRIPPANDO is a *New York Times* bestselling author of suspense and the winner of the Harper Lee Prize for Legal Fiction. *The Girl in the Glass Box* is his twenty-seventh novel. His books are enjoyed worldwide in twenty-eight languages, and his signature character, Jack Swyteck, is one of the most enduring protagonists in the legal thriller genre. James is a practicing attorney at the law firm of Boies Schiller Flexner LLP and teaches the Law and Lawyers in Modern Literature at the University of Miami School of Law. He lives in South Florida.